MW01632253

ELLIS KACKLEY
Best Damn Doctor in the West

by Ellen Carney

— A Maverick Publication —

ISBN 0-89288-199-2

Maverick Publications
Drawer 5007 • Bend, Oregon 97708

Dedication

THE ETERNITY OF ME

(Youthful comments on the Irony of Death)

by Dennis Lyle Carney, written during his high school years

My voice is whispers, visions wild
My heart is ancient, though a child
And tears that burn this youthful face,
Bring laughter to this lonely place.
My God is Truth, in floods of lies,
To drown in sorrow and despise.
Fear so humbled mocks high words,
Like worms which laugh at hungry birds.
Tomorrow says good-by today,
As thoughts of you will drift away.
I dream my world asleep in peace,
Soon sweet time will steal my lease;
And though my life may soon be gone,
My dreams and visioned words live on.

This book is dedicated to my son, Dennis Lyle Carney, whose lease on life ran out on September 1, 1988, at the age of thirty two. Throughout his lifetime he encouraged me to reach toward broader horizons and gave me added courage to try new things. His untimely death forced upon me a greater understanding of the tragedies suffered by the Kackley family.

Acknowledgements

I would like to thank those who have helped in the creation of this book. My newspaper requests for information brought many letters and some photos, mostly from people who had been helped by the doctor.

A most heartfelt thanks to Dr. Evan Kackley who spent over one-hundred hours in personal interviews and telephone conversations, telling me about his father and mother, telling about when he practiced medicine with his father in Soda Springs, helping straighten out unclear information, and separating truth from rumor and legend. He also shared many photographs from the Kackley collection with me and arranged for Boise artist, Steven Poulson, to draw the sketches for the book. My thanks also to Mr. Poulson.

Because of his reputation throughout the western states, Dr. Ellis Kackley became a legend of the area. His activities, though impressive, were often stretched beyond reason, as in the story of the pig's stomach. Through Dr. Evan Kackley's help I have tried to portray these stories about his father as near to the actual happenings as possible.

I would like to thank the Soda Springs library staff, especially Head Librarian Karen Tate, for supplying my constant requests for information and books about the area; Elaine S. Johnson, current president of the Caribou Historical Society and member of other historical boards, and friend, for encouraging me and helping critique the manuscript; Dianna Troyer, Pocatello, Idaho State Journal Regional editor, for helping critique the manuscript; Johann Siebers and Venice Munro for helping with the Scottish brogue; and Rodger Sorensen, Clayton Schmitt and Randy Somsen for computer assistance.

I thank my family and friends for sharing stories,

putting up with my many hours at the computer, encouraging me in the work, and for their willingness to read and critique the manuscript.

Lastly, I would like to apologize to those whose stories are not included in this book. Many fine people worked with and were treated by Dr. Kackley who have not been mentioned in the book because of lack of space. The project grew to much greater proportions than I had originally expected, and some things had to be left out. If you have stories about the Kackleys you would like to share, please send them to me in care of C. Lyle Burton, 19 Grays Lake Road, Wayan, Idaho 83285, in case I decide to do a sequel.

About the Author

Ellen B. Carney was born in Soda Springs, and delivered by Dr. Ellis Kackley. She was raised in the Grays Lake area, later living in the states of Washington, Utah, Alaska, Arizona and Florida, before returning to the Grays Lake area in 1981, where she became highly interested in the history of the local area.

She is currently serving on the Caribou County Historic Preservation Commission.

She has taught elementary school for fifteen years, and been a newspaper correspondent for the *Idaho State Journal*, Pocatello, and the *Caribou County Sun*, Soda Springs, for the past five years.

She received her Bachelor's Degree from the University of Arizona, and a Master's of Education from the University of Utah.

Mrs. Carney is the mother of five children.

Introduction

This book is a biographical novel based on the life of Ellis Kackley, who came to Soda Springs in 1898, three days after graduating from medical school at the University of Tennessee.

He and his wife, Ida, fought to raise themselves from abject poverty in the aftermath of the Civil War. He became a doctor and came west to practice during the epic of American opportunity. He and Ida witnessed the "winning of the West" and the losing of the western opportunity, which culminated with the great depression. He took part in the evolution of medicine from the country doctor, to specialization; from the discovery of germs to the discovery of antibiotics. Their son, Evan, also became a doctor, and contributed to the advancement of medicine through his practice and medical research.

At the turn of the century, Soda Springs was a wild frontier town, with drinking, gambling, and murder a part of everyday life. Kackleys worked, along with many other people of the locality, to help make Soda Springs a better place to live, and to bring law and order to the area. They were great benefactors of the town, helping those in need, putting many young people through college, and donating many thousands of dollars worth of equipment to the hospital.

Ellis was at odds with Anaconda Mining Company, Utah Power and Light Company, Union Pacific Railroad, and the American Medical Association at various times when he felt their policies were hurting the common people.

The Kackley Doctors took part in World War I and World War II. Though opposed to involvement in these wars, they were among the first to volunteer their services to help our country.

They treated outlaws, Indians, the poor, and the well-to-do with equal concern for their welfare, whether or not they were paid for their services. In his early practice, Ellis sometimes faced almost insurmountable odds in getting to patients, but never refused a call in spite of the distance involved or difficulties in getting there. In later years, people flocked to his doorstep from all over the West, filling the hotels and boarding houses of Soda Springs to capacity.

Both my father and I were among the over four-thousand babies Ellis estimated he had delivered. My father, Clarence Lyle Burton, was delivered at the hospital in the Fryar building. I was also delivered by him in the Caribou County Hospital.

In writing this book, the following names have been changed for obvious reasons, or because the name of the person was unknown:

Lawrence Berry, the geologist, identity unknown
The Mart
Mr. and Mrs. Ashler, proprietors of the Mart
Jenny the prostitute
Pat Horton, the merchant
Judge Smith, identity unknown
Jake Frankfurt, who begged for another "rough" treatment.
Joe York from IRS, identity unknown
John, Claire, and Donald from the dog burial scene
Father Lateur, the French Catholic Priest, identity unknown
Mr. Jones, fined for shooting the sage hens
Mrs. Brown, who experienced complications giving blood
Dr. Green

Chapter 1

Ellis Kackley occasionally dozed in the high-back wooden chair, but stayed alert to changes in the breathing of the sheepherder. The injured man was in the bed, in the hotel room Ellis had rented, and Ellis hadn't even had one good night's sleep after his long journey. If the sheepherder died it would be murder—but from what he had seen and heard in the past few days, murder might be the way of life in this wild frontier town he and Ida had decided to make their home.

Three days earlier, Ellis had boarded the train in Omaha. He grasped his bag tightly. In it was a diploma, just received, from the University of Tennessee Medical School. His dark eyes sparkled with excitement, dimmed only by having to leave the woman he loved behind, as he turned and waved to her before entering the wooden coach car of the westbound train.

Ida had fixed a basket of food for Ellis to eat during the journey. She had to keep busy in order to hide her deep anxiety. Though Idaho had been a state for eight years, it seemed more like he was going to a foreign country. She had talked once to a man who went way out West on the train, and he spoke of seeing Indians, buffalo, and all types of wild animals. It sounded like the area was terribly primitive. She had heard stories of bank and train robberies, and worried for fear he might meet with foul play along the way. She worried about his health and whether he would be able to hold up under the rigorous life of the frontier. She kept her worries to herself—she didn't want to make things harder for Ellis than they already were.

"Remember to wear your hat and coat when you get a call," she told him. "It might be warm when you leave, but it could be quite late and cold when you come back.''

Ellis looked amused, "Now, Idie, don't you worry. I'll get along fine, and it won't be long until you'll be joining me.''

"And watch out for Indians. I hear the hostile Blackfoot tribe lives around there. And be careful about grizzly bears, they supposedly have lots of them. . .''

Ellis laughed again, "Don't worry, you know I have a streak of Cherokee blood myself; I'll be right at home. I'll be the best damn doctor in the West,'' he added, kissing her on the cheek.

Ida could see in his dark eyes how excited he was about this adventure. She hoped he wouldn't be disappointed.

Hours later, in the creaking, wooden chair car, Ellis's thoughts went back to the time when he first became interested in medicine. His early education had been broken by a turnover of teachers, who came and went quickly, and also by the necessity of working in the tobacco fields. He had managed to put himself through normal school and get a teaching job. He and Ida were both teaching school. They had met at a teacher's institute.

Before he started teaching he had borrowed a book and "read medicine''—the only kind of training many doctors had in his early youth. A few years earlier, all doctors had to do to set up a practice was hang out a sign or advertise in the newspaper that they were ready for business. More was demanded now.

After their marriage, Ida continued teaching so he could attend medical school. He went one year to the University of Louisville and two to the University of Tennessee at Nashville—two of the finest medical schools in the country. Both had excellent doctors for teachers. His desire to become a doctor was now a reality. "Doctor Kackley,'' he said softly under his breath, and a sharp pleasure came over him at the sound.

Ellis looked over his shoulder. The passengers were a varied bunch. The old man next to him seemed to be sleeping. He said "hello'' to a rotund man across the aisle, as their eyes met, and received a nod in reply before returning to his thoughts.

Many graduates were becoming traveling or "floating" doctors and spending their time going from town to town, working with the sick. Ellis didn't want that kind of life. He wanted a real practice in a fixed geographical area. In spite of their reluctance to be separated, Ida would have to stay with his parents until he was able to save enough money to send for her. He hoped it wouldn't be long.

It seemed the train went extremely slow. The wooden cars creaked and the coal fired engine sent up sparks. The weathered, gray-haired conductor, who was limping noticeably, came through and took his ticket. He returned later and lit the kerosene lamps. A sad-eyed boy was hawking sandwiches and other food items. He didn't look old enough to be working. Ellis lifted, from under his seat, the small basket. Ida had packed it carefully, somehow managing to put in all the things he liked best, including fried chicken and corn bread. He pictured Ida and his parents sitting down to eat their evening meal, and suddenly felt terribly homesick.

As dusk signaled the approach of night, Ellis grasped tighter the small black bag carrying his instruments, all seven of them. He watched the miles fly by, bringing him closer to the small western town and wondered what Soda Springs would be like.

Even though he didn't like the way they had taken the land, and taken advantage of the common people, he was thankful the railroad had been completed to his destination. His previous experiences with rail travel had not been so pleasant. In the recession of the Cleveland administration, he had occasionally, hopped a freight train. The Pinkerton men were always waiting to throw those who used that method of transportation off the train. If you were riding the rails that way, God only knew, you were in desperate need. The railroad didn't care about people, or the sick, only about dollars, which had left Ellis with a sour taste in his mouth when he thought of railroads. Those in charge were too far removed from common people to realize what was going on with the average person.

Ellis scanned the landscape. When they crossed the Missouri River, it gave him the feeling of really being out

West, and his spirits began to rise. Sitting in the seat next to him, the old man with an unkempt appearance, wrinkled face, and skin like leather, struck up a conversation. Soon they were chatting like old friends.

"I'm headed for the Klondike. I'm going to be coming back with a fortune," the man confided. "I've heard say you can pick nuggets as big as grapes right out of the stream beds. You ought to go with me. A doctor could strike it rich there in no time."

Ellis wasn't tempted by the idea of making a fortune in the gold fields. He'd heard of the terrible White and Chilkoot passes, and how people were swarming to the Klondike by the thousands, with only the strong having the endurance demanded by this rugged northern route. People seemed to lose their senses when they started looking for gold. He had decided where they would make their home, and Ida, though reluctant had agreed. He wasn't about to change that decision now. He was anxious to treat the sick, not those crazy with gold fever.

It would be a long, grueling trip, but Ellis had learned to take advantage of every opportunity to get a moment's rest. It was cold in the car, and he was thankful for the heavy, warm overcoat and the hat which covered his head. He took stock of himself as the train sped along. He had a natural capacity for observation, which should be a great help in doctoring. He liked to believe he had a fair stock of common sense, but he couldn't help wondering if he were adequately prepared for what would lie ahead. Though he would never admit it to Ida, or anyone else for that matter, he felt absolutely frightened to death.

Ellis found it hard to believe they were skimming over the prairies of Nebraska, twenty miles per hour, as smoothly as if they were in a sailing ship. So many interesting people were traveling west. Some were going for speculation, others out of curiosity. Some were headed for gold fields, and families were traveling to join their husbands and fathers. Some intelligent young women, going West to teach school, reminded Ellis of Ida. Ellis found the talk about improving schools, locating ranches, discovering rich mines, and securing town sites stimulating.

Practically everyone had a lunch basket packed with goodies for the trip, and a good share of the baskets contained a bottle or two of spirits to fortify the travelers with strength for the journey and to neutralize the alkali water in the West. Some of the men were indulging in a little flirting with the ladies, confident their wives and sweethearts at home would never hear of anything which transpired west of the Mississippi. In general, the travelers were a jolly company.

The train boy came through again, with a basket of apples. They looked tempting, but Ellis knew he must save his small amount of coins for necessities. He had hidden his money carefully—there were always thieves and pickpockets on trains.

They had traveled nearly two hundred miles through the Platte Valley. The country was mostly settled up under the Homestead Act of 1862. Columns of smoke rose thin and straight from cabin chimneys. Thriving towns had sprung up all along the line of the railroad. In contrast to the naked prairies, the area looked beautiful and fertile.

"Last time I was through here, the most terrible storm came up," the miner beside Ellis said. "I wasn't sure we were gonna make it."

Ellis had heard this part of the country was subject to violent storms, both summer and winter. He noticed there was little timber in the area except for small stands of trees close to the river and on the islands.

Though the train was an improvement over horse-drawn vehicles, it was dirty. Ellis would welcome arrival at his destination with a chance to clean up and relax. The car had a pot-bellied, coal-burning stove at the front, but the farther west they went, the colder the April air felt.

Ellis felt he needed to stretch his legs, so he strolled back to the smoking car. There one could find pleasant, warm sounds of husky voices, laughter, and shared jokes and memories. He stood in the doorway a moment and glanced around, then took a seat by a portly gentleman puffing with obvious relish on an intricately carved pipe.

"Where are you headed, young man? Are you a doctor?" the man asked, his eyes resting on Ellis' instrument bag.

"Yes," answered Ellis, "I just graduated from the University of Tennessee Medical School and I'm on my way to Soda Springs, Idaho, to start a practice..."

"Soda Springs!" sputtered the man, "I can't imagine why any promising young doctor would want to settle in Soda Springs, or even stay there over night, for that matter."

"Why do you say that?" asked Ellis with some apprehension.

"I stopped at Soda Springs one night," said the stranger, "and I never saw so much hell in my life. Cowboys rode up and down the streets, shooting in all directions. One came into the saloon and shot out all the lights. I got out of that town as fast as I could, and I never want to see the place again! Whatever made you decide to set up a practice in Soda Springs? You look like a sensible young man. Have you ever been there?"

Ellis had to admit he had never been west of the Mississippi. A tall, slender, well-dressed fellow, also of mature years, who looked like a drummer, spoke up, "The company may be a bit rough, but the springs and bubbling waters are sure something to see. The area is filled with springs of water which bubble right out of the ground in a lot of places, and I've heard tell the mineral water heals the ills like nothing else in the world."

"Well, I imagine they need plenty of doctorin' in that God forsaken town, if you can stay alive long enough to do any good," suggested the first man. "As for me, I'm heading for Denver"

For almost twenty-four hours they traveled up hill all the way, until they reached Cheyenne, known as the "Magic City of the Plains". There was little of note between the Platte settlements and Cheyenne. Ellis went back to his seat and dozed awhile. When he awoke, sunlight had left the sky and the clouds were gray. They passed an occasional Indian on horseback, but they were scraggly, pitiful specimens of the race. Wild animals were numerous. With interest Ellis watched elk, deer, antelope, and occasional small groups of buffalo in their natural settings.

They stopped at Cheyenne, the junction of the Denver

and Pacific railroads and the point to which freight was shipped for Colorado, to rest and prepare for crossing the Laramie Mountains. Here they left the portly, pipe-smoking stranger, whose words had made Ellis question his decision to settle in Soda Springs. He would hate to bring Ida to a place where you had to worry constantly about being shot by ruffians, he mused.

Leaving Cheyenne, the train puffed up a grade of about ninety feet to the mile, the highest point being Sherman, on the summit of the Laramie Mountains. Ellis was awed at being over eight-thousand feet above the level of the sea. This strip found the track lined with sheds to protect it from the great amounts of snow which fell during the wintertime.

From Sherman, they roared downhill to the Laramie plains. Vegetation here contained a great deal of sagebrush, and he could smell its poignant aroma. After another hundred miles they again crossed the Platte, and started up the slopes of the Rocky Mountains. They stopped at Rawlings Springs for refreshments. The man Ellis thought was a drummer sat down beside him.

"My name is Lawrence Berry, and I've been in Soda Springs several times," he said. "Don't let what that old man said bother you too much. It isn't all as bad as it sounded."

"I'm glad to hear that," said Ellis. "I was beginning to wonder what kind of a place I'm headed for."

"Let me give you a little advice," said Lawrence. "Don't let anyone get you into a poker game. That's one of the most popular ways to fleece a newcomer. You can't count on an honest game in Soda Springs. Some of the establishments sell marked cards. They tell you to buy your own deck, and then try to swindle you out of every penny you have. You never know what they'll slip in your drink. It's one town where you need all your wits about you. I was foolish enough to get into a card game once, and if it hadn't been for the station agent getting me onto a freight train in a hurry, I probably wouldn't be here with a whole hide."

"Well, I've played an occasional hand of poker," said Ellis, but I'm not a card player. I haven't had time or money for that sort of amusement, even if I had been inclined toward it.''

"Another thing you want to watch out for is the women. There's two whorehouses there, and as soon as it gets dark, the men start drifting down the railroad tracks to Jenny's place, or over south of town to the one by the Bear River. That's another good place to lose your hide. There's a rough crowd there, and the favorite way to celebrate is to shoot up the place."

"Don't worry," said Ellis. "I left a wife at home and I don't intend to mess around with anyone else."

"I'm sure what that fellow said about his experiences in Soda Springs was right," continued Lawrence. "It's a wild frontier town, and you'll find all kinds there. The two main factions are the Mormons and those who are out to get a buck. Most of the second group don't care how they get it, and anyone who rides into town with a few dollars in his pocket is in danger of not only losing his money, but his life as well. Of course there are some dishonest Mormons and some honest merchants and others who don't belong to either group. The criminal element is strong, and very little is done about it by the law."

The two men finished eating and boarded the train. They sat down together in the smoking car. It was dark now, and clouds were again gathering. The full moon still shone brightly enough to see herds of antelope through the window, watching the train as it passed, and jackrabbits springing out of the sagebrush.

"What kind of people are the Mormons?" asked Ellis. "I've heard all kinds of stories about the practice of polygamy and other strange beliefs."

"Well," laughed Lawrence, "When I went out West the first time, I thought Mormons had horns and tails, and they cut off their tails when they were born. I haven't seen a horn or a tail yet. Like with any other group, there's good and bad Mormons. They've had to band together to protect themselves—you know. In 1838 Lillburn Boggs, Governor of Missouri, gave his infamous extermination order saying: 'The Mormons must be treated as enemies and exterminated or driven from the state, for public peace.' He mobilized the state militia to do the job. The thing he'll go down in history for, is the anti-Mormon riots and night floggings and persecution, and trying to exterminate a whole group of people. The only reason most of them got away and into the state of Illinois alive was because many state militia commanders refused to obey the order. Any people who are put into that kind of position are bound to be defensive, but in general they seem to be pretty decent people."

"I've heard a little about the Mormons, and Brigham Young bringing them west," said Ellis.

"A lot of people look on Brigham Young as sort of a modern day Moses," said Lawrence, "but the land he brought them to in the West was no land of milk and honey. Without their foresight in developing irrigation, they couldn't have raised a stalk of corn on much of the land that's now fertile farms."

"Do you have a sales route through Soda Springs?" Ellis. questioned. "You said you'd been there several times."

"No," said Lawrence. "Actually I'm a geologist. I've been studying the geological formations around Soda Springs and up through the Yellowstone National Park Area for the government. Soda Springs should have been part of that protected area. There's a wealth of unusual springs and mineral formations there, but people will destroy them. Where there's a dollar to be made, people forget about everything else."

"I've heard Soda Springs has the potential of becoming a health resort which could rival those in Europe," said Ellis.

"The potential is there," agreed Lawrence, "but it needs to be developed. It is a place of great contrasts. You'll find high mountain peaks, forests, lakes, and lava beds. Mount Sherman is around ten-thousand feet high, but down by the Bear River, the land is lower and less rocky and has little vegetation. The entire area is of volcanic origin and made up of lava beds with a little soil on top. The soda water is outstanding."

"I've heard about the water and it's mineral content. Do you really think it has medicinal properties?"

"Many people feel it does, and the Indians believed it to have, but I don't know—medicine is not my field. Tasting it was a pleasant surprise. I expected a slight soda taste, but when I took a large swallow, the tears started in my eyes. Add flavoring and it equals the best manufactured soda you can buy."

"How many springs are there?" asked Ellis.

"Oh, there's numerous mineral springs, many of them along a creek known as Soda Creek. In a lot of places there are fissures through which gases of sulphur, carbonate of soda, and others impregnate the water with chemicals. You can hardly walk a few yards without finding springs with some kind of minerals. The creek has a good sized flow and contains a number of rapids and waterfalls. It's full of spotted mountain trout. Do you fish?"

"That's another thing I haven't had time to do," said Ellis.

"Well, you'll enjoy the springs," said Lawrence. "Maybe as a doctor, you can find out if they really heal people's ills.

"There's an interesting place near the junction of Soda Creek and Bear River. It's flat country decorated with occasional large mounds of silicate of soda and other minerals. These are remains of hot springs which must have been as spectacular as those of Yellowstone at one time. There's hundreds of them in about a three-square-mile area.

"Down the river is a group of about seventy springs. Many come up through crevices in the river bottom. A large one known as Steamboat Springs sounds exactly like a steamboat when the steam escapes through the pipes. Every few minutes it throws a stream of water about four feet into the air."

"It sounds extraordinary," agreed Ellis. "I'm anxious to see all these places. There must be a real inferno underneath the area."

"Beer Springs, on the bank of Soda Creek, has been put under a canopy and has a row of seats around it. It must have been a thermal spring at one time. It's said to have intoxicating properties if you drink too much. Hooper Springs is a conglomerate of small springs which looks like a huge caldron of boiling water, but is ice cold. The activity in the water is from gases, not steam. It's water is delicious. The Idan-ha' Natural Mineral Water Company bottles the water of Ninety Percent Springs and fortifies it with carbon dioxide of Mammoth Springs, which is a large spring north of Hooper. They ship it all over the world. As I said, the area should have been included in Yellowstone Park."

Before going back to his coach car, Ellis sat quietly for awhile thinking about all he had heard of this mysterious place he planned to make his home.

Crossing over the "backbone" of the country after a gradual ascent, they rode through gently rolling hills. He thought of Bridger and Sublette, explorers who had discovered this south pass through the mountains, with practically a continuous altitude, so one hardly knew when they were over the pass.

He returned to the day coach, which was not conducive to sleep, but in spite of the discomfort, Ellis was tired enough to doze, while they passed mines and coal fields.

At Montpelier, Idaho, two young frontier chaps, each carrying a book under his arm which looked something like a Bible, boarded the train. Ellis wondered if they might be Mormons until he heard a man behind him mention that they were Mormon missionaries. In spite of all the strange things he'd heard, he couldn't help thinking these two fellows looked quite civilized, and like reasonably nice young men.

Knowing he was finally in Idaho, and almost to his destination, Ellis felt excitement rising inside him. The conductor came by and informed him Soda Springs was the next town on the route. Here they were traveling along the Oregon Trail, as they had on much of the journey. His thoughts went back to his early years, and things he had heard as a child. Many of his ancestors had followed this route west, and he felt intrigued by the thought that he, too, was helping to pioneer this country. Kackleys were always going west, and were still fighting the Civil War—in their hearts if not in actuality. He wondered what battles he would have to fight in this untamed land.

As they approached the town, he noticed Mount Sherman rising to the south with buildings nestled at its base. Some of the buildings looked too modern for their setting. Along the railroad tracks to the north were new homes. Several large buildings in close proximity to the tracks looked like hotels. A gravel road cut through the center of town and disappeared to the north, while the opposite end curved westward just south of the business district. Businesses lined the one main street going north and south, and the railroad tracks going east and west. Mountains rimmed the skyline in almost every direction. Most businesses were housed in modest sized, false-front buildings common to the West, though some buildings were made of rock and brick and some were log cabins. Columns held up balconies, or just adorned the front of buildings. Businesses were set behind a raised board walk.

Ellis stepped off the train and immediately felt the chill of a cold east wind. He pulled his woolen overcoat closely around him, and thought of Ida's concern he might go doctoring without his coat. He decided it was unlikely he would forget his coat in weather like this. There were still some patches of snow on the ground, but mostly it was covered with dark brown dirt splotched with brown grass and mud puddles. Ellis wondered when spring would come to this part of the world.

A massive three-story building to the north with numerous windows, porches, and turrets caught his eye. It had covered walkways around the lower story, pinnacles on the roof, and decorative columns around the doorways. Just down the street from the depot was a smaller building, obviously a hotel. It was a modest sized building with a false front and large windows on each side of three entry doors on the main level. In one window the sign said "Sample Room" and on the other side was a bar. Two old timers were sitting on short wooden benches placed on either side of the center doorway. Hotel rooms on the upper story opened onto a balcony held up by columns where several men were standing in a small group talking.

Ellis glanced around, but no one was there to meet him. He picked up his bag and entered the small, low, Union Pacific Railroad building with tracks running on either side. The only person in the station was the agent—a stout, blonde fellow with a full moustache, who looked up rather friendly like as Ellis approached the ticket window. "Can I be o' ony help to ya'self?'' the Scotchman with a heavy accent asked.

''I'm the new doctor, Ellis Kackley. I wrote the postmaster, Mr. Eastman, that I would be arriving today. I was hoping he'd be here to meet me,'' Ellis explained.

The agent, probably in his early forties, looked at him with interest and smiled. ''I'm Jimmy Strachan, Jimmy they call me. What can I be doon' to help ya'self get settled?'' he asked. ''A sheem 'tis that Mr. Eastman is noot here. 'Tis sure I am he'd be here if your letter he'd goot. 'Tis a bussey man he t'is with the post office oon' drug store oon' everything. A bed you look like ya'd be needin'. Do ya have reservations ot the hotel?''

''No,'' said Ellis, ''but I could sure use a place to wash up and a bed.''

''Six hotels we have in Soda Springs,'' said Jimmy. Inta' ohn ya'd better settle an' get a bit o' rest. 'T' show ya aroond a bit after ya're rested, my pleasure 'twould be.''

''Thank you,'' said Ellis, ''I would really appreciate that.

''What kind o' accommodations would ya be likin'?'' asked Jimmy. ''The Idanha 'tis oor nicest. Aye, the finest—furnished in French Provincial an' fooly carpeted it be.'' He waved his hand toward the huge turreted building Ellis had noticed previously. ''Aye, 'tis where a lot o' the toorists stay. The finest dinin' room, 't has. 'Tis a dinin' station for the railrood.

''A working mahn's choice 'tis the Mart. Just doon the street 't is. Aye, and Mrs. Ashler is a second mither to the cowhands an' stockmen who ride 'nto toon from the range. 'Tis a hospitable place she roons. An excellent cook she is an'a lot o' business deals 'ere made there.''

''I'll try The Mart,'' said Ellis. ''I'll just walk on over and see if they have an empty room. Thanks for the help.''

Chapter 2

Ellis entered the hotel and found a long lobby with wooden benches on each side, being dusted by a sizable black maid with a feather duster. The red-hot stove warmed the room, and the aroma of burning pine filled the air. A table to be used by traveling men for writing or playing cards was set just close enough to the stove for comfort. Toward the back of the room, a short, square young man sat behind a desk.

"We're glad to have you here, Dr. Kackley," he said in a husky voice when Ellis identified himself. "This town really needs a doctor." He called the maid to show Ellis to his room. Her bulky frame proceeded him up the stairs, and opened the door into a small, plain room.

Inside the room, Ellis dropped his bags and looked around. It was simple, but adequate, with an iron bedstead and a wooden washstand. He felt absolutely grimy after three long days on the smoky, dirty train and he hadn't realized how exhausted he was. The people he had talked with seemed friendly and glad to see him. Maybe it wouldn't be such a bad place to live after all, he thought. But everything here seemed strange, like the West had a whole new language, and way of life.

He slipped off his overcoat and jacket, hung them on the hangers provided, and unpacked his bag, hanging his spare shirt beside the coats. He thoroughly cleaned his instruments, which were caked with dust, then returned them to their leather case.

When his personal items were taken care of, he slipped off his shoes, and lay down on the bed to relax for a few minutes before looking over the town. Ellis was soon fast asleep. He didn't know how long he had slept, but it was dark when he was awakened by a loud pounding on his door. He opened it to see a tall, slender man with a marshal's badge. "Dr. Kackley, we need you downstairs. We have a seriously injured man in the saloon."

Ellis grabbed his medical bag and had to take the stairs two at a time to keep up with the long-legged lawman. "What happened?" he asked as he caught his breath.

"One of the sheepherders came into town carrying a lot of money. A couple of thugs wrapped a handkerchief around a damn billiard ball, and knocked him over the head. Some of the fellows found him just outside."

The atmosphere in the saloon was thick with smoke. Strange faces looked at Ellis from a group of unkempt men who were gathered around the old sheepherder laying on the floor unconscious and bleeding profusely from the head. Beside him lay a large, silk, blood-covered handkerchief, wrapped around a billiard ball. Ellis' pulse quickened when he saw the fancy, silk handkerchief. It told him immediately the attacker had been a man of affluence.

"Stand back for the doctor," the Marshall ordered, and the silent spectators sullenly cleared a path for Ellis, who bent over the grizzled old man and parted his hair. He could see badly crushed skull bones as well as a deep gash producing the blood. He felt along the carotid artery and found a weak pulse. The man's hands were cold and moist.

Doctoring was something like playing poker with the Lord and the Devil, thought Ellis. Some hands you would win—sooner or later you would lose. Ellis was afraid the Grim Reaper already had this one, with his sheet white face and clammy cold hands.

He pressed on the side of the injured man's head to slow the bleeding. He had already lost a lot of blood. Ellis asked for some clean sheets. The silence was thick as fog and penetrated only by dirty looks from the crowd which had gathered. He glanced quickly around the smoke filled saloon, looking for a suitable place to operate. His eyes lit on a pool table. It was the only half-way usable place he could see. It wasn't exactly the perfect place, but one of his teachers, talking about kitchen surgery, had said the only essentials for surgery were a doctor and a patient. This case would test that premise, he thought grimly.

"Can someone help me lift this man onto one of the pool tables so I can operate?" he asked.

A small man, about five-ten, with a pencil thin moustache over his thin upper lip and wearing buckskin britches and a silk shirt, quickly stepped forward to protest. "You'll ruin the pool table if you get blood on it."

Ellis looked into a pair of bulging, red-veined eyes, and a wrinkled face which revealed more years of trouble than one might think at first. A spindly-looking fellow with a scrubby crop of whiskers elbowed his way forward to join in protest, wiping his mouth on his sleeve as he nodded in agreement.

"Now Mr. Ashler, a man's life is at stake!" The speaker rose from a table where three well-dressed businessmen were sitting, and walked slowly up to Ashler. All was quiet again for a moment. Ellis hadn't noticed the men at the table before.

"Well," conceded the reluctant owner of the pool table, drawing out the word as though it pained him, "we'll have to cover it. Eva, get some papers for the doctor." he hollered.

Mrs. Ashler was soon there with papers and sheets, holding the door half open behind her as she stood uncertainly in the doorway. "Bring them over here, and get a move on," Ashler commanded gruffly.

"Now help the doctor get this man onto the table, " the businessman ordered when the table was covered. The crowd parted and a couple of husky fellows lifted the injured man onto the table. Mrs. Ashler left and returned with a kerosene lamp.

"I'll need some hot water," said Ellis.

Mrs. Ashler already had one of the kitchen girls heating a dish pan full of water over the white, enameled cook stove. Ellis went into the kitchen to wash up, and the girl gave him a smaller pan to use for boiling his rubber gloves. Ellis put his instruments into the water, along with some pieces he tore from one of the sheets to use as sponges. While the water was heating, Ellis returned to the saloon and shaved the hair away from the wound and washed the area with soap and water. Over the wound itself he gently poured hydrogen peroxide and carefully sponged it dry then returned to the kitchen to prepare for surgery. He could hear the low hum of the men chattering among themselves.

When Mrs. Ashler was out of the room, the young girl slipped up beside Ellis and confided in a voice so low that Ellis could barely make out her words, "I speak not good English, and they think I no understand, but I hear many things. Be careful. I think you in big danger. Bad things happen in this town." Before Ellis could answer, she had disappeared.

Ellis rolled up his shirt sleeves and dropped a few drops of soap into the rubber gloves so they would slide on easily. He cleansed the wound again with warm salt water. He found an unbleached muslin drape with bound edges and a small slit, which Ida had sewed for him, and put over the unfortunate fellow, clipping it to his skin with towel clips. He put a few drops of chloroform on a mask which he held a few inches above the old man's face, using just enough to keep him from wiggling. He looked around to see if there was someone he could ask to help and noticed the kitchen girl had followed him into the bar. He motioned her to come over, and showed her how to hold the mask.

It would be a miracle if the man lived. The wound was extensive and he was afraid there was a great deal of brain damage. The dura, the clear white covering of the brain, had been torn and bone fragments driven into the brain, which would likely cause swelling, pressure, and eventual death.

Ellis moved rapidly as he used the opposite end of his scalpel to raise the crushed bone, and remove broken bits and pieces. The saloon was deadly quiet again as everyone gathered around to watch the new doctor work. He was thankful for his early classes where he had developed a 3-D anatomy in his mind. His professors had drawn pictures of the various body structures on the board and demonstrated them on a cadaver as they lectured. The students were then required to repeat the performance in the dissecting room. He knew well the relationship of various parts to each other, and was not obliged to hunt around for vessels as he went through the operation. He sewed the dura gently together with fine absorbable suture, and inserted a small, flat piece of rubber glove to act as a drain before sewing up the outside skin.

Mrs. Ashler held the kerosene lamp steady as he worked. He was surprised she showed no signs of squeamishness. "Is there a quiet room where we can put this fellow?" Ellis asked.

Again he was met with silent sullen resistance. "He doesn't have any money for a room," Ashler finally reasoned out loud. "unless you want to pay for one for him, Doctor."

"We could put him down at the pest house, if there isn't anything contagious there now," the small, scraggly man suggested, scuffing his beard with his knuckles.

Ellis walked over and picked up the handkerchief and pool ball. He undid the knot in the handkerchief carefully, dropped the ball from his hand, and let it fall with a heavy thud.

He looked at Ashler, and caught his eyes unguarded. For an instant his face was marked with fear, his thoughts laid bare. Ellis read his mind, and put it all together, confirming what he had begun to suspect.

"This isn't the kind of case you put in the pest house. It will probably end up to be a case of murder," Ellis said coolly, taking note of the quick shadow which crossed Ashler's face. "Will someone help me carry this man up to my room?" he continued, anger flashing in his dark eyes. The men who had lifted the sheepherder onto the table obliged rather awkwardly.

"If you need anything, let me know," said the businessman who had been so helpful, holding out his hand. "I'm J. O. Morgan. This is August Largilliere, and Henry Schmidt," he said, indicating his companions. "We're staying over at the Idanha."

Ellis sat beside the sheepherder and wondered why he and Ida had decided to come to this God forsaken place. He thought back to the day, several months earlier, when he had written to the postmasters of two Western towns which needed a doctor. When he received their replies he sat with the two letters before him on the small wooden table. His lifelong ambition of becoming a doctor was about to be realized—a dream which only a few years before had seemed as remote a possibility as being elected President of the United States.

Another dream was about to unfold—a dream of going West. He had no desire to begin his practice in the East, but like his ancestors, had a burning desire to come West. "There's no future for us here," Ellis had told Ida. "If we'd been born a few years sooner, maybe we'd own a tobacco plantation or something of value, but both our families lost everything in the war, and we were born into the bondage of poverty, confining as a prison."

"Don't you think that's putting it a little strongly?"

"Just think about it," replied Ellis. "What happened when you got the scholarship to The University of Indiana?"

"You're right," she sighed. "Even with the scholarship, my family couldn't afford to send me."

"In this part of the country, we're victims of 'white trash' bondage. The West is where the opportunity is," Ellis insisted.

Ellis had checked on places where a doctor's services were needed. He had written to the postmasters of Flagstaff, Arizona, and Soda Springs, Idaho. The two letters before him were their replies, and the choice was a difficult one.

"What do you think, Idie?" he asked his wife, who was drying the dishes from their evening meal.

"Well, Dr. Kackley..." she had begun.

"Not yet, Idie, not yet," he said seriously, brushing the curly black hair from his forehead with one hand. "I have a few more weeks of medical school and some damned hard exams before I qualify for the title, but it's getting close. I still find it hard to believe! But seriously, how in the hell are we going to decide which place to go?"

"I think," said Ida simply, "since you are the doctor, the choice should be yours." It seemed natural to both of them that he should make the decision.

Ellis spread the two letters before him. "I've done some checking on the two places," he said. "Arizona was settled mainly by people who came there looking for gold. Soda Springs was started by a religious group called Morrisites, and soldiers of Camp Connor, who came to protect them from religious persecution and from the Indians. A short time later the Mormons colonized the area. It grew as gold was discovered on Carriboo Mountain, about fifty miles to the north."

Ellis paused and thought a moment, then continued, "It seems that goods and services were at a premium for a few years as prospectors flocked like hungry wolves to the area. Soda Springs is also a railroad town, and as much as I dislike the railroad, it means availability of transportation.

"I have heard some strange stories about the Mormons, and I understand some of them are polygamists. Both towns are wild frontier towns, and undoubtedly have their share of gamblers, swindlers, and unscrupulous characters," he mused.

"The West doesn't have a monopoly on unscrupulous characters. We get our share of them here too," said Ida, "but don't think you're going to take me out West and then marry a bunch more wives."

"Don't worry," laughed Ellis, "You're woman enough for me—I wouldn't trade you for a dozen. By the way, I found a fellow who'd been out in Southern Arizona a few years ago. He said there were hundreds of little towns in the mountains with names such as Goug-em, Hog-em, and Stink-em. How would you like to live in a town with a name like that?" he asked, his dark eyes twinkling.

"If names tell anything," that's all we need to know," laughed Ida, "but Flagstaff is quite a ways to the north and may be entirely different."

"The climate in Flagstaff is probably a little milder than in Soda Springs, but it's in the mountains and isn't warm like Southern Arizona," said Ellis. "Arizona may require state medical exams, and from what I've seen of them, it is usually more who you know than what you know that counts. They're notorious for prejudice, and with my mixed heritage, I probably couldn't pass one if I turned in a perfect paper. Idaho only requires you to register in the county where you live before starting a practice."

"Do you really think prejudice plays that big a part in the exams?" asked Ida.

"I know it does," Ellis insisted, without hesitation. "What

do you think then?" asked Ida.

"I'm rather inclined toward Soda Springs," he said thoughtfully. "According to L. C. Eastman, postmaster and druggist in the settlement, there is no doctor from Montpelier westward to Pocatello, and from Preston northward to Idaho Falls. That's an unopposed practice over one-hundred miles square. I doubt if Flagstaff would offer that kind of opportunity."

He picked up the letter from Soda Springs. "Eastman says any doctor who settles there, tends to business, and does not drink or gamble, will make a lot of money in the big open spaces of Southeastern Idaho."

While Ellis' goals did not include accumulating a fortune, it would be nice to provide a good roof over their heads and be able to raise a family and provide them with the necessities of life. He had seen a lot of poverty in his twenty-seven years, in medical school and through the depression, and it wasn't a pretty sight. Ellis felt a strong desire to administer help in this world, to go into the homes and relieve the suffering—the very things the Savior did. He loved the common people.

He looked at his wife, hanging the dishtowel on a wooden rack attached to the end of the tall dish cupboard, and admired her tenacity. At five-foot-six, she was a little taller than he, and weighed slightly more than his one-hundred-ten pounds.

"This would never have been possible without you, Idie," he said. "Three years of medical school would have been an impossibility for the son of a poor tobacco farmer who entered this world at a time when the Union Army had destroyed everything. Lady Luck smiled on me when I met you, and I'm glad I was smart enough to realize it and make you my wife."

"I hope you'll always feel that way," said Ida. "I'm sure it was my lucky day when I met you."

"Kackley has always been a respected name," said Ellis. "My early ancestors came to Pennsylvania in the sixteen-hundreds from Germany, then moved to Virginia. They could not read or write, but were skilled with their hands. They had built up quite a fortune before the war came along."

"It's too bad war and its aftermath can destroy in such a short time what has taken hundreds of years to build," said Ida.

He reached out and pulled his wife toward him. "You have worked hard, lived in poverty, and sacrificed all but the bare necessities to put me through medical school, but soon I'll be able to give you a better life," he promised.

Ida had saved some money before their marriage for going to the university. She had sacrificed it willingly to the cause, and had never complained about giving up her plans, or the hard summer work at menial tasks to earn a few extra dollars.

She finished tidying up the kitchen and walked behind the chair where Ellis was still examining the two letters, placing a hand on his shoulder. While her husband was small in stature, he was larger than life in her eyes. She admired his super-abundance of nervous energy which kept him going constantly. His dedication to the human race and to medicine, combined with his remarkable memory and a mind which worked with lightning speed had already made him outstanding in his class. She was grateful they had been able to obtain the education necessary for him to realize his dream.

"I think you are right," she said. "Soda Springs may be primitive, but it has a lot of potential. I've heard its mineral waters are considered healing, and rich and fashionable people from all over go there to drink and bathe in the springs."

"Captain John Codman, a retired sea captain and writer, has written about the area. He seems greatly impressed with the natural resources, especially the mineral water. He thinks the springs will become as internationally known as Carlsbad Hot Springs of Czechoslovakia," said Ellis.

Ida didn't voice the fears she felt within. They were flat broke, and it wouldn't be easy to get enough money for a train ticket to that far out territory, not to mention the instruments and medical supplies he would need. She knew she wouldn't be able to accompany him, and wondered just what he would be getting into. She wondered how long it would be before they could be together again, and if he could really make a living in the Wild West, although she didn't doubt his ability for a minute. It was a hard decision to make—this choosing a place to practice, but Ellis seemed inclined toward Soda Springs, and if that was where he wanted to go, it was okay with her. Either place sounded so very different from the life they were accustomed to.

"You're one helluva wife," he said.

Ellis stood and put his arms around Ida, and they both felt the strength of togetherness. Together they would make their new home in a unique frontier town, caring for strangers, in spite of what difficulties they might face. They knew it wouldn't be easy. There would be no hospitals and few supplies. There would be bitter winter weather. It was the center of a wide open territory, with numerous areas not even surveyed yet.

"It will be a contrast to Nashville, which we've enjoyed so much," sighed Ida. "Nashville is such a nice, quiet, beautiful town. There's a lot of history to enjoy here, and the home of Andrew Jackson, and everything."

He saw her mouth twist in spite of her efforts to straighten it out. He reached behind her and untied her apron strings. The apron slipped to the floor. A smile returned to Ida's face. "In Soda Springs we'll be making history," he said confidently. She wished she could share his optimism for their future.

Ellis notified Mr. Eastman he would be coming to Soda Springs as soon as he was out of medical school. Time had flown by until Ellis' graduation. There was so much to do, and so much to think about. He knew a lot of people would soon be depending upon his skill and the responsibility weighed heavily upon him. He took out the recently purchased little black leather bag containing seven instruments and laid them carefully upon the table.

"I now have the tools, both material and intellectual to be a doctor, or so they tell me. I'm sure doctoring is not something conferred with a diploma, but something you must learn by doing, like an Indian learns buffalo hunting," he said. "When the sick and injured come to me, will I be able to find out what is wrong and help them? Will I be able to send them away better off than when they came, both physically and mentally?''

Ida noted the seriousness in his voice. ''You'll be the best doctor in the West,'' she responded. He hoped he would be worthy of Ida's confidence.

A groan of pain from the sheepherder brought Ellis back to the present. He prepared and administered a small shot of morphine to his patient. He wondered what Soda Springs was like. He could see little from the window as he watched a full moon rise in the dark sky. He would not leave the injured man's side.

When the sheepherder was resting better, Ellis again dozed fitfully in the hard-backed chair. When he awoke, daylight was streaming in the window and the blue April sky was filled with cotton clouds. Soon the unfortunate man was moaning in pain. Ellis hated to see him suffer so.

He had worked in the summer time as was required of medical students. He had seen many people healed through the medical arts, and many die in spite of all efforts made to save them. He had never accepted death without wondering what he had done wrong, or what undiscovered secrets might have prolonged life.

To those he could not cure he showed compassion, administering to their needs, and giving what comfort he could to their suffering. The poverty he had seen in Nashville and Louisville had a profound effect on his life. He knew people had problems when they were sick and came to a doctor, and if you could help, it was the thing to do. Helping was the whole rationale behind the practice of medicine, he thought.

That first summer, after a year of medical school, he had gone into the slums and worked among the destitute. He had never forgotten the desperation of the poor and the sick, living in squalid shacks which squatted on damp ground and furnished little protection from the elements and less of the comforts of even a simple home life. There he had met almost every disease human beings were heir to, and gained a mind full of tragic memories. The occurrence of disease was thought to be inevitable, and often met with passive acceptance as the expression of Divine Will.

The hardest thing to see had been the suffering of children. In some homes they had no beds, slept on the bare floor, were sewn into their clothing with the onset of winter, and were never washed, bathed, or cared for.

Epidemics of diseases such as diphtheria, scarlet fever, and typhoid were rampant. He had watched a child, feverish and delirious, it's face grotesque as it turned bluer and bluer in the last stages of diphtheria. The head and shoulders pulled back, the hands twitched, and then the entire body relaxed in death. The picture had never left his mind.

Much of what he learned in medical school was not usable or practical under slum conditions. Patients were treated with home remedies or just ignored until the pain became too great to bear. Often the doctor was not called until it was too late to help. Acute abdominal infections were unrecognized until terminal stages, when general inflammation was established. Old people sometimes lay unconscious for days before anyone sent for help.

Often it was the living, not the dying who suffered most. Some drank whiskey, some cursed, and some prayed. Though it had been awhile, he could still see in his mind's eye every detail of the misery he had witnessed.

There Ellis had learned to bear the hardship of long hours, working to the limit of endurance for the sake of his suffering patients. At times he felt his body not big enough to contain the frustration nor able to hold down his rising anger. Much of the misery was so unnecessary.

These experiences made him more determined to learn all there was to know about the cause and treatment of disease in order to help relieve the suffering he saw around him. Medicine had made great strides and was welling up into a whole field of newly found knowledge. Louis Pasteur had discovered germs; Lister had taught cleanliness and that body cavities could be opened without causing infection. Antitoxin and anesthesia had been developed. New horizons were opening up in all directions—the Army and Navy making great advances in tropical medicine, Public Health Departments organized—a great epic era of discovery was revolutionizing medicine.

"Money will come in when we have a good practice going," he had told Ida. "It will help, not only with our own family, but for building the community and helping others. You can't take it with you, and money is only of value if it is used to do good. I can't understand the selfishness of men who wouldn't hesitate to cut each other's throats for a few dollars."

Ida agreed wholeheartedly. "You're never afraid of hard work, and you're always willing to give of yourself to help others," she said. "That's one of the things I respect and admire about you."

Ellis shook his head. "I can't understand the urge some people have to pile up wealth for its own sake. I have to admit though, a little money would be great right now." he sighed.

It had taken them months of saving to get a new suit, which was considered the only proper attire for a professional man. For the trip west, they had to add a long, heavy overcoat. It was cold in Idaho, and doctors not only had to be skilled and able to make quick decisions, they had to gain the confidence of their patients. If a patient didn't think you looked and acted like a doctor, he might walk out with something like a bad appendix "to think it over" and never live to come back. They ordered the clothing, and one evening on her way home from teaching school, Ida had picked it up.

"Just slip it on," she urged, "and let's see how you look."

Ellis hadn't felt much like giving a fashion show, but he figured the least he could do was try the clothing on after all Ida had done to help him. He took it into the simple bedroom, furnished with only a bed and wash stand, where they washed in turn. He slipped into the white, high-collared shirt and black bow tie. He carefully put on his pants, vest, and jacket, then turned slowly around while Ida looked him over. Her smiling eyes, which showed her obvious pride, told him he had passed the inspection with flying colors.

She had wished out loud she could buy him a large silk handkerchief, which was the style then for the influential or well-to-do. She knew Ellis had always wanted one, but there was nothing for frills. They would be lucky to get bare necessities.

Graduation time had been like a dream. He couldn't believe it was happening, and kept feeling he might wake up any minute and find he was still a school teacher, not a doctor. Shortly after receiving his diploma, he had boarded the train at the Union Station in St. Louis, coming through Omaha and on west to this small frontier town. He already missed Ida. It would be lonely in the West until she could join him.

Chapter 3

For the next three days Ellis sat beside the sheepherder. The prognosis was doubtful, and all he could do was to administer an occasional small dose of morphine to alleviate the pain.

Mr. Morgan, who was running sheep in the area, came by several times with hot coffee and words of encouragement for which Ellis was grateful. When the patient died, halfway through the third night, Ellis felt devastated. He hadn't imagined, even in his wildest nightmares, this kind of a situation on his first night in town—and losing his first real patient. He wondered if there were anything he could have done to save the man, but all of his past training and instinct told him that he had done his best. Now it was up to the law to punish those responsible for taking the sheepherder's life.

He sat slowly down and opened his Bible to the Lord's Prayer. He sat for a long time, Bible in hand, before finally falling asleep, still sitting in the chair.

In spite of losing his first case, as soon as word got around the new doctor had arrived, he began getting a few calls daily. Soda Springs and the surrounding country did need a doctor. There was a semi-retired Doctor Anderson, with great, long whiskers, who had moved to Soda Springs from Utah the year before, and was running the Anderson Drug Store.

Ellis went down and talked to the old man and learned he had received his education in Pennsylvania and Ohio. He had graduated from the Eclectic College of Medicine and Surgery in Cincinnati in 1855. Dr. Anderson was a Mormon and had served as Regimental Surgeon to the Nauvoo Legion of Cache County, Utah. He had also been postmaster thirty years and Justice of the Peace for twenty-five years in Portage, Utah. Ellis liked the old man, who operated a traveling library as well as the drug store, where he advertised a full line of Kickapoo Indian medicines.

One day, shortly after Ellis' arrival, Jimmy stopped in to see how he was doing. "A fellow there iss came in oon the train last night. Oover night in the hotel he stayed. Oon his way to Pocatella t' see a doctor aboot his arm, he is. Aye, thinks broken it might be. Ya' might be interested ya'self in stoopin' by t' see him. Aye, there's noot a mite o' use in his takin' hisself clear to Pocatella when a doctor we have right 'ere in the hotel. He asked myself t' bring ya' by."

Ellis put on his jacket and followed Jimmy down the hall and out the door of the hotel. He hadn't stopped to put on his overcoat, and though the sun was shining, the east wind was cool. Inside the station building a large, bulky man was hovering over a younger man of smaller stature, with a full mustache. The young fellow was sitting on the edge of the bench holding his arm. He was obviously in excruciating pain.

"This is Dr. Kackley, the new doctor I told ya' aboot," explained Jimmy. "Aye, no use goin' clear to Pocatella, a doctor ta' see, when ohn we have right 'ere."

"Would you like me to take a look at that arm?" asked Ellis.

The large man looked at Ellis as though he thought he was too young to know much. "Well, I guess it can't hurt anything for you to take a look at it," he conceded.

Ellis checked the arm carefully and found it was dislocated, not broken. He knew this was a chance to show his skill, and it was clearly a case where the patient wasn't going to drop dead from the injury, though it was painful. He took off his jacket and draped it over a bench. He knew the man's pain could be remedied quickly, but must be done just right or he might break the elbow. He extended the patient's arm, locking his elbow, as he had read about doing in a medical book, then using the arm as a lever, rolled it around and popped the head back into the socket. Everyone in the depot could hear it pop into place.

Relief was immediate. By that time a group of about ten people had gathered and were watching with great interest. The man moved his arm slowly and grinned when he found he could do so without pain. He and his friend were pleasantly surprised and relieved not to have to go farther for treatment. Ellis had always possessed a flair for the dramatic, and knew how to take advantage of that talent when the time was right. Soon the story of how he had fixed the man's arm with a quick twist of the wrist was all over town, and a legend was in the process of being born. Patients began to send for the new doctor.

Ellis was anxious to see the springs Lawrence had told him about on the train. Late in May, after the weather had warmed up, he and Jimmy decided to take a day and ride out and see the area. "A couple o' horses we'll pick oop 't the stables," Jimmy said.

They walked over to the stables. It was a nice day, with only a light breeze stirring. Ellis stopped in his tracks when the attendant appeared and he realized with a start that the small man with the scraggly whiskers, who had agreed with everything Ashler said while he was treating the sheepherder, was one of the stable employees.

They saddled the two horses, mounted, and started in a northwesterly direction toward Hooper Springs. The air was brisk, but the spring sunshine lay on their shoulders and warmed their spirits as well as their bodies.

"I don't trust that man at the stables," Ellis told Jimmy.

"An' right ya' ere," said Jimmy. "Aye, a rascal he is, an' his friends with him," he added.

When they got to the springs, Ellis was not disappointed with the area. The springs were clear, as water bubbled from the earth and boiled like it was in a heated caldron. It made whirlpools before running into the creek. The water at Hooper and Ninety Percent Springs was delicious.

They rode up Soda Creek and examined the numerous mineral springs along its banks. The creek ran strongly, with a firm current. Ellis was fascinated with the area. It was a lovely place. Trees, brush, and grass grew along the stream. He drew in deep breaths of the air, aromic with wetness. He couldn't get over the beauty of the mountains, and stopped occasionally just to drink it all in. They followed the stream to the junction of Soda Creek and Bear River, on the west side of town. Ellis recognized the mounds Lawrence had described to him during his train ride.

"Aye, wee streams still roon from some o' the cones,"

Jimmy explained, "an' things people poot where the water can drip oover an' coat them. Like stone they look in a short time, they do. Aye, great souvenirs they make for tourists t' carry home."

East of town, at Formation Creek a large spring of clear, cool water came up at the foot of a big mountain and ran along the stream for about a mile. It spread out over the country, leaving behind strange formations. There was a large cave, with three fingers, the longest running close to one-hundred-and-fifty feet in length. It was lined with lime formations, which Ellis found fascinating.

The cave was inhabited by furry, rat-sized animals, which seemed to be blind. They lived in the dark recesses of the cave, and didn't react to light. "'Tis blind I think they ere," said Jimmy. "A lot more of them there used to be. Aye, before killing 'em the kids started doon."

Their last stop was at Mineral Heights, where Tom Williams had a bathhouse. "'Tis used mainly by the cattle an' sheep men when to toon they come," Jimmy explained to Ellis.

The structure, near the base of Mineral Heights hill, used water which trickled down from a spring at the top. It was made of rough lumber slabs filled in with mud and clay mortar and was about eight by ten feet. The water was lukewarm.

The place was filled with men. Some looked like they were of Italian or Spanish descent, and particularly from the Basque area. They were covered with dust and dirt, and Ellis thought they needed a dip in the cleansing waters. Jimmy promptly introduced Ellis to the leader. "Mr. Knowlin, woot ya be likin' to meet oor new doctor, Ellis Kackley."

Knowlin shook Ellis' hand warmly. "We sure need a doctor in this town. Sheep men are having one helluva time with eye infections. If you could find a cure for that, you'd make a fortune," he added.

Knowlin called over one of the men, and Ellis examined his eyes. They were intensely inflamed, granulated, and the man tried to shield them from the light. Looking closer, Ellis noticed a pterygium, or wing like growth of the superficial covering of the eye, from the inner margin spreading out towards the pupil. Ellis knew the pterygium was not the primary cause of the disease, for he had helped his summer preceptor, Dr. Zoring, remove a number of similar growths.

"Are all of the sheep men having this problem?" he asked.

"It's like a plague. With the fine dust and dirt of trailing a herd, every sheep man in the country is having trouble with his herders getting eye problems. A. J. Knowlin and Company handles over eight-hundred-thousand sheep a year. We used to trail 'em from the corn belt until the railroad was finished. Now we ship 'em," he informed Ellis, "but we're still trailing the herds up here to pasture in the spring and back to the Southern Utah desert in the fall. It adds up to hundreds of miles."

Eight-hundred-thousand! Good Lord, that's a lot of sheep!" exclaimed Ellis.

"Yes," agreed Knowlin, "and they're the best damn sheep in the West. We have Shropshires, Hampshires, Rambouillets, Oxfords, Cotwolds, Lincolns, and Southdowns, imported from England and Europe. I started out for Swift and Company of Chicago, then started my own company in '94. Now we have six shipping houses at western points and the best purebred flock in the West, but if this damned eye situation keeps up, we won't be able to get herders."

"Have the men stop by the Mart," said Ellis, "and I'll see what I can do for them."

The sun was not far from setting when Ellis and Jimmy returned to town. That night Ellis wrote a long letter to Ida. He wasn't much for letter writing, but he told her about the wonders of the country he had seen, his experiences in medicine in this wild outpost, and his concern about the sheep men and their eye infections. He hadn't told her of his suspicions about Mr. Ashler because he was almost afraid to put them on paper, and he didn't want to worry Ida. "I can hardly wait for the day when we can be together again," he concluded.

Ellis soon discovered that midwives did virtually all the

birthing in this frontier town except when they ran into a problem they couldn't handle. Then they called for the young doctor, who demonstrated his skill with cases where the baby had to be delivered with forceps or turned by hand, where there was hemorrhaging or other complications, or when the birth required more able hands than their own for some reason.

Sometimes he was not called in time to save the mother or child. Ellis found one of the hardest things to do was to tell a new mother her baby had died. He never accepted death without severe sorrow and a nagging feeling of guilt because he had not been able to save the life, as he felt he should have.

There seemed to be a particular problem with mothers of babies delivered in sheep camps running dangerously high fevers for a week or so after delivery. Ellis tried to determine a common denominator for these infections. Then one day he arrived at a call to find the new mother packed in a poultice. Taking it off, he examined the contents to find fresh cow manure. He drew a deep breath and ran his fingers through his hair. "What are you using on this woman?" he asked the midwife. "Do you usually use 'cow-pie' poultices on new mothers?"

The woman explained hesitantly that "cow-pie" poultices were indeed commonly used at the first sign of infection.

Ellis could see he had a difficult job ahead educating these sincere but misled people who relied on such remedies. "Thank God for Pasteur and Lister," he mumbled to himself, "or I might still be treating people with remedies like 'cow-pie' poultices."

He wiped his brow and explained patiently to the woman that the poultice was swarming with germs which cause infection. Then he showed the midwife how to care for the woman properly.

Some of these midwives would later become his nurses. He was careful to teach them the right way and to try and make friends so they would call for him when there was a problem and send him cases which warranted a doctor's care.

As long as Ellis had sterile instruments and drapes, and a

workable place to put the patient, he would not hesitate to operate or do whatever needed to be done. The philosophy of the time was to cut things to the core if there was a situation which might spread infection or cause further problems. The wild frontier way of life at the turn of the century, working with outlaw horses, and other dangers made terrible fractures and injuries commonplace.

Most cuts were sewn up without anesthesia. Speed was the mark of a good physician. When incisions were closed quickly, there was a minimum of trauma to the tissues, and healing was more likely to be prompt. All wounds of any magnitude drained pus. Injuries which might seem trivial in years to come were treated with amputation. In those early times, amputation was considered the most practical way to treat injuries of large joints, fractures of the thigh bone, or others which could lead to infection and death, but Ellis always tried to save a limb if at all possible.

Often he operated on a patient and never saw the person again. To leave something in a case like that, which might breed problems, would mean certain death. He was not able to save some of these early cases, but he did his best to help them, and many a life was lengthened by his medical knowledge and skill. Some he helped gain a few extra days or weeks to straighten out their affairs, while others were restored to health, and enjoyed a long and useful life. Some lived with inconveniences, which without his care would have been serious disabilities. With experience, his skill increased, and he received more and more calls.

Fevers were common, including typhoid and scarlet fever, and others such as Rocky Mountain fever, undulant fever, later known also as Bang's disease, and a score of unnamed ones which had not yet been separated by medical science. It was known that typhus was caused by rats and fleas and typhoid came through water, but their bacterias were not yet separated.

Acute infections also caused fever, and it wasn't easy to sort out the cause when the temperature was elevated. Venereal disease was rampant. Syphilis and gonorrhea were common to this newly settled land, and were dreaded diseases before the advent of antibiotics. Pneumonia was the most common cause of winter fevers and was often a killer. It was especially lethal to children. The young doctor went into the homes with mustard plasters, cough suppressants and often recommending some fresh air and sunshine for the patient. Quinine was used in treating the more serious fevers.

When Ellis saw what he was faced with in this frontier town, he went to see if Mr. Eastman could order more instruments for him. Eastman dragged out a case from under the counter. "These were left by a Dr. Wilson from Scotland who was here a few years before you came. I'll sell them to you cheap."

"That's exactly what I need," exclaimed Ellis, and hurried back to the hotel to examine his new purchase more closely.

Not dangerous to life, but irritating, was scabies, commonly known as "the seven-year itch." The tiny bug burrowed under the skin and as it moved, it caused severe itching. Ellis treated it with a mixture of lard and sulphur, which was used for six nights, even in the hair. After the sixth night, the patient was given a hot bath and clothing, sheets, and towels were boiled to kill the parasite. It was readily transmitted between individuals, and spread throughout the community at regular intervals, particularly among those who didn't know what caused it. Whenever Ellis got a new patient, he always checked to make sure they didn't have the bug.

Ellis never knew just what to expect when someone called for his help. Sometimes a hired man or child was sent for the doctor, and he was told that there was an emergency at the Jones' ranch or home. Sometimes the messenger would say that Mrs. Jones was in the family way, or that the midwife needed help. The lack of information made things difficult. People became excited and gave wrong directions to the doctor. It took far more time to get to his patients than to treat them.

Ellis never refused a call, no matter how great the distance he had to travel to reach a patient. There were no specialists in this western area to treat a case if it was too difficult for the country doctor. Often a long, tiring journey was followed by a difficult operation, but he was tough when it came to doctoring, and could work, even when seemingly dead on his feet. Before operating on a patient, Ellis performed the operation in his mind, taking into account the age, physical condition, and mental attitude of the patient. He had to carefully consider the risk of operation and what would become of the patient if he didn't operate.

Children sometimes became violently ill and required immediate attention, particularly in cases of acute abdominal problems like appendicitis. Delay could be fatal, especially when peritonitis set in and spread all over the abdomen.

Ellis found the Mormon people to be a well-organized, close-knit group. When someone was ill the neighbors were always willing to lend a hand, whether to harvest the crops or sit up all night and nurse the afflicted one. Women from their Relief Society organization were adept at caring for the ill, and when a disease reached epidemic proportions, these ladies were willing to give assistance night and day.

Dorthea Lau, president of the organization, tore up so many petticoats for emergency bandages, Ellis told Ida later, "Her girls never knew when they got up in the morning whether or not they'd have a petticoat to put on."

In spite of having twelve children of her own, this lady often helped late into the night. "Your Relief Society is the only organization I've ever wanted to join," Ellis told Dorthea jokingly, "and I don't qualify to be a member!"

Most of the families had few modern conveniences in their homes. Houses were lighted by a kerosene lamp which could be carried from one place to another, wherever it was needed. Inside plumbing was unheard of, and every family had an outhouse, or privy as it was sometimes called, about twenty yards behind the house. Most featured two holes, but one-holers were not uncommon. While some of the settlers in town were served by the Mormon water system, bringing water into their homes, others got their water from wells, and brought it up by the bucketful using a rope and pulley. None of the residences had central heating. People relied on wood burning stoves for heat. The kitchen range usually heated the kitchen area and dining room if one was fortunate enough to have such a luxury as a separate room for dining. The focal point of the front room was usually a pot bellied stove, which left one hot on the side turned toward it, and cold on whatever side was turned away from the heat source. Bedrooms were usually not heated.

He could adapt to the living conditions, though more primitive than what he had enjoyed in Tennessee, but the biggest source of irritation for Ellis was the horses from the livery stable he was given to ride when there was a call from out in the country.

While he knew country doctors were usually given horses which would not be easily winded and could cover the distance quickly, he was sure they saved the meanest, orneriest cayuses they had, to rent to the new doctor. The men who hung around the livery stable and saloon stood back and guffawed loudly when he was bucked off before he got out of sight.

Because Ellis was small of stature, they seemed to doubly enjoy seeing him unseated by an unruly horse. He made a brave show of strength, but vowed he would get a place of his own where he could keep animals as soon as he could see his way clear to pay for it. He knew the time wouldn't be in the near future, because getting Ida to Soda Springs was his first priority.

It was hardly fair when he had come to the settlement to help people, and often as not received no pay for his services, nor asked any, for these men to put him in bodily danger or have this kind of fun at his expense. But Ellis was spunky. He never let them have the satisfaction of seeing his deep anger or hurt. He promptly got up, got back on the animal, and rode off, whether his buttocks were numb or his limbs felt broken. If they could have seen his black eyes, flashing with anger, they would have had no question about his feelings.

He tried hard not to be bitter towards anyone, and he always treated everyone, even his tormentors, as professionally as he would any other patient if they were in need of his services, but he knew these unfeeling, greedy people were no friends of his, and that his life was in danger as long as he had to rely on them for his transportation. He wondered if the whole group was in cahoots with Ashler, and were accomplices in the murder of the sheepherder. He noticed several of the men who had been present in the saloon that first night hung around at the livery stable and saloon, drinking and gambling.

As he persisted in riding, he became more skilled at keeping his seat. He learned to blend his body with that of the animal, lean the right direction, and stay seated most of the time. His natural love of animals helped and after he had ridden a particular horse a few times, it became easier to handle.

Word soon spread that the new doctor was honest with people and knew what he was doing in spite of his young appearance. He was beginning to be accepted as a good doctor who was serious about his profession. He worked hard to establish himself in the community, and struggled to get to know his patients. Though Ellis never sent a bill for his services, those who could afford to pay gladly did, and he ministered to those who couldn't afford a doctor with the same concern as to those rich in worldly goods.

One day when he asked for a horse at the livery stable, the attendant brought out a white mule. Ellis sized up the situation instantly. A crowd had quickly gathered, and when he noticed Ashler in the fringes of the group, he knew a trick had been planned. The men came out of the barber shop next door; one old man was wrapped in an apron with his whiskers all lathered up. He knew they were all waiting to see him bucked off.

Mules and dogs were the same everywhere, Ellis thought, and if there was one thing he had learned in his youth while cultivating tobacco on his father's few acres of land, it was how to handle a mule. He walked over to the mule, talking to it softly as he walked around it. The animal responded as he stroked it's neck, still talking softly. After a few minutes he mounted the mule and rode off, turning to look at the waiting men with a caustic look in his black eyes. The men were amazed, and noticeably disappointed.

"That mule will get him before he gets back," he heard a gruff voice comment. "There goes the old white mule doctor," said another.

The mule clopped along through the mud from a recent rain storm. The countryside glistened as the golden sun came out. Ellis could taste the flavor of rain upon his tongue. While three or four miles an hour was average speed for a mule, if rushed, the speed would likely drop to half that. The animal seemed to take no notice of anything around him, hardly even paying attention to whether it was fair or stormy. The mule was a most reliable means of transportation, though a less dignified means than the horse. Dignity was very important to the young doctor, but he had a way with the mule, and they developed a quick understanding. Every so often, the mule would feel like bucking. Ellis would slide off and let him buck. When he was finished, Ellis would slip back on.

When Ellis returned from the call, he came into the livery stable past the bystanders and chronic sitters in captain's chairs who looked glum and obviously disappointed to see him. He passed them, carrying the saddle bags encasing his instruments, and tossed the coins to the bar tender for the rent of the mule. From then on, he preferred the mule, unless high speed was required. He soon became known to his friends as the "White Mule Doctor."

His mind was occupied with deeper thoughts as he walked out onto the wooden sidewalk that day, past the men and dogs. A warmth filled him that was not the low, golden sun. He remembered the child, just delivered, who had been named Ellis—the first of many to be named after him. He thought of Ida, who would soon be coming to Soda Springs, and knew they were now a part of the West, delivered from the "white trash" bondage they had been born into in the East. Others had come before him with the same deliverance. The Pathfinders, Bill Sublette and Jim Bridger, had come to this very area, followed by the Mountain Men, Gentiles, and the Mormons in their covered wagons and push carts. Frontier life was not easy, but Ellis was determined he would not let these unscrupulous men get the best of him.

He knew the tide had brought the armed forces, and people by oxen, and by the iron horse on which he had arrived. It would be another half century before the tide of people coming west would slow to ebb tide and die. Now they were coming with anticipation and hope for the future. Later, during the great depression of the thirties the masses would be coming west again, but this future migration would come without hope, with a "Lost Cause." The Manifest Destiny no longer existed; with the Spanish American War, American Imperialism had taken its place.

Many new ideas were popular. Hypnotism was a new field, and a renaissance in spiritualism was in progress. Many doctors during Ellis' time were highly involved in both. Ellis did not participate in either. While he had been raised in the Lutheran faith, he was never involved in organized religion to the point where it entered into his rituals or thoughts, though he often read his Bible. In a day of religious revivals many members of his family had embraced religion like Huckleberry Finn, when he and the two scoundrels, the Duke of Bilgewater and the King, the Dauphin "Louie of France" crashed a religious revival. Soon the King was whooping and hollering and fleecing those attending of several hundred dollars, and a few gallons of whiskey hidden beneath their wagons.

Ellis thought of his mother, a short woman with hard work showing on her face, telling of how her father shook his head and told his family, "I don't want you going to any more camp meetings. If one more person gets religion I won't have anyone left to swear at the oxen to keep them moving."

While Ellis did not participate in organized religion, he always granted full access to elders, priests, bishops, and those who tried to bring comfort to the sick through their faith. He never spoke against any of the churches, and had strong moral convictions of right and wrong. He did not fight the criminal element in town openly, but did everything he could to circumvent their plans and operations, and he knew they recognized that he was aware of what was going on.

Often Ellis was called on to patch up victims of their foul play. All kinds of shillelaghs were used to hit people over the head. A miner with mangled, long hair and unwashed clothing came in with cigarette burns all over his private parts, where he had been tortured by a group of men trying to get him to tell where he had hidden his gold dust when he came to town. Gold was the medium of exchange, and places of business had scales to weigh the mineral, which was mostly found as fine dust or flour gold in this area. Another miner, a large, strong looking man who said his name was Albin Lindstrom, told Ellis of being backed up against a wall by a gang of men in the saloon, and grabbing a chair to fend off his attackers while he made his escape. His brother, who had ridden into town with friends and was to meet him there, was never heard of again.

Ellis knew that quite a few of the business people clothed in the guise of respectability were involved in these atrocities, and cursed their inhumanity.

The sheep men continued to be plagued by eye infections, and Ellis treated them to the best of his ability. He tried various methods of treatment, but nothing seemed to give any permanent relief.

The Indians in the area were the most pitiful people Ellis had ever seen. The troops had tried to wipe them out, killing all the buffalo, and even killing women and children when they were in the meadow bottoms during the winter to find pasture for their horses. The attitude of the town, as first laid down by the military, was that the only good Indian was a dead Indian. The Mormons did not share this attitude. Brigham Young had told his people to feed the Indians, not fight them, and though many of the Mormon colonists were poor, they would share what they had with their Indian brothers. The Indians were a half-starved, broken race, with no immunity to infectious disease, such as measles, smallpox, and scarlet fever. They were herded onto reservations, and children were put into schools, where they picked up these diseases and large groups were wiped out.

Ellis felt a great deal of empathy with the Indian people. He thought of President Andrew Jackson's "Trail of Tears" from Georgia to Oklahoma Territory, and realized that here in the West, similar atrocities were still being committed against his people. Not only did he have Indian blood himself, he had been poor, and felt himself fortunate, not better than these people. He treated them without charge whenever the occasion arose.

Most sickness occurred at night or in bad weather. On a sunny day, the population was likely to be disgustingly healthy. Summers in Soda Springs were short, as was the growing season. Crops were often damaged by frost even during summer months.

As September approached, Ellis noticed the air becoming nippy, at times even during the day. He had saved enough money that first summer to be able to send for Ida. It would be an exciting day for them both when she boarded the train at Union Station and started west to join her husband, whose reputation was growing daily. He had been gone what seemed like an eternity, and though going west on the train alone was frightening, she could hardly wait to get to Soda Springs.

Chapter 4

The three days it took for the arrival of the train bringing Ida west seemed like an eternity to Ellis. Time dragged, and every time he looked back over the years, nostalgia filled him. On the day she was to arrive, he hurried down to the station half an hour early. He had saved conscientiously so his wife could join him in Soda Springs, and now that she was about to appear, a sharp pleasure came over him. He wondered what she would think of the area. He knew she would like the springs, but he was worried she might be offended by some of the townspeople. Raised Southern Methodist, she had a deep sense of right and wrong. He wondered how she would adjust to all the lawlessness and corruption being carried on almost openly in the town. Ida didn't have a lot of tolerance for people hurting other people.

The Mart was not the kind of a place Ellis would want his wife to live, so he had scrimped to get an apartment at the Idanha. The Mart was mostly filled with cattlemen, sheep men, and other businessmen seeking to turn a profitable deal.

Since the episode with the murdered sheepherder, Mr. Ashler had openly showed his dislike for Ellis; and Ellis, in turn, deeply distrusted the man. He would always believe Ashler had been responsible for the sheepherder's robbery and murder. This seemed to be a prevalent notion around town, though the case was not even investigated by the law. When Ellis asked the Marshal why nothing was done about the murder, he said he had no evidence. Ellis came away feeling he would never try to find any.

To press the matter might be extremely dangerous. He would have to be careful what he did until he at least knew who was involved in the corruption and just what was going on. He knew his position was weak, as a newcomer, and that he was looked upon by many as a "white mule doctor." He was hopeful that with sufficient time people would realize what was taking place and rise up against the lawlessness and deceit.

A cool, early fall breeze was rustling the leaves on the trees and blowing the small bunches of grass as Ellis nervously waited for the train. He ran his fingers through the hair on his forehead as he looked around the town. Ida would enjoy looking at the mountains, he thought, as he gazed at the already snow-patched slopes of Mt. Sherman. It had been a lonely summer, but somehow he was just a little bit glad he had left her at home. It had given him a chance to get somewhat established without Ida having to go through all of the pain he had experienced. He had been here long enough to make friends with a few people he respected.

Jimmy stuck his head out the station door and greeted Ellis. "Mornin' Doc. I'll bet 'tis a bundle of nerves ya ere, a waitin' for the missus. Aye, the train shoot be a comin' in about fifteen minutes."

Ellis appreciated Jimmy's friendship. He was one of the few people Ellis knew he could count on, no matter what the situation. He sensed that Jimmy knew exactly what was going on and would quietly, like himself, be a slow mover until people became fully aware of the situation. Ellis had also made friends with the Schmidts, Gortons, Knowlins, Morgans and Largillieres.

He would always appreciate Mr. Morgan befriending him that first night in town when no one else would help with the injured sheepherder.

Mr. and Mrs. Largilliere were such a dignified couple. They commanded the respect of the whole town, and Ellis never heard them called or spoken of by first names, but they had been very friendly to him.

Henry Schmidt had taken time out of his busy schedule to take him boating at Mammoth Spring, and show him around a bit. Schmidts had a trading post north of town at the small settlement of Henry, which had been named for him.

Much of his business had been brought in by Leah Gorton, whose badly broken leg he had fixed when a run-away team had thrown her out of a wagon. They had called Dr. Green, who came on the train, and thought it should be amputated. When Ellis was consulted for a second opinion, he felt he could save the leg, and had. While amputation was the accepted treatment for such a wound, you had to take a chance once in awhile when the stakes were high.

Mr. Morgan, Mr. Houtz, and Mr. Knowlin, and the business of the other sheep men had done a lot to make it possible for Ellis to earn enough to send for Ida this soon. These people were all the type of people Ida would like, he thought with satisfaction. He wished he could take her to a home of their own, but he knew it would still be some time before he could afford to get into one. To the north, the Codman house stood out with two gabled stories. It was as beautiful a specimen of a house as the Idanha was of a hotel. Ida would like the Idanha, he thought, even though it retained only a trace of its original elegance, according to the townspeople.

The train whistle trilled, bringing him back to the present, and his excitement mounted as the huge 4-4-0 steam engine roared into the station amid great clouds of black smoke and flying cinders. Ellis had already made more than one friend by removing the hot, painful cinders from eyes of those who had occasion to meet the train. It wasn't unusual for the hot cinders to start a fire. Ellis had heard that Union Pacific had paid out a lot of money in damage claims because of the cinders.

One by one the passengers stepped out of the coach car, and finally he saw her, even more beautiful than he remembered. He could hardly wait to take her in his arms. He squeezed her so tightly she could hardly breathe, then held her at arms length, and just looked at her. Neither of them spoke for a moment, then they both tried to talk at once. At last they were together again, and as they had dreamed earlier, they would make history in this rugged frontier town.

They had dinner in the Idanha Hotel dining room that

evening. Ida looked about curiously. She was anxious to find out everything about the town, and Ellis wondered if she were trying to do it all in one evening.

"You've written so seldom, I often wondered if you were still alive!" she chided as she cut the thick beefsteak on her plate.

"I know," admitted Ellis with a sheepish grin, "I'm not much for letter writing, but I thought about you every day."

"What are the schools like here?" she questioned.

"I haven't had much time for anything but doctoring, but I've heard they just go to the fourth grade, and many of the students only attend a few months of the year."

"That's terrible," said Ida. "Education has improved greatly in the civilized areas. A good education for every child is the goal. It looks like there is lots to do here."

Ida was especially concerned about the school situation. Schools in Nashville were more sophisticated than in Seymour, Bedford, and Mt. Liberty, where she had taught in Indiana. She loved working with the young people, and her heart was with them.

"Yes," said Ellis, "there is lots to do in more areas than one. The law does not protect the people it should, especially those who ride into town alone. Some of the supposedly respected people are nothing but a bunch of damn thieves, and exploit everyone they can. As soon as it gets dark there is a mass exodus to the 'wild' houses, one down the railroad tracks and one down by the Bear River. Disease is rampant, including venereal disease. On the other hand, there are some damn nice people in the town, and I'm anxious for you to meet some of them."

"What about the Mormons?" Ida asked, glancing around as though she was afraid she might be overheard.

"Well, they don't have horns nor tails," said Ellis. "I've delivered enough babies to know that for a certainty."

"Oh, go on," laughed Ida. "What kind of people are they. Do they accept progress and doctors? How many wives do they have? Are they mean to them? I've all kinds of questions."

"They're people just like you and I. Most of them have

only one wife, but there's a few with more than one, although it's illegal now. I hear Star Valley, Wyoming, has quite a few polygamists. But forget the schools, and the Mormons, and everything else for now. There'll be plenty of time to find out about all those things later," he said softly, as he rose and took her arm, guiding her toward their rooms. "Tonight I don't want to share my wife with anyone or anything. We've been apart far too long."

It was wonderful for Ellis having Ida there. He didn't realize how lonely he had been while they were apart. She was exhausted from the long trip, but when she was rested up, it didn't take her long to become friends with the wives of some of the men living at the Idanha. While Soda Springs was a tough town, the women were respected. Dressed in their high top shoes, corsets, and long dresses, they wore big hats and carried large purses and parasols, and even the roughest men tipped their hats when they passed. The town boasted many dressmakers. Mrs. Strachan had a millinery and dressmaking shop opposite the Union Pacific Depot, and advertised "fancy notions and hats of the latest patterns kept in stock and trimmed to order." Ida fell in love with the Strachans immediately. She enjoyed looking around the shop while they visited. The Strachan family knew how to make her feel at home. The other families Ellis knew and liked had also welcomed Ida with open arms.

Women from the poorer families in the area were respected too. They were hard workers with sun weathered faces, and Ellis thought many of them looked more like men than women. They had accomplished a hard day's work every day of their lives, and it showed on their faces. The log cabins they called home were likely to have dirt floors and sod roofs. Winter blizzards were so severe, ropes had to be strung from the house to the outhouse to keep from getting lost when necessity made them venture out.

These women were often worn out from bearing numerous children as well as from hard work. For some unknown reason, goiters were a common ailment among this group. As Ellis' practice continued to grow, he began doing a little goiter research, and found he could sometimes control hyperthyroidism with administration of very small doses of iodine, instead of the disfiguring surgery generally in use, eliminating many serious surgical complications. However, the majority had to have the thyroid removed to prevent the heart from failing. Often the operation had to be done with a local anesthetic because of advanced heart disease.

One day a man in critical condition, died before Ellis could treat him. Ellis helped the family arrange for his burial. He called the market for a burial cart. The two main markets in town had delivery service twice a day, serving the more affluent housewives, and both markets had sleek, showy teams and light rigs to deliver the groceries. They had one speed—fast, as they sped through town with their wares, which households were billed for monthly. These same rigs were used for burial carts.

One was called to take the body for interment. The fast, high stepping horses went up the turn to the rock store, down the road which crosses the railroad tracks, and at that point the driver lost control of the horses. As they went over the railroad tracks the casket fell off, the lid popped open, and the deceased rolled out. He was wearing the usual burial half-suit of the time, covering just his front half. Ellis had discovered very shortly after his arrival the old saying about being buried with your boots on was not true. Boots were expensive, and no one was buried with them on. They usually didn't put any kind of shoes on the dead.

Ellis helped family members pick up the corpse and re-dress the man, who would have blushed with shame at the indecent exposure, had he been alive.

When Ellis took out appendix, kidney stones, or had to amputate a finger or toe, the fashionable thing to do was to take the part home and put it in a jar on the mantle, where it became a show and conversation piece. "When Gabriel blows his horn and tries to find all these people, and get everyone together, he's going to have quite a time finding all the parts," Ellis told Ida.

When he had patients there, Ellis drove to the pest house on the banks of Little Spring Creek daily. Here residents without loved ones to care for them at home, or those who came into town with infectious diseases such as smallpox, typhoid, or advanced cases of rotting syphilis were housed while they received medical care. Most towns had a "pest" house in those days to isolate the contagious cases. Patients there were often terminal, and Ellis washed carefully and changed his clothing after checking on them. Smallpox could be controlled. A short time earlier it had been rampant with about thirty percent of the cases dying. Ellis began his practice on the tail end of the smallpox era. He saw hundreds with the infection during his early practice, but the disease was on its way out. Vaccine had been developed instead of pricking the skin and rubbing it against the sores of an infected person, which more often than not caused the disease, but sometimes developed immunity.

People were terrified of contagious diseases which were not yet understood. The citizens of Soda Springs remembered well a diphtheria epidemic which had devastated the town. Only a few compassionate and fearless people would care for the victims of contagious diseases.

A large, pretty, brown dog with floppy ears, referred to as Mr. McDougal, was often at one or another of the saloons, and everyone in town seemed to know him. He was a big, friendly dog, with large brown eyes and a fluffy tail. Ellis stopped on the street to pet Mr. McDougal, and looked forward to the time when he could have a dog of his own.

Almost everyone in the locality had large dogs—hunting dogs and sheep dogs. They would lay around the rigs, worn out from miles of trotting on the way to town, waiting for their masters, or following the men into saloons, or accompanying them to the doctor. People loved and respected their animals and relied on them for protection and for help on the farms and ranches.

One afternoon Ellis dropped by the drug store to pick up some medication. The frame building had seven or eight steps up to the door. He had never been quite able to figure Mr. Eastman out. The tall, lean, gaunt man was usually all business, and spoke his words sharply and very distinctly. Today he was quite friendly. "What in the hell are you reading?" Ellis asked seeing the huge book he seemed engrossed in.

"It's a book about mining laws," said Mr. Eastman looking up with a frown as though he had been unnecessarily disturbed. He seemed much more interested in law than in pharmacy, and spent much of his time at the pharmacy reading law books.

"Are you taking up the law?" asked Ellis.

"I've considered it," replied Mr. Eastman abruptly.

He didn't seem to be in a talking mood, so Ellis took care of his business and hurried home.

Ida thought Mrs. Eastman was outspoken, but found her likable as they became better acquainted. You could always count on her to give you an account of what was going on around town. While Ida did not like malicious gossip, she was interested in people.

Ida spent much of her time helping Ellis. In the evenings she would sit at the table and cut up bandages, then sterilize them in a large double boiler. She enjoyed reading when she had spare time in the evenings, and she could get her hands on a good book. Much of his time was spent reading medical books or journals.

In the mornings she fixed ham, eggs, oatmeal, and coffee for Ellis, but he hurried through the meal until she worried about his digestive system being abused. "If you'd take time to eat more slowly, you might add a few pounds," said Ida. "Everything is always 'hurry up'."

"There's so much to do, and so little time to do it," Ellis retorted on the defensive. He knew he should spend more time with Ida, but he was always rushing and sweating to keep up with the demands of his growing practice. In the evenings they shared a cup of tea when he was not on call, and a more leisurely evening meal. When Ellis had a difficult operation or medical procedure coming up, he often went down to the slaughter house and got animal parts to use in practicing his techniques. It was not unusual to find him sewing up a pig's stomach over and over again until he got all sides to come out just exactly right, and was sure he had not left a bleeder on the inside. He practiced to make sure the stomach was air tight and water tight. This helped his surgical techniques, but led to strange rumors that he was putting pig stomachs in human beings.

He came home one night, and found Ida highly

indignant. "Do you know what I heard today? I heard that you put a pig's stomach in the last man you operated on, and when he came to and asked you why he was so hungry, you said, 'most pigs are'."

Ellis laughed, "Where on earth did you hear that?" he asked. "Mrs. Eastman told me the story was going around town. Can you believe that? What a ridiculous thing for someone to be spreading around."

"I guess somebody heard about me getting animal parts at the slaughter house, and had to invent a use for them. Don't worry about what some of the old busybodies are spreading around. If I could substitute a pig's stomach for a human one, and have it function normally, I'd be rich and famous."

Quite late one evening they were preparing for bed when an urgent knock sounded on their door. Ellis opened it to find a short, sandy haired man he had seen around town a few times before, but did not know by name. He was quite out of breath.

"Doctor, can you come quickly!" he panted. "There's trouble down at Jenny's Place."

"What happened?" asked Ellis as he grabbed his coat and his bag of instruments.

"Well, some fellow got to celebrating a little more than usual and started shooting up the place," said the man, still huffing from exertion. "Mary was sitting on the pot, and he shot it right out from under her. I think he got her right in the butt. She's bleeding like a stuck hog."

Ellis hurried down across the railroad tracks into the cool darkness and shadows of night, toward the whorehouse, with the messenger. As they approached the place, he could hear loud piano music, a lot of shouting, and an occasional gun blast.

"Since you know where to go, I think I'll go on home and hope my wife will believe I was working late," the sandy haired man said as he hurried off into the darkness.

A dog barked as he swung open the front gate. Ellis stepped inside the door with some misgivings, but he wasn't one to be intimidated. A large, burly cowboy with sparse black hair and a deep fierce scowl was pointing a six gun at

a small moustached piano player, who was playing with all his might. The music sounded considerably more cheerful than its maker looked. The sweat stood out on his forehead, and it was evident that he was visibly shaken.

The gun wielding bully glanced toward the door as Ellis entered. "You the Doc-tor?" he bellowed, dragging the word out to two syllables.

"I am," said Ellis. "What have you done here?"

"I think I tore a piece of hide off the ass of that old girl upstairs," said the cowboy. "You better go up and see if you can fix her up." He nodded toward a stairway to the right, and Ellis wasted no time getting up the stairs. As he went, he could hear the man yelling at the piano player, "Keep the music going, Professor, and make it louder." The bullets made an unusual sounding 'ping' as they struck the insides of the piano with a resounding musical tone.

Jenny, the small dark haired madam, was bending over the blonde, thirtyish looking woman lying on her stomach on the bed. They both looked up at the doctor, with faces absolutely white. Jenny was sponging the blood from several cuts across the blonde's buttocks which were bleeding profusely. The big, old, ceramic chamber pot was broken into a dozen pieces which were lying in a puddle of urine, and a stream of blood led from there to the bed. The women were obviously embarrassed.

Ellis examined the cuts. He was relieved to see that though the wounds were long, they were shallow. Apparently the ruffian had shot the pot right out from under the old gal, and she had fallen onto the pieces. He cleansed the wound and began sewing up the woman's behind. He could feel his heart thumping in his chest, but his hands were steady. The woman pulled her lips back from her teeth in a grimace of pain, but made no outcry. "Well, that's a pain in the butt if I ever saw one," he said. The women giggled.

A loud commotion downstairs sent Jenny peeking to see what was happening. The piano playing stopped, and Jenny came back and reported, "Well, it looks like the mickey I slipped into his drink finally worked. The sonofabitch is a good customer, but he gets a little rowdy once in awhile. I don't know what gets into him, but he sure likes to raise hell, especially with his six-gun. All in all, it's been one helluva day."

Ellis knew these women would encourage a man to drink away his last dime, but he had also heard stories of them helping those who were down and out. He wondered what circumstances had brought them to this kind of life. He also wondered if they were involved with Ashler and his friends.

He finished stitching up the cut and advised the woman she best not plan to do much sitting around for the next couple of weeks. It was midnight when he started up the tracks toward home. Krug Swain was standing in front of the railway station and as he came toward him, exclaimed, "Doctor, I didn't think I'd ever see you coming from that direction this time of night? What you doin' down at the whorehouse?"

Ellis shook his head and held up his medical bag. "I just put over a hundred stitches in an old girl's behind," he said.

When Ellis arrived home, Ida was still up. He was relieved to be inside the safe comfort of their apartment again. He told her about the evenings experiences. "You could have been killed," she worried.

Ellis told her of the strange sound the bullets made when striking the insides of the piano. "What was the piano player playing?" asked Ida, who was always interested in the cultural side of things.

"Well, I'm not rightly sure," said Ellis, "but I think it was 'Nearer My God to Thee'."

The Codman house remained empty that summer, and

Kackleys never got a chance to meet its famous owner. Rumors were that Captain Codman was ill, and that was why he had not come west that year. They had both been looking forward to making his acquaintance.

One hot summer afternoon Ellis went into the drug store and found Mr. Eastman behind a new typewriter. It was on the desk in front of him. The contraption had two sets of alphabet letters on small keys, one in lower case letters, and one in capitals. The brand name was L.C. Smith. Eastman had rolled a piece of paper into the machine, and it was printing the words as he hit the appropriate keys. Ellis watched with interest. He had heard of typewriters, but he had never seen one in use before.

"Say," he said. "Everybody has trouble reading my handwriting, that's just what I need. Is it hard to use?"

Mr. Eastman looked up at him rather sourly and said, "It's terribly hard to do. I wouldn't get one if I were you."

Ellis figured if Mr. Eastman could master the contraption, there was no reason why he couldn't. He went home and thought about it for awhile, then ordered a typewriter for himself. When it came, it didn't take him long to learn to peck out the words in much more readable form than his handwriting.

By mid October, a clean blanket of new snow covered the land, and made it even harder to reach his patients. Ellis had to resort to snowshoes, known as webs, to get into some places. It was a slow, laborious way of travel. An emergency at Grays Lake, miles to the northeast, found him huffing and puffing over the mountains with his feet fitted into the awkward, webbed walking gear. The cold winter air filled his lungs. After traveling for miles, Isaac Vias from Wayan met him at the cut-off at the top of Neville's Canyon with a pair of skis in hand.

"These will be much faster," he insisted, "try them."

Ellis hesitantly put on the long, thin boards with loops of hide to put his toes through, and started down the hill. He promptly lost control of the skis, and went faster and faster, barely missing trees and bushes. He was too startled to even swear, as he flew down the slopes toward the little settlement of Wayan, at the southern end of the Grays Lake

Valley, originally settled by half a dozen families from Finland. He managed to hold onto his bag of instruments, though his hat went flying off into the snow and the wind whistled through his hair. He never found his hat until summer. Years later he was to brag he had beat Isaac, who was an excellent skier, down the mountain on skis one time during his life.

This little settlement of Wayan included the Sodermans, Obergs, Viases, Petersens, Stoors, Sibbetts, Lewises, Raymonds, Lincolns, and Calls. That skis were faster, he had to admit, and he worked to master their use. He soon became quite adept at skiing.

Opening his door one day to an impatient knock, he found an exhausted looking, unshaven, red-faced man, whose breath smelled strongly of whiskey. "My wife needs help," he gasped. "I just skied in from Carriboo Mountain. She had a baby boy during the night, but I'm no damn doctor and she's having trouble."

Ellis donned his skis and followed the miner over hills and through valleys mile after mile. At last they reached the James Sibbett house at Grays Lake. They paused only a few minutes to rest and continued up the mountain to the mining settlement. Ellis wasn't looking forward to skiing all the way back, and wondered how he'd ever make it. At last a small cabin came into sight, with smoke curling thickly from a stick and clay chimney. A young girl was looking out the window. As soon as they entered, the miner, who had been nipping on a bottle of whiskey he was carrying in his back pocket, slumped across a pile of blankets in the corner, and passed out.

The girl brought Ellis some water so he could wash his hands. He turned his attention to the pale woman lying on the bed, with a husky baby boy cradled in her arm. The man had delivered the baby, but the afterbirth had not come. Ellis pressed skillfully on the woman's abdomen, loosening the matter from the uterus walls. Luckily the cord was tied tightly so she was not hemorrhaging. In a few minutes he had the situation taken care of.

He wasn't sure he could find his way back to Soda Springs, but the miner was out cold. He started tracing his tracks back toward the Sibbett home. He knew daylight wouldn't last long, and he soon noticed silent dog-like animals slinking after him. He had heard stories of wolves, and how they would kill just for the joy of killing. Mr. Morgan said wolves had killed over twenty head of his sheep, but only eaten two. Another man had told him how when deer were weak from a hard winter, wolves would sometimes kill them by the herd, and only eat a few. He was sure they wouldn't hesitate to attack a lone man infringing on their territory.

He went faster, trying to get back to the Sibbett home in Grays Lake before night overtook him. The dark shapes moved in closer, and Ellis' fear turned to near panic. He glanced over his shoulder and stumbled as he tried to hurry even faster. Just when he felt he was finished for sure, one of the animals let out a mournful howl, and Ellis realized to his great relief, he was being followed by coyotes, not wolves, and figured he was in no eminent danger.

Ellis stayed overnight at the Sibbett home and started out again early the next morning, but before he had gone far, a blizzard came up. Snow swirled and blew into his face until he could hardly see. It stung his exposed skin and eyes, and he could not keep track of where he was going. The wind seemed to be blowing in every direction at once, and completely taking away his breath. He realized he had lost his way when he again passed the big pines he had left behind over an hour earlier. He stood a minute, hesitant about which way to go. Delirium had almost come over him. Finally he headed in what he hoped was the right direction. He hadn't gone far when he came to the Little Blackfoot River, which he followed to the small town of Henry. He had been in Enoch Valley, miles east of where he thought he was. He was almost frozen when he stumbled into the saloon.

Ellis had heard about Bill Winschell, the proprietor, who had been a freighter, hauling from Soda Springs to the Carriboo mines. He had built the Winschell Dugway, shortening the trip to Carriboo by thirty-five miles. He had also been active in politics and he and George Gorton had served as delegates to the Idaho Constitutional Convention.

These men were pioneers who could experience hardships, build roads and run stores, and also have the ability to help draft a State Constitution which would be enduring and protect the present and future citizens of the state. Ellis couldn't help but admire them and other civic minded pioneers for their accomplishments.

Bill took him quickly into a back room. "Take off all your clothes," he commanded. Ellis wondered what was going on, but was too weak to object.

The tall man with steel gray eyes disappeared and came back a few minutes later, with an armload of clothing. He tossed the red flannel underwear to Ellis. "Put these on first," he commanded. The underwear were followed by a heavy woolen shirt and pants. "When you go out in this weather, you have to be dressed right, or you'll freeze to death," he explained. "When you get warmed up and ready to leave, take this heavy coat and lap robe," he added. "For now, come have a cup of hot coffee to warm up your insides. In a little while one of my men will be going into town with a sleigh to get some supplies. You might as well ride along with him."

Ellis tried to pay him for the clothing, but he said, "Hell, no. If you're willing to come out here to help us, we're willing to help you."

Ellis dressed and entered the store, which was a gathering place for the locals. A group of long whiskered men with bushy hair and beards of different shapes and sizes, were seated on chairs around the pot-bellied wood burning stove, smoking, drinking, talking, and exchanging stories. They stopped a moment and stared at Ellis so hard his knees began to shake. He decided he was just weak from the cold and exposure. He looked around the room. On one side of the store was the area containing canned goods, cheese, pickle barrels, candy buckets, dried fruits and meats. On the other side was dry-goods which included bolts of material, articles of clothing, show cases of knives, and guns. Saddles, lanterns, harnesses, shovels, and tubs hung from the ceiling. Bill introduced him to the men. After a few minutes of talk, when Ellis was warmed up, he showed him around the place. Bill had a bear caged in the back yard. He brought it out of the cage on a chain. "You've got a helluva lot of guts to mess around like that with a bear," said Ellis.

"He's quite tame," insisted Bill.

"Tame or not, I'd rather deal with people," said Ellis "Even if some of them are more dangerous than animals."

They went into the kitchen, and the spiced smells that came to his nose made Ellis weak with hunger. "Dora," Bill called as they entered, "We have company for lunch. This is Dr. Kackley, the new doctor in Soda Springs."

The quiet woman, who greeted Ellis warmly, would later become his helper in many deliveries in the Henry area. She had cooked a dinner fit for a preacher. Ellis plunged into its spicy and savory goodness with gusto, giving his plate his full attention. He was as hungry as if he hadn't had a bite to eat for days.

Soon after lunch, the hired man with the sleigh was ready to start for town, and Ellis was grateful for the ride as well as the clothing. The return trip was comfortable. When he arrived home, Ida met him at the door. "Thank God you're okay. I've been worried sick about you being out in this weather for so long," she said. It came to him for the first time, how close he had come to freezing to death.

In a small town it didn't take long for word to get around that the doctor had been lost and almost frozen. It was one more thing for Ellis' tormentors to use in having fun at his expense. The next time he walked into the saloon, to pay for his horse rental, one of the local patrons, an old man with a thin voice said, "Well if it isn't the little doctor, who can't find his way through a snow storm. I hope I never get a bad appendix in a blizzard."

Bill Winschell, who Ellis hadn't noticed sitting at a table towards the back, promptly rose and walked toward the man. "Well if you sonsabitches ever got out of town and away from a rope to the outhouse, you'd see what a real blizzard is like," he said.

The man shut up instantly. As soon as Bill sat down, he made a quick exit. Ellis appreciated Bill standing up for him, and from then on, they were close friends. Whenever Ellis was called to the northern settlements he stopped at Bill's place, and changed horses there. He was always willing to lend him a mount, and after seventeen miles of riding, his horses were ready for a rest. Ellis also stopped at Henry Schmidt's trading post whenever he got a chance.

Ellis was glad when the cold of winter gave way to spring, and the world showed its appreciation by sprouting a new carpet of green. When he went out into the country he loved to hear the meadow larks trill, the cranes whoop, the geese honk, and drink in the freshness of the spring air. Squirrels raced up and down the pines, chattering among themselves. He knew when he returned home supper would be ready and hot bread baking in the oven. Ida would shake her head and say he had been gone far too long, and she was worried sick.

Chapter 5

Ellis was coming back to Soda Springs from a call in Gem Valley. Far in the east, lightening rumbled and flashed. There'll be rain before nightfall, he thought. He was just coming into town, when he was flagged down by Henry. "Jimmy's boy accidentally shot himself," he yelled.

"Is he at home?" asked Ellis, and when Henry nodded in the affirmative, he laid the whip on the horses' backs and raced to the railway station. When he entered the station it was unusually quiet out front, but he could hear a commotion in the back even before Jimmy rushed out.

"Doc, I'm sa glad ya're back. It's oor Alan. Playing with a gun he was, and shot hisself right in the face."

"My God," said Ellis, "Is he still alive?"

"Aye," said Jimmy, "'Tis sorry I am ya were away an' we had t' call Dr. Green. They sent him doon oon a special train.

"Let me take a look at him," said Ellis as he followed Jimmy to the back of the depot where the family resided.

The pale faced, young boy's head was almost covered with bandages. Ellis removed the wrappings and examined the boy gently. He found the spent bullet was lodged below the angle of the jaw. It was about two inches from the pneumogastric nerve, commonly known as the vega, which after leaving the base of the skull, goes down the back of the jaw and neck, and branches to the lungs and stomach area to control the muscles of respiration and digestive processes. The boy was breathing steadily, and his pulse was good.

"Dr. Green said 'twas against the nehrve, the bullet was, an' oor Alan, he woodn't make it through the night—likely not 'till the doc was hoome oon the train," Jimmy said sadly.

"The kid is damn lucky," said Ellis. "The bullet isn't near enough the nerve to do any harm. The only complications we might have to worry about are infection or lead poisoning from the bullet, but chances of that are slim. His pulse and respiration are stable. He'll probably live longer than any of us."

"'Tis thankful I am, an' the missus too," Jimmy said with relief. "How we could bear to loose the boy, I doon't know."

Ellis put his hand gently on Mrs. Strachan's shoulder. "You'd better get some rest. An accident like this is a helluva shock to the system, but the boy is going to be all right."

Ellis hurried home. Ida met him at the door. "Did you see the Strachans as you came in?" she asked. Ellis nodded.

"Is the boy going to die?" she asked. "Dr. Green said he wouldn't last long."

"I think he's going to make it fine," said Ellis "It was a large caliber gun, and left a big hole, but if we can control the infection, the kid will do okay. He's damn lucky. The bullet isn't near as close to the nerve as Dr. Green thought, it's at least a couple of inches away, and freely movable."

"How's Mrs. Strachan holding up through all of this?" asked Ida.

"Mrs. Strachan looked like she was torn to pieces, but she'll be okay. She's tiny, but that woman is wiry and has a lot of strength inside that frail-looking exterior. She's one of these people who can surprise you with what they can handle."

"I'm so glad," said Ida. "I don't know how they'd ever survive losing that boy. I think that would be more than I could take to lose a child—girl or boy—and so many of them die in this frontier town, but not near as many as before you came." She paused, contemplating the horror of losing a child, then continued thoughtfully, "These people don't realize just how lucky they are that you decided to come to Soda Springs. If they did, they'd treat you better and not try to kill you on crazy horses and with ridicule and sarcasm."

With a sparkle in his eye, Ellis put his arms around his

wife. "Idie, the 'White Mule Doctor' is going to outlive them all, and you with him." Then becoming more serious, he asked, "Are people being rude to you?"

"Well not exactly," said Ida. "Just smart remarks from some of the fellows about the 'little doctor', and asking if you'd been lost in any blizzards lately, and laughing about your southern accent, and your getting bucked off the livery horses."

"These thugs don't like me because they know I know what's going on in this town and that I know horse shit when I'm standing knee deep in it. Don't pay any attention to them. One of these days the good people here, and there are plenty of them, will get fed up enough with what's going on that they won't tolerate it anymore, and some of these crooks will end up behind bars where they belong."

Ellis hadn't been home an hour when word came that a man was injured at Herman. The messenger said the man's leg was broken, and no telling what else was wrong with him.

Ellis gave Ida a quick kiss as he picked up his bag, grabbed his hat, crammed it on his head, and hurried out the door. He put his instruments into the saddle bags, and headed for the livery stable. He was glad the sky had cleared and the sun was shining.

"I need a horse to go out to Herman," he informed the livery man, who by this time had become a real thorn in Ellis' side.

"I have just the one for a long ride," the man with a small, turned down mouth which curled in a perpetual sneer told Ellis. "We just got this one, he used to be a race horse, and will get you there fast."

"I bet he will," thought Ellis. "I wonder what kind of animal the sonofabitch will pawn off on me this time."

The dog Mr. McDougal rubbed against Ellis' leg, and he reached down absent mindedly and gave him a few pats on the head before he mounted the high spirited horse. He knew full well this was probably another trick. He managed to keep the horse under control through town, but decided if he gave him free rein maybe it would wear the animal out so he would be more manageable. Ellis' small stature made it hard for him to control some of the riding horses, but he had discovered if he let them run at full gallop for awhile, usually they would be winded enough to be handled more easily. People were used to seeing the doctor galloping into the country, and it contributed to his image of always hurrying quickly to a call.

This horse didn't get winded easily. Soon Ellis realized the animal was not going to be stopped, as he galloped mile after mile without slowing down. He passed The Blackfoot River Bridge, north of town, at record-breaking speed. The warm, humid smell of horse sweat rolled back toward Ellis' nostrils. His own shirt had a wide, sweat soaked strip down the back and dark circular patches under each arm. Ellis would have traded horses there at the Tolmie residence if he could have stopped the beast, but it started to buck whenever he pulled on the reins. He hung on for dear life, knowing if he lost his seat he was in trouble and out in the middle of nowhere at that. He was almost to Henry before the horse became tired enough that he could exercise some measure of control over the animal.

He stopped at the saloon at Henry, and got off the horse with relief. Bill only had one horse available, but Ellis was glad to take it. He figured anything would be an improvement over the one he had just managed to get off without getting killed. The horse was an old cavalry horse. "He hasn't been ridden for awhile, but he's a good horse," Bill said.

By the time he got a few miles out of Henry, the new mount was acting strange, and Ellis realized he had probably got a hold of some loco weed recently. Loco weed, when eaten by a horse, caused sporadic symptoms. You never knew how long they would last, and some horses never got over the strange behavior. This horse was taking on symptoms of the loco syndrome. He took the bit and ran like the wind. Ellis knew Bill wouldn't give him a bad horse on purpose, but this animal was also uncontrollable.

He practically flew by the Sibbett house at Grays Lake, and was thankful he was three-fourths of the way to Herman. He wondered if he could stay seated much longer, and how he would get the animal stopped when he got there.

He hoped the horse would be tired out by that time. He had gone many miles, and managed to get two uncontrollable horses in one day.

Ellis was getting a lot of calls from the miners and those supporting the mines at Carriboo. With the miners and sheep men, he could usually count on being well paid. Gold from the mines came and went freely. He wished he could get a place where he could keep his own horses, and reduce the risk of being hurt or killed while out on calls in the country.

He had a warm spot in his heart for these folks in the northern areas. The people at Henry, Wayan, Grays Lake, Eagle Creek, Williamsburg, and Herman treated him well. They were always willing to lend him a horse, invited him to share their homes and meals, and did whatever they could to help him. These people weren't like the group of ruffians in Soda Springs who laughed at his Southern speech, pulled tricks on him, and tormented Ida's life as well as his.

Ellis headed the horse toward the old saloon and store at Herman, surrounded by tent dwellings, and tried to rein up. The horse kept going. They were approaching a barbed wire gate, but like in a steeple chase, the horse sailed over the gate without slowing down. Then he went head over heels into the grass, and Ellis with him. The hard earth hit Ellis like a fist. For a moment he was on the verge of unconsciousness. The impact left him dazed and his head swam. He blinked his eyes and struggled to come around, as he sat up and shook his head. He looked over at the horse, and discovered to his horror that the animal had a big gash in his belly. He wiped away the blood, and assessed the damage. The cut went through one of the large veins which are so close to the surface there. He didn't look mean anymore lying on the grass, out cold, and bleeding. Ellis grabbed his instruments, and started suturing the horse.

About that time the proprietor of the establishment, young Henry Gorton, came out. Surprised to see the doctor sewing up the horse, he shook his head and asked, "Aren't you going to take care of the patient first?"

"Hell no," said Ellis. "I have to ride this horse home."

It only took a few minutes to sew up the horse, and he

was soon checking the leg of the injured man. It was a nasty break, with ripped and torn flesh and blood that had clotted. Ellis cleaned the compound fracture carefully, then hunted around the grounds for a board which would be just right for holding it firmly. At last he found one and went to work getting the bones lined up for setting the leg. The man grimaced and took a large swig of whiskey, but no complaint escaped his lips "You'll have to stay off it for a few months. If you do that, you'll be as good as new," he told the man when he was finished.

By the time Ellis was through with the injured man, the horse seemed to be doing fine, though rather subdued. Young Henry Gorton offered to lend Ellis a sorrel mare, and he was glad to take him up on the offer. "Just leave her with my dad, and he can bring her back the next time he comes this way," Henry said. Ellis was glad he could lead Bill's cavalry horse back to the town of Henry, and not have to ride him. When he got there, he stopped and talked with Bill. "I was just getting ready to go into town," said Bill. "We'll tie the race horse and the mare onto the back of the wagon, and you can ride in with me."

Ellis liked that arrangement much better than the prospect of getting back on a horse. When he returned the horse to the stable, he reached down again to pet the dog, Mr.McDougal. Ellis had become quite fond of the ownerless dog, who was still hanging around town. "He probably gets fed more than any dog with an owner because he's such a likable animal," thought Ellis. Ellis wished he had a place to keep a dog.

"That was one helluva horse you rented me this time. He got me there in record breaking time," he told the stable man who took the horse. He wouldn't let these people have the satisfaction of knowing what had really happened. He knew these men would destroy him as surely as they had others they had disposed of through the years, such as the unfortunate sheepherder, if they had half a chance and thought they could get away with it. The doctor was becoming too well known and liked to disappear without an investigation, and Ida would make one helluva fuss if anything unexplainable happened to Ellis. That was one consolation.

Ida worried about Ellis whenever he went on a call. They never knew what kind of experiences he would have, especially with the horses he kept getting from the stable. If there were just some way they could get into a place where they could keep their own horses, half of their problems would be solved.

Ellis was telling Ida about his experiences of the day when he noticed she was looking a little peaked. "Are you feeling okay?" he asked, giving her his full attention for the first time in a long while.

"Come sit down," said Ida. "I've been trying to talk to you for days, but you're always hurrying off on a call. Ellis sat down, wondering what could be wrong. He crossed his arms across his chest and looked at her expectantly.

"What would you say if I told you you're going to be a father?"

"Are you sure?" he asked incredulously. She nodded. He bounded up and encircled her in his arms. "You couldn't tell me anything that would make me happier," he said, with a hug.

"Don't squeeze me to death," she laughed, "or you'll never be a father."

While Ellis was a very private type person, this was something he just couldn't wait to share with someone. "Well, I'll be damned," said Henry Schmidt when he told him the news. "With you running around the country like you do, I never would have believed you'd had time to father a child."

When Ellis was on the road, which was about the only time he had an opportunity to think about his life, he wondered what it would be like to have a child of his own. He had always liked children and found the idea of being a father exciting.

Jimmy told Ellis one day that the Codman house was up for sale. Captain Codman's health had deteriorated to the point where he could no longer spend his summers in the West. Ellis looked at the house and grounds, and was highly impressed with the barn. He had never seen a barn so wonderfully built. It had a good cemented-up rock base and a heavy wood floor. Inside were four double stalls for horses and also space for tack and buggies which were still stored there. In the top was a hayloft with plenty of room to store hay. A ditch with water ran close by. On the side was an ice house. None of the folks back home had ever had an ice house. Some had a spring house where perishables were kept cool by the water, but an ice house was a real luxury.

Ellis went home and described the wonderful barn to Ida. "There's also a chicken house," Ellis said as he extolled the virtues of the place.

Ida insisted on going to look it over. Ellis got the key from Herbert Horsley who had built the house for Codman, and was handling the sale. The house was mid-Victorian and had a formal appearance. A large living room and good sized dining area on the west side had sliding doors between, and could be opened into one big area, or shut off. Large wall-attached kerosene lamps lighted the six high-ceilinged rooms on the main floor. A back stairway from the kitchen led to four upstairs bedrooms, also with high ceilings. Luxurious windows with large panes of glass looked out over the town. A third floor, up under the eaves, had small windows, was dark, and looked like it had been used as a catch-all. Porches covered the entry ways.

Cabinets had been done by Matt Suhrke, and were beautifully crafted. Three fireplaces, made with fancy inlaid tile and black marble, had fireboxes and log holders. Inside the place was completely furnished, including fine china, silverware, and a huge library of the classics. Ida ran her finger softly along the bindings as she read title after title. She and Ellis had never had access to such a treasure trove, and they looked over everything with awe.

"It's simply beautiful, but we couldn't possibly afford it," said Ida wishfully, shaking her head. "Do you know how much he wants for the place?"

"I don't know," said Ellis, "but I've heard it's dirt cheap. I'm afraid dirt cheap isn't within our budget right now, but I'd sure like to have that barn." He hesitated, then began again, "We don't need a big house like this, and we certainly aren't needing to put on airs, but I'll find out what it's selling for. It might be cheaper than a regular place."

Ida looked at her husband with a hint of amusement in her smile. She was much more interested in the house and the treasures it contained, than in the barn or chicken coop.

Ellis checked on the price. Captain Codman was willing to take two-thousand-five hundred dollars for the house, grounds, furnishings, outbuildings, and buggies.

The terms were reasonable. Night after night Ellis and Ida talked of the advantages of buying, and ways they might be able to make the payments. If they took the house, it would be nip and tuck for quite awhile to pay for it. On the other hand, Ellis could get his own horses and reduce the most dangerous aspect of his work. He could even get a dog of his own. Ida could plant a garden and raise chickens for meat and eggs. They might be able to take in a boarder or two while finances were really tight. Ellis would have space for an office, and might get more patients that way. After hashing over the pros and cons for some time, they decided they could not afford to pass up such a bargain. Likely they would have to pay much more for less if they waited.

Once they had made a decision, they finalized the arrangements quickly, and were soon moving into the home. Ida felt some apprehension about heating the great area, with only fireplaces and a kitchen stove, during the severe winters they experienced in Soda Springs. She wondered if it would be warm enough for raising a family there, but the immediate and pressing problem of protecting Ellis from severe injury or possible death from the horses he was maliciously being given at the livery stable was her greatest concern at the moment.

"'Tis a lucky couple ya ere," said Jimmy when he saw the many treasures left in the house. "Everything ohn could wish fer, ya have."

Ellis proudly painted "Ellis Kackley, M. D." on the front windows in large, red letters. There was no way for him to know in his excitement about getting into such a beautiful home of their own, that buying the Codman place would lead to the most tragic experiences of their lives.

Ellis was ecstatic about the opportunity to be independent of the dray people. He promptly purchased a team of good dependable horses, and had the harness double stitched, replaced the snaps with buckles which couldn't freeze shut, put heavy lines on the harness, and heavy wheels on the buggy. He had done everything possible to make his transportation dependable and minimize the probability of breakdowns.

Inside he set up a waiting room and his office on the main floor. He didn't take long to bring home a puppy which they named "Wink." "Mr. Morgan gave him to us. He says he'll be just what we need," he told Ida proudly.

Inside the house, Captain Codman had left a menagerie of interesting things, including a centrifuge for spinning urine samples to check for blood and pus in the urine. "I'll bet Captain Codman has Bright's disease, a forerunner of kidney disease," Ellis told Ida, when he saw the instrument.

Captain Codman was a landmark figure on the Old Oregon Trail, and had done a lot of other writing, as well as his book called "The Mormon Country." His health continued to decline and he died not long after Kackleys bought the house.

The large place wasn't easy for them to keep up. Ellis tried to do the heavier work, but Ida did the cleaning, including the stables. When Ellis went out on a call, she always waited up for him, and helped unhitch the team. She continued to worry about his health and safety. "Don't worry so much about me," Ellis urged. "Just take good care of yourself and our child. You need to get more sleep."

"I sleep best when I know you're safely home," said Ida. "Besides, jumping into that cold bed alone is like jumping into an icy creek in early spring," she said with a little shudder.

Ellis laughed as he gave her a quick hug. The midwives tell me if you want to warm a bed up, to use a warm flat iron or heat the catalogue. That's how they keep new mothers and babies warm, and their families warm when they are sick. Of course, six or seven in a bed, like many of the settlers have, helps keep them all warm. That's one advantage of a big family."

"Some of these women seem to exist for nothing but having babies," said Ida. "I want a family, but not that large."

The non-Mormon residents of Soda Springs, who were desirous of attending a church, had allied themselves to found the First Community Church. Having a desire to become part of an established creed, they organized into a Presbyterian Church in 1892. Captain Codman had donated land for a building and a home which served as a manse. A rock church was built with stones originally cut to build a railroad roundhouse in Soda, but never used. Most of Kackleys' close friends in Soda Springs belonged to this group. Ida soon became a member and was active in church activities.

One day a sheep man Ellis had been treating for the dust caused eye problem came in with a fresh discharge of pus in his eyes. Ellis quickly realized there was a problem in addition to what he had been treating, and he suspected the man had a gonorrhea infection. Clap, as it was commonly called, caused infection in the eyes quite often, and Ellis saw plenty of it. It was easily treated, but if left too long the germ would burrow into the eye and cause blindness. He questioned the man about his recent activities, and found he had been frequenting the whorehouses. The infection had been bad for about four days.

Ellis put a solution of nitrate of silver, which was later required by law to be used in the eyes of all newborn infants to prevent blindness from venereal disease, into the sheep man's eyes, and told him to come back four times a day for treatment. In a few days, not only was the clap infection cured, but the severe dust irritation was gone also. Ellis didn't know what had cured the dust problem, but figured the clap bacteria caused a counter infection which had stimulated the immune system to get rid of the dust caused irritation, then the clap infection was killed with the silver nitrate, leaving the eye infection-free. It would be approximately thirty years before Ellis would hear of penicillin and understand why his treatment of the eye condition was so successful. That one disease organism could destroy another was unheard of at that time.

Ellis knew he had stumbled onto a cure for the problem which had plagued sheep men in the area for years. He didn't dare let anyone know what he was doing, but he began infecting the eyes of the sheep men with clap bacteria, letting it go for a few days, then using nitrate of silver to clear up the infection. If the medical profession ever found out I was infecting all these guys with clap, they'd hang me from the nearest tree, thought Ellis, but it works, and that's what counts.

Word soon spread that Ellis had a cure for the eye irritation. Sheep men came from hundreds of miles—from Wyoming, Nevada, and Utah, as well as Idaho, to get rid of their eye problems, and Ellis cured them without a single failure. He charged a twenty-dollar gold piece for the cure, and they paid it gladly. Since his discovery wasn't something Ellis could share, he remained the only doctor who could help the sheep men. When Dr. Green asked Ellis what he was using, he replied, "Just good nursing care of the eyes."

Gonorrhea was a disease which was common, rampant both to new and old, not too often killing, but inflicting disabilities for life. It was a scourge to mankind—a common cause of blindness. A child's eyes being infected with clap as it came from traversing the birth canal of the mother was the cause of twenty to twenty-five percent of childhood blindness. Now it was controllable by Crade's discovery of instilling silver nitrate in the eyes of the newborn.

Ellis, who was quick to incorporate new medical discoveries into his practice, had ordered some of the silver nitrate, which came with three or four drops in a little waxy tube, and could be opened with a pin. Its effectiveness had been proven, but it was not widely accepted even by some of the doctors. Ellis encouraged its use and supplied all the midwives who would use it with the drops. He instructed those who were willing to listen in how to clean the baby's eyes with a weak solution of warm salt water, and put the drops in. Some of the less trusting women at first thought he was trying to cause blindness in their patients, but began to use the medication when they discovered he was using it in the eyes of the babies he delivered. Gradually the medication became accepted by most of the midwives in the locality.

The abundant grass which grew over two feet high around Soda Springs and the country to the north made it a sheep man's paradise. Knowlin said he could start out from Soda Springs and go in any direction for open grazing, except for a few ranches. By 1907 there were almost a million sheep grazing in the locality.

One day a sheep man came for Ellis with word that one of the herders at Williamsburg, a small settlement southeast of Wayan, was very sick, and needed the doctor. Ellis hitched up the buggy and went to see what he could do for the man. The sheep camp was in a remote area back in the mountains where the sheep were grazing for the summer. It was beautiful country, criss-crossed with mountain streams and stands of quaking aspen trees, Douglas fir, and lodgepole pine.

There was also a lot of sagebrush which harbored wood ticks in some areas. Ellis was helping Rocky Mountain Research in the Bitterroot Valley, and every time he removed a tick from a patient, he put it in a little tick box and sent it to a doctor there. Rocky Mountain Fever was a lot like tularemia. Scrub typhus and undulant fever also brought high temperatures and similar symptoms. Research was being done to separate these diseases and the germs causing them.

The canvas covered box on wheels known as a sheep camp was quite a sight. When moving, the driver would stand up over a narrow gate at the front of the wagon-type base or camp box, which was covered with canvas like a covered wagon, but closed in the back. The space on each side of the door was utilized to hang various utensils including a small washboard, a tin tub, and a water jug. Ellis was impressed with the compactness and efficiency of the sheep camp. which was home to the sheepherder throughout the summer months.

It was the first time he had been inside one. There was just enough room to stand upright. Furnishings included a narrow two-burner wood stove, a table which let down from the wall, some cabinets, and the little narrow bunk where the herder lay.

The small man who appeared to be in his late thirties, was in severe pain, and it was evident immediately he was extremely ill. He was running a high temperature, which according to the camp tender, had been spiking from normal to high for the past couple of weeks. The pain seemed to be coming from the area of his right kidney.

Ellis nodded to himself as he decided the only way to possibly save the fellow was to operate and see if he could find the source of the trouble. He suspected the kidney was abscessed. How to operate in these cramped quarters was no small problem, but the sheep camp immediately, to him, became a hospital, and the camp tender, two dogs, and three horses constituted the hospital staff.

Ellis enlisted the camp tender to build a campfire and boil some water. When the instruments and some pads were sterilized, he again surveyed the situation. "Do you have a couple of fairly large logs of firewood?" he asked.

"Yes," said the fellow. "What do you want logs for?" "I hope I can use them to get this fellow in a position where I can get to his kidneys. Bring some quickly," Ellis urged, and the fellow obliged.

They lifted the sheepherder in the middle and shoved the logs under him, humping him over the wood to force the kidneys up in back and spread the space between his ribs and abdomen so Ellis could get at the kidney and find the problem.

He showed the man how to give the chloroform, and explained carefully that he should put a few drops on the mask, then hold it about two inches from the patient's nose. "There's only two things to watch out for," he said. "If the man starts wiggling or showing any signs of coming to, give him a few more drops. If his breathing becomes shallow remove the mask."

Ellis washed his hands with soap and water and got the camp tender to help him into an operating gown. He put on his rubber gloves and cleaned the sheepherder's skin with soap and water, then painted it with a diluted solution of tincture of iodine before picking a drape with a long narrow slit to put over him.

Ellis opened the man up, and swore as he swept his finger

around, trying to find the kidney. As he looked, he again thought that the most important thing he had learned in medical school was anatomy, and he was thankful he had bought that old dog-eared, second-hand copy of "Gray's Anatomy" and practically committed it to memory.

The kidney was right up into the rib-diaphragm area almost hidden from every angle, where the Almighty had put it to protect it from harm. When he did get to it, he found it was badly abscessed. To remove it, under these conditions, in a sheep camp would be a difficult operation, but Ellis knew the man had no chance of making it, with the knowledge and medicines then available to medical science, unless the offending organ were removed.

Tying off the large arteries which came directly off the big abdominal aorta, the largest artery in the body, would be a problem, and would have to be done almost blindly because he could not see what he was doing very well in that area. The kerosene lamp lighting the camp left a lot to be desired. He began clipping and tying, using hemostats to clip off the arteries. It was extremely important not to break into the lung cavity or the abdominal cavity by accident, or they might become infected. As he cut, the sheepherder moved slightly and blood pressure from the aorta made the blood squirt out with so much force it hit the canvas overhead which served as a ceiling. Ellis nodded to the camp tender to let a few more drops of chloroform drop onto the mask.

As usual Ellis worked quickly. He had seen the operation done before, and felt if anyone else could do it, so could he. He tied off the tube going into the bladder and the big veins. Even Ellis, himself, was surprised at how quickly he cut the kidney free and dropped it into a granite wash basin.

Hydronephrosis had abscessed the area where the urine had been slowed for a long period of time, going into the bladder, and infection had developed in the kidney after dilation from the obstruction to urine passing. The blood and tissue accumulation, or seepage, in the cavity left from the kidney had to be removed, and a drain put in to let the pus seep from the wound. It wasn't easily done. Ellis shook his head as he closed off the area as deftly as possible under the circumstances, leaving a piece of rubber glove for a drain. It was a good thing he was not a large man, he thought as he straightened up and looked around the small enclosure where he had performed the operation.

Chapter 6

The man's breathing and pulse were steady when he finished. Ellis waited a few hours, hesitant whether to go or stay, but eventually he figured the sheepherder's chances of making it were good, and he had better get back to his practice. He left a vial of morphine and a syringe, gave the camp tender careful instructions about how to take care of the patient and administer the pain killer as needed, and started for home, exhausted. It seemed like it took forever to get there. As the town of Soda Springs came into sight, the Kackley house loomed tall and dark against the red-gold west. He heard Ida's chickens clucking and knew they had just been fed. Ellis was so tired he could hardly remember the ride home. He barely touched his dinner before climbing right into bed.

The man never came into town, but Ellis inquired of Mr. Morgan and Mr. Knowlin and learned the sheepherder had lived and was doing splendidly. People who heard about the operation found it almost impossible to believe Ellis had removed a kidney in a sheep camp.

Over forty years later the sheepherder would walk into Ellis' forty bed hospital—with three operating rooms and a white linened staff—as living evidence of Ellis' early skill in his primitive, Idaho sheep camp operating room.

Outlaw bands were a part of living in the Wild West. On June 2, 1899, the whole town was talking about the Butch Cassidy Gang robbing the Overland Flyer of the Union Pacific Railroad. The news had come to Soda Springs over the telegraph. They had stolen bank money which was being transported by the railway. Jimmy had taken the message. He shook his head, "'Tis a sarry lot these boys 'ere," he said sadly. "Doon't they know the railrood is the lifeblood o' this coontry, it 'tis."

Ellis came home to find Ida highly upset about the news. "These outlaws are really getting daring," she said. I hear they robbed the payroll from the Pleasant Valley Coal Company at Castle Gate last spring."

"When it comes to banks and railroads," said Ellis, "I have to admire their spunk. With hostility and conflicts raging between the small man and the big outfits, the small man always gets the raw end of the deal. Laws which are supposed to protect everyone, more often than not protect only the man with enough money in his pocket to pay off the greedy. Banks and railroads seem to exist only to take away what the poor man has and use it for their own purposes."

"You don't mean to tell me you're on the side of the outlaws, do you?" exclaimed Ida, her eyes wide. "Where's your respect for law and order?"

"There's a fine line between lawmen and lawless men. They both live by the six-gun, and many a man who supposedly represents the law has killed more men than most outlaws. From what I've heard, Butch Cassidy hasn't killed a man yet. He's a sort of Robin Hood of the West, and quite respected by some of the people who know him, though some members of the gang are not as gentlemanly as Cassidy."

"Well, I don't know," said Ida. "There must be a better way to change things than by outlaw gangs and robbery."

"When you've seen half the atrocities I have, which go on under the name of law and order, or respectable business, you begin to wonder whose side you should be on," Ellis sighed.

Ida looked thoughtful. She remembered the Reno Gang who were hung near where her family lived after the Civil War.

"Well, many people where I was raised thought of the Reno Gang, not as gunmen, but as sort of Robin Hoods," she said.

"Although the Cassidy Gang is a group of highwaymen," Ellis persisted, "with public sentiment the way it is, it's going to be difficult for Pinkerton's detectives to make them out as criminals, just as time did not make Robin Hood a criminal. People often feel these fellows are victims of circumstances and the lawmen involved are just trying to look like heroes."

"Well, I just hope they stay over in Wyoming, and don't come this way," Ida said with anxiety showing in her voice.

"I wouldn't worry about it," said Ellis.

Ellis' ideas toward medicine were the same as towards the typewriter. He felt if a surgeon could do an operation, by reading and studying, he could do it too, as long as he followed general techniques of mastered surgery. He accumulated a large library of medical books, and studied them whenever he had an unfamiliar medical procedure coming up. He continued to get animal parts from the slaughter house so he could practice difficult techniques.

He also kept the works of that great Scotch poet, Robert Burns, close by. He had memorized long passages from his poetry. "Burns was an alcoholic," he told Ida, "but he had a dramatic soul and understood people. Reading his poetry and his philosophy helps me deal with the suffering of mankind."

Ida cared for her chickens and a cow and began selling eggs and churning butter to sell. She tended the vegetable garden carefully, and through prudent management, they prospered.

The town was served by a two-room schoolhouse, but enrollment was growing to such proportions that two rooms were inadequate. Ida worked to gain support for a ten thousand dollar bond to build a new building. The bond passed, and a two-story red brick school was built. The old two-room school building was sold to A.J. Knowlin and moved about two-hundred feet to the west, where he added a wing on each side and turned it into a livery stable and barn.

The new school had two rooms on each floor. It was a start toward improving education in Soda Springs, but there was so much that needed to be done. Many of the children in the outlying areas were not getting any education at all. Many of the adults were virtually illiterate.

One quiet Sunday afternoon Ellis and Ida took a buggy

ride out in the Five-Mile Meadow area above Soda Creek. They slowed the horses to a walk so they might pass the changing vegetation tree by tree, bush by bush. Ellis glanced at his wife. She looked fresh and lovely. Being pregnant agreed with her, he thought, it seemed to give her a special glow. They looked forward to having their own child with a great deal of anticipation. "I hope it will be a boy that looks just like his father," said Ida.

"Or a girl that looks just like her mother," laughed Ellis.

They both knew that as long as the baby was strong and healthy, whether it was a boy or girl was of little consequence.

They were intrigued by the abundance of wildlife, and had never seen so many ducks in one spot. Ida shook her head angrily, her face pursed in agitation, when they found a small pile of the birds killed and left to rot. "The people in the West and the nation for that matter, think ducks and other wildlife are an unlimited resource, in fact they view the West in general as unlimited," said Ellis, his face hard. "Some day that attitude will have to change."

The meadows were being irrigated in some spots. Pastures were green and succulent with tender sprouts of young grass. "That's one thing about the Mormons," explained Ellis, "they know the importance of the water, and use it for growing crops, while still protecting the streams. They're way ahead of the times in that field."

In rare instances like this, when there was an opportunity to get away and spend a few hours together enjoying nature and each other's company, they felt closer than they had for a long time. They watched an eagle soaring above, and listened to birds chattering among the willows. They sat on the banks of an irrigation ditch and watched and laughed as a frog wriggled from under the mud. "It's so nice being able to spend an afternoon together without anyone calling you out on a case," said Ida. "I just wish we could do it more often."

"You know I enjoy being with you, Idie," said Ellis, "but there are so many people that need medical attention."

"I know," sighed Ida. "A doctor's wife has to share her husband with the whole world, it seems."

The dusky evening lay cool hands on them. Ida started to shiver, and Ellis reached over, surprisingly tender, and took her into his arms. They didn't start home until the sun had set and a cool breeze started to blow. The mournful cry of a coyote reminded Ellis of his first trip to the mining settlement at Carriboo, and how he had mistaken the coyotes for wolves.

A few weeks later some of the local men got together and decided to see who could shoot the most ducks. They chose up teams of about four on each side, and went on a rampage of destruction against the beautiful birds. Two empty gondola cars were sitting on the railroad siding, and the groups each chose a car and proceeded to fill it with ducks. When they had finished the two gondolas were each about two-thirds full, and every duck within sight had been slaughtered. Periodic hunts, similar to the one they had witnessed, and just as wasteful, would continue to be big events in the region for years.

Ida was angered at the waste and destruction. "Look at all those ducks lying there just rotting!" she complained, wrinkling up her nose in disgust at the terrible smell.

"You're right," said Ellis. "That is an awful waste of food and of animal life."

In a few days, they could hardly stand to be in the yard for the appalling stench of rotting meat.

"I'll talk to Jimmy," said Ellis as the thought suddenly occurred to him. "Maybe he can get the railroad cars moved."

Jimmy got an engineer to hook onto the gondolas and haul them off to be dumped in an out-of-the-way spot.

The hunters bragged about their successful duck shoot for years, and Ida had to bite her tongue on more than one occasion to keep from saying what she thought about the escapade. In those early days, few people in Soda Springs or any other place, in the country, were conscious of conservation practices.

At four-thirty one morning Ellis arose and stumbled through the dark house to answer an impatient knock on the door. The stranger looked nervous.

"What's the problem?" Ellis asked.

"A man out at Williamsburg got hurt by a horse, and needs a doctor," answered the man.

Ellis nodded his head and mumbled, "I'll get my things, How bad is your man?"

"He's hurt pretty bad," said the fellow, "so you'd better hurry Doc."

Ellis went to the bedroom and got his instrument bag. Ida, who had been awakened by the knock, had heard the exchange of words.

"Be careful," she advised quietly. "For some reason I don't trust that man."

"Don't worry, Idie," said Ellis. "I'll be back before nightfall. You know I always return just as soon as I can.

Ellis kissed her quickly and left. Ida worried about Ellis when he was called out into the country. Sometimes she felt she shouldn't have agreed to come west. At least in Tennessee they were living in a civilized area, even if they were poor.

The man had two horses tied to the gatepost. They were typical cowboy horses; smaller, built for endurance, and a cross between the Morgan horse and the cayuse or Indian pony. The Morgan horse was a breed developed in New England in the seventeen-hundreds. They were relatively small, but tough, and could pull heavy loads. They had proved to be an excellent breed for western cattle ranchers because of their high intelligence and abundant energy.

"I brought a good, fast horse for you, to save time," the man said.

Ellis mounted the extra horse and followed the man out of town just as a few streaks of light were starting to show in the eastern sky. The air tasted fresh and the moon cast a soft glow over the sleepy little village before being chased away by the rising sun. They went north through the hills to the Blackfoot River which gurgled with joy at the beauty of the dawning day then followed up the river through the Narrows. Trout were jumping in the stream, having an early morning breakfast of moths and other insects.

There were several camps of Shoshone Indians along the Narrows, where they often camped in summertime to fish and hunt. They made fish traps from willows, and caught large numbers of the native cutthroat trout, which they dried on the willow racks along with what meat they could get. The buffalo and great flocks of mountain sheep near Soda Springs had been virtually annihilated, and the native mule deer had been practically all slaughtered, mostly for their hides which would bring a dollar each. You didn't see the Indians waste wildlife like that, thought Ellis. They took only what they needed to subsist on. Many people liked venison. Ellis had tasted it once, and while it wasn't as good as elk or buffalo, he didn't mind the slightly musky taste of the meat. Many of the Indians lived on rockchucks, porcupines, badgers and ground squirrels. Ellis knew that was probably the only reason they hadn't all starved to death. The squaws were busy cooking breakfast on the campfires. They dug camas bulbs from the marshes for winter use, but in spite of utilizing whatever they could get off the land, and eating those species which did not hibernate, they often went hungry when the snow came and the winter winds blew.

They passed a squaw on a horse with a travois on which the family's possessions, including their small, movable summer house, or tepee, was loaded. The poles of the travois went on each side of the horse and dragged behind, where they were lashed together to form a carry-all.

From the narrows, they headed in a northeasterly direction to Williamsburg and the Middle Dairy. The Middle Dairy was run by the Mormon family of William J. Kunz, of Bern. The nearby Lower Dairy was operated by Sam and Dave Kunz. Farther up was the Upper Dairy operated by John Kunz. During the summer months they boarded cows from Bern and other nearby communities and manufactured high quality Swiss and American cheese, which they marketed in the surrounding communities. The owners of the cows were given shares, a percentage of the cheese for use of the animals, and the surplus was sold. The cows were trailed back to Bern for the winter months, and cheese making operations carried on there. Cows were milked mostly by young women between the ages of fourteen and eighteen. These milkmaids each milked as many as twenty cows twice daily. Men and boys herded the cows. Well chaperoned all night dances and parties were common at the dairies where the milkmaids attracted cowboys and other young men from the nearby areas.

The main settlement of Williamsburg was a tough little area. It had a boarding house, a saloon which was notorious for the hell-raising which was carried on there, a summer tent city which included two prostitutes' tents, and Ellis had been told it was supposed to be the toughest area in the United States besides Jackson Hole, Wyoming. Ellis had heard about several Chinamen being murdered on Williamsburg. When they started a sawmill there, he had been told they had to discard the trees close to the settlement because they were so loaded with sheepherders' and miners' bullets from celebrating with a six-gun, that the lead would dull the saw blades. It wasn't much different from what went on at Carriboo and at Soda Springs, only Soda Springs was more permanent, Ellis thought.

The homesteaders, dairy owners, and permanent residents of these areas were a different type, but a hardy lot. They had to be hardy to survive in these isolated areas. They were always willing to lend a helping hand to anyone who needed it.

They passed the Williamsburg sheep dip on the headwaters of the Blackfoot. There sheep were dipped to get rid of scabies, which had paralyzed the sheep market. The sheep in this area had been put under government quarantine until they had all been run through a dip, and were cured of the bug. Some were quarantined for as much as a month. Dips and shearing corrals were always needed. There were several in the area, including the Doull Dip at Henry, the Morgan Dip at Wayan, and this one coming up Williamsburg. Sheep were run through water containing a mixture of sheep dip and sulphur, which was brought by the wagon load from Sulphur Canyon.

They passed Chippie Creek, which was named after the notorious women of the area. Just west of the middle dairy, a man stepped out of the trees, and waved to the riders. The man with Ellis immediately changed their course to head in that direction.

A blonde, rather stocky young man emerged from the small grove of quaking aspens. He was leading a horse, and was followed by several other members of the group, and their mounts. "I see you got the Doc.," he said. "Did you have any trouble?"

The man shook his head. "Did anyone see you?" he questioned.

"Didn't see a soul except the Doctor. I just slipped in and outa town without even hardly a dog barking."

"Good," said the leader, who by now Ellis recognized as Butch Cassidy. He turned to Ellis. "Hate to have to do this Doc, but one of the fellows is shot up pretty bad. He's over in Star Valley. Sorry to have to kidnap you."

Ellis noticed several of the men had their guns drawn. "If there's someone who needs my help, I'll see what I can do for them, but by God I won't be kidnapped," said Ellis. "If you want this doctor to take care of your man, put your guns away."

Cassidy nodded and the men holstered their guns. "Let's get going. Doc, we've got a fresh horse for you," he said.

The men, looking like typical cowboys with boots, chaps, spurs, scarves, and cowboy hats, hobbled the tired horses in a grassy area and brought fresh ones. When mounted, they skirted around the dairies and headed east again. Ellis knew Cassidy had a lot of friends in Star Valley, Wyoming, where the little town of Freedom was located. Cassidy had been good to these Mormon polygamists who had refused to give up their wives and families. They went down Tincup Creek and through Gardner's Pass where Peg-Leg Smith, the notorious Wyoming trader, had driven herds of stolen California horses three-score years earlier. Ellis had heard a lot about the man who had established a trading post along the Oregon Trail, married several Indian wives, and built up quite an empire in Wyoming in the early days. He was a colorful character and shrewd trader, thought Ellis. Losing a leg hadn't slowed him down much. In spite of his methods he had provided a needed service, and many a traveler was thankful to find a place along the trail where he could get necessities.

"Glad to have you aboard, Doc," said Cassidy dropping back beside Ellis. "I hope you can do something for our friend. He's in one helluva mess."

"I'll go to see anyone who is sick or injured," said Ellis, his jaw firmly set, "But don't ever expect me to go anywhere at gunpoint. Nobody is kidnapping me."

Cassidy nodded, "Can't blame you for feeling that way."

Cassidy rode beside Ellis and they talked about the Credit-Mobilier scandal, in which Union Pacific had been involved. "They made all the investors think the government was backing all the bonds in the credit-mobiliers they set up, then set up another company to take the bonds away from the government. Can you believe that?" asked Cassidy.

"Oh, I know they've really pulled some good ones," said Ellis, "and the methods they used to get the land for the railroad was often scandalous. A lot of people hate the railroad, with good reason, too."

They rode up to a small, log ranch house in Freedom. "Well, let's go take a look at the patient," said Cassidy, swinging quickly off his horse.

He ushered Ellis into a back bedroom, where a pale-faced man, was swathed in bloody bandages. It was evident at first glance the fellow had been badly shot up. Ellis' hand automatically ran through his hair making it stand on end, as he shook his head. "I'll do what I can," he told Cassidy.

A tall, thin woman with her hair tied back in a bun, brought hot water. He washed his hands carefully, put on rubber gloves, and then washed and dressed the wounds. He swore softly under his breath as he worked. He could see that if the man did make it, he would require a lot of care and a long convalescence. The wounds would have to be lanced and drained regularly and the infected areas would probably have to be cut away.

When Ellis had finished doing what he could for the injured outlaw for the moment, he walked slowly to a lean-to in the yard where Cassidy had joined the other men. "It's touch and go," he said. "If he makes it through the next twenty-four hours he might have a chance, if he doesn't get too much infection in those wounds. He'll need a lot of care for a long time."

"We'll just have to keep you, Doc," said one of the gang.

"Like I said before, you damn well better realize I'll not be kidnapped. You don't make this doctor do anything. I'm no lover of the railroads or the banks and I deplore what they're doing to the common man. He stopped a moment, then continued thoughtfully, "I'll never forget the Pinkerton men throwing me off the freight trains when I desperately needed to get from place to place. I don't care what you fellows have done. If a man needs doctorin' I'll care for him, but if you try to keep me at gunpoint, he won't get any care, and Ida will have a posse here in no time."

The men started talking quietly among themselves. There seemed to be a difference of opinion as voices rose. "What do you suggest, Doc?" asked Cassidy. "He's gonna have the best—and that's you, Doc. Besides that, we can't trust nobody else."

Kackley ran his fingers through his hair again. "Well," he said, "what he needs right now is rest. If he can make it through this initial shock, you'd better bring him into town and let me take care of him."

"You're crazy, Doc," said a husky, dark-haired man. "We can't take a chance of going into town. If we did, we'd probably run into some of Pinkerton's men, and end up spending the rest of our lives in the hoosegow or hang from a rope."

"I've been thinking there might be a way," said Ellis. "If we can pass him off as a typhoid case, and take him down to the pest house, or one of the little cabins in town where I sometimes keep such cases, none of the local residents will go near."

Cassidy looked up with surprise showing in his eyes. "Say, you're okay, Doc," he said, with the beginnings of a smile curling around his lips. "Maybe one of the guys could dress up as his wife and go along to care for him."

"Don't look at me," said the dark-haired man in a loud voice, shaking his head back and forth for emphasis.

"I'll do it," said a young, small-framed man, who Ellis thought looked like only a boy.

"You're not going to trust the doctor to do something like that, are you?" protested the first man. "We'll all end up in jail. All he has to do is call the sheriff."

"Shut-up," said Cassidy. "Doc, if he makes it till then, and we can move him, I'll have him at your place in two days at about four in the morning. His 'wife' will accompany him. Can you make it back by yourself, or do you need someone to show you the way?"

"I'll make it," said Ellis.

"Don't worry about the horse, we'll get him when we come by," said Cassidy. "If not, you can keep him. He's a good mount."

Since it was still fairly early in the afternoon, Ellis decided to stop by and check on the sheepherder he had operated on. The man wasn't at camp, but the camp tender told Ellis, "He's as good as new, Doc. You're so damned good with that knife, it's too bad you can't cut out some of the damned meanness around here. A guy hardly dares to go into town, the way they're treated there."

Ellis wished he could cut out the meanness and inhumanity, but he was beginning to think there was no cure for that. It was dark when Ellis rode into his yard. Wink, who by now usually accompanied him when he rode out of town, was waiting by the gate. Ellis reached down and patted his head, then followed the dog toward the house. He felt stiff, abused, tired and hungry from the long ride, but he couldn't help liking Cassidy, even if he was an outlaw. Ida came flying out the door to meet him, and threw herself into his arms. "Thank God," she sobbed, "It really is you. For some reason, I've been worried sick. Who was that man anyway?"

"Just one of Butch Cassidy's gang who was sent to kidnap me," said Ellis casually.

"I knew something wasn't right about the whole situation. I can't believe they didn't kill you."

"You'll believe it when you see how much I'm going to eat for supper," Ellis laughed. "Boy what a reception. I should get kidnapped more often."

"Be serious," said Ida. "You could easily have been hurt or killed."

Ellis' face became serious as he looked into her eyes thoughtfully a moment and then spoke, "Idie, now you must not say a thing about this. I had to treat the man, and I think he will make it, but we must never mention it. You and I have never believed in an eye for an eye and a tooth for a tooth," he added.

Two days later, Ellis awoke to a loud knock on the door at four o'clock in the morning. He opened it to find a small sunbonneted "lady," in a long drab looking dress, with an old shawl and a basket on her arm. "Your typhoid case is here, Doc," he said.

"You look just like a woman in that get-up" said Ellis. "It's amazing what a sunbonnet and a few petticoats can cover. Let me get dressed, and I'll take you to the place I've prepared."

Ellis dressed quickly, then hopped in the buggy beside the driver, and directed him down the street to a small bungalow behind Peck and Enright's Store. He could hardly believe how well the huge sunbonnet and dress hid the sexual identity of the man. "What do you have in the basket?" he asked.

The man lifted the dishtowel inside the basket, and disclosed the large caliber pistol hidden there. "It's my shopping basket," he said.

The injured man was a little shaken up by the journey, but his pulse and temperature were good. Ellis made him as comfortable as possible, dressed his wounds again, and took leave of the two. He took the horses and buggy back to his place.

Ellis quickly spread the word that he had a new typhoid case, and the man's wife was taking care of him. No one seemed suspicious. Typhoid cases were not uncommon, and no one wanted to go near the place. The "wife" shelled peas or peeled potatoes with her basket beside her, day after day, as she kept a lookout for any trouble.

Ellis visited the man every afternoon just as he always did his typhoid cases. He bathed, lanced, sometimes stitched, and rebandaged the wounds, and used his skill to keep the infection under control.

Penetrating wounds usually had to be opened up, sometimes as much as three to six inches. If "proud flesh" grew up around the wound, it would not heal, and had to be treated with silver nitrate so the skin would grow up over it. Skin would not heal up-hill on its own.

Once wounds got infected, they had to be laid open to get drainage, and sometimes stitched up afterwards. If they did not heal from the bottom up, they would form a pocket which would fill with infection. Sometimes hot poultices were used. It was lucky that lead was usually well tolerated by the body. When a person was hit, the trajectory was peculiar, and it sometimes took a lot of blind probing to find a bullet.

Gradually the man's wounds healed and the fellow gained strength. When Ellis released him from his care, he watched as he and his 'wife' headed out of town in the buggy which had brought them, into the early morning darkness, and realized he had become quite fond of the two. He wondered what the good citizens of Soda Springs would say if they knew two members of Cassidy's gang had spent much of the summer in town. This was one of the "lost periods" in the chronicles of the Cassidy Gang, when they were supposed to be hidden out in Star Valley.

My job, thought Ellis, is to help the sick and injured, not to enforce the law, though I might be a helluva lot better at it than some of the lawmen I've seen, who are as crooked as the worst of the bunch. Something is going to have to be done about the lawlessness in this town and the so-called businesses who are killing people while I'm trying to help them, and getting away with it most of the time, too. The Cassidy gang can't hold a candle to some of the crooks hiding behind respectability, he thought to himself.

The summer had gone quickly. As fall turned to winter, the weather became colder, Kackleys found the Codman house impossible to keep warm. When blizzards came up, snow blew in through the cracks and piled up in little heaps inside the house. "I don't know how anyone could keep from freezing to death in this place," said Ida, shaking her head. "It's beautiful and showy, but not practical to live in during the winter. I can see it was built just for a summer home, with only fireplaces for heating. I'm afraid we really got in over our heads this time. We'd be better off in the barn or chicken coop than in the house."

The wind blew for days at a time and made a howling sound like Banshee of the desert as it seemed to go right through the house. They bought two new stoves. One was a big black, shiny, sheet metal stove with a lot of nickel trim. Between them and the big, old cook stove, it warmed things up some, but still not enough to be comfortable. Finally they closed off everything but the kitchen and bedroom and Ellis' office, and only tried to keep the three rooms warm. They practically lived in the kitchen. "If we don't both get pneumonia and die, we'll be lucky," observed Ida. "I don't know what on earth we'll do when the baby comes to keep it from freezing to death."

Ellis had been secretly worrying about keeping the baby warm also. It seemed like he was always cold in the house.

Ellis' horses were good snow horses. They could feel the packing of the snow on the road under their feet, but one day when he was coming home from out by the Blackfoot River in a nasty, cold blizzard, they started falling off the road. During the winter the settlers cut the fence lines, and made the roads the shortest distance possible. They were staked with willows, and drivers would hold their buggy whip out as they drove along. If it hit the willows, they knew they were on the road.

Ellis stopped, got out and checked the horses to see what was wrong. They had gotten so cold, their eye lids were frosted down, and they seemed to be relying solely on horse sense, or their animal instinct, to stay on the road. Ellis leaned against the side of each horse's head until he had the animal warmed up enough to get its eyes open, and finally made it home. One horse had frozen the whole side of its head and in a few days all the hair started falling out of that side. It was a hard winter that year, and Ellis and Ida would both be glad when spring came.

Chapter 7

In 1899, licensing, in addition to registering in the county in which they practiced, was required of those practicing medicine, surgery, or pharmacy in Idaho. Examining boards were established, and one hundred ninety-three medical and one-hundred-thirty-three dental licenses were issued that year. Those who called themselves "Doctor" but had only read a few medical books or had a mail-order diploma from a school they had never attended, were no longer able to establish a practice.

Ida went into labor early one morning before breakfast on what she figured was the twentieth day of her ninth month. Ellis always felt a sense of awe at bringing a child into the world, to suddenly have a new little human being appear on the scene. To deliver his own child made him nervous, though he wasn't going to show it in front of Ida. Tiny beads of sweat instantly popped out on his forehead.

It wasn't often Ellis had a chance to be involved in a normal delivery. He was called by the midwives only when there were problems which made the birth difficult. It was a helluva manipulation nature put the child through to get into this world, he thought. The child's head sometimes took a lot of abuse, especially if the birth canal was malformed or the mother had suffered injury or disease such as rickets—common among these pioneer women—which might cause the head not to engage or to get lodged in the birth canal. Sometimes the cord came ahead of the baby or wrapped around the infant's neck, tightening and suffocating the child. Position of the baby could cause problems. Sometimes it became necessary to sacrifice mother or baby to keep the other alive. Ellis was always prepared for and expecting the worst.

Ida's delivery took place late in the day and went well. As

he eased the slippery little body into the world and saw it was a fine baby boy, he was filled with a joy he had never known before. He picked up his son by the ankles and slapped his behind, and was rewarded with a lusty cry. When the child was washed up and dressed, he set him in Ida's arms and stood silently observing the scene. The baby's bright red hair curled around his tiny face, and they both thought he was the prettiest baby they had ever seen.

Mrs. Rose, across the street, came over to help care for the mother and baby. The next day, there were congratulations and gifts from their friends the Strachans, Schmidts, Whitmans, Morgans, Knowlins, Laus, Horsleys, Gortons and many others.

The baby was a hardy child. When Ida pushed a nipple toward the little puckered mouth, he was soon nursing with gusto, though they were both novices at this activity. He was a good baby and only cried when he was wet or hungry. They christened him Alvin. It was Ellis' proudest day, and he looked forward to the time when his tiny son would grow to adulthood and become a partner with him in the medical field.

Ida's life revolved around the baby. She felt happier and more settled with a child in their home. As the air again warmed with the coming of spring, she took him for long walks in the sunshine. She read aloud to him before he was old enough to understand the words, but he responded to her voice and the warmth and love it contained. The bright-eyed child brought a bond into their marriage which in spite of their love for each other, had not been there before.

While Ida cooed loving words to her son, Ellis uttered medical terms, and told him what a great doctor he would be one day. Things had improved for both of them in this frontier town where life was hard and dangerous because their love had brought this tiny bundle of joy into their world.

Ellis' practice was growing daily. Money was no longer a problem, but as their fortune increased, time became more and more scarce. Ellis was always in a hurry, and rushed from one call to another. When he was home, he enjoyed playing with little Alvin. It seemed like no time at all until the baby was beginning to crawl, and could get across a room and into things before Ida could turn her head.

Ida became increasingly worried about Ellis' health. His hair was starting to stand straight up on his forehead because he kept running his fingers through it whenever he was worried. "You are going to have to quit doing that," she insisted. "Your hair is beginning to stick straight up, and never will lie down if you keep pushing it up like that. The only time I ever see your hair in place is when you're coming out of the barber shop door. It's just a nervous habit and you should try . . ."

Ellis' lips covered hers before she could finish the sentence. "You worry too much, Idie," he laughed. "There's a helluva lot worse things that could happen than my hair standing straight up. I could be going bald, and not have any to stand up. Then you might have something to be concerned about."

Ida shook her head and laughed. "You never take me seriously," she said. "How am I ever going to get you to take care of yourself."

The Next Sunday afternoon Ellis hitched the horses to the buggy and took Ida and Alvin for a ride up Soda Creek and to Five-Mile Meadow. The dog, Wink, trotted along beside the buggy. Ellis seldom went anywhere without his dog. He had removed the top of the buggy to cut down on wind resistance when he was going on a call, and make it possible to get more speed. Ida had to make sure little Alvin was bundled up well and had a hat to protect him from the bright sun's rays.

The new spring vegetation with a background of mountains, showing some snow patches still on the slopes made a striking picture. Grass in the meadows was almost up to their ankles already, which surprised Ellis. Somehow the spring season always took him unawares. They absorbed the sun's warm rays and thought how good it was to be warm.

Ellis showed Ida the large Mammoth Spring north of Hooper.

She looked across it and said, "I didn't realize any of the springs were so huge. I thought they were all only a few feet across."

"Mammoth is so big that George took me boating there shortly after I came," replied Ellis.

As they rode past springs, Ida marveled that there could be a fresh water spring only two or three feet from a soda water spring. It seemed to Ida like she hadn't been out of the house for years. She was full of questions. "Why do some springs have red coloring and others practically next to them black?" she wondered out loud.

"They both have oxide of iron, but one has red oxide and another black oxide," Ellis explained. "Isn't it great to have all of these fascinating natural wonders. I've thought ever since I first saw them that some day I would like to build a health resort here—one that would rival the great health resorts of Europe," he said, his eyes sparkling. "I think there's a fantastic future in treating people with the soda water. It seems to have a soothing effect on stomach problems, and bathing in the water can be healing to certain types of skin irritations. Some of the local people say it heals rheumatism," he continued enthusiastically. "I think there is something to the alleged medicinal properties that have been credited to these springs."

"You really believe they have a healing effect on illnesses?" Ida asked as her eyes met his.

"You know, Idie, I've heard a lot of rumors that many a man who met with foul play in this town, died from knockout drops in their drink, or a knock over the head with a shillelagh was thrown into a lime pit behind one of the saloons."

Ida looked surprised, but didn't speak. Ellis continued, "An old miner up at Carriboo tells about a man who was thrown in and lived to tell about it. He says the fellow had been working cattle all summer, but came into town when he got his pay. He got a room at the hotel, then went over to the saloon. They loaded his drink. He didn't remember anything more until towards morning he woke up in the lime pit with just his head and one shoulder sticking out. He said he could feel the lime working on his whole body, and was badly burned by it, but managed to crawl out and to his surprise found his rifle there on the edge of the pit. After laying there a long time, he remembered what had happened and got up strength enough to go back into the saloon where the men were still talking and laughing. The old miner said the room became deadly quiet and those fellows stared at his friend like they were seeing a ghost. He raised his gun and shot the bastard who had thrown him in the pit right in the head. That's one time one of these swindlers got what he had coming."

Ida's eyes widened in horror.

"The miner also told me they healed the man's lime burns by bathing him in water from the springs. I really think it has a lot of healing properties we aren't aware of."

"You mean to tell me they just threw people in the lime pit, and that was the last anyone ever heard of them?" Ida asked.

"Apparently so, Idie. There's a lot of inhumanity goes on in this town, and I've heard of more than one man who disappeared here, never to be heard of again."

Ida shook her head in disbelief. "I can't believe anyone could do that," she sighed. "How can one human being treat another that way?"

"I don't know, Idie. As the poet Burns says, 'Man's inhumanity to man makes countless thousands mourn!'" He paused a moment before continuing, "I do know these springs are a marvel of nature, and some day they'll be recognized for the potential they have, if people don't ruin them first. It's too bad this whole area wasn't set aside along with Yellowstone Park. Just a few years ago, when the Idanha was in full bloom, many were the rich and famous people who came here to drink the water, and stay in the luxurious hotel, which was reported to be the largest hotel in Idaho, and the finest of its day between Denver and the Pacific coast. It's too bad the hotel has gone downhill," he said sadly, "but the spring water is still in great demand."

He waited a moment for Ida to make a comment. She didn't, but her expression was one of complete interest, so he continued, "Theodore Enders, who manages the plant told me they are shipping the water by the carload to the home office in Salt Lake, and to eastern markets, and even to foreign countries. In the past, European nobility who explored the West always stopped here. The old Beer Spring was a famous stopping place of early Indians, trappers and explorers, and travelers on the Oregon Trail alike. These early people all thought it had healing effects.''

"Mrs. Crawford said that during the trek along the Oregon Trail, women stopped to wash their clothes in the warm water, while the meadows provided a place to rest and graze the horses,'' mused Ida. "I'll bet they really appreciated warm water to wash their clothes, besides having the soda water to drink.''

"Railroad tycoon, Jay Gould visits occasionally, drinks Hooper Springs water from a rusty tin can, and lauds its health-building properties. He's one of those who parks his private railroad car on the siding while he enjoys the town in luxury,'' Ellis said. "Brigham Young was so impressed with the place a cabin was built for him here. Diamond Jim Brady, the railroad tycoon and connoisseur of diamonds, comes here occasionally too, staying in his luxurious private railway car.''

"That's quite an impressive bunch,'' agreed Ida, and no wonder. Look how beautiful it is,'' she said, her eyes sweeping over the area. "I hope to God no one destroys it before it can be preserved for mankind and Idaho,'' she added thoughtfully.

Ida's glowing eyes seemed to cloud over as she thought of the creek and springs which had given Soda Springs its name and birthright, and realized, though it belonged to both the past and the future, it might easily be destroyed through ignorance or greed. She wondered if destruction might even come from the people of the very city which had taken its name.

On Five-Mile Meadow they inspected the ditches bringing water to irrigate the hay fields. "These ditches were mostly built by hand, and represent a helluva lot of time and work by the Mormons,'' Ellis marveled.

Shortly before Ellis and Ida had bought the house, the settlers on the north side of the tracks had piped water from a spring to the southeast, and set up what they called the Mormon Water System. It provided a culinary water supply for a limited number of homes in the town. Ellis had always appreciated the fact they were able to have running water because of these men.

"They seem to be a far-sighted group," agreed Ida.

The idea of turning the area into a health resort was exciting to her. She had an interest in preserving the natural wonders, as well as a good business head on her shoulders. It seemed like a first rate plan, she thought to herself. She would become a strong organizer of community efforts to promote the water and preserve the springs. She silently made a promise to herself that she would solicit the pioneer spirit of the Mormons to help preserve these wonderful gifts from the Almighty. This spirit she had admired more and more in these Mormon people as she had begun to notice and learn about them. Brigham Young and other Mormon leaders had encouraged preservation of the springs, and a spring had been named in remembrance of Wilford Woodruff, who later became the fourth president of the Mormon Church.

It was a special day. Ellis and Ida felt a day in the out-of-doors renewed both body and spirit. He had bought a couple of riding horses, and she was enjoying learning to ride. She took to it easily—much more easily than Ellis had—and was already putting little Alvin snugly in front of her on the saddle and taking him for rides.

"We're going to need some summer pasture for the horses," mused Ellis. "I'd sure like to get some here along Soda Creek."

"That's an excellent idea," said Ida with enthusiasm. "Let's find out if we can buy some. It's a beautiful area. Besides being good pasture, if we could buy some of the land with springs on it, we could make sure they were protected."

"Look at this," said Ellis, lighting a small piece of paper from his pocket on fire, and holding it over one of the springs. The gas being emitted from the spring put the fire right out.

"What makes it do that?" asked Ida, who was intrigued.

"The spring puts off carbon dioxide," said Ellis. "They say a few years back an Indian child fell into one of the springs, and though snatched out before hardly wet, the child could not be revived.''

''Oh, how horrible,'' said Ida, holding Alvin a little more closely to her. I've often wondered how Mrs. Gorton ever survived losing four little girls at once in the diphtheria epidemic. I could never stand such a terrible loss.

''The whole family carries scars from the experience,'' said Ellis quietly. ''They've had more than their share of sorrow and grief. She couldn't bear to see her little girls buried in the cemetery by the cedars, where the water came up to within a few feet of the graves, so they donated land where the new cemetery is and they were the first graves there.''

They sat quietly for a few moments, both absorbed in their own thoughts, before Ellis spoke again. ''By the way, George and Suzie Small have bought the land where Tom Williams' bathhouse was, and applied for a permit to build a new one. They paid one hundred and fifty dollars for the lot,'' he continued. ''George said he is planning to deepen and clean out the spring at the top of the hill, and make a pool about five feet deep and several feet in diameter.''

''That will really be nice,'' said Ida looking a little brighter. ''We'd better be getting back now before it gets too cold for Alvin,'' she suggested noticing a breeze had come up.

When Smalls got the pool built, it was a good outdoor pool in the summer. The water was lukewarm, but hard with minerals. Villagers were allowed free access to the pool, and many who frequented it felt the mineral water cured their arthritis and other ills. They called it Small's Natatorium. Smalls never got around to building a bath house, though they talked a lot about the idea. They were just too busy with other things.

Ellis and Ida bought 400 acres of pasture land along Soda Creek. They were delighted with the purchase, and it gave them a feeling of security to have so much land. They irrigated part of it and raised hay for feeding their horses in the winter.

When Alvin started to walk, he tagged around behind his mother until Ellis came home and then he followed his father around. By fourteen months he was talking quite well.

Progress was coming to the little village of Soda Springs. A Board of Health was organized by the village board, with Ellis as general physician and three other members. T.S. Williams was granted a franchise for permission to build an electric plant.

Some of the townsmen wanted to have slot-machines legalized, and there was a great deal of opposition to the idea from the Mormons who were opposed to gambling. It was discussed at length at town board meetings, and on the streets, and over the dinner table. Ellis and Ida opposed the idea. "We have enough corruption, without encouraging more," Ida sighed. "Do you think they'll ever get all of the people in this town to obey the law?"

"Not the way things are," said Ellis. "What we need is to have someone completely removed from the situation come in—like a Grand Jury. That's the only way this town will improve. The dishonest have too much control over the local people, and many of those who would like to fight for improvements are afraid of them," he said thoughtfully. After a pause he added, "It isn't any different here than in any other boom town in the West. Law and order will some day gain the upper hand."

In spite of the problems, Soda Springs prospered. A new town hall was built. It was a period of growth for the city and Ellis and Ida had plenty of exciting things to keep them busy. As always, Ida was concerned with the schools, and kept close track of what was happening there. Now that she had a son, who would soon be growing up and going to school, she felt even more personally involved in the academic progress of the community.

Both Ida and Ellis were becoming increasingly concerned about patients bringing contagious diseases into their home now that they had a child. "I think I'd better look for an office downtown," said Ellis. "The last thing we need is for a case of diphtheria to walk into our home. Diphtheria is on its way out, but when it's under control, there'll still be typhoid and pneumonia and measles and scarlet fever. Scarlet fever is a helluva disease." he continued. "We've never been able to separate it from strep throat, and long strain strep is a lethal germ. It has a tremendous effect on the kidneys, the heart, and ears. Whooping cough can also be fatal in babies," he worried. Ellis rented a space from Charlie Fryar above his mercantile business. It was one of the few brick buildings in town. Charlie had built it a couple of years before, and had made the bricks himself. Besides the mercantile store downstairs, there were a few hotel rooms upstairs, and a ballroom. Dancers often got out of hand, and resorted to fighting and throwing each other down the steep outside stairs which led to the upper floor. It would soon become a contest to see who could throw the most people down the stairs. The ballroom was losing money for Mr. Fryar, who was a far-sighted man, but didn't take kindly to anything which would not turn at least some profit.

They divided the large room into an office and a waiting room, and partitioned one area off for Dr. Smedley, a local dentist who wanted to put his office there. Ellis used the northwest corner of the upper floor of the building. It had a small closet in one end. More and more patients were coming to Ellis' office, and he kept extremely busy. He used sulphur from Sulphur Canyon, near town, to fumigate. He would wash and clean up everything each evening and change his clothes before going home. Ida sat and cut and rolled bandages at the kitchen table in the evenings after Alvin was in bed, then sterilized them in the large double boiler.

In June 1903, the whole town was excitedly following the progress of Dr. Horatio Nelson Jackson of Burlington, Vermont, who had bet someone at the University Club in San Francisco he could drive one of the new horseless carriages from coast to coast in three months. "That's a foolhardy undertaking," said Ellis, "as undependable as those new contraptions are."

At midnight on the thirteenth of June, Jackson reached Caldwell, Idaho. People in Soda Springs followed his progress as he followed a stream bed toward Mountain Home, was engulfed by a sudden rise of water, had to be pulled out with a four horse team, then followed the Union

Pacific tracks to Pocatello where he arrived June 17, and on to Soda Springs the next day.

He rounded the corner at Whitman's Store at sundown on Tuesday night, the 18th of June, in a cloud of dust. A whoop from cowboys, sheepherders, Indians, and citizens of the town, was taken up and passed along the whole block. Indians camped on the flat completely surrounded the horseless carriage, and their exclamations of wonder were almost as much of a novelty to the townspeople as the automobile itself. Gambling was temporarily suspended, as curiosity about the strange apparition superseded interest in roulette and twenty-one. The whole town, including Kackleys, was soon there to inspect the 20 horsepower, chain-driven, two-cylinder Winton automobile and its driver.

Dr. Jackson arrived with a pit bull sitting in the front seat beside him, wearing a pair of goggles. "Where'd you get the dog?" asked a sheepherder.

"Well, they invited me to a pit bull fight near Caldwell, and I said, 'Hell, no, I don't want to go to that, but I'll take the dog'."

Ellis and his friends, August Largilliere and J. O. Morgan were busily inspecting the car. "That's what you need to get out on calls in a hurry," suggested Mr. Morgan.

"I need something more dependable than one of these horseless carriages," said Ellis shaking his head. "They say flat tires are a real problem and it can take longer to change them than to walk. Besides, they scare the horses half to death. I don't believe the automobile would be practical for me."

"How long did it take you to get this far?" Ellis asked Dr. Jackson when he finally got a chance to talk to him.

"I've been on the road twenty-five days," he replied.

"That's a helluva lot longer than it takes the pony express to get here," he told Mr. Morgan. "What I need is something which would get me around the country faster than a horse."

"The automobile has a long way to go before it is perfected, but it has the potential to completely change the common man's way of transportation," said Dr. Jackson.

"What I wanted to call attention to by the trip, is that potential. It's either horses or human power now, except for the railroad. This invention can put machine power into the transportation of the common man. It would be a lot faster if we had roads built to drive on. Some day I expect to see roadways all over the United States."

"Well, I don't know," said Ellis. "I doubt if it will catch on, but it's an interesting thought. Good luck."

Dr. Jackson stayed overnight in Soda Springs before continuing on his coast to coast drive. His stop in town was the main topic of conversation for some time, and a dream of owning an automobile of their own was born in the hearts of some of the more farsighted citizens. Jim Horsley and Ed Whitman were visibly excited about the future prospects of the automobile.

Jim had a great interest in electricity also. "I think your interest in electricity and building a power plant has a lot more potential than the automobile, Jim," advised Ellis. "If I tried to get around in one of those contraptions, the baby I went to deliver might be half-grown before I got there, but electricity has the potential of lighting up the world. Doctors could do a lot more with emergency surgery if they could see better," he added.

Jim was doing a lot of experimental work on electricity, and Ellis recognized him as being way ahead of his time in the field. He was investing his own money in the projects he was doing, and Ellis enjoyed running by once in awhile and checking on his progress. A lot of people didn't think electricity would become important, but Ellis could envision lighting up the whole world so people could see to work or read night or day.

Mr. Largilliere didn't say much about the automobile, but later, when the opportunity arose, he was one of the first to purchase a wasp like Ford with canvas tires for his personal use. Others soon followed his example. Mr. Jackson's trip through Soda Springs had a great and lasting impact on the town.

One evening after dinner, Ellis realized he hadn't seen Wink around the yard that evening. "Have you seen Wink?" he asked Ida.

"Not since afternoon," she replied.

Ellis went out and whistled for the dog, but he did not come. Again and again he called, but there was no answering bound of energy from Wink, who usually responded quickly to his call. The only answer was the scratching and clucking of the chickens. "I wonder where he went," Ellis mumbled as he searched for the dog, who was nowhere to be found.

Late that evening after dinner, Wink dragged himself home with a bullet in his chest. Ellis opened the door to his whimper, and the dog dragged himself across the threshold before collapsing in a pool of blood. Ida held the dog's head in her lap and cried as she begged him not to die. Little Alvin's large eyes filled with tears as Ellis knelt beside his faithful friend and with trembling hands tried to doctor the animal. The dog emitted a few throaty rumbles and quivered before becoming completely still. Ellis thumbed up his right eyelid, and pronounced him dead in a low voice.

Ellis could hold himself back no longer. He cursed the man who had shot his companion, and swore he would find out who it was and even the score. Ida and Alvin looked with wide, tear filled eyes at Ellis, who was not at all in control of the situation. All of his pent up anger came forth. "What are we doing here, bashing our brains out for God knows what?" he questioned. "All we've done is try to help these people, and what do we get in return? I don't understand how anyone could treat an animal this way," he added angrily.

Ellis went into his room, and shut the door. He sat for a long time before a large picture on the wall of Christ before Pilate, while he struggled with his anger, frustration, and desire for revenge.

It didn't take long to discover the bullet had come from the gun of Pat Horton, a local merchant. Ellis vowed none of his family would ever set foot in the man's establishment. Ellis was a professional man, and he would treat the man's family if they needed his services, but they would never be his friends.

When winter snows blanketed the earth again, Ellis got a call from Grays Lake saying he was needed by a miner from

Carriboo, who was wintering in the hotel at Herman. Mining had declined at the Carriboo mines to where only a few people were still engaged in trying to make their fortune on the mountain. The once busy Carriboo City, which for a short time had competed with Eagle Rock for being the largest city in Southeastern Idaho, had been destroyed by fire and all that remained was the Greenhouse Hotel, and a few other buildings including the powder house, a whore-house, and a small summer tent city. Keenan City on the other side of the mountain had also become a ghost town.

Miners who still persisted in trying to get the illusive treasure of the mountain came in the early spring as soon as the ice melted in the streams. Then water was available to use the hydraulic water guns with which they washed away at the mountain side, reducing it to a pile of gravel and dirt which was washed through sluice boxes to collect the precious metal. They left in the late summer when the water in the streams was too low to continue the placer mining, some just going a few miles down the mountain to the settlements of Herman or Eagle Creek to winter in the hotels there and return early in the spring to pursue their dream of striking it rich.

Ellis headed north, though the snow was swirling and a cold wind was blowing into his face. He stopped at Winschell's Store, warmed himself, and had a sandwich and some hot coffee. "It's a helluva day to go out there," said Bill looking concerned.

"Accident and illness never pick a convenient time to strike," said Ellis. "If I'm needed, I'll get there in spite of the weather. I haven't been in so much trouble since you taught me how to dress for the cold when I was a greenhorn. You saved my life that time. God knows I would have frozen to death if it hadn't been for your hospitality." He stopped talking and his mouth twisted into a wry grin as he continued, "I wondered what in the hell was coming off when you told me to go in that back room and take all my clothes off."

Bill laughed heartily, "Well, I'll fix you up with a fresh team, but be careful. People who have been here a helluva lot longer than you have frozen to death out there. You've *probably heard what happened to Tom Crane and his wife a few years back. He had a store and saloon at Keenan City, on the western slope of Carriboo mountain. They were returning from spending most of the winter out of the area, and got lost in a storm. She froze solid, and he ended up having to have both feet amputated. You have to look out for yourself. A dead doctor isn't worth much."*

Ellis made it to Herman and treated an old miner, who paid him with three twenty dollar gold pieces. He stayed overnight in the hotel, and started back for town early the next morning. He might have been tempted to start, and try to get at least part way that night, but the horses were exhausted, and he remembered Bill's story about the Crane family.

The early morning air the next day was cold and breezy, and Ellis hadn't gone far before he was in a blizzard, which became increasingly worse as he neared Henry.

He was anxious to get back to his office, and his growing practice. "You can't go anywhere in this storm," Bill advised. "You'd better just settle down and enjoy yourself until it clears off. I've got an empty room you can have 'till you can get out of here."

When it did clear, huge drifts had blown over the road, which had been none too good even before the storm. "You'd have to have horses with legs like giraffes to make it out of here," Bill said shaking his head.

"I have to get back to town. I have patients there who need to be taken care of," insisted Ellis. "Do you have a pair of snowshoes around the place somewhere?"

Bill shook his head again, and went for the snowshoes. He hated to see the doctor out on a road like that, but he'd have a better chance of making it on snowshoes than with the horses. He brought back the best pair he had, and reluctantly handed them over. "Be careful, Doc," he urged.

Ellis started toward town, and as he trudged along, he found himself becoming more and more exhausted. He found the three twenty-dollar gold pieces in his pocket irritated him, and the longer he traveled, the heavier they seemed. "What good is gold, anyway?" he asked himself. "It's good to buy food and shelter, but it doesn't help much to have more than what you can use for basic needs.''

Money had lost a lot of its value since he had enough to live a little more comfortably on. ''It has no effect on life and death to have more than one needs,'' he thought as the gold pieces rubbed against, and galled his groin.

A lone fence post came into view near the Blackfoot River Bridge. Some fellows had tried to fence this area off once, but went broke and all that remained of the effort was a fence post here and there. As he approached it, he reached into his pocket and removed the three cold, inert pieces of money, and put them on top of the post. He couldn't believe how much better he felt, as he continued on with empty pockets. He would check and see if it was still there when he went by the next time. He continued on home, and seemed to go much easier without the added weight.

Ida met him at the door, and hurried him inside to change his wet clothing. She rubbed his hands and feet until they regained their normal body warmth. ''I got paid with three twenty dollar gold pieces, but I left them on a fence post out by the Blackfoot River. I just couldn't make it another step with all that weight in my pocket,'' he explained.

Ida wondered how three twenty dollar gold pieces could weigh enough to make much difference, but Ellis was home, and that was what was really important. ''What good is gold anyway?'' thought Ida. ''You can't take it with you.''

The next spring, Ellis stopped and picked up the money. ''Money isn't that important,'' he said. ''You wouldn't believe how many men have died of exhaustion because they wouldn't give up their gold. As I've said many times before, money is only useful to protect oneself from the elements, to provide for one's old age, and to use in helping your fellowmen.''

Summers and winters came and went. Dr. Kackley kept busy treating the sick; Ida became more involved in the progress of the town. At three, young Alvin was a bright eyed, intelligent child. Ellis was teaching him the names of the skull bones. He named them off happily, glorying in the praise received for the accomplishment. Ida worried about the cold winds which blew through the house. Ellis was always cold, with hands and feet like ice, and she fretted over both Ellis and Alvin. "We should just board up this God forsaken icy place and live in the barn," she said for probably the hundredth time.

When Alvin came down with a cold, his hoarse cough struck terror in her heart. Ellis used mustard plasters and sat over his bed night and day to no avail. His condition continued to worsen, as his temperature climbed and his breathing became more and more labored. Pneumonia had set in.

Chapter 8

Ida and Ellis took turns holding their young son in their arms in an upright position so he could get his breath more easily, and sharing their body warmth with the child. Ida warmed his clothes and warmed the catalogue in the oven and put it in the bed to make it warm. In spite of everything they tried to do, the child's condition did not improve. His lungs filled with pus and his breathing became more and more difficult. They felt panic like they had never experienced before, as they worked with their little son, and prayed for his recovery. It seemed like months, but had only been eight days when in the early hours of the morning, little Alvin's body shuddered with convulsions before he gave up the struggle and passed on.

"No, no," screamed Ida, and shook the tiny body, trying to bring life back into the child. Ellis placed his fingers against the boy's neck and felt no pulse.

"It's no use, Idie, he's gone," he said hoarsely.

"I hate this town, I hate this house," sobbed Ida. "You've saved so many people here. Why couldn't you save our son? It isn't fair. Why should our baby have to die?"

Ellis put his arms around her, and she fell into them, sobbing. She felt like something inside of her died with her son, and she would never be quite the same again. She found herself unwilling to believe the inevitable. Friends brought food and condolences, or said nothing because they knew nothing to say to comfort the grief stricken couple. They were inconsolable. For months Ida would find her mind wandering back to that grief-filled night and refusing to believe it had really happened. She found herself listening for little Alvin's voice and the patter of his small feet, and the days dragged miserably on.

Ellis felt responsible for the death of his son. He

shouldn't have bought the house. He should have realized it would be impossible to heat. He had been so intrigued by the wonderful barn, he had put his animals' comfort above the comfort of his family, he thought to himself. He should have known how to save the boy. He was a doctor, and that was his duty. Ellis read over and over the books of the great poets, left in the house by Captain Codman, and tried to reconcile himself with death, which had always been the fundamental concern of the great philosophers. Time pressed heavily on them both as they lay awake night after night, clinging to each other for comfort. Both were tortured by their own thoughts, which came with the shadows of night and haunted their dreams. There was a huge void in their lives—a broken promise of shattered hopes and plans. Life would never be quite as happy as it had been those few short years when Alvin's presence had brightened their world.

Alvin's death drove Ellis to work with even more purpose. He kept busy to drown his sorrow, and dedicated himself to helping others. He worried about Ida, who would sit in the house for hours never speaking unless spoken to. He was greatly relieved when after a few months, she began to resume some outside activities, though not as enthusiastically as before. The spring sunshine helped rejuvenate the spirits of the unhappy couple.

A typhoid epidemic was in full bloom in Gem Valley, south of Soda Springs on the Bear River. Whenever Ellis was called out that way, he could almost be sure it was another case of typhoid. After the settlers there had fought so hard to get water, and get it onto the land, now they were in the midst of a typhoid epidemic. He had one-hundred-twelve cases in the area that spring. If he could just get people to realize they could not throw all of their waste products into the river, and then drink the water, maybe they could curtail the problem, he thought, but as soon as he got people educated about the disease and hauling their water from the springs, someone new moved in, and the problem started all over again.

When he answered a call, the most distressing thing he could see was the sight of bedclothes hanging on the line, which he always hoped meant the patient was being kept in a clean bed, but usually meant death had struck. Typhoid was a dread disease in those days. He wondered how he could impress on the settlers the importance of using only clean water for culinary purposes.

Ellis knew he had a public health problem on his hands—the first he had been faced with during his career. Many people did not yet accept the reality of bacteria, and though people ran their sewage into the Bear River, they still expected it to be clean enough to drink. He had to educate these people to the cause of the disease before he could get rid of the problem. Since the canal ran right by many of their places, they could see no reason not to use it for drinking water as well as irrigation.

Typhoid had a terrible odor associated with it. He could smell the disease the minute the door opened. There were a few cases of what they called "walking typhoid," but most of his patients were incapacitated. They suffered from diarrhea, vomiting, a temperature sometimes as high as a hundred and five or a hundred and six degrees, and tremendous, rapid weight loss.

Ellis had made many, many trips up and down that valley, and was getting to know the settlers in those parts well. Most of the people were of extremely limited circumstances; so limited that to many, hunger was a well known companion, and suffering from the cold was the normal situation. He had helped the midwives deliver many a baby for these hardy settlers, and had become close friends with several, like the Mickelsons out in Lago. Sadie was a hard working woman, but always willing to help her neighbors or nurse the sick.

Ellis was having a good deal of success in treating the typhoid, and loss of patients was limited, due to his effective care. He was becoming highly loved and respected by the settlers, especially the women, who were in the homes and had to deal with the disease, pick the doctor, and follow his recommendations. He had to teach the womenfolk how to care for the ill, giving them soft foods and frequent feedings, keeping those who had contracted the disease clean and bathed, boiling linens, sheets, and bedclothes to kill the bacteria, and keeping dishes separate and sterilized to keep the disease from spreading to other members of the family.

Ellis had learned very early in his practice the importance of keeping a patient's hopes up. "When a patient loses hope, you may as well get your pen and start filling out the death records," he told Ida.

His genuine concern for his patients, unconcern about ability to pay for his services, upbeat attitude about the practice of medicine, and willingness to teach others endeared him in the hearts of the people. He became their friend.

Ellis marveled at the irrigation system the men there had built to bring water onto their land. Many of these settlers had homesteaded bench land which was hard to grub out. They had built cabins and cleared the land, but the only land worth anything without irrigation was the lower land near the river or the rare piece with springs on it.

Their first attempts to divert water from the Bear River had been costly in human resources, and complete failures, but the settlers didn't give up. They had put forth one more giant effort, and named it "The Last Chance Canal Company." They had built a complicated system with a dam across the river, canals, and flumes. Ellis admired the tenacity of these men, who wouldn't give up their efforts to cultivate the dry land, and had gone to almost impossible lengths to get the precious water onto their farms and make them productive. They had started the project a year before Ellis came to Idaho, and had persevered in spite of the many difficulties they encountered, until irrigation was in progress and there was water available to farm the land, though many of them practically starved to death meanwhile.

With water, the land was growing good crops. Gem Valley was different than the area around Soda Springs, and dry farming was not successful in these parts or the area south of Five Mile Meadows. You could tell at a glance where irrigation was being used, as the fields became productive.

While they had started with sixty-four original stockholders in the Last Chance Canal Company, money was so scarce most of the initial stock issues were paid for with labor at a dollar-and-a-half a day. Using locally available timber and rocks, the men had built log "cribs" which they positioned across the river on the ice during the winter to form the foundation of the dam. They hauled huge timbers, up to sixty feet in length. Some they cut in the mountains along the river earlier in the year and floated to the dam site, others were hauled from the nearby canyons on wagons or sleds.

To hold the timbers down, boulders were loosened and rolled down the hills. Some Ellis had heard were "as large as a load of hay." When the ice melted, this construction sunk into the river, and they had the foundation of their dam.

It was a major engineering challenge, and required rough, dangerous work, which was done mainly with crowbars, shovels, picks, and hand saws. The project was hampered by extremes of weather and climate. Men worked without having adequate clothing, sometimes using sacks to make overalls and burlap to wrap their feet to protect them from the frost. Food was often limited to bread and gravy.

When they went to install the headgates, they ran into so many problems, they ended up contracting to have another dam put in about 40 feet below the first, and borrowing money to get it done, but whatever it took, they were willing to somehow do, and with their own limited resources. A few years later, the United States Bureau of Reclamation would be involved in many such projects, and financiers on Wall Street would make gigantic profits by building great irrigation and power projects, and accompanying towns, hotels, and transportation systems, but these men had none of that kind of help.

It was an ambitious project for these early settlers in Idaho. Plans were for one hundred miles of canals to irrigate almost all of Gem valley, from Bancroft and Chesterfield at the north to Grace and Lago to the south. Now over 29,000 acres were being irrigated. The canals and flumes were already giving the system trouble, but Ellis was sure problems would be worked out as time progressed. Water rights were guarded jealously, and he had a feeling that sometime in the future he would see some real fighting over water, which was a scarce commodity in dry years. In normal and wet years, the Bear River could be a powerful force, as the men had found out when it's raging waters washed out the first canal they built to divert the water onto the land.

The Mormon settlements followed the rivers from the Salt Lake area, both north and south. They had come up the Bear River and started Franklin, the first settlement in Idaho, then on into Gem Valley and to Alexander, just west of Soda Springs, and into Soda Springs. Meanwhile, they settled the Bear Lake area—Paris, Montpelier, and Georgetown. They had turned the Soda Creek meadows into a fertile farming area, and opened the whole vast lands to the north, which had become prime sheep and cattle raising area.

Rustling of cattle had become quite a business for some of the less than honest, and more than one herd had been started with a running iron, made to alter brands. Running irons came in all shapes. He had heard Susie Small tell of the murder of Dutch John, who was appropriating part of the herd of the Hacke Cattle Company. His body was found on Carriboo Mountain, and after a long trial, people were astounded at the confession of a seemingly innocent man. Several years later, when the confessed murderer was out of jail, he promptly got drunk and told how he had been paid a sizable sum to take the rap for the murder.

Susie was a first-rate midwife. She aptly applied her trade, and called for the doctor when there was a problem. She also raised five children, taught for years in the children's department of the Presbyterian Church, and acted as a judge at elections. Ellis had heard that during the diphtheria epidemic in Soda Springs the winter of 1889-1890, when everyone else was afraid to go near the sick and dying, Susie had nursed the ill and cared for the children, with no thought for herself.

The disease had been devastating as multiple deaths reduced families to being childless or deprived of their father or mother. Children were extremely susceptible. Fear was in the hearts of the townspeople, and they took the dead out through the windows and buried them in the dark and cool of the night. That was when Gortons had lost their four little girls, all the Beus family had been stricken and three of their children were buried in the old cemetery in the cedars, Chesters who had homesteaded on Chester Hill north of Soda Springs and the surrounding land lost their mother and two children.

It was a miracle Susie had not contracted the disease which came on very suddenly and in about a twenty-four-hour period, left its victims unable to get their breath, intoxicated, and unable to swallow. It was toxic, and many died a terrible, but swift death.

Besides Susie and some of the other non-Mormon women, quite a few of the Mormon women were also excellent midwives. The Mormon church had taken some of the women from the outlying areas to Salt Lake and given them a short training course with a doctor, where they were taught to care for their sisters in the church when they were in the family way and through the birth and recuperation period. The Mormon women felt they should be cared for by another woman, and hesitated to call the doctor unless absolutely necessary. Ellis' life had become so fast paced, he found it extremely difficult to sit through a long labor, though he always went when called.

Ellis encouraged doctors and nurses to come into the area. He set up additional training for ladies who were willing to work as midwives, but many learned from experience as the necessity arose.

He taught Dr. Anderson to give chloroform for him when he did operations in his office. He liked Dr. Anderson with his great long whiskers, a high forehead, receding hairline, and sideburns. "He's a good assistant, and a fine old fellow," Ellis told Ida, "though I don't know how anyone can keep whiskers like that clean, especially a doctor."

Ellis was always clean shaven. He attended medical school after germs had been discovered and surgeons had come to the conclusion that whiskers could not be kept clean, and could be a source of infection. Ellis didn't realize he was a member of a new breed of doctors, which came between the poorly trained early frontier doctor and the specialists who would soon appear on the scene, dissecting medicine into multiple fields.

The hotels were keeping quite full with Ellis' patients. People were coming from all over Idaho, as well as Utah and Wyoming, to see the young doctor as his fame spread beyond the confines of the frontier town. "You bring in more people than the springs and natural attractions," Charlie told him one day. "Your office is small, and you need hospital facilities. I think we should build you a hospital. Think the idea over."

Ida was pregnant again and was approaching full term in her confinement. Her sister, Minnie Sarver, decided to come out and teach school at Eight Mile. Ida enjoyed the company, and having someone to help with things during her pregnancy. Minnie rode a bicycle to work during good weather, and a horse when the bike became impractical. Ellis felt good about having someone who was family there with Ida when he was gone so much.

Ida gave birth to another baby boy. Ellis delivered the child, and noted with satisfaction he was healthy and strong. They named him Evan Morgan, after their friend, J.O. Morgan, and Ellis once again had dreams of having an eventual partner in the medical field, but he was a little cautious about giving his dreams full reign after losing little Alvin. Ellis and Ida had never recuperated fully from the loss, and whenever a child Ellis was treating died, it seemed he felt the full impact of the pain all over again. Ida did too, whenever she heard about a child dying, especially from pneumonia.

Ellis was in even more of a hurry now to get back to the office when he went out into the country, and he ran his horses hard, but changed teams often if he had to go very far, so top speed could be maintained. There was always someone willing to meet him with a fresh team when an emergency arose. He and Ida cared for his horses carefully, and made sure they were well fed, grained twice a day, and kept in top shape.

It was again a period of prosperity for the village of Soda Springs. August Largilliere started a bank. It was the first incorporated bank in Idaho. He was also in the brewery business, and had purchased the Peck and Enright Store which carried a full line of hardware, clothing, and food. Their stock included corsets and high button shoes which were fashionable for the women of the time, and button hooks for doing up their buttons. They would eventually add farm machinery. He also owned land and had several hundred head of sheep. Ellis and Ida were one of the first couples to open an account at the bank. "I thought you didn't trust banks, or want anything to do with them," Ida told Ellis when he suggested opening an account.

"This is a different situation," said Ellis. "I know and trust August Largilliere, and I feel sure my account is safe with him. I don't trust big banking systems, and would never put money into an account with someone I didn't know. Mr. Largilliere was driven from France by persecution, with other Huguenots and served in the Franco-Prussian War. The French Army was humiliatingly defeated, and soldiers wore paper soles in their shoes and their guns were equally bad. I've heard him tell a little about it, but he doesn't say much. I think his bank will be a safe place for people to put their money. Though his fortunes are good at the moment, he has been through enough times of boom and bust to be concerned about the common man rather than feel superior to people who are less fortunate.

"It's strange that he and Henry Schmidt should meet up together and become friends," Ellis said thoughtfully. Henry fled Germany before the Franco-Prussian War to avoid being a part of Germany when it was becoming amalgamated into a militant state. It's a peculiar set of circumstances which allied this Frenchman and German in friendship."

Largillieres were a progressive couple, and well liked by the Kackleys. Catherine Largilliere taught piano lessons to many of the young people in town. Their son, Edgar, was a partner with his dad. Ellis almost envied the relationship, but now he had high hopes of having his son as a partner in a few years.

Smalls sold their place on Mineral Heights to Denver Smith, who had big plans for commercializing the area, and building a bath house which would attract more than the villagers, though those plans, like earlier plans of George and Susie's would never be carried out. When a group of men drilled for what a government geologist said would be a hot water source, they hit a rampaging geyser which lowered the water table on Smith's property. The geyser was capped and became an important attraction of the city. It was later listed in Ripley's "Believe It or Not."

The town was trying to pass a bond issue for five-thousand dollars to buy Jim's electric plant for the Village of Soda Springs. Earlier T. S. Williams had been given a franchise to build a power plant, and in the spring of 1904, the village had agreed to take four arc lights and contracted to light up the town. To appease those who thought electricity would never become popular, they cautiously agreed for the contract to go thirty days at a time. Williams never got the plant built, but after some time, and one or two others considering it in between, Jim had come up with an operational plant.

Now the city was considering buying the power plant. Only taxpayers could vote on the issue. Ellis fully supported the idea. When the votes were counted, only one was against purchase of the plant, so the city went into the power business. The original cost had been estimated at five thousand dollars, but before all was done, the plant cost seven-thousand-five-hundred dollars.

It was a great day when the lights were turned on in Soda Springs. It was only a few years after Broadway, New York, was entitled "The Great White Way" by the founder of Telluride Power Company, which would later become Utah Power and Light Company.

Electricity changed the way of life of the women in Soda Springs. Soon they were freed from much of the drudgery of housework, as vacuum cleaners, washing machines, and other appliances made their work easier.

Jim told Kackleys electricity could be used to heat things, as well as provide lighting. Ellis and Ida decided to have the place wired for electricity and put in electric lamps. The system only carried eighty watts. Very few people under-stood electricity and its great power. When the sockets were all in, Ida, Ellis, and their friends all took turns sticking their finger into one and feeling the shock it caused. Ellis even held Evan up so he could feel the tingle of electricity. Then they screwed the bulbs into the sockets. "Look how bright the lights are," exclaimed Ida. "Now I can see twice as well to read in the evening."

"When the good Lord said, 'Let there be light,' he created a dynamic force," said Ellis. "What a difference it would make if everyone had electricity to light their homes and businesses. Can you imagine no more delivering babies by kerosene lamps, no more trimming the wicks and cleaning the chimneys, no more hunting for a match to light a candle in the middle of the night, no more fires caused by kerosene lamps. At the flip of a switch, the whole world could be lit up!"

That was his vision, but he didn't foresee great combines of light denying electricity to farming areas and taking a line past a home, but refusing to give them service. Because of this, he would still be delivering babies by kerosene lights until Franklin Roosevelt, during his administration, would break up the great electrical monopolies with government financing of rural electric powerplants as cooperative businesses.

Jim brought down an old wringer washing machine. "The women won't know what to do with their spare time with all these modern conveniences." said Ellis.

Ida purchased an electric iron. It was almost as heavy as a sad iron, but didn't require heating on the cook stove before using and periodically throughout the ironing process. Jim started selling vacuums, and called to show one to the Kackley family. Ida and Annie cleaned the big green rug in the front room. Jim took them into the kitchen and dumped a whole bag of dirt the machine had sucked up. They were astounded.

"It sounds like a threshing machine, but boy does it pick up the dirt," Ida told Ellis. "I thought that room was clean, but I was embarrassed when I saw the dirt that came out of there."

It was the beginning of a whole new era of improved living, especially for those of the female gender, but the Kackley house was still impossible to heat adequately and electricity was never utilized for heating. Their three stoves, the big round-bellied one, the slightly fancier sheet metal stove, and the cook stove all consumed numerous cords of wood and coal from George Small and Jim Horsley, but the family found it impossible to keep comfortably warm.

Soda Springs now had five hotels, eight general stores, three restaurants, four saloons, three drug stores, two blacksmith shops, three livery stables, a newspaper, a saw mill, the soda water bottling plant, two meat markets, a photo studio, a new creamery, two opera houses, two churches and a grade school with four teachers.

While the town was still a hot-bed of iniquity, according to the standards of many of the citizens, with gambling, cheating, two whorehouses, and two dances every Friday night, there was a cultural side for the honest settlers, which people like Idie had worked hard to develop.

Soda Springs was a prosperous town. Its population had grown to about five-hundred, with many more summer residents. There was a great demand for houses to rent, but few were available. A number of Mormon couples from Salt Lake City came to Soda Springs for the summer. Many of them stayed at the Wetzel Hotel. A Doctor Clawson accompanied the group, and often talked with Ellis, who enjoyed an opportunity to discuss what was going on in the medical profession.

The mining activity at Carriboo Mountain had continued to decrease, but a few people were still bringing out gold. W. H. Stocks was down from the placer mines in June, 1905 with a good sized gold brick, estimated to be worth at least a hundred and fifty dollars, and predicting big doings at the mine that summer. The Monte Cristo Mine owners, who were mining for copper, levied a one-cent share on all stock. They were also predicting big things to happen at the mines.

Mining was opening up in the Enoch Valley where copper ore had been discovered. A six hundred foot tunnel was completed there that summer, though little came of mining in that location until years later when Soda Springs was discovered to be the center of the largest phosphate beds in the United States.

There was an excellent hay crop in the areas to the north.

Farming was a rather dangerous business and Ellis usually was called to treat several accidents each summer. This year, the only injury Ellis treated was a lady from Wayan who was kicked by a horse while driving a hay rake. The injury healed without any serious consequences.

The town had become a valuable shipping point for sheep and cattle, the most important west of Omaha. Sheep were selling for three dollars and thirty-five cents per head, and cattle for thirty-five dollars. Wool was becoming an extremely valuable commodity with over two million pounds having been shipped out after shearing that spring. It sold from sixteen to twenty-two cents per pound. Grays Lake clip was the most sought after wool of any because it was always clean and never weighted with rocks.

Ellis was still getting a considerable business in treating the dust caused eye problems of the sheep men. John Petersen, a sheep herder for Grass Sheep Company dropped a gun which went off and shot him. He was not found until the wounds were fly blown and when carried to Herman, he was beyond medical help. He had no known relatives, and was buried where he died.

The Idan-ha' Bottling plant was doing extremely well, and enjoying ample demand for their mineral water throughout the country. It continued to be shipped out on the railroad by the car load. Idan-ha' Bottling Works took first place on their water at the world's fair in Paris, France that year. The city water system was run down Dillon Street two-thousand feet from the Idanha Hotel, giving running water to all of the town. The City Water System had been constructed for the villagers not served by the Mormon System, under the able supervision of the village dads. A reservoir was built just below the dip on the Hooper Springs road.

Later, as new village dads came along, they extended power production along Soda Creek. They refused to sell out to big private power companies which gobbled up many an adjacent municipal system, realizing they could not finance proper growth of the town with tax monies only. Some, like Charlie Fryar, felt electricity should be made available to everyone at a nominal rate, not used as a money maker.

Having a baby in their home was bringing joy once again to the Kackley family. Ida fussed over the child, and worried every time he let out a cry, which he did more often than Alvin had because Evan was prone to an occasional bout of colic.

The game of baseball was becoming extremely popular with the townspeople, and in the outlying areas. Nearly every Mormon ward or congregation in Gem Valley, Soda Springs, and the settlements to the north had a team. Mr. Eastman carried quite a line of high-grade merchandise as well as baseball equipment at the drug store. He told Ellis there was a ball game on the Fourth of July at Eagle Creek between Gray and Freedom, Wyoming, and there was a considerable amount bet on the game. Betting on the games became quite common among the non-Mormons. A game between Herman and Soda Springs on the 24th of July had a two hundred and fifty dollar purse.

Ida was a top rate manager. Ellis only had time to practice medicine, and was too busy to care about management. His practice had grown to the point where he had to shrug his shoulders and say "to hell with everything else."

Ellis thought he and Idie made a good team, with his medical skill and her management skills applied to help keep order in their lives, Ida had a lot of self-discipline, and she saw that things were done right. She hated lies, theft, and destruction, and worked hard to keep their home in order and to help make Soda Springs a better place for honest people to live. It bothered Ida to see anyone mistreated, and she fretted about Ashler and his friends and the way they were taking advantage of people. She would never feel completely at ease as long as she knew they considered her husband their enemy.

One day when Ellis returned to town after a call, the whole place was in an uproar. A Mormon bishop's son had gotten himself killed at Jenny's place. The fellow was not a local man, but the townspeople were in an uproar. "What on earth he was doing down at Jenny's, I don't know," Ida told Ellis. "You'd think a bishop's son would know better.''

''Now, Idie,'' Ellis chided, ''it must be hell to be a preacher's or bishop's son. If they do anything out of the ordinary, the public is very critical of them. It isn't any worse for a bishop's son to be down there than for anyone else to be there.''

''Well, I guess that's true,'' agreed Ida reluctantly, ''but you just expect better of someone like that. I hear he was down to Jenny's, carousing around and raising hell when bullets started flying and he was killed.''

''Most people like to gossip. It's a common bad habit. You know how it is in this town. By the time it goes through the pool hall bunch and the women folk, I imagine it will be one helluva scandal. Some people are awfully good at minding everyone's business but their own, but things like that happen everywhere. We don't like it, but it's true, and the Mormons or any other religious group aren't exempt from such problems. Remember what Christ said, ''He who is without sin, let him cast the first stone,'' he added.

Many of the women, the Mormons, and other church groups were determined to run the prostitutes out of town. The honest citizens of Soda Springs were totally fed up with the outrageous things which were happening in their town and were determined to clean up the place. ''This was the last straw,'' said Ida. ''I think there'll be some changes around here this time.''

Ellis had to agree there were plenty of things happening which needed to be changed. Ida was right, the citizens of Soda Springs were fed up with the lawlessness. There was a lot of talk about getting a Grand Jury investigation of the crimes going on in Soda Springs. Maybe the time had come when something would be done. Ellis and Ida certainly hoped so.

The town had improved some since they had arrived. The honest citizens had a lot of civic pride, and tried hard to improve the town's image, but the lawlessness continued.

Chapter 9

One January afternoon in 1907 Ida picked up the local newspaper, *The Idaho Chieftain,* "Listen to this, Ellis," she said, reading from its pages, "Sunday's snowstorm caused many problems. People walking home over well-known routes were obliged to follow fences, etc. in order to keep their course and at times it was impossible to see at all. . ."

"That's for sure," agreed Ellis. "It was the worst storm I've ever seen."

"'Dr. Kackley was out in most of the storm and had a rather hard time of it. . .'"

"That's putting it mildly," Ellis said, walking behind her chair and looking over her shoulder.

"'While trying to get home from the valley, he was blown out of his rig twice, at one time landing against a fence with such force that his big fur coat was all that prevented a broken arm. He was over an hour finding the bridge across Bear River at Grace and about the same time finding a crossing at Soda Creek. His team was blown down once and was so exhausted that they lay still for sometime before attempting to get on their feet. The Doctor finally made his way home, exhausted in both mind and body.'"

"The second time I was blown out of the sled, I almost didn't make it," noted Ellis. "I was lucky I was near that huge culvert under the railroad by Davisville and could crawl into it until I recovered enough from the chill of the wind to find the horses and get them back on the road and to crawl back into the sled. I've had some mighty close calls, but that's the closest I ever came to freezing to death, except maybe that time I got lost out by Henry." He paused a moment lost in his own reflections, then continued, "Ashler and his cronies won't have to worry about me if I get into many storms like that."

The sled was a double bob, open sled, and offered no protection from the terrible blizzard. When Ida, who was waiting up for him, had heard the sleigh bells, she had run out to the barn to help him unhitch the horses.

"When that team came home, I thought they had come without you," she said. "Then I found you lying there in the sled bottom, the lines clasped in stiff hands, and you were barely conscious. She paused, then continued earnestly, "Oh, Ellis, I worry so much about you when you're out on a call and a bad storm comes up. It seems to me like every time the weather gets bad, that's when people get sick or hurt."

"Don't worry, Idie, the Good Lord always guides me home, one way or another."

"Well let's not press our luck," said Ida.

Toward spring Ellis came home one night to find Evan was running a slight fever, had a runny nose, and a dry cough. "What do you think it is?" asked Ida anxiously.

"I hope I'm wrong, but I'm afraid it's whooping cough," replied Ellis with a frown. "There's a lot of it around now."

"Whooping cough has a high fatality rate in infants this age," Ellis thought to himself. He examined the baby and found the mucous membranes of his nose and throat were inflamed. He put his arm around Ida and said, "Idie, I'm afraid that's what it is. It's a dangerous disease, but we'll just have to watch him very closely and nurse him carefully for the next few weeks.

Ida's eyes filled with tears, terror written all over her face. "We've lost one child. It just isn't fair. It's this damn cold house. We should never have bought it."

They both rushed for Evan as he went into a severe coughing spasm. His tiny body fought to get air in the lungs, then because of the heavy mucus, didn't have the strength to force it out. In a day or two, the spasms were ending with Evan throwing up or his face turning blue.

Ida, an excellent nurse, hardly left his side, even to eat or sleep. She kept the temperature in the kitchen, where they kept the sick child, as even as possible.

In spite of the attention Evan received, he was losing

weight. She worked by the hour to get a few ounces of water down the child to keep him from becoming dehydrated. Ellis was getting almost as worried about Ida as about Evan. He hired a girl to help with the housework, and tried to spell her off as much as possible.

In the fifth week of the illness, the coughing spells began to be less frequent, and Ellis knew they were past the most dangerous stage. Evan was pale and thin, but gradually he began to pick up a few ounces of weight and have more spark. The weather was warming up and the spring sunshine made some days warm enough so Ida could take the baby out for a few minutes.

"Thank God, Idie, he's going to make it," Ellis told his wife one night. "Now you've got to get some rest."

As the family gradually regained their strength, Ida got back into her usual activities. She never took Evan out if it was cold or stormy, and they watched closely for additional problems, but none developed. Evan was soon crawling all over the place. He found the pots and pans in the kitchen cupboards, and they could hardly keep him out of them.

That summer Ida learned to smoke hams and bacon, and set up a work place on the third floor of the house. It was hard labor, but Ida was a hard worker. She raised chickens and put-up vegetables which she raised in the garden during the summer.

The next summer one of her friends suggested she use salt instead of smoke to cure the meat, and showed her how to cut it into pieces six inches square, then rub each piece with salt. They were packed closely in a barrel, then brine made of salt and saltpeter was poured over the meat. It was weighted down and kept in the brine until used, or after several weeks taken out and placed into sacks to keep out larva. After two or three summers, Ida was almost an expert on the womanly arts of gardening, cutting up meat, salting it, and bottling the things raised in the garden. She always shared her knowledge with the young girls of the community.

Often when Ellis treated someone who had no money to pay, to show their appreciation, they would bring him some beef or vegetables or whatever they had to trade for his services. He accepted such things graciously, whether he needed the item or not. If he couldn't use it, there was always someone he knew who could. Several sheep were given to him to butcher, but instead, he kept them around the place and they became pets.

Evan, in spite of a difficult start, at two and a half was a robust toddler, and seemed none the worse for his bout with whooping cough, except possibly a little spoiled. Ida was pregnant again, and it hadn't been easy for her, sweltering over a hot stove on steamy hot summer days of harvest time, but the putting-up of endless jars of vegetables and produce and curing of meat, paid off during the chill days of winter.

When Ellis walked up the street from his office to his home, or wherever he happened to go, he was constantly stopped and asked for medical advice. "You do more practicing of medicine between the barber shop and the office than most doctors do in a week," Charlie Fryar told him.

One autumn day Ellis got a call saying he was needed by the Michael Mickelson family in Gem Valley. From the garbled message, it sounded like Michael was badly injured. He galloped to their home, and found Michael lying on the floor where he had fallen when he stumbled into the house. His wife Sadie had covered him with blankets, but hadn't dared move him.

When she carefully uncovered her husband, there was a huge gash from his chest upward along the neck, and Ellis could see the carotid artery pulsating deep in the wound. He was barely conscious. "What happened?" Ellis asked Sadie.

"He was up in the timber, and a horse fell on him, and drove the big ax—it weighs about five pounds—into his chest. He managed to drive the wagon two and a half miles, and walked two more miles to get home. When I untied the coat he had tied around his neck and ripped his shirt open, I couldn't believe the wound. I threw a pan of flour into it to coagulate the blood and stop the bleeding. His pockets are chuck full of clotted blood."

"Good Lord, Man," Ellis told Michael. "Any other sonofabitch would be dead, but it looks like you're too damned ornery to die. That ax grazed your jugular vein; an eighth of an inch more, and you'd be dead, but thanks to luck, your iron constitution, and your wife's good care, you're going to make it fine."

Ellis cleaned and sutured the wound. Michael, a native of Denmark, had come west with the Mormons. They had come for freedom from religious persecution and to get a hundred and sixty acres of land, which they had to clear, cultivate, and build on, in order to prove-up their homestead. It was a rough life, and they had to be strong to endure, but how Michael had ever made it home with such a wound was almost a miracle. One of the things that saved him was he had foresight enough to take off his undercoat and wrap the sleeves tightly around his neck, almost like a tourniquet. It had slowed the flow of blood to where it was only oozing instead of flowing freely, but he had lost a lot, and was weak.

Ellis was amazed that Sadie would have the presence of mind to throw flour into the wound, and wondered where she had learned of its coagulating properties. The gluten it contained had caused agglutination or what might be simply stated as flour pasting together of the wound. That knowledge must have been handed down from the old country. Few women would be able to deal with a wound of that magnitude, he thought.

What was commonly known as old wives tales often became extremely useful in an emergency, and while some cures, such as "cow pie poultices" were dangerous to a person's health and welfare, many others were based on good common sense, Ellis mused as he cleaned and sutured the wound.

As he rode home he thought about the settlers in this area, and marveled at their hardiness. He would check on Michael whenever he got out that way, which these days was quite often.

It grew late as he passed miles and miles of farms. The wind whistled around Soda Point. It was cold and as dark as midnight by the time he got back to the sleeping little town of Soda Springs, but Ellis felt his happiness was complete as his eyes traced the shadows of his home place.

Ida was waiting up, keeping his dinner warm in the oven.

It took Michael about six weeks to regain his strength, but soon he was back at work. He and Sadie had a good sized family of six small children. Ellis was getting to know them well, and was thankful he had been able to help save Michael's life. His young family needed their father.

In 1908 Ida gave birth to a beautiful baby girl. Ellis was delighted to have a baby daughter, and she captured her parents' hearts with their first glimpse of her. Now the Kackley family was complete—a son to learn medicine and share his practice, and a beautiful little girl to help Ida.

The little lady fascinated her parents, and they excitedly followed each stage of her development. It wasn't long before Ida noticed her little girl, christened Ida Margaret, had a temperament much like her father; lovable, but impatient.

The Kackleys also had a house dog named Crab, and a flock of tame ducks, geese and guinea hens which strutted around the yard as though they owned the place. The family who managed the Idanha Hotel had a large flock of peacocks. They liked to light on the freight trains when they were parked, and hitch a ride until the trains started going fast, then fly off. They would often fly into Kackley's trees on their way back to home base. Their cries at night were a strange mournful sound. Ellis and Ida both enjoyed their animals. Evan and little Margaret, as soon as she was big enough, spent many hours playing with them.

Henry's Schmidt's wife, Annie, was not well. A daughter of Mr. and Mrs. Eric Eliason, born in 1863, she was known as the first white child born in Soda Springs. Her parents were Morrisite settlers, some of the first who came to the area, and started a settlement on the west side of what was now the town of Soda Springs. Most of the Morrisites had given up and left after a few years of poor crops and severe weather.

Henry had sold his interest in the trading post he established at Henry for white trappers and Indians to William Chester and his partner, Frank Merrill, and moved into town. Later Chester would buy out Merrill, and the Chester family would run the store for many generations.

Henry went into the brewery business with August Largilliere. Ellis examined Annie Schmidt and found she had heart trouble, probably as a result of rheumatic fever as a child. Damaged heart valves didn't always give problems immediately, but often worsened as they wore out quicker than the rest of the body.

They were an interesting pair, and Kackleys found Henry and Annie's stories of the early days entertaining. They had taken a great liking to the Kackley kids, especially Margaret, and were frequent guests in the Kackley home.

Since Ellis had no trained assistants, he took local women with an inclination toward nursing and trained them to help him. Things were set up a little better now in the office at Fryars. He had a glass topped table on which to set his instruments. He had been lucky, shortly after he opened his home office to find a used operating table for twenty-five dollars. "It's heavier than hell, but one great advantage is it won't tip over," he told Ida.

He used it as an examining table, an operating table, and a gurney. After operating on a patient, he would wheel them, still on the table, through the double doors into one of the few upstairs hotel rooms, and put them into a bed. The beds were two person iron beds, which were low in height and close to the floor. It wasn't unusual for two or sometimes even three people to have to share a bed. They brought meals for the patients up from the cafe below. A spring house out back was utilized for washing, but sheets were extremely hard to dry in winter.

Ellis had always preferred chloroform to ether, which was highly explosive around open flames such as cook stoves and kerosene lights. Patients having ether were susceptible to fatal ether pneumonia, a dreaded complication in surgical cases. Ellis felt ether was much more difficult to give under frontier conditions, and by untrained assistants.

A big drawback of chloroform was the person administering it sometimes got a whiff of the fumes. Ellis had a problem with his assistants getting sleepy. He kept one eye on Dr. Anderson, and whenever he started nodding, Ellis knew it was time to give him a gentle nudge. Ellis sometimes inhaled a sufficient amount of the fumes himself to become drowsy. When a person was operated on in those days, other members of the family usually came in to watch, so the operating room often had a number of spectators.

Ellis still felt there was no reason why he couldn't do anything being done by anyone else at that time if he studied and practiced and made use of the facilities and people available.

He was taking out appendix not long after the first appendix operation at Harvard. He did his first stomach-resection there in the office, and soon was doing many stomach operations. Where he needed the stomach to be stretched so he could sew cut edges together, he put long sutures through the tissues and midwives and other assistants held the stomach tissue taut by pulling on the sutures they held. He soon became adept at working on the stomach. The skill it required was something like that of being a seamstress. If one side was getting a little short, he took a longer stitch on the other side to bring the sides together and make it come out even. Before long Ellis was spending a good share of his time doing major operations.

Before operating he scrubbed with boiled water containing creosote or alcohol, doused his arms with alcohol, and had someone undo a sterile gown and tie around in back over his business clothes. He put soap drops in his rubber gloves so they were easy to pull on. With a mask and cap, he was ready. He had no operating nurse to anticipate and put the instrument he needed next into his hand, which makes operating so much easier.

He purchased a shelved office case, about four feet wide and seven feet tall. He added instruments regularly, until he had a very complete set of surgical tools. Drapes for the table, and for operating were made by Ida on her "White" sewing machine which came with the house. She also made towels and small ones for sponges. She spent many hours cutting and folding fine cotton-like material, closely woven mosquito netting which came in rolls three feet wide, to make gauze pads which she sterilized for Ellis to use as sponges. She would package everything in cloth and put it in the sterilizer on the stove to heat.

Young Evan was soon helping his mother cut sponges,

and do other tasks. One day he opened the double boiler sterilizer, and was shocked to find it contained a severed leg. When limbs were amputated, they were usually tossed into the fire.

"It's just one of those things that we have no control over," Ellis told his son. "Sometimes a limb has to be cut off in order to save the life of the patient." He looked at Evan thoughtfully as he explained, "I never amputate unless it's absolutely necessary. 'Aunt Leah' Gorton was thrown out of a runaway sled shortly after I came here, and Dr. Green said the leg would have to go or the wound would become infected. She had a helluva bad fracture of her upper leg bone, and that was the common way to treat such injuries."

He shook his head remembering the wound. "Gortons called me in for a second opinion, and I told them I thought I could save the leg, and by hell I did. She's walking pretty well now, and though she has a limp, it doesn't slow her up much. She's just as busy as ever, running the store and everything." He paused again, then added, "Things don't always turn out that well; sometimes you have no choice but to amputate."

Charlie wasn't joking when he suggested to Ellis he needed a new hospital. "I'll build you a building, and all you'll have to do is put your patients in it. You won't have to worry about a thing," he suggested to Ellis.

"That would be a lot of trouble and expense for you," said Ellis. "Why would you want to do that?"

"I'm smart enough to see your practice is growing," said Charlie. "We could put a few hotel rooms and our living quarters on the ground floor, and the hospital on the top. I could build it right here next to the store." he decided, stroking his chin. "A lot of your patients are not sick enough to hospitalize and they would keep the hotel rooms filled." He turned and looked at Ellis, smiling with enthusiasm, "You're the best damn doctor in the West, you know."

By this time, Ellis was finding the office far too small, and needed rooms for convalescing patients. There was seldom ever a vacant room in the hospital, and the hotels in

town were getting a sizable amount of trade from Ellis' patients.

"It would be great to have more space," Ellis agreed. "If you're willing to build a hospital, how can I say no."

Charlie started immediately to plan the building. He made the bricks himself. They were quite soft, and many young people of the town were caught carving their initials in the brick of the hospital walls almost as soon as they were up.

While Charlie was an astute businessman, he was also far sighted. By the summer of 1910, the new private hospital was completed and ready for use. Ellis could walk right up the same stairs to his office, and by turning left, instead of right, he could enter the hospital.

Fryar both built and operated the hospital. He paid the nurses, and his wife did the cooking. Ellis had only to bring in the patients and treat them. The Fryar children played in the hospital when their mother was busy helping there, and Ellis enjoyed their little escapades and their natural curiosity.

While Ellis didn't have to put up a penny for the construction of the hospital, the one thing Charlie seemed easily upset about was the electric bill. He felt it was way too high a price to pay for the privilege of having electric lights.

The old double boiler sterilizer was soon replaced with an alcohol sterilizer that would boil and make steam to sterilize things. Every once in awhile the alcohol flame that heated the sterilizer would come close to setting the place on fire.

Ellis was getting a lot of patients with extremely painful arthritis from untreated gonorrhea. After a short time, if the progress of the disease was uninterrupted, the symptoms would disappear, but the germ would invade the blood stream, irritate the joints, and eventually fuse them together.

One thing Ellis would not tolerate was for his assistants to gossip about what was going on in the hospital. A patient's confidence was considered sacred. As Ellis began to get the help of trained nurses, they were quietly called on the carpet if he learned they were talking about patients, and it was drilled into everyone that they never say anything about a patient outside of the hospital. Ellis was getting a lot of out-of-town patients, attracted by his growing reputation, and the privacy of being unknown in a small Western town. He did not appreciate anything in the newspaper about his patients or any unnecessary talk.

The staff, as well as his family were reminded tactfully that when people came in they were sick, or they wouldn't be there, and no one was better than anyone else. "When people suffer, they have pain just like us," he explained to his son. "Never take on airs and think you are better than someone else."

In the summer time Ellis bought quite a lot of things from the Indians who came through, and always paid the first price they asked for items. He treated them through illnesses and accident, and delivered babies that were turned wrong or had to be taken Caesarean. He had started taking the baby through the abdomen in extremely difficult cases of childbirth with only the midwives to help him, before he had a hospital. He continued to treat the Indian people without charging for his services. "A doctor can't choose his practice; he has to help everyone who needs medical attention," he told Ida and Evan.

Ellis returned to the hospital for rounds at nine o'clock each night, his dog, Pal, at his side. Hospitals always had the smell of infection. Wounds drained, frequently for long periods of time, and there were no antibiotics to facilitate healing.

One day when Ellis opened his office door to frantic pounding, he found an old sheepherder there. The man looked disoriented and extremely ill. He was having convulsions, which came and went with no apparent rhythm, and was foaming at the mouth. His jaws were locked up and Ellis could not understand what he was trying to say. The man stopped suddenly and dropped his britches, and Ellis noted an erection of the penis. The man was trying to tell him it was causing pain. Ellis suddenly put the symptoms together and realized he was dealing with the first case of rabies he had ever seen.

Rabies, with no available treatment, was extremely infectious and Ellis knew the infectious agent which caused it through a bite, was also contained in copious saliva.

Ellis put the old fellow in the hospital and tried to make him as comfortable as possible, but in spite of being heavily sedated with chloral hydrate—commonly known as knock-out drops—when it started to wear off, he chewed the bed post until the corners of his mouth split open. Paralysis and inability to swallow were early symptoms of the disease, and previous choking had made him afraid to try and drink, but he suffered from thirst, and constantly wanted water. Ellis gave the unfortunate fellow small doses of chloroform for twelve hours before he died. In medical school Ellis had seen pictures, under proper staining, of a microscopic, bright body that was always present in brain cells of a rabid victim, and was recognized as specific to rabies infection. Little was known about the disease, and when he had been in medical school at the University of Tennessee, they did not have slides which showed the effect of the rabies infection on the brain.

Ellis knew the germ was lethal and the man's corpse had to be handled with care. A small cut or scratch while he was working with the sheepherder, which came in contact with saliva containing the causing organism, could infect him. In spite of the risk, he sawed off upper part of the skull enclosing the man's brain and took it out. He sent the infected brain to the University, so students there could have slides to study.

Ellis made numerous inquiries, but was unable to find out anything about the man or where he had come from. He figured the poor fellow had probably been bitten by a rabid coyote. The story of the sheepherder with rabies precipitated several cases of pseudo-rabies, and he had to diagnose

Photo of Ellis and Ida Kackley taken in 1895, shortly after their marriage.
(Kackley Collection)

Photo of Idan-ha' Hotel in 1890.
(Kackley Collection)

Kackley home (Old Codman home) in 1908. *(Kackley Collection)*

Old Kackley House about 1978.
(Elaine S. Johnson photo)

Tall building at right housed Kackley's first office in Soda Springs. Lower floor was Fryar's Store. Next building to the left, not quite as tall, was Kackley's first hospital, built by Charlie Fryar. (Kackley collection)

A 1940 view of the Caribou County Hospital, with 36 beds and 4 bassinettes. It was usually full, often operating with beds in the halls.

At Hooper Spring in 1914. The wooden barrels are being filled with soda water to take home. No one on this photo has been identified.
(Kackley Collection)

The light-weight Ellis (at 100 lbs.) and heavy-weight Charlie Bunn (at 350 lbs.) of Soda Springs in front of Stock X Bar, 1904.
(Kackley Collection)

Photo of Ida on horse Dempsey.
(Kackley Collection)

August Largilliere had the first incorporated bank in Idaho in early Soda Springs.

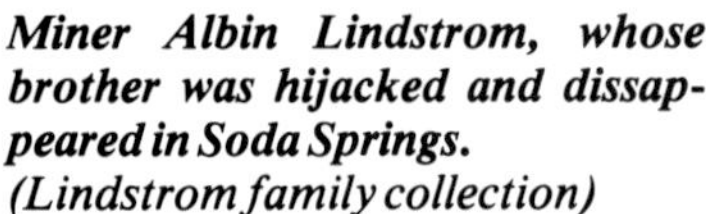

Miner Albin Lindstrom, whose brother was hijacked and dissappeared in Soda Springs. (Lindstrom family collection)

Neighbors, Otto and Nora Petersen.
(Petersen Collection)

Haying time in the country near Soda Springs.

Le Grande Gurre Cemetery, France. One-forth mile to the east was the field hospital where Ellis served during World War I while stationed at Saint Mihiel. (Earl J. Carney collection)

Amercan army trucks in downtown Saint Mihiel during World War I. (Earl J. Carney collection)

French underground fort called "Fort Camp of the Romans" used during World War I. Tunnels went for miles in all different directions, and the fort was several stories deep. Railroad tracks went into barracks, offices, and ammunition storage. *(Earl J. Carney Collection)*

Montsec, Monument of Americans. The U. S. Government had this monument built after World War I in honor of Americans who served in France. It pays for the maintenance of the monument. Around the top are the names of the major battles. A large map inside the center shows the locations of the battles and American divisions that fought there. *(Earl J. Carney collection)*

One of the first Henry Stampede and Stockman's reunions held at the meadows of Henry. *(Forrest Mann Collection)*

Bert Sibbett - World Champion Cowboy who often rode at the Henry Stampede. The fans were duly proud of his skills. Bert was born in Grays Lake. *(Sibbett Collection)*

Evan, while at Stanford in 1926. *(Kackley Collection)*

Evan, Ellis, and Jim Swenson in front of offices on ground floor of Caribou County Hospital in 1940. *(Lavonda Lallatin, R. N. photo)*

***1934 or 1935 photo of Dr. Evan Kackley.** (I. Madsen collection)*

***Recent photo of Dr. Evan Kackley.** (Kackley collection)*

Ellis Kackley in front of Caribou County Hospital, 1934 or 1935.
(I. Madsen collection)

Ellis Kackley in later years.
(Kackley collection)

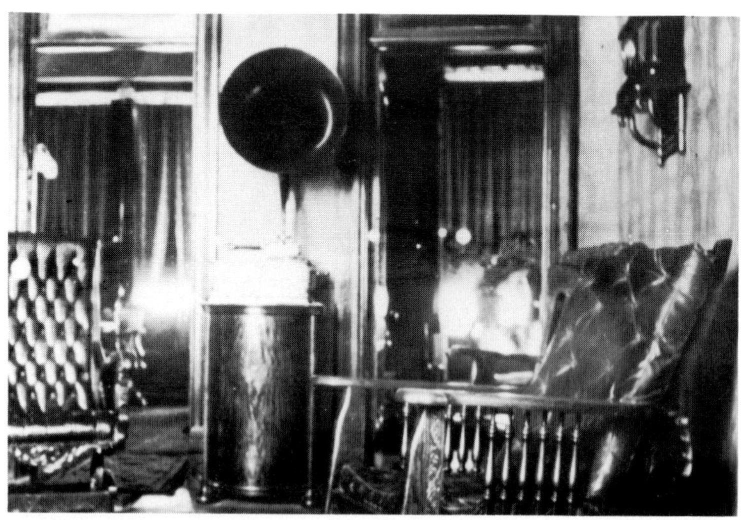

The large room in the Kackley residence shows both Ellis and Ida's chairs, with a Thomas Edison phonograph in the center. This is where the late Dr. Ellis Kackley was viewed by numerous patients and friends, who came to pay their last respects. *(Kackley Collection)*

Six-Shooter Sal and Evan in foreground taken in Soda Springs. "Six-Shooter Sal" was Grand Matra and Evan, Grand Marshall of the Historical parade in 1982. Back left, Vance Birchfield. Back right, Don Cook, author of "Six-Shooter Sal" book. (Elaine S Johnson photo)

Evan Kackley Family: Alvin, Evan, Lois, and Ellis at home in Boise, Idaho, 1985. (Kackley collection)

The historical instrument display in a walnut case upon the lectern in memory of Ellis Kackley, M. D. in the Hugh Young Memorial Library of John Hopkins Medical School in Philadelphia. The oil paintings are of Dr. Hugh Young and James Brady, founder of the James Brady Urological Institute. *(Photo courtesy of Dr. Patrick Walsh, professor of urology of Johns Hopkins University Medical School, and director of the Brady Urological Institute.)*

the problem, then talk the patients out of it. This was a form of hysteria, and the patient would get on their hands and knees and bark like a dog, or do other strange things.

Ellis never ceased to be amazed at what the mind could do to people. When their minds were confused by all this talk about an illness, they could easily talk themselves into being sick. He was occasionally called upon to treat hysteria. These types had to be treated differently than other illnesses. A shot of apomorphine to induce vomiting—which had a relaxing effect on the patient, who would arrive at one position and stay put for hours—would usually bring a person out of the state of mind.

Ellis had to be careful to sort out physical illnesses such as tuberculosis or third stage syphilis, which often had similar symptoms to mind induced illnesses.

Many of his patients suffering from what was later known as psychosomatic illnesses were hard working, successful people. Never did he establish chronic hysteria, or label the person neurotic, or the disease chronic, for far too often symptoms precluded serious disease such as brain tumors.

Ellis often told Ida, "It's all this damn advertising, which hammers at people until they are sure they have the condition. It's worse than the old medicine shows they used to have." He thought a moment before continuing, "Many people just need to be reassured in a nice way. You have to let them talk to you, like you were a priest or bishop. Sometimes you have to give them a little medicine which won't do any harm, like soda tablets or some bit of medicine to impress them, to get them feeling better."

Ellis took time to talk to these people who needed reassurance, but did not encourage them to keep coming back. A doctor with a busy practice like he had, didn't need to prey off peoples' fears as some doctors of the time were doing.

Mrs. Schmidt's condition continued to worsen. She developed Bright's Disease, which often accompanied heart trouble. Ellis didn't give her much chance for improvement, and felt sorry for his friend Henry, who was broken up by the prognosis.

Ellis bought a 1910 automobile put out by R.E. Olds called a "Reo." It had no top, not even a windshield, and was run by a chain drive similar to a bicycle. The old chain drive was a common source of annoyance for early automobile owners.

To start the contraption there was a large brass crank on one side. It had two cylinders, but no real spark plugs. The point, which looked something like a spark plug, got red hot, and set off the gasoline. In those early days, if tires failed, you simply removed the tire and continued on the rim to the next town where you hoped you would be able to buy a new tire.

Ellis found the machine totally unreliable, and if curses could kill, it would have been dead shortly after he bought it. It was prone to premature explosions, and went through the spark-like contraptions at a ridiculous rate. Sometimes they had to be changed as often as three times in a mile.

Ellis not only did not take kindly to the contraption, when it came to awful drivers, he became known as one of the worst. One day he was driving along, with Evan accompanying him, and the steering wheel came off. Evan was thrown out into the road. Ellis was furious.

"That's the end of that," Ellis told Ida. "I won't have my son getting killed in some damn horseless carriage. That's the last machine for me. I just feel lucky to have gotten rid of the damned thing."

"What did you do with it?" asked Ida, who rather liked the car.

"I traded the sonofabitch for a harness," said Ellis. "That's the first time in my life I ever cheated a man, but he seemed happy with the deal."

Soda Springs continued to develop new industries. East of town, in Sulphur Canyon, there was a cold water spring highly charged with sulphur, which enterprising citizens tried to recover. They could not economically capture the particles.

In the canyon area, volcanic action at least 13,000 years before had left deposits of sulphur which could be gathered up by the wagon load with a shovel. The sulphur came up with gases in fumaroles, or small openings, and condensed in the cooler air. It congregated in clumps and small veins. Pieces the size of an egg were plentiful in Sulphur Canyon.

Most of the sulphur used in the U. S. came from Sicily. A competitive market led local men to decide there was a sufficient amount in the canyon to support mining activity. A small office building and a boarding house were constructed, and mining began. As the mine began to produce, Soda Springs began shipping out sulphur.

Ellis was pleased to see sulphur being mined in the close proximity of Soda Springs. He used it in his medical practice, it was used in the sheep dips, and a great deal was used to make gunpowder.

One night the smokestack off the big sulphur mine disappeared. It had been lost in a card game to the Idan-ha' Mineral Water people and soon appeared on their building.

Both industries were run by steam engines fueled by wood. Gambling was big business in Soda Springs, and businesses, ranches, and anything a man had, was likely to be lost at the tables, especially when gambling and a little whiskey were mixed.

After the accessible sulphur was mined, the mineral became increasingly difficult to remove. Sicily's long monopoly on sulphur was broken when great domes were discovered in the United States and injected with steam which made the sulphur flow out. The mines in Soda Springs could not compete either, and soon were put out of business by the new technology. The mining activity in Sulphur Canyon had lasted only two seasons.

Besides having a coal delivery service, George Small was appointed deputy sheriff. He had worked earlier as a federal marshal, and was known for being fearless, but it was impossible for one man to clean up the town. When he did arrest some of the culprits, they were back on the streets in no time.

George kept all of his business records scratched on shingles and stored under the eves of the log cabin. "That's different, but I guess if it works, its okay," Ellis told him.

Ellis came home highly excited one day in 1910. "Morgans have had the telephone line extended out to their place in Grays Lake," he told Ida. "I think we should get a telephone." He stopped a moment waiting for Ida to reply. When she didn't, he added, "Wouldn't it be great if all the people in the outlying areas could call when they needed a doctor instead of having to come or send someone clear into town to get me."

The phone line was called the Rocky Mountain telephone line. A two wire line ran from Mink Creek through Gem Valley, into Soda Springs, and a single wire north to Henry. Now it went clear to the Morgan Ranch in Grays Lake. Ida was agreeable to the idea, and Kackleys soon installed a phone. It was quite a novelty to be able to talk clear to Grays Lake. The reception was poor, but they were usually able to get messages through, though they sometimes had to be relayed from Henry. While most people had party lines, Kackleys were privileged to have a private line since he was the doctor. Their numbers were six at the house, and forty-one at the office. Listening in on the party line became a major entertainment of many of the ladies.

The town soon had telephone operators. They were always helpful. Their duties entailed a lot more than running the switchboard. Mert Gorton, who married one of the Gorton boys and later worked at the hospital for years, was a telephone operator. Whenever the line broke down, she would go up the pole with a pair of spikes and fix it. The single line wire Morgans put in to Grays Lake allowed people to talk one at a time, similar to a CB. Whenever the line would break, the first person who came along would fix it with a piece of barbed wire from the fence, and soon the expression "talking over the barbed wire" became common for talking on the line to Grays Lake.

In July of 1911, the Whitney brothers were terrorizing the area from Salmon to Butte and from Utah to Wyoming. The desperado, Hugh, was reported by an Idaho Falls newspaper to be in the area and headed toward Soda Springs. He had shot a deputy who recognized and tried to arrest him, and killed a railroad conductor named Kidd. He was charged with murder.

Governor James Hawley was asked to bring out the state militia. He referred the request to his adjutant general, who decided the capture of two boys was hardly reason for calling out the militia, but Fort Hall Indians were used to track the fugitives and bloodhounds from Boise to sniff the trail. Whitney rode to Menan bridge near Idaho Falls, across the Snake River. Rube Scott waited on the other side, and commanded him to stop. Whitney firing into the early dawn light, shot off Scott's trigger finger.

Whitney went from Idaho Falls through the hills to Grays Lake—a lonely region. He stopped at a homestead, in the area called Chub Springs, about twenty miles north of Soda Springs, for dinner. His horse was getting lame, so they gave him a horseshoe and helped him shoe the horse.

Telephone stories came in on the newly installed Morgan line to the north about the man who rode by. Then the line was cut by Whitney, and no one bothered to fix it.

At Henry they knew he was going through, but no one tried to stop him. It was like "High Noon"—while the citizens of the area kept close track of his progress, he rode openly by the saloon, waving at those he was acquainted with. Henry was peopled by men equally deadly with the six-gun, but no one wanted a gun fight with Hugh.

In Soda Springs people repeated rumors and stories about him at the dinner table each day. Whitney was a boy from the Cokeville area, and had been considered a good kid. He had worked out north for some of the livestock owners around Henry and Grays Lake. People felt there was something decent about Hugh and his family in spite of the binge of lawlessness which had begun with an altercation over a card game at Monida, Idaho, near the Idaho-Montana border. He and his brother Charles felt they had been abused. They got their money back by robbing the joint, then ended up in several shooting sprees.

Hugh came closer and closer, with six-guns on his hips and a rifle in a scabbard, stopping only for meals. At Martin's Flat north of Soda Springs, he asked to stay overnight.

Young Evan, who would be starting school in the fall, was on a horse down at the stockyards by the railroad tracks listening to the stories on Hugh's progress brought in by sheepherders and range riders. Beside him, on another horse, was Bessie Small, daughter of Susie and George.

Bessie was a tomboyish girl a year or so older than Evan.

Whitney was past the Blackfoot River, only eleven miles away. Evan and Bessie hung on the words they heard about the killer coming to town rumored to be riding a bronco he had roped and busted from the open range. He was riding along, head and shoulders above the sage, on a road that was ankle deep in dust from the flow of livestock. One lone desperado, but many people thought the National Guard should be called out to apprehend him and protect the state from his wave of crime.

George Small drove up to the stockyards in a democrat, a light spring-board wagon, with a rifle across the seat beside him. He was tall and angular, but stooped. While clumsy with the six-gun, he was a master of the rifle. He kept the sights on his gun blackened by smoke from a match. He had picked a twig off a juniper tree just above one fugitive's head while being peppered at with a six-gun. When he said the next rifle shot would be just two inches lower, the fugitive had quickly surrendered.

Last rumored reports to George were that Hugh Whitney had shot his horse which had become lame at Three-Mile-Knoll, and was afoot. George was going out to get Whitney. He didn't ask for a posse, and the other men quickly thought of reasons they couldn't go with the deputy, but six-year-old Evan and Bessie begged to go along. He finally consented, and the two children piled into the back of the democrat, their feet over the open end-gate. They rode northward toward where the desperado had last been reported. They went quickly along, with George prodding the horses. This was no kid's game of cops and robbers, they were after a killer. Three-Mile-Knoll was coming up fast, with its "quakers" or quaking aspen trees, where the dead horse lay, and Whitney was supposed to be in those trees.

As the lawman and two kids approached the trees, a cloud of dust in the distance caught Evan's eye, and as it came closer, the kids realized it was a lone rider following them. The rider was cutting corners off the road, going across the sage and coming closer by the minute.

Chapter 10

Bessie urged her father to go faster, not telling him a rider was drawing close, because that rider was one the kids in the wagon wanted to keep their distance from. The rider, with a divided skirt and broad brimmed hat held on with hat pins, sat high on her Morgan horse. The horse, from the great Potter strain at Lava Hot Springs, was named Dempsey after the creek there.

They were only about a quarter of a mile from the trees when Ida galloped up in a whirl of dust and reined in beside the team pulling the wagon. They knew she wasn't interested in helping bring in Whitney, but was after the kids beside George.

"Sheriff Small," Ida said quietly, "do you have guns for these two?"

"No," drawled the sheriff. "Don't reckon I do."

"Then I think I'd better take them back with me," she advised, "They're a mite young."

The kids were hoisted up behind Ida, and in spite of their reluctance, there was no appeal as they returned home without a glimpse of the gunman. The silence was broken only once when Ida said to Evan, "I don't think your father is going to like my coming after you." Then as though to reassure herself, she added, "But he isn't your mother."

The words sounded strange to Evan, who didn't know his father was the doctor who had saved the life of one of the Cassidy boys when he was shot up, and cared for him in Soda Springs while he was supposedly hiding out in Star Valley.

Deputy Small didn't find Whitney either. The day after their aborted ride, Evan and Bessie rode out to see the dead horse, slipping between Rocky and Rooster Tree Peak of Chester Hill, to throw off those who might suspect their destination. The horse and saddle and rifle scabbard were there, but not Whitney. His trail was lost at Soda Springs.

Several years later Evan was playing with Kenneth Burton, who became a lifelong bosom friend, on the west side of Chester Hill. On a ledge beneath Rocky Peak they found a rusty rifle and two tin plates. Even then they realized these things must have belonged to Whitney, and that he had probably hid out in the hills and jumped a freight train one night as it slowed on the Soda grade. Years later, Ellis told Evan that Whitney had come by the Kackley house that night to see the doctor, as he had been slightly injured in his long flight from the law, and told him he had seen two kids on horses ride between Rocky and Rooster Peak within a hundred yards of him.

Ellis had known and treated Whitney before he got into trouble with the law. Though he was still just a kid, he was known as one of the best sharpshooters around, and it was said he could hit a dime flipped into the air or stood sideways on a fence post.

Whitney disappeared, changed his name, and changed his life. Many years later, in June of 1952, his brother Charles turned himself in to the authorities in Montana, for his part in the crimes they had committed. He said he had not done so sooner because of the murder charges against his brother, who had died in Canada in 1950.

He said he and his brother had served in France with Allied troops in World War I, and went straight under assumed names. A judge in Kemmerer, Wyoming, pardoned Charles because he was an old man, those he had stolen from were then dead, and he had led many years of productive life under his assumed name. So ended the story of the Whitney brothers. Hugh's initials, cut in a piece of timber of a corral gate, are preserved in the Kemmerer, Wyoming Museum.

One day Ellis ran into Deputy Small in town, and he was hopping mad. "I don't know what I'll do," he told Ellis. "You know I kept my records on shingles tucked under the eves of the house. Well the other day Suzie got short on wood, and burned them for kindling. I don't even know who owes me for coal."

"She didn't know they were your records?" asked Ellis incredulously.

"No, the damned woman just stuck them in the fire," exclaimed George. "You have to keep an eye on these women. You never know what they'll do next". He paused a moment, then added in a more mellow tone, "But I don't know what I'd do without her."

"I don't know what the county would do without her," said Ellis. "She has done so much for everyone, risking her life to help others, and so often without any kind of pay. He shook his head and laughed, "You're so damned honest, George, no one would doubt your word if you didn't tell anyone what happened."

Prohibition was becoming a hot issue in Idaho as well as many other parts of the country. The Mormons were always opposed to liquor, and the Women's Christian Temperance Union (WCTU) was fighting the consumption of alcohol. Ellis figured the way the good ladies of Soda Springs were backing it, prohibition would soon come, even though the business interests of the town opposed it rigorously. The women had become a powerful force in Soda Springs, and they objected to the men spending time in the saloons and whorehouses.

Prohibition was the top topic of conversation in Soda Springs in 1909 before the vote on the local option law, and many of Kackleys friends were highly involved in the controversy. It would eliminate Largilliere and Schmidt's brewery business. Largillieres were involved in many other business ventures in the area. Henry Schmidt's interests were less diversified. Widespread prohibition would raise havoc with the Idan-ha' Bottling Works because most of their large orders from around the country were for mixing with spirits.

Ellis and Ida opposed heavy drinking and Ida leaned toward the prohibition side. "You'll see stills in half the cellars in town, and the moonshine business will become a big problem if prohibition passes," Ellis told Ida.

"If they make the stuff illegal, at least we won't see the drinking and carousing which goes on in the saloons now," Ida countered. "Maybe it would cut down on some of the lawlessness that goes on around here."

"Many of these old men are physically dependent on alcohol," Ellis explained. "They drink, but are seldom drunk. These sanctimonious old ladies, who are a lot better at minding other folks' business than their own, will have the town full of the delirium tremens, or what they call D. T.'s, if they take liquor completely away."

He walked over and looked out the window, then finally he spoke. "Some men, though you may never see them drunk or out of line, must have a nip of the bottle now and then, to function. I know it's bad, but I don't think outlawing whiskey will deter them, he added shaking his head. The liquor business will just go underground."

"I don't see what anyone sees in the stuff," said Ida. "Remember in Tennessee when we decided to go down and buy a ten cent pitcher of beer, just to see what it tasted like? Neither of us liked it, and we ended up throwing it out."

When the vote did come up, Bannock, Bear Lake, and Franklin were the only southeastern Idaho counties that went dry. Soda Springs was then a part of Bannock. Establishments which sold spirits in those counties had until April 1, 1910, to phase out stocks of liquor. Surrounding states of Wyoming, Nevada, and Montana remained absolutely wide open. Of forty-seven states in the nation, twenty-one went dry during the local option period.

Ellis talked to Theodore Enders who told him, "It isn't just prohibition that's killing the Idan-ha' Bottling plant, it was just a matter of time, anyway. Since somebody invented a seltzer bottle that carbonates ordinary water, the business has been going steadily downhill." He looked sentimentally at the old bottling plant before continuing, "We used to ship it out on the railroad by the carload, but now it usually goes by the case. With railroad freight rates so high, we just can't compete."

It saddened Ellis to see Soda Springs industries going downhill, especially those concerned with the mineral water and springs. He felt that if the local merchants were a little more aggressive, they might see more progress.

Charlie summed up the situation when he said, "In Soda Springs the people think the Lord owes them a living, and in

Pocatello they think the Union Pacific Railroad does. If there were a change of attitude, there might be more progress."

Ellis felt this was true in a lot of cases, though many people worked hard and had progressive attitudes. "If more of the people around here thought like Charlie Fryar and Jim Horsley, we'd see a helluva lot more progress," he later told Jimmy.

The Bear River was extremely high that spring. Ellis was called out to help deliver a baby which was turned wrong and was not coming naturally. He reached the river bridge to find it had been washed out by the high water. Ellis looked at the swirling stream, and thought of the young woman on the other side who desperately needed his medical knowledge and skill. Without it, she and her baby could both die. He wouldn't have been called if it wasn't an emergency. It was most frustrating that he could see the light in the house on the other side of the raging river but there seemed to be no way of getting across. Then the answer came to him. He quickly tied the team in a safe spot, took off his overcoat, coat, and shoes, tied his forceps around his neck with a piece of bandage, put a vial of chloroform in his pocket, and plunged into the cold waters.

Ellis wasn't a good swimmer, and the only stroke he was proficient at was the breast stroke. He threw every ounce of his strength against the current as he pulled toward the small island midway between the banks. He reached the island and pulled himself onto the bank, teeth chattering, but didn't hesitate to plunge into the water on the other side as soon as he had his breath.

He grabbed hold of some bushes and pulled himself up on the opposite bank. He was slightly below the house where he was needed, and he took off toward it running at top speed. A cow gave a loud moo, as if lauding the accomplishment.

The midwife who opened the door could hardly believe her eyes, when she saw the wet, shivering doctor leaning against the door frame, hardly able to breathe. She took charge of the situation quickly. "Get out of those wet clothes, Doctor, and I'll find you something dry to put on," she instructed. "I'll hang yours over the stove to dry."

Ellis was soon warmed up, washed up, and had delivered the baby. He delivered it buttocks first, but it was a healthy baby boy, and both mother and child got along well. In spite of their protests, Ellis swam back to his team and hurried home. "If I got here that way, I sure as hell can get back the way I came," he insisted despite their objections.

When he got home, Ida met him as he drove into the barn, and unhitched the horses while he went in and got out of his wet clothes and into a hot tub of water.

"If you don't take care, you'll kill yourself trying to help someone else, and dead doctors can't do any good in this world," she scolded. "I'll be surprised if you don't get pneumonia."

Ellis came down with a cold, but didn't get the pneumonia his concerned wife was predicting as a consequence of the exposure.

It was soon evident keeping up with everything was too much for Ida. Kackleys hired Anna Enlund to help care for the children. She was capable and dependable. There was quite a migration of people from the Scandinavian countries, especially Finland, in the Soda Springs area. Ida hired two other Finnish girls, Edla and Mary, to help in the house. With two children to care for, taking care of that big place and keeping everything up in the house, yard, and barn was too much for one person, especially when she had so many other interests and obligations. Ida was getting more and more involved in the church and community. Every night after supper, she would have the girls around the table, teaching them to read and write English. It took a lot of time, but Ida enjoyed it and they were anxious to learn.

She put little Margaret to bed early in spite of her protests, but Evan was allowed to stay up until 9:30. After the girls had left, Ida continued to read the classics—which were left in the large Codman library—aloud to Ellis, sometimes for hours after bedtime. She was determined to take full advantage of the wonderful learning opportunity at their disposal.

Summer went by quickly. In the fall Evan started to school. He decided he would like to stay home one day. He felt fortunate when both of his parents left early that morning. It wasn't hard to convince Anna he was not feeling well enough to go to school. He was sure he wouldn't miss much just skipping school for one day. When Ida returned before time for school to let out, and found Evan still at home, it didn't take long for him to wish he had gone, and when Ellis got home and heard about his activities, he got it from both parents. He ended up grounded and was unable to go to the last episode of "The Clutching Hand" at the local Friday night movie, where the scoundrel of previous episodes was to be identified. He couldn't ride his horse, or hang around the stockyards and listen to the men, or see Bessie, George, Ken, and his other friends. After that, he attended school faithfully. He hated to come inside in the evenings and do his homework, but Ida kept close tabs on him and made sure he did his lessons well.

Evan was a little more successful in getting out of going to church, but when he did have to go, he managed to get a lot of teaching about Christ. Early pioneers of the church had given the big stained-glass windows to the Presbyterian Church, and Evan enjoyed looking at them and at the large pictures of Christ on the walls, and listening to the old pump organ.

When Mrs. Rose visited California in the winter time, she always brought back small gifts for Ida and the kids. "The Mormons have taken me into the community, and never tried to change my religion, but they've been great friends," Ida told Mrs. Strachan. "I enjoy going out and helping when there's a need and I can assist, and so do these women."

There were often guests at the Kackley table in the evening, the only meal Ellis took time to enjoy at leisure, and the kitchen was filled with lively talk. When Henry Schmidt's wife died, he was welcomed into their home, and usually joined them for their evening meal. Little Margaret had taken a great liking to him, and they all felt he was almost a part of the family.

Patients would come from Gem Valley or farther away, and when they were released from the hospital, Ida and Ellis would take them into their home and take care of them during convalescence. It wasn't unusual for people to stay as long as three months in the Kackley home.

There were still a few emigrants coming through Soda Springs, and occasionally a family would get caught in inclement weather and have to winter in Soda Springs before going on. Ida would bring young people up to the house, and make sure the families were okay, and had enough food and clothing.

Sometimes people convalescing or traveling through just needed a place to soak in a warm tub and have a hot meal. They were welcomed into the Kackley home.

Ellis hired a young man from Grace named Cyril Rich, who had dropped out of school and was drifting. One day he came to Ellis and wanted to work for him. "The boy is sharp as a razor, and thrifty too," Ellis told Ida.

Cyril soon took it upon himself to clean the dirty medical instruments, put new gauze on the chloroform inhalation masks, and replenish Ellis' medicine bag with new supplies each day. Ida and Ellis both knew he was interested in medicine, and waited until the time when the subject would spontaneously open up. They agreed they would help him. Soon they were helping to put several young people through college. "You never lose when you invest in young people and education," Ellis maintained and Ida agreed wholeheartedly.

Ellis and Ida purchased a ranch in Grace from Edward J. Turner, one of the men who had first visualized the Gem Valley as a great farming area irrigated with Bear River water and had worked assiduously to bring that about. He had known the people of the valley did not have the necessary money and realized the irrigation project would have to be done by their own sweat and labor. Ellis admired the beautiful farming area created when water was brought onto it by these good hardworking people.

Ida ran the ranch. When Mr. Turner turned the ranch over to them, Ellis and Ida found the Joe Garner family, good, hard-working, high-visioned people with great experience to carry out their thoughts and plans. A lot of land had never been broken out for irrigation, as it was beyond practical feasibility to do with horses. This Ida broke out with oxen which were able to tear out the sagebrush with a walking plow, then available. She went into beef and hog business, and soon the ranch was doing well.

The ice house Codman left as part of the barn, was filled each winter with ice cut from Bear River. For long term preservation of meats, Ida filled five gallon crocks with sausage, partially cooked and covered with lard, and placed deep in the ice house under sawdust.

Ida continued to put up all their vegetables from the garden, and fruits when they were available. Peaches and apples were favorites, and she always saw that her family had good substantial meals, with skillet corn bread every night, and occasionally ice cream for a treat. "I'm lucky to have an old fashioned cook," bragged Ellis as he stood up from the table.

Stockholders of the Last Chance Canal Company—who led the valley to realize it was the last chance settlers would have to build a canal for irrigation—were upset with Telluride Power Company, and concerned about their water rights. At a hearing on April 11, 1907, Secretary of the Interior, Garfield, had approved Telluride Power Company's application for right of way and to turn Bear Lake into a reservoir controlled by Telluride.

Bear Lake had been set aside on the basis of "Temporary Reclamation Withdrawal," by the U. S. Department of the Interior several years before, and Garfield, after a long discussion of places where beneficial uses of water could be made for both power and irrigation, approved the application without rescinding the earlier order withdrawing Bear Lake reservoir site from public domain. Ellis hated to see the Bear Lake project approved, because it would convert one of the most beautiful free flowing lakes in Idaho to nothing but a reservoir.

Those wise in water law mentioned "the understanding that the right-of-way would be used for the development of power, as subsidiary to the main purpose of irrigation and drainage," but some of the irrigators were afraid the power company would try to take more and more of the water, and problems would arise, especially in dry years. The early settlers had worked too hard and sacrificed too much to lose their water, which was their financial life-blood. Their canal project, costly in so many ways, would have turned back the faint of heart, but these people were pioneers of the West. They had fought to complete the canal, by themselves, against overwhelming odds, so they could get the precious water onto their land and produce crops.

A power plant had been constructed in Black Canyon, near Grace, in 1908, with two eight-thousand-five-hundred horsepower spinning Westinghouse generators, and six transformers which would increase voltage to forty-four thousand for transmitting the power to Salt Lake City. The electricity was for use in the mining districts of Bingham and Eureka; it was not sold to local customers. High voltage transmission of power was a new concept, and this was a pioneer project to prove it could be done. The plant was the largest one west of Omaha.

With the purchase of the Grace ranch, Ellis became involved in the water controversy. Irrigation was necessary to produce crops, and he could see the power company gaining more and more control over Bear River water rights. Ellis was worried the power company would try to negate the irrigators' water rights. Last Chance's diversion was about two miles upstream from Telluride's dam, and when water was low, there was not enough to fill the power company's needs. Last Chance had an earlier water right, but the power company had little regard for a small group of Mormon farmers, and the company had the backing of those on Wall Street who were making money through development of power.

Ellis' family, though impoverished, had been landowners, and he felt owning land was the only thing which was of tangible value and would bring security for old age. The original Kackley few acres was in Virginia, close to where George Washington had lived. When Ellis was called to Gem Valley, and looked out over the fertile lands, he felt a sense of pride in owning a part of the land, and being involved in the activities of the settlers. He and Ida had saved their money carefully in order to add the Grace ranch to their holdings, and they both felt good about it.

Ellis seemed to be working double time. He was always in a hurry, and those who worked for him soon realized it was always "Hurry up" and "Time is of the essence" when they were doing something for the doctor.

Ellis had been appointed Union Pacific Railway doctor, and regional doctor for the big Grace Telluride Plant. While he hated the big business interests of the railroad and the power company, and those who didn't care about the rights of the individual person, he found both jobs mainly entailed caring for the workers, and working with them to get compensation when injured. Ellis had no qualms about standing up to the companies when he felt they were not treating an individual right.

The train would stop anywhere and pick Ellis up, or let him off anywhere between stations. He became well acquainted with and well liked by the engineers, brakies, conductors, signal men, and section foremen. Only the policy setters of big businesses were on his black list.

Prohibition had the exact effect upon the town Ellis had expected. It wasn't long until the deputy sheriff started confiscating bootlegged whiskey. Often he would bring it up to the hospital, to see if Ellis had any use for the brew. "Can you use this stuff, Doc. I just picked it up out north," he said as he deposited several jugs on the doctor's table.

"Is it any good, or will it kill somebody if I use it for medication," asked Ellis.

"Hell, Doc, that stuff is so rotten it will corrode the stomach lining of anyone who tries to drink it. I don't think you'll even have to lock this batch up," he drawled.

"That's good," said Ellis. "My big locker is chuck full of booze you've already brought me."

"Well, Doc, you know some of these old boys around here can't get along without the stuff, an' I know you can write prescriptions for medicinal use."

"I'll tell you what," said Ellis, "why don't you just keep the next batch you get, and if I have to write prescriptions for it, I'll just send them down for you to fill," suggested Ellis.

"Well, I suppose that would be okay," said the deputy. I have plenty of room. The drug stores have plenty to last a good long time.''

There were soon stills in the basements of the hotels and in many of the other businesses and private residences. Some of the older men would stop by once in awhile and get a prescription for a bottle to ''make it home on.'' Ellis felt sorry for the old fellows, who were already starting to get the D. T.'s and usually prescribed a bottle for them.

One spring night he arrived home to find Ida visibly upset. ''What's wrong?'' he asked.

''On my way over to the ranch in Grace, I saw a mountain of whiskey bottles along the side of the road by Davisville. I stopped and checked, and every one of them was a prescription written out by you. I don't think prohibition will do any good if doctors go prescribing it for every old drunk in town.''

''Gosh, Idie, most of those fellows wouldn't have made it home without a bottle. They were shaking like a leaf by the time they came into the office. You wouldn't want to see them frozen to death in last winter's blizzards because they couldn't make it home, would you?''

He could see by the way her body stiffened that she disagreed with him. ''Well, Ellis, I've never doubted your medical knowledge and decisions, and bow to them now. You know more about health problems than most anyone, and certainly more than I do.''

''Idie, I really believe drunkenness is a sickness,'' sighed Ellis. ''You know I don't like it any more than you do, but these old fellows are in bad shape. You can't take a man who has been toting a bottle since he was knee high to a grasshopper and suddenly take it away from him without ill effects. You wouldn't believe the guys I've seen for the D.T.'s since prohibition went into effect.''

One day Ellis was called out to the mines. As he headed toward Caribou Mountain, he passed China Hat, which was a hill just out of town shaped like a coolie's hat. It had received the name because some of the Chinese miners had supposedly been killed there. It had become a landmark to the people of the area.

In January of 1907 the U.S. Forest Service had created Caribou National Forest, and the spelling of Carriboo was changed to Caribou along with name changes to many other localities appearing in the geography books of the day. Many of the old timers in the Grays Lake and Caribou area were still indignant about the government changes.

"Those government assholes have no business changing the names of our places out here," a grizzled, old man told Ellis. "Who in the hell do they think they are? They've changed the spelling of the mountain to Caribou and pretty soon people will think it was named after the animal instead of Old 'Carriboo' Jack Fairchilds."

Ellis chuckled as he rode past the Eagle Creek Dance Hall. The weekly dances out here sometimes got pretty wild. They needed to fix the outhouses, which were terribly run down.

He kept getting ladies from the area with poison ivy rash on their behinds, and finally found they were selecting a secluded spot to relieve themselves instead of going into the dirty outhouses, not realizing they were squatting in poison ivy which seemed to be growing all over the grounds.

Last time Ellis had been called to the mine, a Chinaman had been shot. They carried him over the mountains toward the settlement, but he died on the very top of Caribou. He was buried there. "That's a most fitting place to bury him, for there he is master of all he can see," one of the men told Ellis. The remains of most Chinese who died at the mine were taken back to China.

A Chinaman's life wasn't worth a plugged nickel to many of the people here. The Chinese worked the mines at the same time the whites did, which was unique to this area. In most places, the Chinese were allowed to come in only after the whites had removed the most valuable ore and were ready to give up mining an area. In general, there were not a lot more problems than with the lawless element at any mining town, but racial prejudice flourished and was manifest in many ways. The Chinese were willing to work for low wages, and were hired to cut wood, wash clothing, and many other menial tasks the white miners did not want to do. The whites felt far superior to the Chinese. Ellis hated the cruelty and inhumanity of people who did not care about their fellowmen. He thought of Ashler and the lines of his mouth hardened. He often wondered what possessed people to make them act like they did.

As he went past a small, log schoolhouse, Ellis thought about how the area had advanced since he and Ida had arrived. When the Soda Springs Independent School District was created, Ida and Jimmy Strachan were both elected to the board. The others on the board were Mormons, yet they fully accepted these two into the group. When they held their first meeting, Jimmy was elected president, and Ida secretary of the board. Other members of the board included T. H. Horsley, Mrs. Minnie Horsley, J.E. Lau, and O.H. Lovejoy as principal of the school.

Ellis was glad to see Ida's efforts to improve the schools were being recognized. She was excited about being on the board, and they had all kinds of ideas about things to improve the schooling, which included a new building with more than two rooms on each floor, an auditorium, adding high school, running schools year around, and picking up students in outlying areas with sleighs and wagons, so they too could attend school even in the winter.

Ellis thought their plans were rather ambitious, but practical, and was glad to see Ida was involved in something she enjoyed, and that she was accepted by and liked working with these people. Deep friendships were developing. She hadn't been quite as enthusiastic about life since they had lost Alvin, and he worried about her, though the arrival of the two other children had been a blessing to the family, and helped ease the pain of their earlier loss.

Since Evan had started to school that fall, little Margaret seemed lost without him there to keep her company. The children played so well together. Margaret would often walk part way to meet Evan when he came home from school, and he loved the attention she gave him. He usually brought home little cards he made for her or other surprises. Ellis thought how lucky he was to have two beautiful children, and the joy they brought into the Kackley home.

Ellis stopped at Herman to change horses. Gortons kept horses at their store there, including some big dray teams that hauled supplies to Herman. Besides the store there was a post office, eating house and blacksmith shop. There was a little cabin where a prostitute lived, and during the summer, there was still a city of tents. He couldn't help but laugh when he thought about the time the horse went right over the barbed wire gate with him. Young Henry Gorton was so surprised to see him sewing up the horse when he came out.

When Ellis arrived at Caribou, the old miner had a badly broken forearm. Injuries like this were common when working with heavy hydraulic mining equipment. He looked around until he found a piece of board about the right size to make a splint and set it. Few people were working at the mines now, compared to when Ellis came to Soda Springs, but the gold on Caribou had provided at least a modest living for a few miners for quite a number of years. Ellis always dreaded the long ride home from this part of the country, and as usual it would be after dark before he arrived.

On the way back he thought about Evan and his plans for his son. He was all boy, and got into his share of mischief both with the other kids and by himself. Last week one of his little friends was playing with matches down by the old whorehouse on the creek. He had accidentally set the place on fire. It was lucky the girls had moved out a short time before. Houses of prostitution had almost vanished from the area, but there were still a few in some of the outlying areas.

As Ellis' reputation grew, and more and more people were coming into the town for medical care, Ashler and his friends were losing ground. They no longer dared fleece newcomers as openly as they had when the town was dominated mainly by mining and the sheep and cattle business, but they still took advantage of people when they thought they could get away with it.

Ellis wondered what had happened to the miner, Albin

Lindstrom's brother, who had disappeared shortly after he came to town. He was sure he had met with foul play, as many a man had in that town, but there was no way to prove it.

Chapter 11

The outcry for a Grand Jury investigation of the corruption in Soda Springs continued, and Judge Smith ordered a Grand Jury to be called to investigate whether or not the law enforcement and judicial officials in the town were doing their job. Soda Springs had started out originally as part of Oneida County, then became part of Bingham, then Bannock, before becoming Caribou County. When the county seat was in Pocatello, there was very little local control.

"Are you going to testify?" Ida asked Ellis.

Ellis folded his arms and looked out the window, then at last said softly, "I've thought seriously about it, Idie, but I can't. I know too damn much to testify without violating the confidence of my patients, which I can't do either by law or by the dictates of ancient medical heritage." He was quiet for a few minutes, then said suddenly, "I think you should testify."

"Me," said Ida surprised. "The idea never even crossed my mind. You're teasing—aren't you?" she asked.

"You know enough about what's going on around here to testify, and I think you should," he urged.

The Grand Jury was called, with mostly Pocatello people serving. Ida, as well as many other local people, was asked to testify. They were instructed that the proceedings were to be kept secret, and no one need be afraid to talk because they would not be in any danger of prosecution or repercussion from their testimony, except for cases of perjury.

Table talk, shop talk, and just about all the talk in Soda Springs centered around the Grand Jury, and while some hoped they would finally clean up the town, others trembled at the thought. Testimony was taken for several days, and many poured out their hearts and their fears to the group, hoping the prostitution, the illegal gambling, and the violence would be eradicated through their efforts, and the lack of concern by the law improved.

After several days of testimony, and a couple of days of deliberation, the group left town without recommending any charges be filed. "I can't believe it!" said Ida bitterly.

"I think they were more interested in quieting those who were complaining than in doing anything about the lawlessness," said Ellis. "Maybe Pocatello is too close for bringing about any action. I didn't know the influence of these crooks went that far, but it must."

While the Grand Jury didn't bring about a change in the town, time gradually did. More and more people who settled in Soda Springs were honest, upright citizens who didn't like the settlement's reputation of being one of the toughest little towns in the West. They wanted their lives and those of their families to be different from what had previously been offered in the town.

While Ellis didn't feel automobiles were dependable enough for use in his business, Ida thought they were great, and missed having their car which Ellis had traded for a harness. In 1913, they purchased a four-cylinder, two-geared Ford touring car for Ida to use. It cost four hundred dollars. Alvin Meyers, a former Utah Power and Light Company electrical engineer, who had moved to Soda Springs so his wife could receive continuing care from Ellis, showed Kackleys how to put a self-starter on the car so it didn't have to be cranked.

In 1910, Charles Keetering's electrical ignition system had been made standard equipment on Cadillac in spite of critics who felt the self-starter was an unnecessary frill. Henry Leland, general manager of Cadillac, had lost a close friend in a cranking accident. Crank handles had a tendency to kick sharply as the engine caught, and accidents were all too frequent. By 1914 ninety-three of the automobiles at New York's auto show had electrical starters, and the average person could start these cars without undue exertion.

Though Ida enjoyed it, Ellis wouldn't even ride in the automobile. "There's nothing more dependable than a good horse,'' Ellis still insisted. ''I have trusted my team to get me home many a time when the snow was coming down so thick I couldn't even see my way,'' he observed for the hundredth time. ''I've sent them home without me when the going got too rough and continued on by foot. You can't do that with an automobile. Give me a good animal with plenty of horse sense any day. When I'm called out, I need to get there, people's lives depend on it.''

One day an Irish family seven miles north of Soda called for Ellis. The wife was in severe pain, and from the message Ellis received, he figured she must have an acute obstruction of the small bowel, of several hours duration. It had been raining hard for about a week, and there was mud all over the place. Ida picked up Ellis' sense of urgency, and realized it was a life or death situation. They both knew that with the team and buggy, it would take a long time to go out and get the woman back to the hospital.

Ida knew the family well, and with some trepidation, she offered to drive Ellis out to get the woman in the Ford which he had always shunned. Ellis, because of the emergency nature of the situation, accepted somewhat reluctantly.

When Mr. Meyers had put the self-starter on the Ford, he had given Ida instruction in driving. His admonition was to never lose momentum, and to always shift before the car slowed down to a point where a lower gear would not take up the momentum lost. She had mastered the technique on trips to the Grace ranch, passing through heavy black sand for four miles north of Grace, which taxed teams and oxen. There was also deep, treacherous puddles in the road, due to the common practice of irrigators to send waste water into the road, where it would puddle.

Ida opened up the hand throttle as far as she dared, and the car bounced from one side of the road to the other, jerking and bucking like a bronco. The primitive steering system transferred every bump to Ida's hands.

Ellis hung on as she plowed through mud holes. She held her breath, hoping she could make it up Five-Mile Reef. The roads were muddy and sloppy, with eight to ten inch ruts, and slick as only clay roads could be after a rain. ''Looks like its been coming down harder than a cow peeing on a flat rock,'' Ellis observed.

Evan, in the back seat, was getting mud splattered, as Ida backed up, then plunged forward again, but she made it much faster than they could have in the buggy. They loaded the woman and her husband into the back seat of the car and brought her in to town.

As they pulled up by the hospital, Mike, the husband, carried the patient up the steps, and Ellis followed. Without a word, they left Ida sitting in the car, and no one looked back. Ellis operated and found she did have an obstruction of the bowel. Because they were able to get her to the hospital quickly, he had been able to save her life.

Ellis never mentioned the case at supper time, and only later did Ida hear through the hired man that ten inches of small bowel, which had been gangrenous from the obstruction, had been removed, and the woman was doing well. Ida felt she was no longer a part of Ellis' medical practice; it had superseded her.

She was lucky now to get an occasional quick kiss on the cheek as Ellis rushed out the door to care for his patients. He never discussed things with her, like he used to. She was becoming more and more unhappy, and felt he had turned his back on his family.

She thought back to the many years of sacrifice to help Ellis become a doctor—the giving up of money saved before their marriage to put herself through school, teaching and doing menial tasks during summer months to earn money for his education, working side by side with him and sharing his joys and his sorrows. Was she now unneeded? What a blow the thought was to her. Ellis' practice had grown to the point where they had escaped the poverty which plagued their early lives, but she would give anything, she thought, to go back to those early days when they were so young and carefree, and so much in love.

That was the end of Ida's exclusive use of the car. From then on, Ellis was always using it, so she seldom got to drive. He appreciated the speed, and if he killed the motor on a call, he no longer had to stop and crank the machine into action. Ellis thought of his friend's automobile with the crank placed so that when it high centered on the deep ruts, he had to take a shovel and dig a hole in the road under the crank, then reach under and try to start it. The new starter was a blessing to the Kackleys.

The Ford, with seventeen inch clearance, was not easily high centered in the deep ruts from the ungraded and ungraveled roads. It was built with simple and practical mechanisms and motor, which even the village blacksmiths were usually able to repair. There was a good owner's manual for the do-it-yourself man.

Ellis took over the car, but his driving didn't improve. He had many an accident with posts and other objects which got in his way—obstructions he was unable to avoid with the primitive steering mechanism of the early automobile—yet he never hit another vehicle or injured a person.

In the fall Ellis would bring the car into the barn and jack up the wheels. As soon as spring came, he would bring it out and get it started. When that car wore out, he got a Model T Ford for Ida, but it was the doctor people always saw driving it. As with the buggies, he took off the tops to cut down on wind resistance and increase the speed with which he could travel.

When that first car to enter Soda Springs, driven by Dr. Jackson, came around Whitman's corner in a cloud of dust, it made a gigantic impression on the townspeople. Besides Jim Horsley, Largillieres, and Kackleys, Charlie had bought a Ford. Mr. Whitman became interested in the automobile, and not only bought himself one, but built a garage and started a Ford agency which he ran for many, many years. Jim Horsley sold Studebakers and EMF's. Jim was always twenty years ahead of his time in seeing the great future developments before they appeared, thought Ellis. The "machine," as it was called, had become an integral part of community life.

Ida and Ellis' interest in protecting the springs led to a community project in which Ida became highly involved. The ladies worked to raise money to fix up the most used springs. There was a tremendous amount of civic pride among some of the residents of Soda Springs who worked to improve the town's image, soliciting help from the business community. The ladies raised enough to put concrete around Horseshoe, Barrel, and Octagon Springs. They developed Woodruff Spring and improved the area, and did some work on Ninety Percent Spring.

Woodruff Spring became known as Lovers' Delight. It was a secluded and lovely place where the bank dropped steeply about twelve feet to the small spring. One had to step carefully from rock to rock while holding to the willows growing on each side of the trail to descend safely. The drink, always cool and refreshing, under the canopied limbs overhead, made it well worth the effort required to get there. The water cascaded as it flowed by. A fence was put around the spring to keep children from falling into the creek there. It was visited frequently by the residents of Soda Springs, especially the young couples. The ladies arranged to have a rustic bench, just big enough for two, placed amid the willow trees at the top of the ravine.

Kackleys remodeled the house and added a wing on the south side. The stairs to the second floor were changed from the kitchen to the large front room where they looked impressive with their two landings. They did some insulating and fixing to try and make the house warmer and more habitable in the wintertime. Ellis had a central heating plant installed, but it never worked well enough to make a significant difference in warmth of the house.

Chautauqua programs came to town several times a year. They lasted two or three days and brought educational programs as well as plays, black minstrels, singers, and other entertainment. The second floor of Gorton's storage warehouse was turned into an opera house where speakers, stage plays, and programs were brought to the people of Soda Springs. William Jennings Bryant, Maude Adams and Jane Cowl all appeared there. Fashionable ladies of the town showed their appreciation for the performances by fainting or hysteria. Hypnosis and Mesmerism were demonstrated to captive audiences. Spiritualism was the vogue.

Ellis was asked to operate on a man under mesmerism instead of anesthesia. The patient didn't seem to feel any pain, but the muscles were absolutely rigid when he cut through them. While in the hypnotic state, Ellis told him to come back into the office in three months, on a certain date at a specified time, and sure enough he showed up right on time.

The hospital was crowded. Patients drifting in carried Ellis' name to communities all over the West. He made fewer and fewer house calls, as a steady stream of patients began coming to him instead of expecting the doctor to come to them.

One day he was treating Jake Frankfurt, a Jewish patient who had tuberculosis of the large bowel and was in the hospital periodically for treatment. Ellis prescribed a healing solution put into the large bowel like an enema. The patient would retain the medication, and it would relieve the symptoms for some time.

The nurse applied what she thought was vaseline to lubricate the equipment, and was surprised when he shrieked that his bottom end was on fire, and jumped out of bed. Ellis, whose back was turned, whirled in time to see Jake streak through the hospital, his short, white hospital gown which was open down the back, flapping in the breeze he created. He took the stairs three at a time, and disappeared running top speed down Main Street toward the Enders Hotel where he was staying.

The scene looked so comical, Ellis struggled to keep from smiling with limited success. He tightened his mouth, and asked, "What on earth happened? I've never seen that man move so fast in all the years I've known him. He was going like a bat out of hell!"

The nurse who was still standing, open mouthed, looking toward the stairs, checked and discovered to her embarrassment she had used capsicum, a red pepper ointment, commonly used on the chest and body as a counter irritant for pain, instead of vaseline.

"Good Lord," said Ellis, "that's like using turpentine. The way he went down those stairs with his gown flapping reminded me of what it must have looked like when Jacob was climbing the ladder to heaven, except Genesis doesn't mention him taking the steps three at a time."

The conscientious nurse was highly embarrassed and

concerned about her mistake. A week later, Jake came back into the hospital. "I'm sorry about taking off without paying the bill," he apologized before she could speak. "That was a damn rough treatment, but it did me more good than any I've ever had. What do I owe you?"

For years when he came in for periodical treatment, he always talked about how well that treatment had worked, giving him six months of complete relief, but much to Jake's dismay, the nurse refused to repeat the remedy.

Ellis always kept several dogs, and mourned their passing when they met with accident or foul play. He made a cemetery in the back yard, where he buried his animal friends. The coming of the automobile had made the streets unsafe for dogs. Many were run over, some accidentally and some because the owners of the machine swerved to purposely hit animals. Ellis' dogs were loyal, more devoted than human friends with their changing fancies, and he developed a strong attachment for them and took them everywhere with him. "A dog will never do anything to hurt his master," he observed. "The only thing a dog might do to harm you is take needed food out of your mouth."

You have the strangest way of naming dogs I ever heard of," Mr. Eastman observed, after being introduced to Ellis' dog, Sippio Africanus, named after the old Roman lord who won Africa. You never knew who Ellis would name one of his dogs after next. He had Crab, Longfellow, and Grady, and one was given the common name of Shep.

Evan and Margaret played around the house during the day. Ellis had his fumigation room up on the third floor, and didn't want the kids up there, so he told them the devil lived there. Evan had heard about the devil in Sunday School and Bible School. He didn't want anything to do with him. When Margaret, who was rather independent, decided to go up the stairs it frightened him almost speechless, but he ran up, grabbed her, and gave her a lecture which brought her down immediately.

Ida was teaching homemaking skills to eighth and ninth grade girls, who met at Kackleys twice a week. She was trying to get home economics into the school, but meanwhile she took time in the evenings to teach these necessary skills herself. Evan and Margaret often tried to sneak off when the girls came.

Without warning, the winter of 1912 again brought tragedy to the Kackley household. One day when Evan was playing with Margaret, she began throwing up. Highly concerned, he held a pan for his sister, then saved the contents for Ellis to examine. It contained a lot of phlegm. Margaret experienced a severe chill, and her temperature struck one-hundred-and-four degrees that evening. With a heavy heart, Ellis realized his little daughter, who by then was experiencing a lot of pain, had pneumonia.

Evan had heard about his brother Alvin, and was terribly frightened. When friends of the family came and went, and brought in food and emotional support, he watched his parents' reaction and felt sure his sister was going to die.

As Margaret's condition worsened, Ellis called Dr. Roberts, a Union Pacific Railroad doctor in Pocatello, and arranged for a special train to bring him to Soda Springs at Kackley's expense. They sent a stub, a set-up with just an engine and caboose, to transport the doctor. He used the newest method of treating pneumonia, making oxygen on the kitchen table by combining chemicals with fluids which came in small cans the size of condensed milk. The combination gave off oxygen, which the doctor collected and had Margaret inhale to relieve the stress on her heart. He couldn't make it fast enough to help the child's breathing. She needed oxygen continuously.

Later, the use of an oxygen tent and compressed oxygen in iron bottles would save numerous pneumonia patients, but Dr. Roberts' primitive set-up could not save the little girl. Kackleys always thought the world of Dr. Roberts for trying to save Margaret with a new technique, even though the treatment was not successful.

Ellis and Ida were frantic as Margaret's temperature climbed and climbed. The tragic death of little Alvin eight years earlier was imprinted on their minds and hearts, as they enacted the same scene over again with Margaret.

Day and night blended together as they worked over her, but treatment brought no improvement. Over and over again they both relived that terrible night when Alvin had been taken from their lives. Ellis cursed, and prayed, and used all his medical skill, but to no avail.

As the life left the child's small body, Ida screamed, "It isn't fair, it just isn't fair. Why should we have to lose two children, when you work day after day to save lives. Why couldn't our child be saved?"

Ida's words stung Ellis to the quick as she voiced the feeling of inadequacy that he was unable to do anything to keep his daughter from dying. His mouth tightened into a line of grimness, but he reached out and put his arm around his wife, as she shuddered in the horror of their loss. She felt limp, a spark gone out of her forever as she retreated into her own world of grief. Why, she wondered, had the Lord singled them out to lose two children. It was something neither of them could understand.

Hardly a word was spoken as the grief stricken couple went down to Whitman's furniture store, which carried caskets in a curtained off area, and picked a small wooden box to bury another child who had brought so much joy into their home. Ida was close friends with Blanche Whitman. She was also a former school teacher, and they had much in common, but there was little Blanche could say to comfort her now.

Ida aged visibly with the passing of her daughter. Anna took over with everything she could do in the house. Mrs. Rose, and numerous other neighbors brought in food, but Ellis' throat knotted so he could hardly swallow, and Ida didn't pretend to try and eat, though she coaxed a little nourishment down Evan. Their friends tried to give comfort to the family. As was the custom, they washed and dressed the little girl, laying the ice packed body out for viewing. An endless procession of neighbors came to look at the chalk-white remains of the child who had once been so full of life. Henry Schmidt mourned as if she had been his own.

Jimmy had refused to let anyone else ring the bell atop the beautiful little rock Presbyterian church, where the funeral was held. A short time earlier, the congregation had been so proud of acquiring a bell for their church. He tolled out the slow rhythm, which announced death, with a heavy heart and a great deal of empathy for his good friends. To him the voice of the bell lived and could speak, bringing the congregation together in happiness of a marriage, to worship, or to call those who were grief stricken to feel the strength of the Almighty.

The Strachan family picked up the Kackleys in their buggy and took them to the church. There were no pews yet, just chairs. Mrs. Crawford played the old foot-pump organ. Reverend Lindsey preached the funeral sermon as the family sat there broken hearted amid the beautiful stained-glass windows that depicted the life of Christ in his understanding. There was no alternative but to accept the hand of death.

They felt almost numb as the wooden box was lowered into the grave and the sexton began shoveling dirt on top of it. The hollow thud as each shovel full of earth hit the casket, seemed to penetrate their very being. When the grave was about two-thirds filled, they slowly turned and started walking toward home. "Let me give you a ride," Jimmy offered, but they wanted to walk, and to be alone with their thoughts.

Evan walked along sadly beside his parents. The pathetic little trio was wounded to the point where they would never completely heal from the emotional wounds, sometimes more fatal than physical ones. He wondered what his mother and father were thinking. At the tender age of seven, he had more acquaintance with death than most young people of many more years. He had felt the results of tragedy in his own family, and was acquainted with the cycle of life and death in his father's hospital, but this was an experience which would mark the balance of his life.

As they walked up the old wooden side walk, past the rock store, and back to their home which had been instrumental in inflicting so much sorrow upon them, Ida spoke for the first time since the beginning of the services. "I hate this house, I hate it," she cried.

Hate for their home of the past twelve years became a symbol of her grief. During the next few weeks, they went about their duties automatically, without thought for what they were doing, without joy and laughter in their lives, and haunted by the scenes which they tried to avoid, but which returned over and over to clutch at them. They no longer knew an hour of peace. They each felt alone in this dark and hostile world, where they no longer shared special times together, reading, driving in the country, discussing their goals. Tension tugged at their insides. They forced an outer cheerfulness they didn't feel.

As they drifted farther and farther apart, Ellis decided he must go for additional training in the latest advances in medicine. Maybe he could have saved his daughter if he had known about new techniques, he thought to himself. He enrolled in a post graduate course at Bellview Hospital in New York.

Ida turned most of the domestic duties over to the household help and work on the ranch over to the hired men. She no longer cared about her earlier interests and the activities she had been so excited about. Because she hated the house and felt depressed when she had to be there, she spent very little time at home, and tried to keep busy doing other things, but her heart was not in any of it. Even her love for education and the schools seemed unimportant at that time.

Evan had his own horse, and with the mobility riding afforded, had the run of the town. He liked to go down to the stockyards and railroad depot. He enjoyed doing things with Deputy Small and Jim Horsley, and with Ellis Davis, George Davis, Kenneth Burton, and Vance Birchfield, who were his age.

He was especially interested in Mr. Meyers, who had taken a job with the city of Soda Springs. Evan was intrigued with all he knew about the mystical force called electricity. Mr. Meyers shared Charlie Fryar's sentiments that the charge for electricity in the town was too high. Evan had heard him telling Ellis that when Charlie's verbal protests were ignored, he went out and wired around the meter, directly into the hotel and hospital.

"He's right about the charges being too high. I just wired the line back through the meter, and charged him a little extra each month until I figured he and the city were about even," Myres said weighing the situation. "I'm going to try and get the charges lowered to a more reasonable rate. The city is trying to run the entire community on the revenue from power. Electrical power is no longer a luxury. It is absolutcly indispensable to the welfare of people, and should be furnished at reasonable rates. If more people would protest, like Charlie, something would quickly be done about the price."

The neighborhood kids would go up to Mineral Heights and put small items where the water from the springs would run over them and coat them with rock like mineral substance, which they called petrifying. A whittled stick took on a whole different appearance when covered with the mineral coating. Sometimes they could even trade these things for other things they wanted.

The kids all knew how the ladies of the Presbyterian Church had talked George Schmidt into making a wooden chair with a round hooped back, and the letters "SODA SPRINGS" cut into the wood. They had put the chair on the west slope of the mounds where mineral water would flow over it and turned it a bit every day, until it was completely coated. They had shipped it off to go in the Idaho Building at the Chicago World's Fair in 1893 where it was reported to have amazed the crowds who viewed it.

Evan enjoyed riding, and when he and Kenneth thought their mothers were well enough occupied so they wouldn't be missed, they sometimes went as far out as the Blackfoot River. They particularly enjoyed exploring the springs along Soda Creek.

The boys occasionally rode with the moving of livestock from the Grace ranch to the Soda Springs ranch, a distance of twenty miles each way. With a slow herd it sometimes took two days for the trip; with a fast herd it could be done in one day working from early morning until late at night.

While Evan thought he could get away with almost anything, he soon found out differently when he started snitching an egg now and then from their chicken coop and trading it for treats at the store. One thing Ida would not put up with in a child of hers was dishonesty. Evan thought all hell had broken loose when she began whipping him with the horsehair bridle, which was the nearest thing at hand when he was caught.

Not only was he stealing, he was going into the store run by Pat Horton, who had shot their dog, Wink, years before. He knew he wouldn't get any sympathy from his father either when Ellis heard about his behavior, and he was right. Ellis was just as angry as Ida had been.

One day Charles Lau and Evan spent the afternoon playing in the hayloft of the barn. They decided to try and learn to fly. "If we flap our arms hard enough, I know we can fly," reasoned Evan.

Charles went first. When Evan saw the crash Charles made, after jumping about twenty feet, he temporarily gave up his interest in flying, which as with many other young boys, had been generated by the Wright Brothers first flight a decade earlier.

Ellis wrote and asked if his family would like to join him in New York. Ida packed up their things, left instructions for the help, and she and Evan started east to be with Ellis. They rented an old apartment across from the Children's Hospital. It had gas lights. New York was not yet completely served by electricity, except for Broadway, then known as "The Great White Way" because of the lights. Some of the street cars were still being pulled by teams of horses, but some were modernized to use electrical current.

Young Evan was intrigued by the subways, elevated railway, the horse drawn cars, street cleaners, and other unfamiliar sights. Even though he was only a child, he was extremely interested in the ways electricity was being used, partly as a result of Mr. Meyers influence over Evan and his friends in Soda Springs. He and his friend Max Snell, who eventually became engineer of Soda Springs and Star Valley plants, were both greatly influenced by Meyers during their boyhood. Evan and his friends wanted to know all about how and why electricity worked, which few people understood in those early days.

It was at that time Dr. Hugh Young of John Hopkins Medical School and his family were in New York. They were being shown the "Great White Way" as guests of Diamond Jim Brady, in appreciation for what Dr. Young had done for him. "The Great White Way," was a name intimately connected with Diamond Jim Brady, who had been in Soda Springs in the early days in his private railway car parked on a siding near the Idanha, while he enjoyed the benefits of Soda Springs water. There were many stories about his visits to Soda Springs in the early days.

Diamond Jim had been stricken with an obstruction of the urinary tract so severe that the bladder could only be partially emptied and urine back pressure pushed into the kidney and damaged the secreting portion, causing infection to spread into his whole system, severely affecting his heart, also.

At that time, removal of the prostate was the only solution, and the operation was not too successful, having a debilitating effect. Most men considered it only as a last resort, and were poor risks for surgery. Diamond Jim had been to urologists in New York and Boston who could do nothing for him.

Finally he went to see Hugh Young at John Hopkins. Hugh was a young professor of urology there, and was vibrant and alert to great changes taking place in medicine and surgery. He had been faced many times in his medical practice with the life destroying condition of prostate obstruction and had devised a hollow metal tube about the diameter of a pencil, which could be slipped into the bladder through the urethra. Enclosed in the metal tube was a sliding tube with a circular, cold, sliding-type blade which could cut parts of the prostrate away. The operation was done under local antiseptic. Visibility was by means of a small electric bulb about the size of a grain of wheat, which gave poorly reflected light.

Dr. Young was the first surgeon in the world to accomplish recanalization of the prostatic urethra, under vision, to relieve the death dealing condition. This was one of the first applications of the use of electric light to see inside the body. When the Kackley family was in New York, Dr. Hugh Young was on the verge of being honored as the "Father of Urology" by his colleagues.

Hemorrhage was always a complication one had to deal with when using a cold knife. The control of hemorrhage followed, and was developed by Dr. John Caulk, who had been a student at John Hopkins, and had his surgical training under Hugh Young.

Diamond Jim Brady recuperated magnificently after Dr. Young's removal of the obstruction and soon the exuberant Irishman was as happy as if he were back on Old Sod of Ireland from whence his parents came. In his gratefulness he wished to use some of his wealth to establish a great urological institute in New York City with Dr. Young as head. Dr. Young was too completely dedicated to John Hopkins to consider leaving, and so Diamond Jim established the Brady Urological Institute at John Hopkins Medical School, and one in New York also. "Hugh Young has been the brains of the urological world," Ellis told Ida.

Ellis had no idea then that his son would one day design instruments which would be a part of the refinement of those developed by Dr. Hugh Young and colleagues who followed for transurethral rechanneling of the urethra in prostatic obstruction under vision. This would make the relief of benign prostatic obstruction, though one of the first ten causes for admission to the hospital, a relatively minor operation in skilled hands.

Chapter 12

When they returned home, Ida looked at the house standing out against the sunset, and shuddered. It brought back so many tragic memories, she wished she could stay in New York and never have to face the place again. She yearned for the moral support of Ellis' arms around her, but he was in his own world, and she burned with loneliness.

Ellis had learned a lot of new things, including a great deal about surgery. He studied and practiced techniques. To be successful, he should be successful one hundred percent of the time, and he hadn't even been able to save his own children, which left him with a deep and hopeless feeling of inadequacy. He tried to fill the void in his life by throwing all his energies into medicine, and his practice continued to grow taking more and more time away from his home. As with most highly successful doctors, his practice soon seemed to own him.

One day a visitor, rather skeptical of Ellis' reputation, said, ''Your patients place you right next to God himself. Don't you ever make any mistakes?''

Ellis waved his hand toward the cemetery. ''There's a whole damn graveyard full of them,'' he said soberly.

Ellis rarely came home until bedtime, and the same routine went on seven days a week. He had the same office hours on Sunday as any other day, and except for a couple of hours Ida spent in church, and an occasional special dessert, there was no change in the daily routine. The practice of medicine came before everything else.

Ida again began taking an interest in the schools. She and the other board members worked to get an upstairs addition onto the school and a high school started. They were finally able to arrange for wagons and sleds to pick up children in the closer outlying areas so they could attend school even in the winter, as Ida and others had envisioned earlier. Chris Lallatin was elected to the school board. Ida began taking interest in the Grace ranch again, and it was turning a nice profit.

Ellis and Ida's lives were taking totally different directions, and they seldom spent time together. Ellis missed the companionship of his wife, the good times they used to have, and the warmth which had been such an important part of their life. He felt helpless to change the situation. He slowly began to realize their relationship would never again be what it had been, and he felt a deep sense of loss. Daily he went up over Soda Mound to the cemetery, where he visited the graves of his children, and continued to mourn for them.

Home alone, Ida tried to cope with her loss and feelings of depression. "I think we should send Evan to California to stay with his Aunt Grace for the winter," she told Ellis. "She wrote and suggested they would be glad to take him."

Ellis walked to the window and looked out across the town. "I don't get much time to spend with the boy," he said with his back still to Ida. "Maybe it would be a good thing for him to be in a warm climate with an even temperature."

Evan thought it would be a wonderful adventure, so he was packed up and sent to California for the school year. When winter winds came and the world around Soda Springs lay under a deep covering of snow, and the house was cold, Ida and Ellis felt secure in knowing their son was in California where the winter weather was mild and the sun was shining.

Grace's husband, Fred, was a railway agent for the Southern Pacific Railroad south of San Francisco at Hanford. Evan had the run of the area, and spent most of his time out of doors in the warm weather. He gave the teachers a merry time, and learned very little, but he had a good year that he would never forget.

When he returned home, it didn't take Ida long to see he hadn't been attending to his studies, and she took him quickly under her wing and worked with him until he was caught up. It only took about six weeks.

In 1913 the income tax law was passed. "I'll be damned if I'm going to pay half of my income to the government," said Ellis.

"It's a federal law," said Ida frowning. "If you don't, you'll probably get into a lot of trouble,"

"I don't think the damn law is constitutional," fussed Ellis. "even if it is a Constitutional Amendment. Before that it was ruled unconstitutional by the Supreme Court."

He paced back and forth across the living room. "Some day it will crush us all to support a runaway arm of government in addition to financing all the wars governments like to fight. Already we're meddling in Mexico's affairs, and have an army down there to show them how to run the government. Let the Mexicans and all of the other countries settle their own affairs, just like we settled ours with England."

He set his jaw in determination, "If they want my money, they'll damn well have to come and get it."

It took the federal agents awhile, but that is exactly what they did. One morning a short, stocky, well-groomed man in a navy blue pinstriped business suit appeared in Ellis' office. He didn't wait to be called in, but strode up to Ellis and showed his identification. "I'm Joe York, with the Internal Revenue Service," he said with an air of authority. "It has come to our attention that you did not file tax returns for the past year as required by law."

Ellis took him into the office. He later complained to Ida, "It was a damn rip-off, but I had to give the sonofabitch two-hundred-and-fifty dollars to get him off my back."

One day a messenger came running into Ellis' office, with the message the deputy sheriff needed him down by the Post Office. "They were digging there, and dug up a body!" the excited man volunteered.

Ellis hurried down by the post office and found a crowd gathered there. He jostled his way to the digging, and found that the remains of a good sized man had been found, buried in a shallow grave. He immediately thought of Albin Lindstrom, whose brother had come up missing, and wondered if this was what had befallen the man. They took the remains over to the hospital, and Ellis found the man had been dead somewhere in the neighborhood of fifteen years. It was evident by his crushed skull that he had been the victim of foul play.

They interred the corpse in the cemetery, in the good sized section where unidentified or indigent people were laid to rest. "For the size of the town, we have a bigger Potter's Field than most communities several times this large," Ellis commented to the deputy, as they gazed out toward the west.

"Yes," he agreed, "this town has had more than its share of unidentified deaths over the years."

That night at dinner, Ellis told Ida about the body which had been dug up.

"Though the town in general has been improved in a lot of ways, I hear since the Grand Jury didn't do anything about what was going on around here, Ashler is bragging that he can get away with anything, and the law doesn't dare touch him," Ida said.

The mention of his enemy brought an angry glint to Ellis' eyes, and his mouth tightened in a grim line. He shifted in his chair trying to dispel the anger. He squinted at her for a long minute, then sighed, and went back to eating.

Henry came into the hospital one day quite out of breath. "Some girl out north of town said the hired man raped her and the sheriff sent a posse out to pick the fellow up. A mob is trying to string him up, right on Main Street." he panted.

Ellis put on his hat and hurried down the street towards the group. "Hello, Doc," said one of the men preparing the rope.

Ellis didn't stop. "I hope you know what you're doing," he said quietly, then continued walking down the street.

Looks of perplexity came on the men's faces and they stopped to talk it over for a minute. "Maybe we should take Doc's warning, and let the law take care of him," said one fellow.

"Doc usually knows what he's talking about," said another, who had been operated on earlier by Ellis.

At last they decided to take the man to the jail instead of hanging him.

Ida and Ellis were no strangers to trigger happy mobs with a rope in their hands, and to peace officers and courts determined to right a wrong, even where there was no wrong to right. A few days later the girl admitted she was in love with the fellow and he had rejected her advances, so she had become angry and lied about being raped.

"Good Lord, Doc, I'm glad you came by when you did and stopped us from stringing up an innocent man," one fellow told Ellis.

Ellis never fully trusted the men involved, after that. "Anyone unstable enough to go along with a lynch mob can't be counted on in any emergency. They're just like those who followed the Pied Piper," he told Ida.

A newspaper man came to Soda Springs from Cripple Creek, Colorado, and bought the *Idaho Chieftain*. He was a member of the group in the newspaper profession known as a "boom-town printers." For years he had transported his equipment in a wagon, and moved to towns where sudden growth occurred from gold rushes or other activities.

The medical profession also had its share of these transient people, known as "boom-town doctors" and "tramp nurses." They had made quite a name for themselves. An occasional doctor of that group would come through Soda Springs, but never stayed long when they found the town had a doctor. Several settled temporarily in Gem Valley.

When a "tramp nurse" came through, Ellis tried to get her to stay because these nurses were often some of the best and had nursed at many of the big hospitals around the country.

Mr. W. H. Hildreth was a fluent editor, and his articles delighted the citizens of Soda Springs. He had been at the center of big labor problems and the rise of labor to protect itself, and he had always sided with the common man. Appalled at the rich and their underhanded doings while they tried "to thread their way into heaven" with grand philanthropic projects, he wanted to get away from it all. He came first to Bancroft and finally to settle in Soda Springs, which he promptly dubbed "Sunny Salubrious Sunkist Soda Springs." Soon they were supporting a semi-pro baseball team known affectionately as the "Fizz-water Team."

The newspaper equipment was single-print, and each letter of each word had to be picked out with a pair of tweezers and put into place, one at a time. Ellis became well acquainted with the man, and helped him finance purchase of a line-o-type machine, which was a tremendous step forward in the newspaper business in Soda Springs. The new equipment cost a thousand dollars, which was a large amount of money at that time.

Mr. Hildreth was a very intelligent and highly educated man. He quickly became friends with the town's stray dog, Mr. McDougal. The dog was getting old, but was still a beautiful animal, and a favorite of many of the townspeople as well as the pool hall group.

It was a solemn bunch at the bar and gambling tables, when they discovered Mr. McDougal had vacated his earthly body and left his friends behind. "He was a great pal, one of the best," declared a man named Claire. "I'll sure miss seeing him around."

"He hadn't even seemed sick," said the bartender, shaking his head. "It was a terrible shock to learn he had died."

"I wonder if dogs have spirits and will be raised in the resurrection," questioned John. "Mr. McDougal was almost more human than animal."

"I'm sure they do," said Claire. He thought a minute. "Doesn't the Bible say something about God making all things before he placed them on the earth?" he asked.

"Well, if any dog had a spirit, it was Mr. McDougal. It seems to me he was a lot more deserving of resurrection than some of the men around here," added Donald.

"Seems to me he ought to at least have a decent burial," insisted Claire.

"Well, what are we doing sitting here. The cemetery is just a stones throw away. Let's go give him a proper burial," quipped John.

The sad group of half a dozen men filed out the door of the saloon, picked up their shovels, and met at the cemetery. They picked a choice spot, a little higher than some of the surrounding area, and began to dig.

Soda Springs had quite a few Masons, and they had a fine Masonic Hall. Some of these men belonged to the order. It was an exclusive group, and membership carried a good deal of respectability.

"With a character like McDougal had, he should have been a Mason. He'd have been an honor to the lodge," said Donald, downing the last drop in a fresh bottle of whisky. "I'll run back over to the saloon and get a few drinks to soften the blow of our great loss," he told the others.

Donald was soon back with drinks around. The hole was getting deep enough so the inebriated little group of mourners was having some difficulty staying above ground rather than in the intended burial spot.

"I propose we make McDougal, who certainly deserved the honor, an honorary member of our lodge," said Claire.

"Aye," chorused the group.

"And it isn't too late to bury him with Masonic honors," said John. "Let's go have another drink on that," he proposed.

The burial detail trooped back to the saloon and had several drinks to try and drown their sorrow, then returned to the task at hand. Claire inserted his shovel into the hole, and got a prompt, "Hey, watch it," from the depths of the grave.

"Who in the hell's down there?" asked John.

"I don't know," said Claire, but it didn't sound like McDougal. They fished out the unlucky man who had fallen in before the last round of drinks and finished opening the grave, then trooped over to the Masonic Hall for burial clothing and arrangements. When they had donned their robes and had McDougal dressed, they each walked by for the viewing. "He looks so natural," commented John, his eyes damp. "The sheepskin apron looks so fitting on him."

"Yes, if anyone ever led a pure life, he did," commented Claire sadly. "He never done anyone wrong."

"Sit down, and we'll have the services," said Donald. "Fellow mourners, lend me your ear. We are gathered together at this time to pay our last respects to our friend, McDougal. He was a loyal servant of the Master, and we shall all miss his friendly brown eyes and wagging tail. He was our friend, and we all loved him, but as Shakespeare said, 'The evil men do lives after them, the good is oft interred with their bones,' and so be it with the noble McDougal."

"McDougal didn't do any evil," John broke in.

"Be quiet—that's the way it goes," declared Donald.

"It's my turn to speak," said Claire. "This loyal beast will be remembered by us all. It is a sad parting, and we will all miss him. What few honors we can give him now are but a paltry reminder of our inevitableness. Let us all be inspired to follow his example of kindness and love. He came to our town many years ago, and suffered great hardships. He has met his friends daily with tail wagging and barking hello in spite of hunger and thirst. He has been an asset to our community..."

John hopped up and waved his arm. "Oh ye of little faith, why mourn this noble creature, when we should be celebrating his entry into the spirit world. Christ brought us hope through the resurrection, and this, our friend, will be resurrected in that glorious day appointed. Let's carry these earthly remains to the site we have prepared to house his earthly body until that great day."

Just a minute, said Claire and he began to read: "Brethren—The melancholy event which has caused us to assemble on the present occasion cannot have failed to impress itself on the mind of everyone present. The loss of a friend and Brother—especially of one whose loss we now deplore—conveys a powerful appeal to our hearts, reminding us as it does of the uncertainty of life, and of the vanity of earthly hopes and designs.

"Amid the pleasures, the cares, and the various avocations of life we are too apt to forget that upon us also the common lot of all mankind must one day fall, and that Death's dread summons may surprise us even in the meridian of our lives, and in the full spring-tide of enjoyment and success.

"The ceremonial observances which we practice during the obsequies of a departed Brother, are intended to remind us of our own 'inevitable destiny,' and to warn us that we also should be likewise ready, for we know not the day nor the hour when in the case of each of us, the dust shall return to the earth as it was, and the spirit shall return unto God who gave it.

"Then Brethren, let us lay these things seriously to heart; let us strive in all things to act up to our Masonic profession, to live in accordance with the high moral precepts inculcated in our Ceremonies, and to practically illustrate in our lives and our actions the ancient tenants and established customs of the Order. Thus in humble dependance upon the mercy of the Most High, we may hope, when this transitory life, with all its cares and sorrows, shall have passed away, to rejoin this our departed friend and Brother in the Grand Lodge above, where the world's Great Architect lives and reigns forever."

"So mote it be" chanted the others.

"May we be true and faithful, and may we live in fraternal affection one towards another, and die in peace with all mankind."

"So mote it be," sung the little group.

"May we practice that which is wise and good, and always act in accordance with our Masonic profession."

"So mote it be."

"May the Great Architect of the Universe bless us, and direct us in all that we undertake and do in His Holy Name."

"So mote it be."

They solemnly loaded the dog into one of the buggies and transported him to the cemetery and deposited his remains in the open grave. Donald threw his roll into the grave.

"Glory be to God on high! On earth peace! Goodwill towards men!" said Claire.

"So mote it be, now henceforth and for evermore!"

"There is a calm for those who weep,
A rest for weary pilgrims found;
They softly lie and sweetly sleep
Low in the ground!. . ."

responded the men in song.

"With due respect to the deceased, this is enough," said Donald. Let's consign his body to the earth without further adieu.''

He broke a sprig of evergreen off the nearest tree then walked around the grave several times and tossed it in, to symbolize eternal life. Claire broke off a larger limb and dragged it to the grave. Just then the train roared by, and it's shrill whistle startled the fellows. They all came close to falling into the open grave, but only Claire did. Donald tipped his tall black hat to the train solemnly.

''Look what you've done. You've messed him all up,'' said John, helping his friend out of the grave, almost being pulled in himself. He picked up a shovel and threw the first shovel of earth in on top of the dog's body.

''I can't do it,'' cried Donald. ''Let's get another drink to give us courage to do the task which must now be done.''

They jumped into the buggy and went back to the saloon where the mourners consumed another shot of courage. It took several shots for some of them before they could return to finish filling the grave.

Their escapade would probably have gone by unnoticed if Mr. Hildreth hadn't heard about it and seen fit to write a glowing obituary about the stray of the Salubrious Sun-kissed Soda Springs, complete with burial account, to put in the next newspaper.

Many of the good ladies of Soda Springs were shocked to learn that a dog had been buried in their cemetery, and quickly demanded the animal be removed. After several days of badgering by their female companions and friends, the men agreed to exhume and move the remains. They went out one night, and stirred up the dirt at the grave, and said the dog had been moved to a more suitable location. This quieted the uproar.

Doctor Anderson died and the drug store was purchased by a couple of enterprising young fellows who started a club there. "What kind of a club is it?" asked Ida.

"Well, said Ellis with a grin," there's a lot of card playing going on, and I hear they call it 'The Ring 'Em, Sling 'Em, Pop 'Em Club.' or 'The Chamber With the Broken Handle'."

"What on earth do they call it that for?" asked Ida, shocked at such names.

"I suspect," said Ellis, "the name comes from taking canned heat, crushing it and putting it in the women's silk stockings, and slinging it around until the alcohol separates. Then they wring the alcohol out and drink it. It's damn hard on stockings, but the resulting drink carries quite a wallop, I hear."

"What on earth will these young people think of next!" exclaimed Ida, looking shocked. "I can hardly believe what goes on in this town."

"I hear they also get spirits of niter and boil the alcohol off, but when they don't get all the niter out, it affects the kidneys, and boy does it run them to the outhouse." added Ellis.

In 1915 Dr. Russell Tigert settled in Soda Springs. He was a cousin of Charlie Fryar. Dr. Tigert had graduated from the University of Tennessee also, which had been moved to Memphis by that time. Ellis welcomed help to share the burden of caring for the community which was becoming too much for one doctor. He soon was steering many patients, especially maternity cases, to Doctor Tigert.

That year a gymnasium was added to the school and athletics introduced into the curriculum. The upper floor of the building was used for the high school, and the lower floor for the grades. An auditorium upstairs was used for all school functions. Ida was excited about helping get the first yearbook for the high school started. She felt it helped unify the school and increase school spirit when they came out with the first edition of "The Crest." The new gymnasium, and the advent of basketball, helped keep kids who were inclined to drop out, in school. Those who had dropped out soon started a team and played at the old Gorton Hall, often challenging the school team.

Mr. Eastman had taken up law, and was extremely successful as an attorney. He seemed much happier than he had been in the drug store. Before long he was appointed probate judge.

Katherine Petersen brought her eleven-year-old girl, Sophie, in from Grays Lake with severe stomach pains. Warren was out on the trap line, and it had been some time before the worried mother had found a neighbor who could bring them into town. The four little girls in the family were frail and sickly from inadequate diet. Ellis had suggested the spring before when he stopped at their place that they plant plenty of turnips and see the girls were allowed to eat all they wanted.

A previous appendectomy had caused adhesions which blocked the intestine and caused infection to spread through her abdomen. Ellis could tell peritonitis had already set in from the board like rigidity of the abdominal muscles, and said he must operate immediately. Katherine wanted to wait and try to get word to Warren first, but Ellis told her the girl must have surgery without waiting if she were to have a chance.

Though Ellis did his best, he wasn't sure the child would make it. She had that fragile, almost translucent bluish-white coloring, and a peacefulness about her which made Ellis uneasy. They wheeled her into a hospital room. Every step she heard in the hall she asked if it were her father.

"He'll be too late," she said as she opened her eyes and looked toward the upper corner of the room as though she could see someone there. "Will you play with me all of the time?" she asked. "Here they say I'm either too young or too old to play with."

She smiled as if she had a satisfactory answer. "I'll sing you a song," she said, and started singing "All Through the Night" softly in a weak voice. When she got to the second verse, it was a whisper, on the third, she was only mouthing the words, but no sound was escaping her parched lips. When she finished the song, she looked toward the corner again. "You want me to come with you?" she asked, then closed her eyes in death. Ellis tried to say the right things to comfort the distraught mother, but the words stuck in his throat, and he felt he was of little help. His own heart was heavy, as her grief brought back the tragic loss of his own children, reopening an old wound and causing it to throb.

Ida felt like an unnecessary piece of furniture now that Ellis' practice had become so intense and time consuming. She continued to be depressed by the house, and she began to contemplate leaving Soda Springs.

One night when Ellis was particularly late getting home she waited up for him, which she hadn't been doing since Margaret's death. Ellis was surprised and wondered why she was still up.

"I have to talk to you," Ida insisted.

"It's rather late," said Ellis wearily.

"I know it's late, but this can't wait," said Ida. "I hardly ever get a chance to talk to you. You're so concerned about medicine, you don't give a damn about your family any morc. We always come second," she accused. "We might as well not even be here."

A swell of caring arose in her throat and made talking difficult. This wasn't how she'd meant things to be.

"Now, Idie, that's not true," said Ellis. "You know I've always loved you and Evan, and the other children, too."

"I'm sorry it has to be that way, but I can't stay in this God forsaken house any longer. Ellis, I'm already packed and I'm taking Evan and leaving." She had to work to keep her voice from shaking.

Ellis looked at Ida with a startled face. He walked to the window and looked out over the sleeping town for a long while. It was some time before he could speak. He reached up and ran his fingers through his hair, which perpetually stood on end. Ellis looked tired. He hunched his shoulders. The lines in his face had deepened during the past few months more than Ida had realized. "Where are you going?" he finally asked sinking into a chair. The arms of the chair felt cold and unfamiliar.

"I'm going to Pocatello for now," said Ida. "After we get things settled, I'll probably go to California where the climate is warmer," she added.

"I don't suppose I could talk you out of leaving?" he asked quietly in a flat voice. One quick glance at her face, filled with resolve, told him there'd be no budging her.

"No, Ellis, my mind is made up," said Ida drawing a slow breath as she walked out of the room.

Ida slept peacefully that night, relieved that she had finally made a decision and made a stand. All night Ellis lay awake feeling progressively weaker with the aftershock of Ida's stated intentions. He thought of his life, and what had become of it. He imagined Ida as she looked the day he left to come West, and her arrival on the train. He went over and over the early days of their marriage when they had been so much in love. They had been dirt poor, but they were happy. How he had wished in those days that he could give her the fine things she deserved. So much had happened since that time. He had failed to provide the love and attention his family really needed. It seemed tragedy had always been standing at his bedside, staring him in the face. He felt exhausted and defeated.

There was no divorce, and neither of them ever sought or had any inclination toward remarriage. They drew up papers of separation, and Ida took Evan and left. It was agreed that Evan would spend the summers, when he was out of school, with his father.

Ida took most of the furniture and the car, but only enough money to get by on. She had an excellent business head on her shoulders, and was soon doing well financially on her own. After a few months, she traded the car for a more dependable one, and took Evan and drove to California. The trip was a nightmare. It took fifteen days. The roads were terrible, and the engine choked up with penetrating dust. Even trains stopped to help Ida and her son when they had trouble, which seemed to be unending.

It wasn't long until Ellis bought a Ford "Run-About." It was a one-seater, but Shep usually rode along with the doctor. Ellis found the house unbearably quiet and lonely. He went about his duties and found the only thing which kept his mind off his personal problems was the practice of medicine, which had always been an overpowering influence in his life. His time at home was spent motionless, sitting in his chair staring at first one thing and then another. Without his family there, his life was very different. The house seemed strange, silent, and hostile. Sometimes he felt his greatest misfortune was that he was not in his grave long ago.

After the first year, Ellis hired Walter and Maggie Bolton to live there. She did the housework, and Walter cared for the Soda Springs Ranch.

Daily Ellis cursed Ashler and those who had made their lives less than congenial in Soda Springs. He told himself he had to go forward, not look back, and silence the past. He began reading again. He read and digested thousands of pages of medical writings, and continued to read the poets, in whose words he found some comfort and meaning for life. His practice continued to grow, and he continued to be a benefactor to the community.

Phil Revell, a young man from Ogden, Utah, heard about Dr. Kackley from a friend who had been operated on by Ellis. He drove his father, who had a tooth pulled and got an infected jaw, to Soda Springs. The doctor in Utah had wanted to operate and scrape the jaw. There were no hotel rooms available in Soda Springs. They were all filled with Ellis' patients.

Ellis checked the man and gave him a prescription. "If it doesn't get better right away, bring him back," he told the boy. "What do we owe you, Doctor?" he asked.

"Just pay for the prescription, and be damn careful driving back," Ellis said.

The husband of a family homesteading at Chub Springs died from flu. While most young women would have given up trying to homestead after being widowed at twenty, Laura, the wife, had stayed and was trying to eke out a living in the isolated outpost. She had two little girls to support, and was having a helluva time of it.

Laura dressed like one of the boys, with a pistol slung on her hip, and matched the men with drink and language in the western saloons. Because of a clash with a sheriff when she and her husband were first married, and because she had shot the heels off the boots of a cowboy who tried to get out of line with her, she soon became known as "Six-Shooter-Sal."

Ellis stopped in for a minute to see how she was doing whenever he had a chance. One late summer day he rode up to the homestead. Her cabin, the southernmost in a group of three, stood below a large outcropping of lava rocks, with tall quaking aspen trees and large beautiful pines growing among them. Ellis thought it was one of the prettiest settings he had ever seen.

The cabin was almost lost in the trees and the immense lava ridge above it. It was a single room about fifteen by twenty feet, with a door at the front and windows on each of the other sides. There was a lean-to on the back, and a rock storage cellar next to the lava outcropping behind the lean-to.

He found Sal cutting wood for winter. To survive in the wintertime was not easy. In this country to run out of wood would mean suffering from cold and possible death. She had roped fallen trees and dragged them with her horse to the cabin, and was sawing them up for winter wood. Ellis was surprised at the size of the pile she had accumulated.

Sal invited the doctor inside for a cup of coffee. She appreciated anyone she knew and trusted stopping in to help dispel the terrible loneliness she felt since her husband's death. Inside, a stove in the center of the room provided heat and was also used for cooking.

"How's it going, Sal?" Ellis asked.

"Not too good," she admitted. "I've tried to get on as a cowhand at the ranches in Grays Lake, but couldn't get hired, even though I'm a lot better hand than most of the men around here,'' she confided. ''I may have to get someone to watch the girls and go out of here to find work.''

''If you do, I know a woman in Soda who would probably be glad to watch the girls for you,'' said Ellis. ''Just let me know if you need help.''

''Thanks, Doctor,'' said Sal. ''I'll keep it in mind.''

Ellis thought about the lonely girl as he rode home. Being widowed at twenty years of age, and trying to support the girls by herself was certainly a difficult undertaking. He admired her spunk.

Chapter 13

On June 28, 1914, the world had been shocked by the assassination of Archduke Francis Ferdinand and his wife Sophie, heirs to the Austria-Hungary throne by a young Bosnian student who lived in Serbia. On July 28, Austria-Hungary declared war on Serbia. By October thirtieth the Central Powers—Austria-Hungary, Germany, and the Ottoman Empire were at war with the Allies—Belgium, France, Great Britain, Serbia, and Russia.

The United States tried to remain neutral, but as German submarines began sinking passenger ships and committing other atrocities against U.S. civilians, Ellis felt certain it was just a matter of time until the U.S. would enter the war.

The Kackleys had always gone to war, and Ellis felt it was his duty to enlist if the country did become involved in the fighting. He agreed with George Washington's warning in his farewell address, and was strongly opposed to the United States becoming involved in the constant wars in Europe.

Kackleys had both received and lost their lands and fortunes as a result of war. A lot of his ancestors had seen service in the Revolutionary War, some were mixed up in Indian wars, and they were involved in the Civil War—the outcome of which had devastated their economic lives.

When a national law was passed during George Washington's administration entitling veterans to land, many family members had moved into Ohio, into the county where Johnny Appleseed hailed from, and under the Northwest Territory Act became landowners. The Civil War, with subsequential governorships and troops stationed in the south by Lincoln, had reduced family members from being landowners to living in poverty.

Ellis objected to slavery, but in all other aspects his

sympathies were with the South. While the Civil War was over, as civilization crept into the West, even in far off Idaho, people still quarreled and fought over Civil War loyalties, and more than one friendly drink turned into brawling and gun fighting. Rarely did it reach a point as did one episode Ellis heard of in New Mexico, when a man's head was blown off by his father-in-law's shotgun after mentioning at the dinner table that he had fought for the Union side in the Civil War. However, people's feelings were often strong and unbending.

Americans followed the events of this new war in Europe, which was involving much of the world, and the battles of Marne, Ypres, and Verdun. They sent supplies to the fighting forces. They saw the advent of poison gas used by the Germans in the second battle of Ypres, and the sinking of the British passenger liner Lusitania with 1,198 passengers aboard. One hundred twenty-eight were Americans.

Fighting at the Western Front was at a standstill from early in 1915 to 1917. Troops dug in and built a network of trenches for about 600 miles across France and Belgium. Some places only a few hundred yards separated opposing lines—an area known as no-man's land.

Second and third lines of trenches were built parallel to the first. Huge underground dugouts served as first-aid stations, supply stations, and temporary living quarters. Doctors stationed at the front worked in rain filled trenches and dugouts, sometimes in water up to the waist, with all the troops eventually infested with body lice commonly called "cooties." The trenches and surrounding areas, including dugouts, were swarming with rats, devouring the dead, and biting the living.

New and improved weapons with greater killing power were developed and tanks, trucks, automobiles, machine guns, motorcycles, airplanes, and bombs, trench mortars and heavy artillery were utilized to inflict destruction upon opposing sides. After Ypres, greatly improved lethal gas warfare was used by both sides at every opportunity, even to including in the heavy bullets, gas, which on explosion would attack those back in the lines.

On April 6, 1917, the U.S. declared war on Germany.

After a few months, which it took to put his affairs in order, Ellis enlisted in the army. He was commissioned as a first lieutenant in the medical corps. With Dr. Tigert there, he would not be leaving the area without a doctor, though Tigert would have his hands full.

He left Dr. Tigert in charge of the hospital and highly recommended him to his patients. Ellis was scheduled to leave for Ft. Riley, Kansas on Sunday March thirty-first.

Hearing of his planned departure, twenty ladies of the community met to plan a farewell party for Ellis. Committees were appointed for a reception, program, amusement, decoration and refreshment. A special committee headed by "Aunt Leah" Gorton was appointed to get Ellis' approval and promise to attend.

On Saturday, March 30, 1918, Ellis entered the school house auditorium and gymnasium to find one of the largest crowds ever assembled in any public place in Soda Springs. Friends and patients had come from all over; there were around 350 people in attendance. Even Pat Horton was there. An emotional, patriotic program of music and recitation was followed by a speech by Judge Eastman. "Dr. Kackley never failed to respond to a call, night or day, and no matter what the condition of the weather. He is one of the best surgeons in Idaho and his leaving is a sad blow to Soda Springs," he said.

The emotional crowd called for a speech by Ellis. He responded with heartfelt thanks for the friendship shown him on the occasion and during the twenty years he had resided in Soda Springs. "I promise to return after the war is over, and end my days in the most perfect and best of towns in Idaho—Soda Springs," he said.

He realized as he looked at familiar faces, saddened by his impending departure, that in spite of all that had happened to him in this western town, it was home, and he loved the area and most of the people here.

The decorations of the auditorium exceeded anything ever seen in the town. On the north wall was a great and glorious American flag and to the left a small rebel flag.

"Dr. Kackley is a rebel Democrat, you know, but he's not dangerous," said Ellen Woodall laughing.

The name Lieutenant Kackley was worked in red, white, and blue on another wall. "There must be a million streamers," said Mrs. Strachan.

Some one proposed the Virginia Reel and two strings of dancers were at once formed, with Dr. Kackley and Mrs. Woodall heading one of the strings. After dancing for some time, a bunch of "southern minstrels" entered thc hall and entertained the group for half-an-hour with singing and dancing. At eleven o'clock, punch and cake were served.

Again Ellis' flair for the dramatic surfaced, as he made the moment memorable by standing at attention at the door and shaking the hand of each guest as they took their leave, wishing them a kind good night and goodby.

Several people hung back until the crowd thinned out and they could get a minute to talk privately with the doctor. Pat Horton was one of these, who waited to speak to Ellis. Ellis wondered why. He had never cared for Pat since he had shot Wink some seventeen years earlier, though he had treated the family with the same professional consideration he gave to any other of his patients.

Pat approached him hesitantly. "Doctor, I'm sorry to see you go. I know you've never cared for me since I shot your dog, and I just want you to know I'm sorry. I didn't want you to go to war without getting a chance to apologize. "Can you forgive me?" he asked holding out his hand and looking into Ellis' face.

Ellis was touched by his sincerity. Seventeen years of animosity began to melt with his apology, and Ellis shook the outstretched hand.

"It's damn good of you to apologize, Pat," Ellis said sincerely. "This isn't the time for holding grudges."

They both felt relieved by the reconciliation of good will.

One old fellow from Gem Valley whose severe cases of the D.T.'s Ellis had treated for years, came up with tears in his eyes. "My God, Doc, what am I going to do when I get the D.T.'s?" he asked.

"Stop by and see Dr. Tigert, he'll take care of you," Ellis assured the man.

Ellis wondered how the ladies had put together such a grand affair in the three days they had known he was leaving. He was touched by the kindness and concern of the people of the area.

He was at the train depot early the next day, and even though it was Sunday, most of the town was there to see him off. The station platform was jammed with well-wishers. At forty-seven, Ellis was much older than the typical kid enlisting in the war. The train was filled with soldiers, sailors, and other young men who were joining the armed forces. As he swung on board, the townspeople were yelling at the boys on the train, telling them what a good doctor they were getting. One with sense of humor, yelled back at the crowd, "Hell, we don't need doctors, we need good cooks."

Ellis stared out the window of the pullman as the countryside rolled past. He thought about the trip, twenty years before, when he had first come to Soda Springs. So much had transpired since that time. He had experienced the best and the worst times of his life, yet he couldn't help feeling he hadn't really lived until he came West.

Changing engines, changing trains, they worked their way toward their destination. Ellis thought about the library of great classics he and Ida had enjoyed so much after buying the Codman place. They had become acquainted with the great poets and their philosophy of life, which had influenced his way of thinking so very much. Through them he had developed understanding of and reconciliation with his life, the tragedies which had been such an integral part of him, the fleeting joys of children's voices, lost love, the satisfaction of devoting his life to helping others. The last nine lines of Thanatopsis were to him an infinite future and promise of the Great Creator. He often quoted these lines of Bryant, and now went over them in his mind:

So live, that when thy summons comes to join
The innumerable caravan which moves
To that mysterious realm where each shall take
His chamber in the silent halls of death,
Thou go not, like the quarry-slave at night,
Scourged to his dungeon; but, sustain'd and soothed
By an unfaltering trust, Approach Thy grave
Like one who wraps the drapery of his couch
About him, and lies down to pleasant dreams.

One of the few non-essential items Ellis took with him was a volume of Robert Burns' poems. Burns, Bryant, and Gray had sustained him through the hard times of life.

When Ellis arrived at Ft. Riley for basic training, he soon found out there was very little military training for doctors. It was almost like a family reunion when he saw so many of those he had known in medical school, who also had answered the call of their country, and were awaiting assignments.

Units were being assembled and shipped to the front as rapidly as possible. Ellis was assigned to the Forty-third Coast Artillery. It wasn't long until he was on his way to France. As the troop ship sailed out of New York Harbor, Ellis stared at the Statue of Liberty and wondered if he would ever see American soil again. It was the first time since he came West, fresh out of medical school, he had felt the terror of wondering if he could handle the situation in which he was voluntarily placing himself. Here he was on his way to war. The enemy would be shooting at them. Though doctors were non-combatants in the U.S. Army, the troops he was with would soon be shooting at the enemy. He would be there to try and patch up the wounds of this crazy activity called war, which made no rhyme nor reason.

Much to Ellis' embarrassment, he became violently seasick. One of the telegraphers had taken a liking to Ellis, and helped nurse him through the nausea and vomiting. He raised his head, with some effort, when Bill brought a cup of warm broth to his bunk. "Come on doctor, try and get a little of this down. Even if it doesn't stay for long, it will help some."

Ellis was too ill to even feel like answering, but he tried to stammer out his thanks between bouts of vomiting. Here he was on his way to help the sick, and he couldn't even hold his head up. They were headed for the Western Front—six-hundred miles from the English Channel to Switzerland, of men in trenches and barbed wire barriers—separating hand-to-hand combatants in the largest armies ever seen to that time. While air warfare was in it's infancy, it was beginning to be used, as airplanes met in "dogfights." The words from Burns' poem, which he had read over and over, came to Ellis' mind:

More pointed still we make ourselves
Regret, remorse, and shame!
And Man, whose heav'n-erected face
The smiles of love adorn—
Man's inhumanity to man
Makes countless thousands mourn!

The troops were assuring each other that the war would be over in a few weeks, but few believed what they were saying.

When Ellis arrived in France, he and the other doctors on the ship went to field hospitals. The Forty-third went by railroad car as far as they could, then marched the rest of the way. Though quite a distance from the front lines, casualties were pouring in faster than they could be treated. The Germans were well entrenched, had broken through the lines, and were periodically lobbing shells into Paris. Morale of the French soldiers was low. Fire power was in the hands of the Germans. In the Somme drive, the English poured in hundreds of thousands of troops.

England and France wanted to integrate the American troops into the French and English Armies as individual replacements to be absorbed by their armies—their lives lost to history and to their rightful honors. Gen. John J. Pershing insisted on keeping the American troops intact as units, rather than letting them serve as individual replacements. These units formed the American First Army, and took part in thirteen major operations of the war.

Ellis' unit, the Forty-Third Coast Artillery, took part in four major battles. They were stationed where the first battle of Verdun had been fought. There as a medical officer, he was working alongside two companies of French. Ellis and his companions went through the communication lines, the back up lines, and into the trenches and dugouts. Wherever the stretcher bearers were, Ellis went. They had to cut passages through heavy barbed wire with huge barbs. The medical personnel would try to cut their way through and bring out the wounded in the middle of the night. They would hide in shell holes half full of water, but had to stand up to carry the stretchers which had one man in front and one in back. Occasional flares would light up large areas. They were instructed that even if standing, not to dive for shell holes, or the enemy would notice the movement and be sure to fire on them. Patrols from both sides were always trying to pick up prisoners. Doctors would get into dugouts which had curtains so the enemy could not see the light, and treat the wounded as best they could under the conditions. Doctors stationed at the front line trench saw absolute hell.

The front line was sandbagged with rifles sticking through the bags. Periscopes were extensively used. Occasionally, during the day, both sides had such heavy losses they declared a short truce to pick up their dead and wounded men.

Besides the Forty-Third Coast Artillery, Ellis was soon assigned as medical officer to the two French Companies which had no medical officer. While doctors, Red Cross personnel, and chaplains in the American Army were non-combatants, the French had no such category. Ellis became good friends with a Catholic Priest in one of these French units.

As a medical officer, Ellis had an orderly assigned to him, which he felt was unnecessary. When the man reported to him every morning, Ellis would dismiss him and that was the last he would see of him throughout the day. Ellis had no interest in rank and privilege.

Eventually, with the assistance of General Pershing and his American troops, the Allies began to drive the German troops back. The English brought horses to the front, which was a luxury most of the units did not enjoy.

The first major battle Ellis took part in was Aisine-Marne, also known as the second Verdun. It was one nasty battle, and Ellis' introduction to battlefield warfare. The hill was small, compared to Western standards, and was known as Dead Man's Hill. It had been fought over many times before. The men fought side by side. When it came to picking up the wounded, Father Lateur, went beside Ellis to administer last rites. Ellis had only his medical knowledge and ability, which didn't furnish much of a shield of protection from flying bullets. American casualties were extremely heavy, and as Ellis assisted bands of men in rescuing troops who had been wounded, he instructed them, "Don't worry about the dead, just see if you can find anyone alive."

In spite of his instructions, the stretchers brought back many who were dead or died on the way to receive medical help. "Over here," he shouted to Father Lateur, as he knelt beside a soldier who was nearly dead, and losing so much blood it was only a matter of time. The young man was asking for last rites to be administered to him. As the men went about, looking at the torn and mangled wounded for signs of life, Ellis stopped again and again, doing the best he could for each man. From everywhere cries of anguish rent the air and mingled with the sound of distant fire. As Ellis bent over a young soldier to tend to his wounds, a sniper, not honoring the short truce, leveled his gun on the doctor and a bullet whizzed past his head. Father Lateur quickly picked up the injured soldier's gun and shot the sniper. Without his quick action, Ellis knew he would have been dead. The bond of friendship was cemented, and from that moment on, Father Lateur had a profound effect on Ellis' life and thinking.

The artillery fire was blowing up the dead as well as killing and injuring the living. Remains of a Karl Mueller had been uncovered, and Ellis picked up the skull, which was lying at his feet. To Ellis, the skull was a tool to improve his medical efficiency, and he took it back to his dugout to study.

Ellis' second major battle was the Saint Mihiel battle of September, 1918. This was the first distinctly American offensive of the war, when Brigadier General William Mitchell directed the war's largest aerial assault, with one-thousand, four-hundred-eighty-one Allied airplanes taking part.

The Allies swept toward the Meuse-Argonne region and took over a large portion of the battle line, helping break through the fortified Hindenburg line which stretched almost across France. Here Ellis was involved in his third major battle.

"The history of great American land battles has always been to throw in heavy troops and try to obliterate the opposing lines,'' Ellis told Father Lateur with some bitterness.

This great sacrifice of human lives, smashed the Hindenburg line and sent Generals Ludendorff and Hindenberg running with their troops, many surrendering. The two generals were in a panic, signaling Kaiser Wilhelm II, that they could not stop the breakthrough and should get out of the war.

About one million two hundred thousand American troops participated. One of every ten, one hundred twenty-thousand, were killed or wounded—more casualties than at Gettysburg or any of the Civil War battles. Ellis was horrified by what men were inflicting upon each other, as he continued to apply his skill to patching up the mangled bodies of his fellow soldiers, their trauma burning in their eyes.

This battle was followed by one in a defensive sector. Ellis used all his skill and surgical speed on those who might be saved, and cursed the effects of war and the death and destruction it brought. He felt helpless when casualties came in and there wasn't enough help or facilities to care for them. All he could do was work on as many as possible. Father Lateur gave a great deal of emotional support to Ellis, cementing their friendship.

With the intervention of the airplane and tank, trench warfare had decreased. As the soldiers fought, Allied airplanes dropped thousands of copies of the ''Fourteen Points'' Wilson had announced as a basis for a post-war peace settlement, over enemy territory, giving many enemy peoples hope for a just peace settlement, and encouraging them to overthrow their governments.

The Austro-Hungarian empire was crumbling rapidly. The Hungarians, Czechs, Slovaks, and Poles declared their independence. On November third, representatives of Emperor Charles I agreed to an armistice, and left Germany standing alone. Mutinies flared among German troops as supplies of food and munitions dwindled. Germany was plagued by riots. At five o'clock in the morning on November 11th, delegates from Germany signed an armistice. Fighting was stopped on all battle grounds at eleven that morning. World War I had ended.

Ellis was having good success with the boys he treated on the front lines until a flu epidemic hit, and after the cold trip back to the hospital, many came down with secondary lung infections, and they died by the thousands. When the flu came on, the boys ached all over for two or three days. Those who survived came down with a second spell of aching and fever in about ten days. Many were carried away with lung infections, toxemia, and heart failure. It was demoralizing to work so hard to save the men, only to lose them later.

When the outfit was shipped back to the U.S. and disbanded, the men Ellis had served with gave him a gold pocket watch for his outstanding service. On the outside they had "Verdun" engraved on the watch. An inscription on the inside said "1st Lt. Ellis Kackley, M.D., by the boys of Battery F, 43rd Artillery CAC AEF 1918."

Besides the watch, Ellis came home with a crucifix given to him by Father Lateur pinned in his inside coat pocket. From then on, when he changed suits he always pinned it inside his coat. He also received permission to bring the skull of Karl Mueller home with him, for medical use.

Ellis had returned to the U.S. still under military orders, and went to Washington, D. C., where he requested a discharge, but was refused. Now that the European war was over, Ellis didn't want to waste any time getting back to Soda Springs. He knew Senator Borah from Idaho well, and went to request his help in getting discharged.

"You'll be out of the service tomorrow morning," Borah, who was known as "The Lion of Idaho," promised Ellis, and he was, in spite of the fact he said "To hell with you," when they instructed him in the long procedure of officially checking-out, which included getting receipts from commissaries within Maryland and Washington, D. C., many places where he had never been stationed.

Chapter 14

As the train pulled into the Soda Springs station, Ellis looked wearily at the familiar scene. He was tired and disillusioned from months on the battlefield, trying to bring help and comfort to the injured, but something inside him could not rest until he was home again.

As he stepped off the train, Jimmy hurried toward him and grasped his hand eagerly. "The doctor, it be!" he exclaimed. "Happy to see ya back, we 'ere. Aye, 'tis missin' ya we've been."

Jimmy's face sobered. "While ya've been away, sa much has happened, Doctor. In trouble the farmers an' stock men 'ere right noo. Aye, feed the coontry, they did durin' the war, an' noo we doon't need them anymoore the government thinks."

It was good talking to Jimmy again, but Ellis was anxious to get home, so after a few minutes, he picked up his bags and started down the street toward the house—the house which had helped to ruin his life. It was a warm day for the time of year. As he came up the walk, the house seemed strange and silent until Shep recognized his step and began to bark. As Ellis entered the porch, the dog nearly knocked him down with his exuberant welcome. He stroked the dog and followed it into the house. As he opened the front door, he felt a wave of nostalgia, followed quickly by the painful remembrance of happiness long gone.

Maggie and Walter had continued to live there and take care of his interests while he was away. He greeted Maggie, then walked through the rooms. Things were essentially like he had left them. He ran his fingers across some of the books in the bookshelf and thought of the many evenings he and Ida had spent reading the classics together. Here he had found his greatest happiness and suffered his greatest sorrows.

Ellis found the area in recession, as Jimmy had said. The monetary resources of the country had been unable to take the shock of the abrupt change from war to peacetime economy. Banks went broke; farmers were having difficult times and many were losing everything they had.

Some leading citizens of Soda Springs had gone together and opened the Bank of Soda Springs, only to be caught in the economic slump. They were honorable men, and used their personal fortunes to make up the losses until they had paid back every penny invested. Some of them never recuperated from the losses.

Ellis loaned money to a lot of people, to help keep their farms and businesses intact. He never worried about getting paid back, but several who owed him money decided to give up, and brought him the title to their land, to pay their indebtedness before they left the area. They had practically starved to make the land produce, but some land, especially in the higher northern areas, was not suitable for growing crops because of the short growing season. In other places where irrigation was not feasible, there was not enough moisture for good crops. They were apologetic for not being able to pay back the money Ellis had loaned them. Ellis watched a gaunt couple, worn down by poverty, a large family, and struggling to get by, come up the walk in the dim evening light. They looked old, tired, gray, and sad. There were tears in the eyes of the plainly dressed woman. She had done everything she could, even taking in washing and boarding the school-marm to bring in a few extra dollars.

"Are you sure you want to leave?" Ellis asked. "You don't have to worry about what you owe me," he added putting a hand lightly on the man's shoulder.

"Doc, I wish I could give you back more than a piece of worthless land nobody will pay a nickel for," said the man. "There's no way we can make it here."

Ellis watched sadly as the couple went down the stairs to the street. He had seen their fortunes go downhill; seen them put a lien on the ranch to get a buggy, a harness, for seed to plant. He had treated them when sick or injured.

While the worst times only lasted about a year, it was devastating to those of the business and agricultural community who did not have sufficient funds to carry them through that short period while money was so tight.

Ellis found his services were still highly in demand. As soon as they heard he was back, patients came from all over to see the "Little Doctor" again, and soon it was business as usual.

Evan came to spend the summer with his father. When Dr. Tigert went on vacation, Evan gave chloroform and assisted his father while operating. Ellis enjoyed teaching his son about medicine.

Mr. Whitman, was a great-grand-nephew of the renowned Marcus Whitman, founder of the Walla Walla Mission in the Columbia Basin. In 1919 he was a state representative from Bannock County. He presented a bill in the House of Representatives proposing the creation of a new county in Southeastern Idaho with the county seat at Soda Springs.

Though Mr. Whitman made personal contacts with them, little interest was shown among the legislators. One day he was in conversation with a group of northern representatives discussing the pro and con of municipal power. He mentioned that Soda Springs had its own power plant which helped considerably in the financial promotion of the city. Through this avenue he gained a captive audience and was able to present and gain support for his proposition for a new county.

During days of heated debate, Mr. Whitman, with the help of the Citizen's Club in Soda Springs, which was sponsoring the creation of the new county, kept those legislators who appreciated a nip of whiskey supplied with amble booze to keep their throats wet. In March of 1919, the measure finally passed by a narrow margin. Caribou County was formed and the Fifteenth Legislature went down in history as the "Thirsty Fifteenth."

Idaho had one of the coldest winters ever known. The jet stream pushed across the Arctic Circle, and brought frigid air which plunged the mercury way below zero. Cattle froze to death, and animals had to be destroyed for lack of hay to feed them. Many of the cattlemen were financially wiped out. People would go into their chicken coops to find their chickens had frozen to death on their roost and were lying dead on the floor. Water pipes froze in the Kackley house and caused a lot of damage when they burst.

Ellis had a coal box in his office. When George Small delivered coal, he always charged for a ton-and-a-half, but when Ellis ordered from the other suppliers, they always charged for two ton. Ellis referred to it as a long-ton and a short-ton. George told Ellis that even though Susie had burned his accounts on the shingles under the eaves a few years earlier, people had been very good to pay, and he thought everyone had come in and paid him what they owed.

"When anyone is as damned honest as you are with other people, they ought to be honest with you," Ellis told him.

As if an outgrowth of the historical old fur rendezvous where trappers and Indians met, traded, and celebrated, the people from Caribou County and surrounding areas began gathering yearly at the Meadows, a large open range along the banks of Reservoir Lake two miles west of the Chester Store at Henry, and near the Fort Hall Indian Reservation. They called it the Henry Stampede and Stockman's Reunion, later dropping Stockman's Reunion.

That first year was held at the Hogan ranch at Chub Springs, but the second year the celebration was moved to the Meadows. It was much like the old rendezvous. There were no buildings or stands—just a corral for the horses and a newly laid out track for the races. Cowboys and Indians rode wild horses, raced, drank, and gambled. The Indians always won their share of the prizes. Great historical families of the Shoshone Bannock Reservation, as the Dixeys, Edmos, and Georges participated in the events. Some participants became nationally famous.

The rodeo itself was under the administrative abilities of early settler families and great cattle families whose brands were known far and wide in the West. These families included the Bittons, Larkins, Chesters, Reynolds, Hogans, and Owens.

"It's a time and place where no law of man or God holds good," said Ellis, who usually took time out of his busy schedule to spend a few hours at the Stampede each year. "That's why everyone has such a good time."

The three day celebration became a family event. Wives came along to enjoy the festivities or to protect their husbands from the "wild women" attending. Buckboards, rigs, and horses crowded the flat as the population of Henry swelled from around fifty to several thousand. Tents were pitched and families set up temporary quarters. Willows were in abundance and provided shade for the campers. During morning hours, men fished and hunted, or practiced with the lariat. Women visited, cooked over campfires, washed the family's clothes, and hung them on willows to dry.

In the afternoon everyone gathered for bronco riding, calf roping, bull dogging and racing. A bowery was built to protect the spectators from the hot sun. Occasionally a woman participated in the bronco riding or other events. Anita Studnick, who also rode in London; Louise Hardwick, from Miles City, Montana; and Laura "Six-Shooter Sal" Edwards were some of the female participants.

Capture and mastery of mustangs, which roamed wild over the plains and mountains, was a matter of intense pride. Cowboys, both Indian and white, tried to prove their ability to stick on the backs of the meanest horses that ever lived. Cinch straps were put on these wild horses, never ridden before, and it took a lot of skill to stay on their backs. There were always injuries; injuries were part of life for a cowboy. Ellis tried to attend during the afternoon when they were most likely to occur. He would return about five o'clock to his office, which would be overflowing after a few hours absence.

Afternoon events at the Stampede were often followed by all-night dancing, singing, and merrymaking. A large piece of canvas would be stretched on a flat spot of ground and waxed for dancing. Dust was so thick it took two or three days to settle after the festivities ended.

Every year the facilities improved as profits were turned into a grandstand, smaller stands, better advertisements, and camping grounds. In 1923 three professional riders came to participate in the stampede. By 1924, it attracted twenty-one professional riders, three of whom were local boys. The Henry Stampede continued until 1956, though moved to Soda Springs in later years. It became known as one of the oldest and best rodeos in the West.

The men involved were tough, hard-riding cowboys, who were born and bred on the cattle range. The events they participated in were every day activities for these Westerners, and many who started there, went on to big time. Homer Holkum from American Falls became the world's champion cowboy clown. He went each year to Madison Square Gardens, at a salary of one hundred dollars a day, plus expenses, where he delighted the thousands present with his queer makeup and antics. He had to be in the arena with the meanest broncos and the most vicious bulls, and even learned to ride them to make fun for the spectators.

Henry Hart from Pocatello became world champion bulldogger. Bill and Foss Lewis from Grays Lake became world champion riders. Bert Sibbetts, born at Grays Lake to homesteaders Samuel and Evelyn Sibbetts, became world champion of bareback riding. He received the silver saddle in the New Westminster stampede in Canada. In the 1924 Henry Stampede he made one helluva ride on "Broken Bones," the horse which had thrown Bob Askens, winner of the fourth place money at London that year and bucked off veteran rider C.R. Williams, with his five hundred dollar ruby and diamond set spurs and ninety dollar beaver hat. Area residents were duly proud of his skills. In 1928 he received the silver cup awarded by Sperry Flour Company, as world champion bull rider at Salinas, California. In 1929 he won silver spurs and silver adorned martingale—a forked strap for holding down a horse's head by connecting the head gear with the bellyband—in a rodeo in California.

Everet Colburn from Blackfoot furnished stock for the rodeo and later bought a large ranch in Texas, where he put on rodeos for Roy Rogers. One of the well known early cattle companies was the Warbonnet Outfit. John Sparks, cattle king who later became governor of Nevada, sold to the Warbonnet Outfit in 1879. Their headquarters ranch was on the south side of the Blackfoot River. They ran about ten to twelve thousand cattle, and were first to bring Durham cattle into this part of the country. Later they brought Hereford bulls to run with their herds.

They had some outstanding horsemen in their ranks, including Bill Brace and Bill Oliver who later joined Buffalo Bill's Wild West Show and toured Europe, playing Italy, France, and England. Warbonnet Cowboy Charles Russell became famous as a painter of western scenes.

When the cowboys came to town everyone knew they were there. They were wild and fearless; drinking, shooting, and gambling. In spite of their rough and uncouth appearance and behavior, they were known to be brave, big-hearted, and true blue.

Injuries from working with cattle and horses were not confined to rodeo times. Charlie Whitworth, a young fellow from Chesterfield in Gem Valley, jerked his thumb completely off while roping a steer at home. He got to Bancroft before he decided to go back and get his thumb. Dr. Kackley sewed it back on, and it healed and continued to be functional until he carried it to his grave.

Industrial medicine was in its infancy. In 1920 Anaconda Copper Company established the town of Conda nine miles north and east of Soda Springs on a spur of the Union Pacific Railroad. Vast quantities of phosphate ore were shipped from Conda to Montana, where it was processed as commercial fertilizer.

The plant was the only phosphate plant of Anaconda, and was built to use the abundant and overflowing supplies of sulfuric acid, a by-product of refining copper. When demand for copper was low, the Conda mine slowed down; when high, it went at full speed. Power was furnished by Utah Power and Light Company. When industrial accident insurance came to Conda, the men came to Ellis, but he was soon having problems with the company. Officials thought he was seeing too many people and seeing them too often.

"These big companies don't give a damn about the men. They're used to taking men like ore and throwing them into the slag pile when they're done with them," he told Henry. "They think because the men come in for treatment when they are sick, they are abusing the privilege. The big companies are fighting industrial insurance, but soon the day will come when they will have to have some kind of plan to take care of their employees."

"You're probably right," said Henry. "These big shots act all pious and like they're doing so much for the fellows, but I doubt if many of them really care a bit about the men."

The recession crippling the country gave way as the roaring twenties brought good times. Businesses started to expand, along with opportunities for work. The business district in Soda Springs enlarged. "Mom and Pop" stores became popular. In 1921 the town of Soda Springs became a second-class city.

In the fall of 1923, Evan entered Stanford. It was an enormous transition for him, like for most college freshmen, to be away from home and on his own. The first quarter was not quite understood, as if following a meandering compass; then came a realization that youthful Stanford, only about a decade older than the freshman students, did not want to regulate, regiment, or fence in the student.

A quarter of the first year was spent on a great, moving course called citizenship, a requirement for doctors-to-be, as well as all other students. This history of mankind covered from the pre-cave era to the present, and the way to live with laws, justice, cruelties and frailties of man. No effort was ever made to take sides, to grandiose an era, or to influence the thoughts of the student. There at Stanford, the history of mankind was left to the student to assimilate as he thought—to swallow, to regurgitate and ruminate on, or to expel it all.

Close by was San Francisco, where a Stanford card would admit anyone to every speak-easy in town, no questions asked. San Francisco, the town of Jack London and his stories, was an ageless, fighting crossroads—through the Stockton Street Tunnel to the largest Chinatown outside of the Orient, their Barbary Coast and Hipperone Saloon—in that decade known as the Roaring Twenties and the age of the flapper.

In the San Francisco Park, was the statue of the hopeless Indian on his horse, driven to the end of the trail and complete defeat. The grave in the Stanford Arboretum, of a Stanford family member of a tragedy, was marked by a carving of an angel weeping with the insurmountable tragedy of men—death. The stone mosaic on its church carried what was spoken as the Sermon on the Mount—"Ye have heard it hath been said, an eye for an eye, and a tooth for a tooth: But I say unto you..." This, the hope of mankind.

It was no greasy grind at Stanford, though by the third year course work had become increasingly difficult. Evan came away with a Phi Beta Kappa Key. Stanford was exhilarating to him, like the West he had known, with wide open spaces, horses, Ken Burton, cattle, Indians and Hugh Whitney. In some ways Stanford was the West, with the founding of a university and a president, still there, who could look back but not lose the ability to see the new horizons—as had settlers from each generation, who moved ahead into the next, like the first settlers from New England had moved away from the hard, rough glaciated hills of New England toward Western horizons.

Ellis had always assumed Evan would take up medicine. Evan had been trained to do so without making a conscious decision—he knew his father looked forward to the time when he could join him in his practice. Summers with Ellis were a great change from Stanford. He helped his father in the hospital during the day, and they read medical literature at night.

One evening in late summer, Ellis and Evan were sitting at the house, reading. The lights were off in all of the other rooms, and though clean, the place still had that run-down appearance. The dogs started to bark and Ellis looked out the window. In the dim light, he saw a lady in a silk dress with a white coat over her shoulder, helping a young girl in obvious pain, approach the house. They stepped around the three dogs on the porch, knocked on the door, and asked for the doctor.

When Ellis said he was the doctor, she looked at him with a critical eye, and glanced around the place as though she wondered what kind of doctor would be living in such circumstances. Even his suit had a worn appearance.

Ellis examined the girl, who was having severe stomach pain, and said she had a hot appendix and needed immediate surgery. The mother was unconvinced that the country doctor knew what he was talking about. "I think I will take her on to Montpelier," the woman said.

"If you do, you'll be taking her life in your hands. If that appendix breaks it could kill her even if you do get medical help," he warned.

In spite of his warning, the mother had made up her mind and remained firm about taking the girl to Montpelier. She departed with her nose tilted slightly skyward, after again stepping around the barking dogs to exit.

Ellis sat back down in his chair with a sigh. "I hope to hell that kid makes it," he told Evan. "She's a time bomb waiting to explode any minute."

A short time later, the woman returned and frantically pounded on the doctor's door. "I got just out of town a ways and I smelled this awful smell, and I knew her appendix had broken, just like you said they would, Doctor!" she gasped.

Ellis dashed the girl to the hospital, where Evan gave the chloroform, and he removed the appendix, which was ready to rupture at any second. He didn't tell the high-class city woman the smell of the wind blowing off sulphur canyon, carrying the odoriferous hydrogen sulphide, had saved her daughter's life. "If she hadn't smelled that sulphur, and turned around, it would have been a case of peritonitis at best," Ellis told Evan.

Ellis was known for his tiny incisions for appendectomies. Doctors throughout the country could identify Ellis' appendectomy scars at a glance. He would draw a small length of intestine out of the incision, not much larger than a stab wound, tie off and remove the appendix, then poke the intestine back into the small opening. People marveled at his ability to get the intestine into such a tiny hole. When Otto Petersen expressed this concern, while Ellis was operating on one of his boys, Ellis replied, "The damn thing has to go back in—it came out of there."

Progress came to Soda Springs in many forms. Almost everyone purchased an automobile, and roads were built and kept plowed so they were open year around. The livery stable business slowed considerably. Many of the more adventurous citizens started taking airplane rides, as the airplane came into more common usage. Sometimes an enterprising flier with a small plane, offering short rides for a nominal fee, was an added attraction of the Henry Stampede, or other events.

Electricity was being used for more and more of the manual labor, and people freed from the drudgery which had ruled their lives prior to this time, expanded their interests into other areas. Women broke out of their traditional role and began to make a space for themselves in other pursuits.

Ellis began to do many new things at the hospital. He started plating bones. He bought a lot of special equipment, including a newfangled Wappler x-ray machine with a Roentgen tube. It took many minutes to get a picture of the hip. First he had to measure and gauge the depth of penetration needed. Then he set the spark gap, and kept setting up controls on two protruding electrodes or sparks until current would spectacularly jump like lightning arcing into the air between two transformers which had been set to measure approximate distance of tissue—a procedure sometimes quite frightening to patients. Big bare wires ran across the ceiling to the tube stand. The air was often so charged with electricity that the hair on people's arms would stand straight up. Paper colored film was kept in a lead box so the rays would not penetrate and ruin it. It produced a poor picture, compared with later standards, but showed if the bones were straight. Working out voltage and watts, doctors applied jolts to cadavers and found they would make a dead person's eyes open. This created inspiration for Frankenstein type stories.

Later the machine was improved by putting in a Coolidge tube. With the advent of the x-ray machine came bone surgery and the ability to fix breaks and injuries which had been treatable only by amputation in earlier years.

As prohibition continued, bootlegging brought a fortune to those who were willing to take a chance and didn't get caught by the law. Drinking was prevalent among all classes of people. The stills in hotel basements occasionally exploded. One by one, the hotels were being lost to fires from this cause. The famed Idanha Hotel building, one of the oldest landmarks in Idaho, had been destroyed by fire on June 7, 1921. Ellis had watched with horror in his eyes as its elegant columns, turrets, and pinnacles went up in flame. He felt almost hypnotized as the massive structure, which had been so much a part of his early life, was destroyed.

The Caribou Hotel, first known as the Clemens House, which was built by William Clemens—cousin of Samuel Clemens, popularly known as Mark Twain—burned in 1923. By then, Billy Clemens was an old man with long whiskers covering his chest. He smoked a long-stem pipe which was a good two feet long.

The Mart went up in Flames, and Ashler, though momentarily devastated, was soon heavily involved in the same kind of business in a different location. The Soda House Hotel had burned a few years earlier. When the old Anderson Drug building was torn down, it, too, had a still in its basement. The Woodall Hotel, earlier called the Stock Exchange burned. Theodore Enders built the Enders Hotel. It was one of the few which survived.

Interest in education was increasing, and many of the young people were going to college. Ellis continued to help support a number of them, and he began giving ten dollars to each student who graduated from Soda Springs High School. Ten dollars was a lot of money in those days.

One of the young men he was sending to school was Johnny Wallace, who after returning from the service, had bought Eastman's Drug Store. He had worked at the Rexall Drug Co. for a year-and-a-half before going into the military and decided he liked that line of work.

Jimmy Strachan told Ellis about the young fellow. "From Mississippi, he came. Aye, at nineteen a ticket he boot from a fellow in Dumas, Mississippi, who a roond-trip ticket had boot, then decided noot t' come back. A difficult time he had findin' a job, but oon the Ping Pong Railrood he finally goot." Jimmy shook his head and continued. "He's a hard worker, that booy. Twelve hours a day, seven days a week he worked, an' oon a cot 'n the corner o' the roondhouse at

Montpelier he slept. Aye, soon the job o' bill clerk he goot, though they thought moore responsibility t'wood be than a chap that yoong coold handle, but fine he did. Happy he was t' get oon 't the drug stoore. A fancy fer 't, he seems t' have. Now he's goone an' boot his oown."

Ellis went in and talked to Johnny, who was anxious to go to pharmacy school so he wouldn't have to hire a pharmacist. "I'll loan you the money to go," Ellis told him. "How much will it cost?"

"I don't really have any idea," said Johnny, shaking his head. "There aren't any pharmacy schools around here. I figured I'd go back to Michigan."

Ellis pulled his checkbook out of his pocket and tore out a few blanks. "Just write out what you need, and I'll have it charged to my account," he instructed.

Johnny went to school in the wintertime, but each summer he would come back to Soda Springs, sit down with Ellis, figure out what he owed him, and sign a note to the doctor for that amount. When he was out of school, he worked hard and repaid the loans quickly. For the next thirty years he ran the drug store as well as building up interests in several of the area's industries.

He was always grateful for Ellis' help. "I was just a kid with no credit. To me Dr. Kackley is an example of a 'real man', and I'll always be grateful to him," he later told Jimmy.

Mr. Eastman had become a probate judge, and did an excellent job. He served six terms in this capacity. He was right in his element, and so much happier than he had been in the drug store. He became known for his wisdom in handling cases, and like Ellis couldn't walk down the street without constantly being stopped and asked advice in matters concerning the law. Whenever a case was being misrepresented or people were being persecuted, they could always go to Judge Eastman, and he would listen to them. His sentences showed profound respect for law and justice. He and Ellis became close friends.

Ellis was keeping the rooms in the private hospital filled and the numbers of people coming from out of town to see the doctor continued to increase. Money was flowing freely but the citizens of Soda Springs took little notice of or interest in the hospital except when they became ill. Little thought was given to improving the facility, or building a new hospital.

One evening when Ellis was about to go home, a group of men entered the waiting room and asked if they could talk to him. "Of course," said Ellis. "Won't you sit down?"

They sat, except for one white bearded gentleman, who was apparently spokesman for the group. "Dr. Kackley," he began, "we are representing the people of Lava Hot Springs. As you know, Lava is a progressive town, and capitalizes on its hot springs and other natural attractions to bring visitors into the area." He paused and glanced around the group before continuing. "Soda Springs has not taken good care of their springs, and has even had some of them filled in." He looked at the doctor for his reaction. Ellis shook his head in agreement.

"Like the natural attractions, you, Doctor, have been taken for granted. If you would be willing to move to Lava, we would build a new, modern hospital to accommodate your practice."

Ellis was stunned. He sat still a moment, not saying a word.

"We know this is sudden and we don't expect a quick answer; all we ask is that you give the proposition your consideration." the man continued. "We know you would bring enough people into town to repay many times the expense of building the hospital."

Ellis was both surprised and touched by the offer. "Let me think about it for awhile," he said. "I assure you I'll consider it carefully."

The man shook his hand and thanked him, and the others rose, shook his hand, told him of their admiration for his skill and knowledge, and said they hoped he would decide to come to their town.

Ellis lay awake that night thinking about the proposal, and wondering what he should do. While Soda Springs had improved his material fortune greatly, and he had become well known for his surgical skill, his personal life was in shambles. He had been unable to save his own two children from the dread clutches of pneumonia and death. Ida had left him and taken Evan to California, except for summer-time visits. He had made friends in Soda Springs, but he had also made enemies. It would be wonderful to have a new modern hospital in which to practice, and townsmen who appreciated his hard work and efforts to help those in need. On the other hand, he would be leaving the place which he knew, and the town whose sod sheltered two of his children.

"We'd hate to see you leave, but I have to admit it's a great opportunity for you," said Henry. "I couldn't blame you if you decided to go."

Ellis looked at the house, which to he and Ida as a young newly married couple had seemed so inviting. It epitomized his feelings of anger and frustration. He had been a fool to buy the place. The exterior paint was beginning to peel and the fence had started falling down. The inside looked like no one who cared had lived there for a long time. Ellis had shut off most of the rooms, and those he still used were given no upkeep, though kept spotlessly clean by Maggie. He hated that house, but yet he continued to live there, while it tortured his soul, he had never considering lightening his burden by moving from the place.

The Charles Rose home was directly across the street. The Rose family had been good neighbors. Mrs. Rose had come in to help when the babies were born and when they lost the children. Mr. Rose had been one of the first homebuilders in "Upper Town." His home was built of adobe with two rooms, later remodeled and turned into a two-story brick house. After raising six children there, the Rose family had recently sold the house to Otto and Nora Petersen from Wayan, and moved to California.

Nora was a good homemaker and set about fixing up the house and yard. She soon had several schoolmarms boarding there. Petersens had six children of their own, four which were still at home. Ellis enjoyed the family next door until they decided to make musicians out of the two boys, Pharis and Carl, and bought Pharis a trombone and Carl a trumpet. The noises that emitted when the boys touched their lips to the mouthpieces of those instruments sent shivers down Ellis' spine. Even the hired help murmured and made unkind comments when the boys began practicing their instruments. The three dogs which were then members of Ellis' family, tuned up to the music coming from across the street and began to howl. Ellis couldn't believe how much racket the combined chorus could make.

Carl wasn't too enthusiastic about spending time with the trumpet. Making music was precluded by his deep interest in the flying machine; in flight, engineering design, and building of these new gravity-defying contraptions. Pharis, on the other hand, practiced night and day. Ellis shut the doors and windows, but the racket still invaded his home. One day Ellis came home and saw Nora out in her yard working in the flower garden. He stopped by to pass the time of day, and then casually suggested, "If I were you, I'd get a different instrument for Pharis before he ruins his lungs on that trombone."

Nora, inclined to worry about every little thing anyway, hurried down and traded the trombone for a saxophone, which if possible, emitted even worse sounds.

Chapter 15

Ellis decided he would take the good citizens of Lava Hot Springs up on their offer, and informed them he would be willing to move there and run their hospital when it was built.

When some of the businessmen in Soda Springs, who would lose considerable business from loss of Ellis' practice, heard he planned to leave, they immediately started backing a bond issue to build a new county hospital.

The thirty thousand dollar bond passed, and Ellis agreed to stay. He put in three thousand dollars of his own, for hospital equipment. He suggested Dr. Cyril Rich would make a good doctor for the town of Lava. Cyril was an intelligent young man, and Ellis was sure he would make an excellent doctor. After he had worked for them, Ida and Ellis had recommended him for a job with J.O. Morgan, who by that time was living in Blackfoot, Idaho. Cyril worked for Morgans while he finished getting a high school education. Ellis and Ida had helped him through college and medical school, and he was ready to start a practice.

Ellis was listed as superintendent of the hospital, and agreed to work with Dr. Cyril Rich when needed. Dr. Rich went to Lava, and remained there for the rest of his life. Evan could not understand why his father had backed out on the people of Lava Hot Springs, and felt some resentment about the decision.

The new Caribou County Hospital was completed the following year, in 1925. It was small, with six private rooms, and two with four beds each, making a total capacity of fourteen beds. It had two modern operating rooms, a large one and a smaller one. It also had a huge, twenty-five foot electric sterilizer with a water distiller which put out both hot and cold distilled water. The sterilizer included a three by four foot utensil sterilizer, and an autoclave for dry sterilization. Ellis could now scrub for surgery there, with distilled water, which was considered the most sanitary way.

Dr. Ellis Kackley was listed as superintendent and Chief of Staff and Miss Ella V. Estes as head nurse. Drs. Russell Tigert, Sr. and W.E. Smedley of Soda Springs and Dr. G. G. Fitz of Bancroft were on the staff.

Miss Estes, who had been an army nurse, ran a taut hospital. She slept in the room, which had been built for an x-ray room, for a couple of years until an x-ray machine was purchased by Kackleys, and saw that things functioned well night and day.

Charlie, far-sighted citizen that he was, took the building of the new hospital in stride. He worked to get the bond issue passed. When the hospital was built, he turned the upper floor where the private hospital had been into a boarding house which was soon filled with Ellis' patients. A short time afterwards he put in a second movie house. Henry Gorton had put in the first one. He also purchased the Feeny Ranch and went into the sheep business. Ellis kept his office at Fryars.

Walter and Maggie moved into their own home. Margie Bolton, Walter's sister, who was a hard working girl and a daughter of a Bear Lake pioneer family, came to work at the Kackley house. Margie was soon fixing up the house and yard. The weeds in the yard gave way to nicely mowed lawns. She made sure Ellis' shirts were washed and ironed neatly, and encouraged him to buy new suits to replace his tattered looking ones. The atmosphere began to improve, and Ellis began to step livelier. Guests again frequented the Kackley table.

"Six-Shooter Sal" and the girls stopped by to see Ellis one afternoon. The waiting room was filled, but he motioned them into his office, and grabbed both girls up in his arms as he greeted Sal. Times had been increasingly tough for her and the girls, as they had for many people in the area. In desperation, she had turned to bootlegging to keep food on the table for herself and the kids. A near miss at being caught by the federal officials, and she had decided to leave the girls in Soda while she hit the rodeo circuits in Las Vegas.

"Have a seat, Sal," Ellis said motioning her to a chair. "I hear you've been in Vegas. How did it go?"

"Bronco riding paid good there. At twenty-five dollars a ride, I could make seventy-five or a hundred dollars a day." She hesitated, then confided, "but the work was dangerous and I kept worrying about what would happen to the girls if I was hurt or killed. I missed the kids terribly."

"It's no damn life for a mother having to be away from her kids," Ellis agreed shaking his head.

"I worked on an Arizona ranch for awhile, and ended up with a string of twenty half-broken mustangs for pay. I tried to drive them five hundred miles to the Army garrison at Fort Douglas, where I could have gotten a good price for them, but a bunch of damn Indians stole the sonsabitches from me southwest of St. George. I couldn't do a thing about it by myself, so I just came on home."

"Good to see you back," said Ellis. "You're all three looking great."

Sal went back to the only way she knew she could make a living for herself and the girls. Soon Federal marshals arrested her for bootlegging. Though it was common knowledge she was making whiskey, they hadn't been able to find any evidence except a little whiskey in a bottle in her cupboard, and half the town had a little whiskey in their cupboards.

She was put in jail, but months went by and no charges were filed. The case was federal, and the local sheriff was unable to find out anything about what was going on. To pass the time, she began sketching on the jail walls. The sheriff left the door unlocked, and she cleaned and helped around the office.

Sal got sick, and Ellis was called to check her. He took her right to the hospital and took out her tonsils. A couple of days later, one of the federal agents who had arrested her came by when Ellis was not there, and demanded she be returned to the jail immediately. There she started to hemorrhage, and almost bled to death before Ellis was located. "That sonofabitch had no business taking my patient before she's released from the hospital," he stormed. "If I could get my hands on him, he might be the one almost bleeding to death."

Ellis got her back into the hospital. "Don't worry, Sal, in a short time we'll have you fixed up as good as new." His eyes murderous, he continued, "If that federal agent shows his face around here again, I want to see him."

The agent returned a few days later and wanted her back in jail, the nurse promptly went for Ellis. When Ellis got through with the man, he got out of there as fast as he could go, and let Sal recuperate until Ellis was ready to release her from the hospital six weeks later. When the case came to trial, Sal had been in jail almost a year. For lack of evidence, it was thrown out of court.

After the brewery business was killed by the advent of prohibition, Henry Schmidt began working as a watchman for Largilliere's Store. He slept in the store at nights. When Henry slept, he slept soundly, and one night when the store was robbed, he supposedly slept right through the burglary.

The safe, way down in one end of the store, had been blasted open. "How in the hell did you sleep through the noise of the burglars dynamiting the safe?" asked Ellis.

"When those men saw me sleeping there, one of the robbers turned to the other one and said, 'If he wakes up, blow his head off.' I'd have been a damn fool to wake up," said Henry.

In 1928 Ellis was appointed to the State Board of Medical Examiners. He was unconvinced of the validity of the exams and was always extremely lenient in his judgment of the applicants. He still maintained, as he had told Ida years before, that just like early Indian hunters learned buffalo hunting by hunting, doctors learned doctoring by doctoring.

In California, Evan had become used to the friendly, easy-going atmosphere of Stanford. Classes were small, professors were interested in the students, and people greeted everyone whether they knew them or not. David Starr Jordan, first president of the university held occasional open houses in the evening, where students could visit and participate in discussions. The school was remarkably cosmopolitan, with scholars from many nations, and gave students a broad outlook on life. It made little difference if students were in class or on the golf course, if they could pass the tests on the material.

Evan's interests had been vacillating between medicine and chemistry. He had about made up his mind to go into organic chemistry, though Ellis would be disappointed. Harvard took in a few undergraduate medical students each year, and Evan, in his third year at Stanford, was encouraged to apply. He did, and was admitted to Harvard. The decision was made by his acceptance.

He first saw Harvard Medical School from afar, where the Avenue of Louis Pasteur meets Riverway, like an Acropolis of Greece, with great columns rising up and up to a shrine. It was like a three-sided temple with no statues and a courtyard of green grass. A long walkway traversed each side, as if one were in the court yard of a great mausoleum. Starting up the steps, it was as if each step covered a century of medicine, almost from primordial times. Chiseled into the deep stone of the building, a part of the edifice, were the words:

Life is short,
Art is long,
Decision difficult,
Experiment perilous.

Standing on the threshold and pulling open one of the great doors, he found life inside, if not outside, passing by in white or green coats. This was the beginning of placing each year, a segment of the four lines upon the back of the novice, a cross to carry. A cross the emerging doctor—as all doctors, from all schools, from antiquity to the present—must bear, and never be free of, day or night until entering the grave.

Harvard also made sure its students had a broad outlook on life. Those aspiring to become doctors were required to work in the "District," where they became acquainted with severe poverty as well as in the Irish community of South Boston, and the Boston Lying-In Hospital, patronized by the wealthy. Ellis was proud of his son, though there was a reserve between them which prevented freely sharing their innermost thoughts. He had always been afraid to get too close to Evan after losing his other two children. He didn't want to leave himself that vulnerable.

As the "Roaring Twenties" crashed into the depression of the thirties, the future looked grim across the whole country. Evan's last two years at Harvard, going out among the poor, were followed by a year at Los Angeles County Hospital, where he saw first-hand the effects of poverty. At Los Angeles he treated everyone from those in the jail ward to impoverished Mexican and Chinese people, to the new poor who were once residents of Wilshire Boulevard and Hollywood and even Beverly Hills, but had recently lost everything.

The hospital was a receiving hospital for the insane, where people were evaluated and court was held before they were committed to the state hospital. Many were there because of alcohol and drug abuse and syphilis, others were dangerously insane.

After interning, Evan started to work with his father in 1931. He had turned down several excellent job offers, to join Ellis in Soda Springs, though for the life of him, he still couldn't imagine why Ellis had decided to stay in Soda Springs instead of going to Lava.

Fresh out of school, he brought enthusiasm and new ideas to the hospital. There was a surprisingly large number of deaths from pneumonia. Evan tried to interest his father in the use of oxygen, but after his experience with Margaret, Ellis had no faith in it. Evan was extremely fearful of pneumonia. Not only had he watched it kill his sister, he had seen many old people succumb to it while in medical school at Boston City Hospital.

Evan talked Ellis into having oxygen available, which had progressed to a plastic tent standing over the bed, with oxygen piped from large cylinders. Ice was used to cool the air and bring down temperatures. Without oxygen people would turn blue, their heart rate would increase, and their lungs would be unable to get the necessary oxygen from the air. With oxygen, high fevers could be brought down, and usually twenty to twenty-five beats taken off the pulse rate. When the crisis passed, the patient would begin to sweat profusely, and be likely to recover.

Evan was called to a sheep camp one winter day when the temperature was near forty degrees below zero, and found a man and his wife, both from long known, old time pioneer families of Grays Lake, with pneumonia. He brought them in and with the use of the new oxygen tents was able to save both.

Shortly after Evan started practicing with his father, Ellis decided to start taking occasional short vacations. His practice was so demanding he needed to get away once in awhile, and now he could, he decided. It would give Evan a chance to gain confidence in his own knowledge and ability, and he wouldn't be gone more than ten days at a time. He left his son in charge of the hospital.

People were coming in steadily from three or four states. During his first absence, there was a ruptured, perforated duodenal ulcer, a six-year-old child with a mastoid infection which required immediate surgery, badly broken bones, a dislocated hip, and countless other emergencies. On top of everything else, a hemophiliac patient came in gradually choking to death with hemorrhage into the neck.

It was a challenge to Evan, a year out of medical school, weighing on him like an avalanche. Then he thought of his father, a few days out of medical school in the vast areas of the West, faced with a patient dying from a hit over the head with a billiard ball wrapped in a silk handkerchief, a sheepherder whose kidney must be removed in a sheep camp, and swimming the Bear River to deliver a baby. Evan had two fine operating rooms, a large case of surgical instruments, a great sterilizer and an x-ray machine. He realized how fortunate he was, and waded into the problems confronting a country doctor.

Like his father, Evan was a voracious reader. He covered over a thousand pages of medical literature, journals, and books each month. When discussing treatments of various diseases, Ellis told Evan about how he had cured the sheep men's eye infections. Evan could hardly believe his ears when he learned his father had infected all of those men with clap bacteria to clear up their eye infections.

One of the few things Ellis and Evan sent to specialists was cataract operations, though they took out eyes, and did almost everything else.

Returning home one day, Evan looked at the house where he was born, and decided something must be done. Heating in winter time was the biggest problem, so he remodeled the old central heating plant installed by Ellis, which had never worked properly, and put in a used electric stoker. It used tons of coal during the coldest winter months, but the new system improved the livability of the house considerably. Delivered coal was selling for three dollars a hundred at that time.

He told Ellis he would share the cost of repairing ceilings where plaster had fallen when pipes froze and were broken, and wallpapering and fixing up the place, and Ellis agreed to put in an equal amount. They even had the gingerbread trim on parts of the porch remade. The house again looked beautiful, it was surrounded by a picket fence and cottonwood trees, typical of the Brigham Young era. Evan stood back and looked at the place. The old house had dignity though he knew it was a shallow, thin-walled home. It had always reminded him of Dickens' story title, "Bleak House."

When he touched on the death of his brother or sister, he found it was still a subject neither of his parents could talk about, and he knew they had buried much of themselves with their children. Though it had been over twenty years before, they still went about their lives without the sentiment of earlier times. Ellis still visited the graves daily, but he never saw his father go out to the old barn except one time when it caught on fire, and then he left as soon as he made sure the animals were all removed from danger.

The Indian people still came through town. Evan was reminded of the years when he, as a young child, used to play with those who camped on his parents' property along Soda Creek during the summertime. He and Ken Burton used to spend many hours playing with the young Indians. Evan still had to stop and think before mounting a horse, or he would get on from the right side like the Indians did, as he had become so used to doing in those carefree childhood days when you could buy an Indian pony for five dollars.

Public Health Doctors were put on the reservations to treat the Indians, but Ellis and Evan were getting a steady stream of them coming in for treatment because Congress did not appropriate a sufficient amount of money to the Bureau of Indian Affairs to operate a proper medical facility. Not only were they getting those who had difficulty subsisting, but the well-educated and leaders of the Indian nation were coming to the Kackleys for treatment and for surgery. They were never charged or sent a bill. The Indians didn't trust most of the white people, but Kackleys were different; the Indian in Ellis came out in his feeling toward these native Americans.

In spite of all the people they were treating without charge, the hospital continued to make money, even through the great depression. It was operating profitably from the first month it was in service.

Caribou County was suffering hard times, but people in the country seemed to fare some better than those in the cities during the depression. Once again the Oregon Trail became a well traveled roadway, as people who were destitute and without hope tried to better their condition by trekking west. Ellis and Evan treated the sick and impoverished without question. They didn't worry about money, but about getting people well and on their way again. Often one of them would buy lunch or a tank of gasoline for some of these unfortunate people. Sometimes they hospitalized patients, then took them home and cared for them until they could forage for themselves. Some were so thin their bones nearly showed through their skin.

A man from northern Idaho died and his relatives brought a rough hewn box on an old fashioned flatbed truck to take the body for its final ride. The box was held in place by chains. They had nothing to protect the corpse but the man's underwear, no money for an undertaker, and had dug their own grave. Evan called the nurse. "Bring a blanket and give to these people to wrap the body in or he'll be full of slivers and all torn up before they get him home for burial," he instructed.

When Evan told his father about the incident, he looked at his son thoughtfully. "You made a mistake," he said shaking his head sadly. "You should have given them two blankets."

One evening just before closing time, Evan and Ellis were in their offices, when about a dozen men from Grace came in. They trooped into Ellis' office, and Ellis recognized them as men involved with the Last Chance Canal Company. "Do you have time to talk with us a minute?" a tall, lanky, poorly dressed man asked.

It had been a light winter, and water was scarce. Drought conditions were threatening the farmers' crops, and while there was water in Bear Lake, it was not high enough to go over the diked north end of the lake without being pumped, so it was not coming down the Bear River. Utah Power and Light Company said they could not pump the water out because they were getting sand in their pumps. They claimed the farmers were wasting water. The farmers felt the Power Company was not trying to pump the water out.

"Hell Yes," said Ellis. "You know I'll always take time to talk to you, but let me get Evan first."

He called Evan over to his office, then sat with the men and gave them his full attention. As Evan sat and listened to the conversation, he could hardly believe his ears.

"Doc, we're going to blow up the Utah Power and Light Company dike at Bear Lake and let the water down the Bear River," a burly fellow said. "We have to get water on our crops, or we won't have any. We've worked too hard for our water to let those sonsabitches at the power company leave us dry and without food for our families," he added angrily.

Ellis looked at the men and marveled at the dynamic force generated when people were put in a position where their backs were up against a wall. He had no doubt Utah Power and Light Company wanted to break the farmers they had experienced so much conflict with in the past.

The power company had a lot of influence and wealth backing them, compared to the farmers, barely making a living on their land, and numbering only about sixty in all. These men didn't have much chance against a company like that, Ellis thought.

He listened carefully. What they were talking of doing

was against the law, and taking a big chance. Ellis knew if they did blow up the dike, legal repercussions were likely. He leaned back in his chair, ran his fingers through his hair, and looked thoughtfully at the desperate group of men. "What are your plans?" he asked.

"Well, we thought we'd just blow a hole in the dike big enough to let some water down..."

"Hmm," said Ellis as though he were thinking out loud. The men looked at him expectantly. "First of all, if you do blow open the dike, blow the whole damn thing wide open. If you're going to do it, don't do it half way, for God's sake do it well."

Evan, startled, looked at his father in disbelief.

Ellis looked at the gaunt, poverty stricken farmers, and felt a kinship with them. He knew they had just begun to get on their feet after a long court battle with Utah Power and Light, when the water had been adjudicated. The "Dietrich Decree" in which Judge Dietrich had been favorable to these men was the only thing which had saved the farmers. Dietrich had left a club in the decree which could be grasped by these men if the need should arise. The date of priority of Last Chance water was mostly superior to that of Utah Power and Light Company and the decree stated in no uncertain terms how much water could be diverted for use out of the state.

The farmers were suffering the effects of one of the worst droughts ever to hit the area. With mortgages on nearly all of their lands, they had planted their crops. Without water they would be financially ruined and some might even starve to death. "There just might be a better way to solve the problem," Ellis said thoughtfully, running his fingers through his hair again.

"What'd ya mean, Doc?" several of the men asked at once.

"Before you resort to blowing up the dike, why don't you go down and talk to Fred Cooper at Grace. He's close to both the Mormon Church and the state, and I think he might be able to help you. You might also want to talk to Tom Heath at the sugar factory in Preston. Let's see if they can help before doing anything drastic."

Ellis thought some of the men looked disappointed, "I know you fellows have built one of the best reclamation projects in the country, and without any help from anyone else. You've put sweat and blood into it, and fought off every obstruction Utah Power and Light and nature have put up against you," he told them. You should have the water you need for your crops."

Evan watched in wonder as the most lean, haggard looking bunch of men he had ever seen agreed to talk to the men Ellis suggested might be able to help. After they left, his father turned to Evan and said only, "What think?"

"You were right when you said if they blow up the dike to blow it wide open, but you gave them an alternative, which was good. I'm all for it," agreed Evan.

There's an old Revolutionary War saying, 'when you kill the king, kill him dead.' If they blow up the dike and only blow a small hole in it, they won't accomplish anything, and they'll be worse off than before," Ellis reasoned out loud. "Actually I thought the idea was great, but I had second thoughts that they might end up in jail, and decided I'd better suggest some negotiation first."

Ellis called Utah Power and Light, and gave them a tongue lashing, and suggested they consider the situation into which they were putting the farmers. Fred Cooper and Tom Heath talked to the power company, and let out the word that if they didn't get some water down to the farmers, there were rumors the dike might be blown up. Utah Power and Light knew the men were capable of blowing up the dike; they had done a lot of blasting in making the canals. They didn't take the threat lightly. At last an agreement was reached, and some water was pumped out of the lake for the farmers' crops.

Game laws and regulations had been set up, and a game warden appointed. There was little enforcement of the laws unless wanton waste was involved. Game wardens, without uniform or gun, looked the other way after seeing the poverty about them.

One night a group of fellows, including the game warden, were out at one of the sheep camps. After a few too many drinks, the party got rather rough. Before the evening was over, they had picked up the game warden and thrown him into the creek. He was highly offended.

"I'm going out and arrest them," he told Ellis and Evan. "They shoot chickens out of season right and left."

When the game warden went back to their camp, he found one of the men with several sage hens, and hauled him in to see the judge.

"Mr. Jones, I'll have to fine you five dollars for shooting chickens out of season," said the judge sternly.

"That's okay, Judge, I'll pay, but I request you award me the chickens after I pay the fine."

The judge thought a moment. "That seems fair enough," he reasoned.

"Thank you, Judge," replied Mr. Jones, a wry grin lighting up his face. "Your Honor, would you come over and have dinner with me?"

The judge accepted the invitation. A short time later they sat down together to eat deliciously fried sage hens.

Evan's friend Jay Edward Beus was a soft-eyed, soft-hearted bachelor sheep man, who packed a six-shooter on his hip and a bottle in his back pocket. He went out and bought a bunch of cheap land from the government when the depression came, and fenced it. Gradually he built up a good sized herd of sheep. Evan's other old childhood friend, young George Small, was running sheep with him. Neither of the men were married. They came into the office one afternoon with a diaperless, sniffling baby, about eighteen months of age. Evan was astounded to see them with a baby.

"Will you take a look at the kid, Doc?" Jay requested casually. "I think he has a cold."

Evan looked at the baby and then questioningly at Jay. "Where'd you get the youngun, Jay?" he asked, shaking his head.

"Well, Doc, you wouldn't believe me if I told you."

"Give me a try," insisted Evan.

"Well," said Jay, "George an' I was gettin' ready to go

out on the range, and was a drivin' the ol' pickup down the road between Blackfoot and Pocatello, when we came upon this pretty young gal, sittin' spang in the center of the road." He paused a moment, then continued. "She was sittin' on a suitcase and holdin' a bawlin' baby on her lap. She had an ol' box o' crackers an' a bottle with a little milk, but that didn't seem to satisfy the kid, who was hollerin' up a storm."

"Where's the mother now?" demanded Evan.

"Just hold on a minute, and I'll explain," said George. "We offered the girl an' her kid a lift, and she said she was goin' to Ogden, Utah, but didn't have a penny to her name. We took her to Lava, an' got her a room at the hotel, and gave her ten dollars for a ticket to Ogden. Later we found the baby's sweater in the pickup, so we turned around and went back to Lava. There she was at the junction of the highway, right back on her suitcase, bawlin' kid an' all.

Evan shook his head again. It sounded like the girl was in a bit of difficulty.

"That kid had taken a likin' to us, an' he climbed right

into the pickup." Jay continued. "Our sheep came along an' we had to get goin', so we quick an' struck a deal. We gave the gal ten dollars down an' a promise of ten a year rental for the kid."

"You mean to tell me you rented this baby, and the mother let him go—just like that?" asked Evan wide eyed.

"You got it," said Jay. "Bet my boots she'll be back after her kid before long, but George and I'll take care of him 'til she comes. Fact is we're gettin' mighty fond of the kid. We just thought we'd rent him awhile and help the gal out. 'Twas a good excuse to give her a little dough, till she's settled."

Evan knew these men had a habit of helping people who were down and out on their luck or in special need of help. They were the first ones around to hire the handicapped, and those considered unable to work by most of the businessmen. It was like them to try and help the girl, Evan thought, but renting a baby was something else!

"Who was the girl?" Evan asked.

"Well, the one thing we forgot to do," said George, "was to get her name, but I figure she'll be findin' us before long. We can take care of the kid until then. We're both good sheepherders, an' have raised a lot of bum lambs on the bottle in our day."

"You think caring for a baby is like caring for lambs?" asked Evan. "It might prove a little bit more complicated than you think."

"Don't worry, Doc, she left a pair of shoes, two pairs of coveralls, socks, a hair brush, and a little piss pot. What more could we need?"

Evan again shook his head in disbelief as he looked at his old friends.

"We call him Bunky," George added. "He had a cold, so we high-tailed it to the drug store and bought some Castoria, but the kid just shit all over the place an' still had the sniffles. We had to buy something to give him a bath in, so we bought a big bread pan, and thought we could use it for bread makin' between times."

Evan examined the child, who seemed to be in excellent physical condition except for the sniffles. He gave them a prescription and some sage advice on the rearing of children.

"One thing I'll have to say about this town, is you never know what you'll see next," he told friends that evening, after they had brought up Jay and George's names as potential kidnappers, instead of renters of a baby.

"How are those two old bachelors ever going to take decent care of a baby?" an indignant woman asked. "That's the most ridiculous thing I ever heard of. They'll probably think they can turn it out to graze with the sheep or tie it with the dogs. The poor child will have pneumonia before long."

Evan smiled, "They've raised many a bum lamb on the bottle. They'll probably do okay with the child."

"They're going to be in for problems with the women of this town," Ellis predicted that night.

While the two bachelors were to incur the wrath of the "Whirling Spray Society"—as the ladies advocating birth control were jokingly called, after the whirling sprays used for that purpose—and other concerned citizens, the baby seemed to stay healthier than most children.

The sheriff was called out to check on the child and insisted he was doing fine. He didn't mention that the kid had slipped up to pee on his leg like a dog on a bush, which Jay and George thought was really funny.

The baby's mother did eventually return, and by that time Bunky and the sheep men had formed such an attachment, it was difficult to part. She started back home, but Bunky cried so loud and long, she returned and stayed a month, while the baby got used to her again. The sheep men never heard of Bunky after his mother took him, until a story in a national magazine many years later put them back in touch.

Karl Mueller's skull in Ellis' office—buried once, then rolled from its grave after a short time—served as a constant reminder to Ellis of the horrors of war and man's inhumanity to man. The skull, always with due respect, was used by Ellis and Evan to visually map out skull fractures in accidents. It was also used to help localize opening the skull in sub-dural hematomas in accident cases, a problem which usually came on several days or a week later. This was an ever increasing medical complication as the automobile came into more common usage.

Evan also used the skull to practice a procedure to relieve pain in certain patients by inserting a long needle into a nerve that exited from the base of the skull and caused pain so severe victims sometimes entertained thoughts of escape by suicide. This palliative treatment relieved the pain for several months while the patient became reconciled to having a top rate brain surgeon cut the nerve from the involved pain centers in the skull.

As usual, the townspeople didn't understand what he was doing, and rumor was that Ellis talked his most difficult cases over with the skull.

Ellis would quote the poet Robert Burns or the poem "Thanatopsis" to his son whenever he felt the philosophy of the poets would help to fortify him against the problems to be faced in life, and the life and death situations and emotions doctors must deal with. Evan thought of John Greenleaf Whittier's, "Maud Muller," exchanging her name for Carl Mueller, in the fatal lines of that poem:

For of all sad words of tongue or pen
The saddest are these: "It might have been!"

The jail in Soda Springs was usually empty. It was one of the favorite over-night stopping places of migrant people going through town. Half starved, half clothed men, caught in the now phantom adage of "Go West, young man," would often come and ask to stay at the jail overnight if there was room. Compounding the problems of the thirties was the most severe winters the area had experienced for years. Snow practically covered City Hall.

A severe epidemic of scarlet fever broke out during the cold, blizzardy winter of 1931-1932, with the roads closed for months. Evan took care of thirty-nine cases of this dread disease, which was feared almost as much as diphtheria had been. A man who lived out by Five-Mile Meadows to the west, had two of his children down with it. Evan drove out as far as he could take the car, then walked the balance of the way over the crusted snow to treat the children. With his recent training, Evan was aware there was a new antitoxin which would control the affliction, but it was extremely expensive, and had to be given at first diagnosis of the disease.

The wholesale cost of six dollars a dose, was at that time a stupendous sum. Eggs were wholesaling at three cents a dozen, turkeys at twenty to twenty-five cents each, and for a quarter one could get five pounds of pork chops. The government had closed the banks without any notice, which left the financial system in utter chaos. When gold was devalued and possession made illegal, individuals found themselves short-changed of two-thirds of a lifetime's work and savings. The nation went on the egg standard, or whatever commodity was indigenous to the region. One could barter an egg for other food.

This was not true of slums or industrial segments of the country, for while the egg had a value of a quarter of a cent, labor had no value. This was the chaos of the nation during the great depression, not "We have only fear to fear." Luxuries were soon forfeited. The horse made a come back, and there were as many hay burners as gas burners on the streets.

Evan went to Johnny Wallace and asked if he would be so good as to get in a supply of the medicine, allow him to carry two vials of the antitoxin with him at all times, and trust the people he gave it to for payment. John accepted the charge accounts, not knowing to whom the medicine would go, and charging people only the wholesale cost. While others were not so lucky, all thirty-nine of the cases Evan treated recuperated without serious complications of scarlet fever, which then included eye damage, heart damage, kidney disease, brain catastrophes, and collapse of the heart or circulatory system.

About a year later, Evan checked with Johnny to see how many of the accounts were still outstanding, thinking he would reimburse him for any which had not been paid. He was told that every one had been paid, and with great thanks and appreciation.

Michael Michaelson brought his family in to see Ellis. The family cat had disappeared, and came back, acting strangely. Each of the four younger boys had received scratches and bites when they grabbed it and tried to calm it down, before Michael and Sadie had realized the cat was sick, probably with rabies. Ellis had to give each child the series of rabies shots which were an ordeal, but he was thankful they were available.

Chapter 16

A man named Fred, who could hardly speak a word of English broke his leg working at the mine. It was a nasty compound fracture. "Why don't you just amputate the leg, and not worry about trying to save it," one of the mine officials suggested.

"You take care of your mine, and let me take care of my patients," Ellis retorted angrily. "I sure as hell don't tell you how to do your job."

The leg became ulcerated and developed bone infection. Behind the scenes, the mine official continued to try to get Kackley to amputate the leg, which was taking a long time to show even gradual improvement. Ellis sent the man to Salt Lake for a second opinion, which the mine official thought was unnecessary. They were at odds for a long time, but Ellis refused to amputate the leg as long as there was some chance it might heal.

Mine officials called in the Industrial Accident Manager. Several doctors met and evaluated the case and decided the leg should be cut off. Still Ellis refused to amputate the leg. It took close to a year, but it finally healed.

Contention increased between Kackleys and the mine officials. Ellis kept trying to get them to put the change rooms closer. "With the mine hotter than hell and the men sweating from the humidity, you'd save money to hike that change room up on blocks and move it closer to the mine entrance so they wouldn't have to walk a quarter of a mile to get a shower and clothing change." Ellis suggested. "Sometimes it's forty degrees below zero in the middle of the winter," he added trying to reason with the man. "These guys are hot, sweaty and tired when they come out, and prone to catch colds or pneumonia."

The man wouldn't listen.

A young, newly married kid came in with pneumonia. He had been working part time at the mine for two weeks. His temperature had climbed to 104 degrees, and he could hardly get his breath. Ellis called Conda to see if the boy could be admitted, and was told they would not pay for his treatment.

Ellis admitted the boy anyway, and put him in an oxygen tent. It was touch and go for eight or nine days, while his temperature went up and down between 100 and 104 degrees. Abscesses developed around the lung, and pus filled the lobe. Ellis removed a rib and put in a drain. "You are so damned cold blooded that I hope you're in heaven while I'm in hell," Ellis told the mine official.

"These guys will spare no expense to put on the dog, or make it look like they're benevolent," Ellis told Evan, "but when it comes right down to it, they don't give a damn about the men."

One summer evening when Ellis and Evan were sitting at the house, both reading, as they often did that time of day, one of the mine officials burst into the house without even knocking. As usual the place was mostly darkened, except for two reading lamps behind their chairs. The dogs on the porch started barking and growling, and the hair raised on the backs of their necks. Ellis fairly leaped out of his chair.

"You're charging us too much and treating too many people," the man accused. "You doctors think we can fork out two dollars for fees every time there's some little thing wrong with a fellow or his family," he added, his voice becoming louder as he spoke.

Evan had never seen his father look so tall. In stunned silence he watched the exchange of angry words. "I'm here to treat the sick, and if there's something wrong with a man or his family, the way I see it, they should be treated. That's what insurance is for," he said in a voice neither loud nor calm.

The man's eyebrows shot up. "Well, I'm going to bring in another doctor who will have some concern for the company," he shouted shaking his fist, his face so flushed he appeared near a stroke.

Evan had seldom seen his father rise up and show his

feelings of anger. He had never seen fire in his eyes like he saw now, so different from his more guarded, bedside-type manner.

"Go ahead," he said, his dark eyes flashing. "Evan and I will be here long after your man has come and gone."

The man turned and dashed off without answering. He shoved the door open, passed the dogs on the porch, and walked briskly down the sidewalk. Evan, feeling a surge of adrenalin, rose and accompanied him to the porch to make sure the dogs, snarling and showing their teeth, didn't bite him on the way out. He petted the animals until they were calmed, then returned to his chair and sat down. "God, damn the corporations," he muttered.

His mind went back to a tenement section in Boston, and he was again climbing the stairs to the third floor. It was an area of terrible slums in the district, and he had been called to deliver a baby. There were no lights and he shined a small flashlight on the stairs to show him the way. One door was ajar, and he figured that was probably the place. He flashed his light inside and saw a man on the left. His whiskers were scroungy and he was dressed in dirty rags. As he flashed the beam on around the room, he saw two iron post beds, one filled with two half naked kids, covered partially by tattered garments.

He looked for a light switch, but a moan from the floor diverted his attention. His flashlight beam revealed a woman lying on an old rug, obviously in hard labor. He dropped to his knees beside her, and as she went into another pain, saw that the baby was crowned, and coming fast. He set the flashlight on the floor, and delivered the baby, then fumbled to open his medical bag and get the forceps, which he doused in alcohol, and clamped on the cord before tying it. "No lights," the woman managed to get out when he asked where the switch was, "the company turned them off months ago."

Before he could catch his breath, the afterbirth started to come. He quickly handed the baby to the husband, as blood started gushing from the woman. A full year from being out of medical school, this was his first case of post-partum hemorrhage. He thought of what his professor of obstetrics,

Chubby Newell, a favorite of the medical students of his time, had taught, and he had read many times in his textbook. He pressed his open right hand on the thin woman's stomach and grabbed hold of her uterus, which was too tired and ill nourished to contract normally. As he began to knead it in his hands the stimulation soon caused it to begin contracting on its own. He knew this process was extremely painful to the patient, but she never flinched or cried out. The bleeding slowed considerably, and Evan glanced toward the spot on the floor where he had dropped the afterbirth. To his surprise, it was gone. A small dog was sitting there licking his mouth, with a satisfied look, like he'd had the best meal he'd eaten in a long time.

The woman got up, produced a small bottle of oil from somewhere, took the baby from her husband and started to clean the infant. Evan couldn't believe she had the strength to get up, after what she had just been through. He wiped up the blood on the floor and looked for a place to wash his hands. He found a bucket of water and wash basin. He cleaned up and started down the stairs, appalled by the extreme poverty, and still seeing the hungry little dog, the woman lying on the rug on the floor, and the new baby he had brought into this hopeless environment.

He stepped into the square, and the area was as light as day. He looked at the huge factory, hardly noticed when he arrived, and in contrast to where he had been, it seemed to be emitting the brightest lights he had ever seen. "Gillette" stood out in large letters across the building. He had frequently heard the Gillette Razor Company's Slogan on the radio: "The sharpest blade ever honed." Evan would never forget the contrast of great wealth and great poverty he witnessed that night.

"Here we are in the West," he thought. "My family came here to escape the quagmire of poverty they were immersed in at that time. Here comes a big company, who pretends to care about its workers and be interested in their health, and they're threatening us because we're treating the men. The books all talk about the 'winning of the West,' but the 'losing of the West,' would be more fitting."

Evan thought how his family and others who came to

Soda Springs had worked for the benefit of the people and to improve the town. Now a big company had come in to mine the country and the people as well. The land was now homesteaded, the range rights and rivers were being controlled by the government, and the opportunity of the West was gone.

He remembered one of his history professors at Stanford who had maintained that when the West was gone it would bring a drastic change, and times would get tough. "When the grass-root resources—one hundred and sixty to six hundred and forty acres of land, almost free for the asking—are gone, the United States will not be able to absorb emigrants, the opportunity to escape poverty by going west will be gone, and times will change," he had insisted.

Now Evan understood what the Stanford professor was trying to get across. He could see the cycle was changing. The raw lawlessness of the developing West his parents had been required to contend with was disappearing, but so was the opportunity the West had afforded.

Ellis interrupted the long silence. "What did you say?"

"I said God, damn the corporations. If He doesn't, they'll take over the whole world. They're something created by the courts with a body, but without a head. They've even named themselves from corpora, meaning body." he continued. "That man who lives in a big white house to the side of the village, and invades our privacy like he had a right to, is nothing but a mouthpiece for a legal body without a head, a conscience, a soul; a body which had the breath of life breathed into by law, and one which can never die like us human beings." He said angrily.

"They are even able to reproduce forever like the head of Medusa of Pagan mythology. Through their subsidiaries—like children—they're blessed with life forever, building great domains that become stronger and wealthier until their strength surpasses that of states and governments that operate the same throughout the world. In the meantime, we mortals born into life with a head and soul, have our meat picked to the bones during our lifetime."

It was the first time Ellis had ever heard Evan speak out

with such deep feeling in reaction to those about him and the times in which he lived.

"We'll treat them without charging if we have to," Ellis said.

One of the few times Ellis used the whiskey the sheriff brought in was after someone donated blood, when he would always offer them a shot. Mrs. Brown came in one day to donate blood, and when Ellis offered her the customary drink, she replied, "I haven't ever tasted the stuff, but give me just a tiny sip."

Ellis poured a small amount from the bottle and handed the glass to the woman. Just then he was called from the room by a minor emergency. About twenty minutes later he returned to find Mrs. Brown lying on the small cot, barely conscious.

"That's pret-ty goood stuff, Doc! How 'bout a lit-tle more?" she drawled.

Ellis glanced at the bottle on the counter, and couldn't believe how much was missing from it. "Good hell, Mrs. Brown, you're soused!" he exclaimed. "Miss Peterson, I need you!" he yelled to the nurse.

Miss Peterson appeared in the doorway. "Bring a stretcher and let's get Mrs. Brown into the hospital and put her to bed. She's had a little too much to drink!" he instructed.

"But Doctor, that's impossible. Mrs. Brown doesn't drink!" insisted Miss Petersen, looking shocked.

"If you don't believe she's inebriated, take a whiff of her breath!" said Ellis.

They put Mrs. Brown in the hospital and kept her for two days before the "complications she experienced from giving blood" wore off and she was able to go home. The hospital did not charge her for her stay.

Talking later about the unexpected "complications," Evan told his father one evening, "I really got my eyes opened in Boston. I'll never forget the poverty and suffering. Some of those women had so many children they knew more about having a baby than I did." He thought for a moment. He could remember the people vividly. "One family had a bunch of youngsters and a new baby, and only a couple of spoons, so they had to take turns eating what little they had—a stew out of a pan." Evan paused again as he thought back. "One time I asked a husband who had been drinking to get me some ice because a lady was hemorrhaging, and all he did was try to smack me."

"You never know what in the hell a person will do when they get a little liquor under their belt," said Ellis. "You see a lot of drinking in the slums. I'll never forget the poverty and suffering I saw when I was going through medical school either."

"I got into East Boston a bit too, but people there had a little more money," Evan continued. "but I got mixed up with some gangsters there once. I went to deliver a baby, and was met by a man with a gun, and escorted to the apartment. After the delivery he told me to dress the baby and I told him that was his job, but I changed my mind quickly when he pointed the gun straight at me and said, 'DRESS THE BABY'."

"The Cassidy Gang tried to pull that kind of stuff on me, too," said Ellis with a short laugh, "until I told them I wasn't about to be kidnapped. A doctor runs into all kinds of things."

Evan laughed, "One time I was taking a history on a big fellow at Los Angeles County Mental Receiving Hospital. I was locked into a cell with him, with just the peek hole in the door as a link with the outer world. I asked a few questions, and the next thing I knew he was sitting on top of me, and I was looking straight up into his face."

"What did you do?" asked Ellis.

"From the look in his eyes, I knew I'd better keep quiet or I'd be dead, so we just looked at each other for about ten minutes, then he finally released my arms and I got up, and we went on taking history and doing a physical. I saw a helluva lot of strange things there, too," Evan mused.

"While Caribou County these days resembles what I saw in Boston in some ways, we're weathering the depression a little better here in the country," reflected Evan. "The Mormons care for their own in times like these and that helps out a lot—not only for their own faith but for others too.''

"We're the only county hospital around that isn't running in the red,'' agreed Ellis. "Even if most of our patients are paying only a dollar or two a month, those who can, are paying.'' He rose from his chair and looked out the window for a few moments. "These people who come through and get medical care know there'll be no lawsuits for collection, but they send a little whenever they can, and tell others about the care they received.''

"We get a lot of people from out of the area,'' Evan agreed.

"Eighty percent of our patients are from out of the county, and a good fifty percent from out of state. We're getting almost swamped with patients from all over the country.'' said Ellis. "Our practice is already exceeding the capacity of the hospital. We keep having to put beds in the halls, and that isn't good when you're treating people who are seriously ill. It can make the difference between life and death.''

Evan agreed, "What we need is a new wing on the hospital, but I wonder what the public would say if we were to add on.'' They thought about the situation for a few minutes in silence. "We do have the money in the county hospital fund. You can bet your boots if we don't use it, the county will want to take it over for something else, no matter how hard we've worked to put it together for the hospital,'' mused Evan.

"Anytime there's a little money available, politicians will try to get their hands on it and blow it,'' agreed Ellis.

"We need a new lab,'' said Evan. "I'm tired of doing blood chemistry out of that little closet in the office. It makes for a big problem with transfusions.''

"We certainly need more lab space than that little coat closet you've turned into a lab. We need space to carry out more complete blood cultures and blood chemistry,'' agreed Ellis. "We need a deep x-ray machine and a portable x-ray at the hospital, with all the serious fractures we're treating.''

"We need a delivery room, and a place for our offices at the hospital,'' added Evan.

"The big question about adding on, is whether or not we could keep enough patients in the hospital to operate without losing money, but I don't think that would be any problem," said Ellis thoughtfully.

A new wing of the hospital was designed, and became a reality, more than doubling the bed capacity and bringing it up to forty. Ellis and Evan discussed what they could realistically treat there, and decided between the two of them, there were many things considered specialties they could handle. One of Evan's contributions to the hospital was seeing that there was a good laboratory. A lab had become a necessity for newly discovered medical diagnosis and treatments. Evan had always been interested in urology and diagnosis and treatment of the urological and genital system. While interning at Los Angeles he had acquired experience in the field of urology and working with prostate problems.

He wanted to go back and study urology. Hugh Young's cold knife used on Diamond Jim Brady had been followed by the electric cautery for cauterization of hemorrhage by Dr. John Caulk, once a student of Young, but now professor of urology at Washington University in St. Louis. These new developments interested Evan. He didn't want a residency there, just further training, so he arranged to work under Dr. John Caulk.

Dr. Caulk's instrument which controlled hemorrhage, using reflected light to illuminate the area, was highly successful. Evan worked on attaching Dr. McCarthy's wonderful new telescope for oblique, with an electric bulb approximately the size of a grass seed, on the instrument called a punch which was developed by Dr. Caulk for prostate surgery. He made a punch using the telescope and tried it out. The instrument was presented at a urological meeting. Here he met and became friends with Dr. Hugh Young.

After eight months study and work at St. Louis, Evan returned home to Soda Springs. He brought the new instrument, but Ellis showed little interest in it until Evan demonstrated its use and got him to try it. Evan had a medical paper on a number of his cases published in the

"Journal of Urology" which Dr. Young had helped to establish. Doctors throughout the nation continued to work on the problem of hemorrhage, particularly at Brady Urological Institute in New York, using high frequency radio currents, until treatment of benign prostate obstruction by transurethral resection, a highly technical, but simple, operation was perfected.

Evan and Ellis spent a small fortune on urological equipment in the hospital, including a cystoscopic operating room with an x-ray built into the base of the special table.

Evan had become quite interested in cancer, and cancer patients were coming from all over the Western States. They purchased radium equipment to treat cancer of the cervix and other malignancies. Evan went back to New York and spent time studying the use of radium, learning its dangers and its merits. He became acquainted with several of the experts in the field, leaders of that science, who had learned from those who pioneered the use of radium. The time there again awoke his interest in chemistry, physics, molecular and atomic structure—disciplines that had once almost wooed him from medicine.

Soon after the Kackley acquisition of radium for the treatment of cancer, they realized its limitations in the treating of malignancies. Beyond that, if they were to advance treatment of cancer, it must be by deep x-ray therapy. Again a trip to the East and study. Finally at Soda Springs building of a heavy lead lined room at the hospital with a door so heavy with lead that it opened with difficulty. A thick leaded glass was installed to observe the patient and protect the doctor as he closed an electrical switch, adjusted currents, and charged monitoring devices to control the dosage.

They had the best setup then available to protect patients from the harm and danger of radiation, through early atomic bruising—not atom splitting, that could destroy the cancer cell. It was effective only in a narrow band. Excess had power to produce cancer, the very disease they were trying to cure.

Miss Hazel Leison was taught to handle the radium and deep x-ray therapy. She was capable and knowledgeable, and monitored the placing of patients and the timers which controlled the dosage. Kackleys had no idea this experience would qualify her for a future job which would result in a terrible death from radiation sickness, after giving mouth to mouth resuscitation to a victim of an explosion of one of the first nuclear reactors built.

It was a double bladed ax, thought Evan, that brought him to that long walk to the steps of Harvard Medical School—decision difficult, experiment perilous—now poignant in reality and responsibility. Each time he opened the massively leaded door, and a patient entered, he looked through the leaded glass before closing the electric switch, and he felt the responsibility of a trust in him beyond that door—that he would not harm those in his care.

Literature, monographs, and books poured in monthly. They relayed information that man had opened a Pandora's Box in radio-activity. In 1939 and 1940 studies—principally of the thyroid gland and metabolism, through radio active isotopes, using the then sensitive instruments available—warned that man had better stop, look, and listen before proceeding recklessly forward in experimentation. The sole thing left in Pandora's Box was hope. Hope man would heed that which man had opened.

Ellis knew his son was a damn good doctor. He was proud of him, and respected his medical knowledge. At times he was almost jealous of the training Evan had in the medical field.

At the few times now available, from joy of healing and relieving man's physical suffering, Evan and Ellis talked of what they controlled in that leaded room. Ellis related experiences in France at Verdun and Dead Man's Hill, of when Germans used deadly gas at Ypres early in the war and the retaliation with deadlier gases, hurled in by large shells, a step forward—in vagaries of wind to carry a deadly chlorine in the right direction.

His father's words brought remembrance to Evan of when he had gazed at the great facade mosaic at the Stanford Church of the Sermon on the Mount. Ellis, as if reading his son's mind spoke softly:

If I'm design'd yon lordling's slave—
By Nature's law design'd—
Why was an independent wish
E'er planted in my mind?
If not, why am I subject to
His cruelty, or scorn?
Or why has Man the will and pow'r
To make his fellow mourn?

Kackleys soon became known for having a good record on breast, cervical, uterine, and prostate cancer. Though still in the depression, Kackleys purchased a portable x-ray machine, and by that time they had put another ten-thousand dollars into x-ray equipment.

They purchased a cardiograph to diagnose and monitor heart conditions, and Evan took a course on it's use. Next were bronchoscopes and a course from Chevalier Jackson and his sons and other associates who had developed the instruments. Dr. Jackson was also a well-known artist, and he gave Evan one of his paintings.

Ellis and Evan figured they could handle orthopedic problems without much trouble. They had two orthopedic beds in the new hospital, which were usually in use. All the splints, traction apparatuses, pins, and nails for various breaks was a far cry from the boards Ellis had used in the early days to splint fractures.

At a time when eggs were three cents a dozen, and it would take four hundred hens laying an egg a day to get one dollar, Kackleys had spent a fortune on equipment, equivalent to hundreds of thousands of eggs.

"We can't do everything, but we can do many of the things specialists are doing to take the medical practice away from the country doctor," Ellis said.

The hospital had become one of the biggest steady payrolls in the county by this time with around 20 people employed, and four or five private nurses. Many patients also came to Soda Springs who were not hospitalized, but added to the economy of the city. Their practice still continued to grow. Ellis and Evan employed and paid two or three lab technicians. When they weren't busy with Kackleys, they sent them up to help in the hospital. They ran all their own tests, but double checked some of them by sending duplicate samples to Boise.

When they got the new wing, they added an obstetrical delivery room, a nursery, an incubator, and began to pull in the maternity trade. To encourage women to come to the hospital to have their babies, they cut the fees to where they were just breaking even—forty-five dollars, which included twenty-five doctor bill and five days hospital stay for mother and baby. Since their time was limited, Ellis and Evan avoided maternity cases, but encouraged their patients to use Dr. Tigert and other doctors on the staff. Kackleys always saw the doctor was paid, even if the patient did not pay the bill and they had to pay him themselves. Long time patients, who didn't want another doctor, were still cared for by Kackleys.

Lyle Burton from Grays Lake, Albin Lindstrom's stepson, brought his wife, Benda, granddaughter of Otto and Nora Petersen, in to have her first baby. Ellis delivered the child. It was a difficult birth, and the umbilical cord was wrapped around the baby girl's neck several times, tighter than a human hand could have tied it. He came close to losing both of them.

Ellis had delivered Lyle, and treated both of these young people since they were babies. He had given them a ten dollar bill instead of charging them when they had come in for exams before their marriage.

Ellis stopped in the room as soon as Benda came out of the anesthetic, and explained the problem to the young couple. "If you would have had your baby outside of a hospital, she would have been born dead," he said. "The hardest thing I ever have to do is tell a mother her baby has died. You are very fortunate that you came to the hospital to have your baby," Fourteen days later, when mother and baby were ready to go home, he stepped into the room with a twinkle in his eye, and shaking his finger at the young mother, said, "Remember, I helped bring this child into the world, but I have done nothing to spoil her. The rest of the job is up to you and your husband. If she is spoiled in a few months, don't blame your doctor."

Young Rex Maughan was brought into the hospital by his

parents. He had fallen out of an automobile and the roadway, now gravelled, had inflicted multiple cuts and abrasions. Ellis' mind went back to the day when young Evan had fallen out of their first automobile, and the expletives that unconsiousloy escaped his lips made the young boy's eyes widen in surprise.

When the American Medical Association regional organization was located in a nearby town, they would periodically recruit one of the new members to visit Ellis and try to get him to join. Though nearly all doctors belonged to the AMA at that time, Ellis wanted nothing to do with it. He did not wish to bind himself, or circumscribe his freedom.

The unsuspecting young man was always very professional, and armed with numerous facts about why Ellis should join. He did not realize sending him to Soda Springs was a joke which had been played on numerous others.

Ellis was always nice to the young men, and gave full credit to what the AMA had done for medicine, but now for some time he had felt the AMA was too far into monopolizing medicine, controlling doctors and medical schools, nurses and nursing colleges, specialists, and everything connected with medicine. He pointed out that he felt they hurt hospitals and brought on nursing and doctor shortages.

Though he did not wish to be affiliated with the organization, Ellis had a particularly warm feeling toward Morris Fishbein, then head of the AMA, who was pleading openly and vigorously that the medical profession not become entangled with the federal government in a manner where it could exert power on doctors in their relationship with patients. Ellis pointed out to the young doctor that Dr. Fishbein's advice was not being accepted and the government was making inroads like a camel into a tent. The young doctor sat and listened then asked Ellis to show him around the hospital. Ellis explained what he and his son were doing. When the new doctor left town, he had plenty of food for thought from the experience.

Evan, who joined the AMA mainly for the journal, was appointed to a regional committee in Idaho, and was appalled to find the whole theme of the meeting was about socializing medicine and trying to get the government to pay for medical and doctor bills. He knew Morris Fishbein and his staff were fighting tooth and toenail in medical journals to keep from becoming involved in any way with the federal government in decisions affecting treatment of patients, admittance to hospitals, and setting of fees.

Evan told Ellis that after listening awhile he pointed out the historical obligation of medicine to treat the sick, which had brought honor and respect to doctors, whether high or low in the echelon. Doctors had historically and in the great literature, with few exceptions, been portrayed as beyond reproach. "I mentioned your experience with the state insurance manager, and their wanting you to cut off a man's leg to save a few dollars. I pointed out that sooner or later, if involved with the federal government, we would be straight-jacketed at every turn."

"What was their reaction?" asked Ellis with interest.

"I think I had no more standing there than Morris Fishbein has," Evan concluded.

"You were absolutely right," agreed Ellis. "Medicine is getting to be a farce these days. They would like us to believe major surgery has to be done in the big cities, and the local medical doctor is getting a lot of unnecessary trouble from doctors in these big hospitals." He paused for thought. "We can take care of most of what the specialists are doing, right here, with just the two of us, and we're not out trying to make a fortune while we do it, but if anything goes wrong, they try to hang us." His eyes clouded as he thought back to his early practice. "When I started practicing, the country doctor or general practitioner was the mainstay of medicine, but they'll soon have the general practitioner going the way of the dinosaurs," he lamented.

Chapter 17

Evan's practice was growing rapidly. Some days it seemed there were a lot more people on his side of the waiting room than on Ellis'. One unusually slow day, Ellis complained to his son, "It's sure been slow over here today. It seems you had nearly all the patients."

"That's okay, it will give you a little time to rest," replied Evan who had noticed his father often seemed tired.

"I don't want to rest," Ellis said quickly. "I can do that in my grave."

A fellow named Ike was brought in from Eight-Mile one day with horrible, multiple, compounded fractures of his lower leg bones. He was unnaturally pale and Evan worked to get the fellow's blood pressure and heart beat stabilized, and then set the break. He used low spinal anesthetic, putting a pin through the bone and attaching a traction apparatus to the pin.

An hour or so after the anesthetic wore off, he instructed Miss Peterson to give the fellow a quarter of a grain of morphine for his excruciating pain. She gave the shot, but the young man was sensitive to morphine, and forgot to breathe except when reminded by a light rap on his ribs. Necessary drugs were injected, and Evan stood worriedly over the patient.

"For God's sake, breathe," Evan instructed rather loudly. He started breathing for a few seconds, then stopped again. Evan again told him to breathe, and he started breathing again.

"Get a coffee enema ready," Evan instructed Miss Peterson. The caffeine in the retention enema would gradually be absorbed and Evan hoped it would stimulate the man to start breathing on his own.

"You can't give him a coffee enema," Miss Peterson

insisted.

"Why not?" demanded Evan hastily. "The man needs it."

"But he's a Mormon, and Mormons don't use coffee," insisted Miss Peterson.

"Well this is one Mormon who's getting coffee," said Evan with a concealed smile, "under pressure from the opposite end."

It became a private joke around the hospital about Miss Peterson's reluctance to give the Mormon man a coffee enema.

Ike recovered and his leg healed so well it was almost impossible to tell it had ever been broken. He fought as a foot soldier in three great land battles in World War II. So did two compression fracture cases Evan treated, in spite of the protests of the State Industrial Accident Manager. Compression fractures were not recognized by many doctors at that time.

Evan operated on one of the mine officials for a ruptured appendix. The man was a confirmed bachelor, though not immune, for later he would marry one of the fine ladies of the area. There was no apparent reason why his condition did not improve as fast as it should have, but he continued to remain in retarded recovery.

"What the hell's bothering you," Evan asked after studying his condition for some time. "The peritonitis is under control, you're not running a temperature, and you're well on the way to recovery, surgically."

The man confessed he was worried about his dog, Rusty, and was afraid he wasn't getting good care.

"Well, it's about time you told me what was wrong," said Evan. "I'll have the dog brought in right away, and we'll see that he's taken care of."

Evan brought the dog into the hospital, by his master, and had some of the orderlies see that it was walked daily. The man began to improve almost immediately and soon left the hospital.

Evan became particularly fond of this mine official, who when he became high enough in the echelon there, stopped the practice of medicine in the mine's front office. Though he tried valiantly, he was not able to save the Conda mine from financial demise due to nineteenth century mining practices. For years the mining company had been sitting in the center of the greatest deposit of phosphate ore in the United States, if not in the world, with the future on fire all around them, but they were not able to capitalize on their advantageous position.

When the mine was on its last legs, a young fellow by the name of Jack Simplot, who had found it necessary to drop out of school in his early teens during the great depression, acquired the mine for a song. His sister was a school teacher in Grays Lake, and many years later, died in Grace. She was a patient, of the Kackleys.

Today Jack Simplot has become one of the greatest industrialists of the century. His private company neither plundered Wall Street like Drake and Morgan plundered a gold laden galleon of Spain, nor became affiliated with the junk bonds which poured out as if from a junk bond bucket shop to finance that plundering.

Mrs. Larkin from a ranch near Grace, one of the grande dames of the West, was not recuperating as she should. Her daughter told Evan she was worried about her parrot, which had been her companion for over fifty years. Evan had it brought right in, and the bird spent fifteen days in the hospital.

Evan and Ellis both kept their dogs with them. They accompanied them on rounds, and they didn't want any of their patients having to worry about their pets while they were hospitalized. If there was a problem with a pet, the hospital doors were open to the animal. Children with sick or injured pets, often without permission of their parents, brought them to the hospital. The doctors gave preference to these young ones with problems. Patients who had to wait seldom seemed to mind.

Once in a great while Evan's dog and Ellis' would start fighting in the waiting room. "That's the quickest way I know to clear out the waiting room" said Ellis.

With patients somewhat dispersed and the office quieted down, the dogs were soon asleep, as if they had done their duty between patient and doctor in the practice of medicine.

Evan and Ellis worked together when Evan first came, but soon their practices were getting so large they decided to overlap them in care. Ellis would make his rounds early in the morning and Evan in the evening. Evan handled late cases that came into the office. This way one of the Kackley doctors was at the hospital from five-thirty in the morning until nine-thirty at night.

Lyle Burton came in from Grays Lake one day with a porcupine quill embedded in his leg. He had been trapping coyotes for the government from Grays Lake to the head of the Blackfoot River and accidentally met up with a porcupine.

"How long's it been there?" Ellis asked.

"About a week. I was trying to cut it out myself, but the wife, who was holding the kerosene lamp fainted, dropped and broke the lamp, and almost fell onto the hot stove. I decided maybe I'd better come in."

"Good hell, man," said Ellis with a poker face, "if it's been there a week, it may be clear up behind your ear by now, but I'll get it out if I have to take your whole leg off."

Lyle looked worried for a few seconds before realizing Ellis was joking, then he laughed. Ellis soon found the quill and removed it.

"That little lady of yours may pass out once in awhile, but she's okay," Ellis laughed. "Back her into a corner and she'd fight like a tiger."

Garrett and Mattie Somsen from Grays Lake brought their young son, Leith, in on Thanksgiving afternoon. He had bit into a goose leg and let out a yell. Something was stuck in his throat. His mother examined the drumstick and found it contained several porcupine quills. Apparently the goose had met up with a porcupine, which likely approached too close to her nest.

Ellis gave the child chloroform and Evan was able to remove the deeply embedded quill from the soft tissue, where only the black end was showing. It was lodged approximately one inch below the point where the windpipe separates the throat from the gullet. He removed it through Chevalier Jackson's Laryngoscope with a sturdy pair of short-boxed forceps.

As the great depression deepened, the high school age kids were unable to get any work. Many of their parents were also out of work. With a lot of time on their hands, some of the youngsters began getting into trouble, and were classified as unruly by the townspeople, though many of the trouble-makers were from prominent families. People in town were especially down on the youngsters being hauled into town from outlying areas.

Russ Lloyd was Soda Springs chief of police and Charlie McCracken was sheriff. They both worked with the kids to try and keep them from becoming criminals and keep them out of jail. They kept publicity down as much as possible.

"These men have great insight into how to handle kids," Ellis marveled. "We must do whatever we can to help them."

Evan had treated Russ' youngest boy and pulled him through a serious sick spell, and they had become close friends. Often he would come over to Evan in the early morning, and together they would work out something they felt would help turn a kid in the right direction, while keeping people from getting down on him and demanding retribution.

"All most of these kids need is something to keep them busy," said Charlie, the understanding Caribou County sheriff, as the two doctors and the two lawmen set about trying to find something to occupy the youngsters.

Charlie was another local lawman who seemed fearless. One time he spotted one of J. Edgar Hoover's ten most wanted men, followed him thirty miles, tricked him into thinking he had several men with him, and brought the man in all by himself. The episode was written up in the Readers Digest.

Evan visited his mother in California for the holidays. While he was away, Ellis examined a seven month old child of Alma Lloyd, and after listening to his parents account of what had happened, decided he probably had a peanut in his lungs. He sent them to Salt Lake, where doctors had worked an hour-and-a-half, and two attempts were made to remove the peanut. In cases like this, when the foreign object was removed, there was normally a dramatic recovery, but this child was still coughing and showing symptoms of lung problems. Ellis was highly concerned. If not removed, such an obstruction could be fatal or leave a child an invalid for life. He wished Evan were there with his experience in bronchoscopy.

As soon as he returned, Ellis sent the Lloyd family across the waiting room to his office. Evan x-rayed the child and could see nothing—peanuts are not opaque to x-ray, as he well knew, but the lung did not show any reaction to a foreign body. However, Evan came to the conclusion after talking with the parents, listening with a stethoscope, and tapping on the child's chest that the peanut was still there. He was concerned it would get rancid and give off oil, causing chronic bronchitis at best.

Evan explained to the distraught parents that after the physical examination and history, he thought the peanut was still in the lung, lying sidewise so air could both enter and leave the lungs. If so, inflammation from reaction to the peanut could soon reach a point where air could neither enter or leave the lung, and the child would become a chronic invalid or die.

"Can you take it out, Doc?" asked Alma.

"I appreciate your confidence," said Evan, "but if it were my child, I'd take him to Philadelphia to Doctor Chevalier Jackson or his son, Chevalier L., who pioneered the instrument for bronchoscopy. They've removed hundreds of foreign bodies, usually in two or three minutes, but this will be extremely difficult. The peanut will be brittle by now, and I don't think the baby could stand another unsuccessful attempt to remove it."

The tearful parents agreed they'd be glad to try Dr. Jackson if they could get the baby there, but being practical, said they didn't have the resources to get the infant to Philadelphia. Evan told the Mormon family to get in touch with their bishop while Evan contacted someone he knew. Evan called Chevalier L. and talked to him about the baby. "Can you get the baby here to Philadelphia so I can look at him?" asked Dr. Jackson. "I won't charge anything, if you can get him here," he added when Evan told him about the financial situation of the family.

"I don't know," said Evan. "The family doesn't have any money at all, and neither does anyone in the town right now with times as hard as they are. People are just barely staying alive. I'll see what I can do. They're members of the Mormon church, and I know Julian Clawson, who's from a good old Mormon family in Salt Lake with influence and a lot of business contacts. He just might help. We'll get the money somehow."

Evan called Julian who said he was sure the church would help. "I don't know about the fare," he said, then contemplated the situation a minute and suggested, "I'll go and talk to United Airlines, we don't want to take a chance on the train, it might be too slow."

United agreed to fly the baby and one of the parents there, but said they would have to find their own way back to Soda Springs. The mother was ill, so Alma took the baby. He showed up at the airport in typical western dress—black cowboy boots, big black hat, Levis, and cowboy shirt—which later made a big hit with the newspapers. The airline had registered nurses as stewardesses on the flight. They took right over, taking care of the baby. An enterprising journalist put the story on the wire, and when the flight got to Denver they were met by reporters. The same thing happened at St. Louis and Philadelphia. The word was soon out that the baby had been to Salt Lake doctors but the peanut was still in the child's lungs.

Evan had no idea the situation would generate so much publicity. In those days doctors carefully avoided publicity of any kind except by word of mouth and in medical journals. When he realized his name was headlined in newspapers all across the nation, and he just a "country doctor," he became extremely apprehensive. "What if the peanut isn't still there?" he thought. "If I've made a wrong diagnosis, I'm really in trouble. About all I could go on was the stethoscope exam."

Evan was the best known country doctor in the United States that week. He was relieved when Dr. Jackson took time from his busy schedule to call and tell him he had found and removed the peanut. It had taken thirty-five minutes to remove it, when most foreign bodies could be extracted from the lungs in anywhere from two seconds to three minutes. "But why all the publicity, Evan?" he asked.

"Believe me, I had no idea this was going to be picked up by all the newspapers," said Evan, as he thanked the doctor for taking care of the baby.

"Our doors are never closed to foreign body cases when they come," said Dr. Jackson.

Meanwhile in Philadelphia, people were recognizing Alma from his pictures in the newspapers, and when he walked down the street people would stop him and want to give him money, which he would not accept. Big chauffeured limousines would stop in the street and ask him into their homes, even sending limos to pick him up at appointed times. These people wanted to know about the West which was getting big play on radio programs, which often included a country doctor. It seemed radio programs were about the only place a country doctor had any standing at that time.

United decided the unexpected publicity had been fantastic and they should finish up their good deed as the Biblical man of Samaria had, and fly the father and child back to Salt Lake.

Evan was the only one who wasn't faring well with the media. Doctors in Salt Lake were saying they could have gotten the peanut out if the country doctor hadn't sent the case clear to Philadelphia, and newspapers made similar statements from most places the plane stopped. It seemed he was catching hell from all directions. Every time they removed a foreign body from a person's insides, the Salt Lake doctors publicized it.

Then about three weeks after the peanut baby case, they had a fatality while trying to remove a part of a watch from a baby's lung. Metal should have been much more easily removed than a brittle peanut, and as suddenly as it had started, the criticism of Evan was put to rest.

Evan never saw the mother of the Peanut Baby again for nearly fifty years, but when he ran into her at the funeral of a mutual acquaintance, they both found their eyes filling with tears.

Kackleys knew the country would probably get into the war which was spreading throughout Europe. "There's no chance of staying out of it," Ellis told Evan. "I've always been against getting involved in war on foreign soil, after the nation once became independent. European wars have been nothing but destructive to America," he mused looking out the window and remembering the battlefields of World War I. "It's always those who fight to keep out of war who are the first to volunteer to save that which we treasure—our country and families. So often 'war hawks' become 'immediate and essential' men—too important in the war effort to fight face to face," he added bitterly.

"If we get into war, I'm enlisting," said Evan, who was now married and had a small son.

"I understand," said Ellis. "Your mother and I would expect it of you. The Kackley men and those from your mother's family, the Sarvers, have always gone to war."

President Roosevelt pushed a state of national emergency through the Congress by one vote, and the draft went into effect. Many youngsters who got into trouble in Soda Springs were offered a chance to have charges dropped, or not filed, if they would enlist. Ellis and Evan thought it was a death sentence for the boys, which it turned out to be in many cases. They continued to work with Charlie McCracken and Russ Lloyd to help the young people stay out of trouble, but futilely, because the draft board had taken over nearly total administration for the peace officers.

"These county draft boards are usually a bunch of old fogies who think they should decide who goes to war and who doesn't, and insist on taking their frustrations out on our kids," Ellis told Evan sadly.

Evan and Ellis were having problems with some of the county commissioners, especially as election time approached, who were trying to use the hospital for political gain. They would send people in and tell the doctors to hospitalize them without charge. "We'll put a stop to that," Ellis said, and managed to get a tax of one-half a mill levy passed to care for the indigent. Then when they were asked to hospitalize special people, they could threaten to take the cost for care out of the mill levy of that commissioner's district. Cost of indigent care was published in the newspaper under auspices of the district. Soon the commissioners thought twice before sending people for free hospitalization.

Though anyone who was in need of hospitalization was admitted and kept until well enough to be returned to their homes or to friends, the hospital fund was building into a substantial surplus. Each month a sizable amount was added to the account.

Ellis and Evan spent a lot on trying to preserve the springs in the area, with the idea of bringing a great health resort to Soda Springs, as the Idanha Hotel had been at its peak, and utilizing it in their medical practice. They had carried out clinical studies on the springs and felt they had medicinal values as did the hot water springs and hot mud baths of Lava, and that many afflicted people could be helped by what nature had provided. French Lick Springs in Indiana was attracting people to its mineral waters from all over the East, as was White Sulphur Springs in West Virginia. Then there was the great "watering holes" in Europe such as Boden-Boden, that for centuries the would-be royalty and common people had frequented periodically to take the waters.

In 1938 Evan planned to go to Europe, but war in Europe circumvented their plans as all hell seemed to break loose there.

Again the hospital at Soda Springs was overflowing, and beds were being put in the halls. Numerous patients were coming from as far away as Nebraska, Arizona, Nevada and Alaska. Kackleys were planning another new wing for the hospital in 1941.

The morning of Sunday, December seventh was a cold day with thick ice on the roads requiring heavy chains on the cars. Evan, on his way to the hospital, stopped at Eastman's Drug Store for a Sunday paper. Stools at the soda fountain were filled with those who came for the same purpose, sitting in stunned silence listening to the radio, expressing occasional words of disbelief and shock. A quiet grimness pervaded the old drug store as Evan picked up the newspaper which carried no mention of the attack, a few hours earlier, on Pearl Harbor and devastation of the Pacific Fleet based there.

According to the drug store radio, the Japanese had suddenly appeared out of the sky, and just as suddenly left the fleet, a mass of setting ducks, torn and mangled, with some capsized. Evan listened a moment or two, then returned to his car and turned on the radio. He automatically drove to Hooper Springs as he listened. Evan often went down to one of the springs in the cool darkness of the shadows to meditate when he felt weighted down with the cares accompanying the practice of medicine.

He had watched the great Pacific fleet, transferred from the East, arrive at Long Beach not too long after World War I. Everyone there had become a part of that fleet, visiting it as often as they could. His mother had become close friends of some of the senior officers' wives and they had been invited to the Senior Officer Ward Rooms for dinners on the big battle wagons. To Evan it was a Navy of no nonsense, of great officers and crews like the history of the American Navy from the Revolution through World War I—an impeccable and victorious fleet.

Now the radio buzzed with what wasn't. Evan knew the Navy he had known and loved had been shortchanged somehow at Pearl Harbor, bringing on the great debacle now being flashed all over the world, with America being ridiculed, even by those who had once been her friends.

Before going to the hospital he returned home to his wife, Lois, red-headed Irish lady, a nursing graduate from St. Patrick's Hospital in Missoula, Montana. She already had two brothers in the armed forces. The first World War had not been good to her family and neither would World War II be. Evan turned on the radio and listened with her. They kept it low so the baby, young Ellis, only a few months old, would not be awakened. She knew Evan would soon go to war.

Evan enlisted in the Navy. He became the medical officer on a ship in the Solomon Islands that was perpetually in areas being bombed. They were charting the bay, up front, to find new channels for ships to travel outside the regular routes, and thus foil the Japanese in their plans to invade

Australia.

With gasoline rationing, Ellis' out of town and out of state practice declined. He stayed quite busy, but for the first time in his life had occasional time on his hands, which dragged. He straightened a picture hanging slightly askew on the wall in his office, and thought about his son, and about Ida. Evan had been gone several months now and he missed his help in the hospital and wondered if he would be one of the lucky ones who survived to return home, or if he would have three children's graves in the little town cemetery. He wondered why the past kept suddenly coming back to him.

His thoughts were interrupted when an accident victim was brought in to the hospital, and the nurse came running for the doctor. The man had been kicked in the head by a horse and had a bad skull fracture. He was barely conscious. Ellis looked at the familiar face of Ashler, and knew death had caught up with the man. Ashler was trying to say something, and Ellis leaned close so he could hear him. "You win, Doc," he whispered, and closed his eyes. Ellis felt mesmerized as he looked at the face of his dying enemy; the face which had haunted his life for so many years; the enemy whose harassment had forced him to buy the cold, death-dealing Codman house to protect himself from being injured or killed by the local livery stable horses; the man responsible for driving a wedge between himself and Ida. He didn't know whether to hate or pity the man who epitomized the corruption and lawlessness of early Soda Springs.

As life left the man's body, Ellis felt no triumph, only overwhelming tiredness. He thought of Ashler's words, "You win, Doc," but felt none of the joy of victory. The town had changed, and he knew he and many others had been instrumental in affecting that change, but he was older and wiser now, and knew the struggle between right and wrong would continue throughout the ages. Ashler was gone, but others would carry on where he had left off—not the same evils, but evil would always be present. Ellis went home that evening and sat in front of the picture of Christ before Pilate for a long time trying to sort out his mixed feelings. After cursing Ashler for over half of his life, it was hard to let go of the feelings of anger he had felt for the man, but anger now was useless. He wondered what his life might have been without the problems Ashler had caused, which were constantly lurking in the background of his memory, but quickly reminded himself of the words of the poet:

For all sad words of tongue or pen
The saddest are these: "It might have been!"

He got very little sleep that night, as his mind continued to go over his life, seeing faces of the past, remembering long gone events and conversations.

A few days later, an old sheepherder came in to Ellis' office in the new hospital. "Remember me, Doc?" he asked. "You took my kidney out in a sheep camp on Williamsburg when you first came here."

Ellis looked at the man and a wry grin turned up the corners of his mouth. "By damn, you made it, too. I had heard several times you did, but never was sure till I could see you with my own eyes," he said extending his hand which the man shook warmly.

"In those days, we made do with what was available," Ellis continued. "There wasn't a bed pan south of the Oregon Short Line Railroad, and if there was one north of the railroad, I never saw it, but we could saw off a board and lay it across an old milk pan. Times were primitive, but you people were survivors."

"You've got a pretty fancy set up here now," the sheepherder said, glancing around the hospital.

"Let me show you around," said Ellis. "I'll give you a grand tour; by damn you deserve it."

As Ellis showed the man around, the sheepherder was highly impressed with the facilities Ellis now had available. They reminisced about early years in the area. "It was truly a pioneer life, but we had pioneer people equal to the occasion, and above all they had kind hearts and willing hands," mused Ellis.

"But no more than the doctor, who has continually had the kindest heart and most willing hands of any," said the sheepherder. "You've done a lot for this town."

Ellis went home that night and thought for a long time about the early days, and how the town, his life, and medicine had changed. The raw, old West was gone, he concluded, and with the passing of Ashler, so were his bosom enemies. He had chosen to give his loyalties to medicine and the forty-four years he had been practicing had been a lonely life, though rewarding in many ways. He figured he had delivered well over four thousand babies. A great many of them were born under pretty hard circumstances, in little log houses, with dirt floors and roofs. Even then it had not been hard to carry out sanitation. Fire and water were available and heat would sterilize instruments and dressings whether in a hospital, a modern home, or a dirt floored and roofed cabin. Premature babies had been placed in a drawer on the oven door to keep them warm. It wasn't like the modern incubators, but they had pulled many of them through.

He thought of all the neighbors and midwives who had assisted him in those early days. They were willing cooperative helpers. They hadn't had bed pans or hot water bottles, but they had used catalogues, beer bottles, hot rocks and stove lids to heat beds.

Chapter 18

Ellis felt unusually tired. Evan had been gone a year-and-a-half now. After he left, Ellis had delivered his second son, another grandson, who had been named Alvin Evan.

Doctors Hugh Young and Chevalier Jackson had written Evan's recommendation to the Navy immediately after Pearl Harbor. Evan was still somewhere in the Pacific in the Solomon Islands Campaign. Ellis knew the Navy was fighting to foil the Japanese in their plans to invade Australia. They had bombed Tokyo, but Japanese submarines were still able to operate in Sidney Harbor as the Navy fought back after the tragedy at Pearl Harbor.

The decisive battle of the Pacific had already been fought, as Evan must also know—one of the great Naval battles of all history—at Midway. The shattered fleet after Pearl Harbor and the obsolete planes had effectively destroyed the Japanese naval fleet superiority. A fleet had been destroyed at Midway, greater than that at Pearl Harbor, and the retaliation within seven months. Evan had always said the Pearl Harbor tragedy had shortchanged the fleet stationed there.

"Never," Ellis wrote Evan, "has the brass shined brighter than at the Admiral's Command Post at Pearl Harbor."

Two months later, Evan had replied in cryptic letters of highly censored mail. "You are right about the brass shining bright. The stain is gone. It will still shine brighter."

Ellis had felt perpetually tired for months. He often thought about Ida and the early joys and sorrows they had shared. He had never stopped loving her, though their lives had drifted apart. He knew he had neglected her when he had become lost in a practice which completely engulfed him. Yet she had been a part of that practice—making it possible, through her sacrifice, for him to go to medical school, and working at his side during the early years in Soda Springs.

He thought back to his two beloved children whose lives had been cut short by the dread disease pneumonia. He had been unable to do a thing for them. If they had been born a few years later, he could probably have saved their lives. Technology had advanced so far during the years of his practice. The great strides made in medicine were almost unbelievable.

He felt lucky to have a son who had followed his footsteps in the medical profession, and Lois his wife, and two beautiful red-headed grandsons, as his own son Alvin had been.

He thought of his dogs, who had been his closest companions. Rags, a big woolly, powerful Australian shepherd, was part of the parcel. Pal, an Airedale by breed and his favorite, had shared his hardships. If he went on horseback, snowshoes, or walked, Pal was always right with him. He rode in the car beside him and when it failed, Pal always followed him as he walked away. He slept beside his bed and ate by his side. "If there's another world and I don't find Pal over there, then I'll know there has been a mighty big mistake made somewhere and St. Peter will be called on to make an explanation," he thought to himself. The lonely house seemed to echo his thoughts.

Most of those early settlers who had been his close friends were dead now. Henry Schmidt, Jimmy Strachan, J. O. Morgan, Bill Winschell, Judge Eastman, Aunt Leah Gorton, and Dorothea Lau. Susie Small was one of the oldest living residents in the community. He smiled as he thought of Susie. She had helped so many people, through hardship and illness—caring for her family, nursing the sick, working in the church and at elections, fighting for woman suffrage, and working for prohibition—and she was still going strong.

He had enjoyed the friendship of a lot of far-sighted people who had helped make Soda Springs, the second oldest settlement in Idaho, a progressive city. Jim Horsley and Mr. Meyers had pioneered the use of electricity. Charlie Fryar, Horsleys, and Laus, the stock men, sheep men, farmers of Gem Valley, and many others through their foresight had brought progress to the area. Six-Shooter Sal, Jenny, Hugh Whitney, and the Cassidy gang had added color to his life.

He had worked with a lot of outstanding nurses. Early ones who helped him care for his patients around Soda Springs included Susie Small, Sister Bertha of the Mennonites, Elsie Woodall, Mrs. Knight, Miss Childs, Mrs. J.J. Call, Elizabeth Richardson, Mrs. Lau, Lil Mather, Sarah Horsley, Rhoda Davis, Louise Horsley, Elizabeth Crawford, Hannah Swensen, Lula Thirkill, Lydia Hawker, Iona Mikesell, Mrs. Winschell, Mrs. Condie, Miss Petersen, Miss Estes, and many others.

He'd practiced a lot of medicine in his day and had seen a lot of progress in technology and methods, but he liked to think back to the good old days when he had removed a kidney in a sheepcamp, swam the Bear River to deliver a baby, cured the sheep men's eye problems, and rode horses to Grays Lake and the mines at Caribou. Times had been tough but the people had been equal to the tasks required.

He remembered the abject poverty of his early life. One time he had walked a girl home from grade school and her parents had objected, a slight which Ellis had never forgotten. His wounded pride still throbbed when he thought about it. Even when he was a young doctor in Soda Springs, one of the families there would not let their children play with Ellis' kids. He had handled what life dished out to the best of his ability, and had become a highly respected member of the community. He had tried to soothe, comfort, and heal the ills of his fellow men.

His sleep was interrupted by many shadows of days gone by and he seldom felt rested.

When needed, Ellis scheduled surgery at eight in the morning and at one and five in the afternoon, a routine he and Evan had begun. He was just finishing his one o'clock surgery one day in November of 1943, when he felt excruciating pain in his chest cavity, and was almost unable to breathe.

He knew he was having a heart attack, and felt sure he was going to die. The head nurse, Miss Leison and Dr. Russell Tigert, who was giving the anesthetic, got him into bed and did what they could for him. He knew his life was slipping from him. He was glad neither he nor Evan kept a record of their accounts, and no one would ever be billed for anything Kackleys had done for them. He didn't want anyone harassing his friends. He always said if people didn't want to pay him, that was their affair and it took too much time from the practice of medicine to keep accounts and try to collect.

Ellis wasn't a good patient. He was impatient to dispense with the inevitable. He told Miss Leison to get the hell out of the room and come back and take care of him in two hours, feeling sure he would be gone by then. Throughout his life, he had been in a hurry, and impending death didn't change the lifelong habit. When the nurse returned in two hours, he was upset he hadn't died yet. He only lingered a few hours after "wrapping the drapery of his couch about him, and lying down to pleasant dreams," as he had so often quoted to his son from "Thanatopsis."

The whole town was in shock as word went forth that the "Little Doctor" had received his summons to join His Maker. The good ladies of the Relief Society helped Margie Bolton lay the doctor out in the large room of the old house, with the stairway leading to the second floor. People came by the hundreds to mourn his passing. Even those who had not supported him in life, mourned his death.

The room was filled to capacity, with the crowd spilling over into the hallway and two other large rooms. Some came in their Levis and work clothes, others were dressed quite formally, as all classes of people mingled together to mourn the loss of their friend. Ed Whitman, one of his few lifelong friends who was still living, had become the city undertaker by virtue of owning a furniture store which sold caskets. He stood quietly beside his friend. He glimpsed the Catholic rosary barely showing from the interior of his coat pocket. The cross and beads had been carried there since World War I.

The two dogs, Pal and Rags, had taken their position by

the casket, as if standing sentinel beside their master. There was a steady hum of voices.

"Our family owes a lot to Doc Kackley. He delivered my twin brother and I at home. He fixed my leg when it was so badly shattered many doctors probably would have cut it off," said Eldon Beus. "I still have the beautiful pocket knife he gave me after using it to cut off the hip to ankle cast." he continued. "My twin brother, who died as a kid, was named Ellis Kackley Beus, after the Doc. My brother Jay Edward always thought the world of him, too. He was quite a man!"

"He was a great humanitarian," said "Ham" Petereit. "A young boy I knew as a kid badly needed five dollars, which was a lot of money in those days. He was getting desperate about it until he suddenly thought of asking Doc if he would loan him the money. He came back from the doctor's office with a big smile on his face. 'What did the doctor say?' I asked. 'He said what in the hell do you need that much money for? But when I told him, he just pulled out his wallet and handed me a five dollar bill'."

"That's the way the doctor was," agreed his companion. "He'd help anyone who really needed it."

"He was a modern day Robin Hood," said a well-dressed man. "He charged me plenty for my operation, but he knew I could afford it, and I didn't mind paying it because I knew he did so much for so many people for little or no charge."

"The Doc had quite a sense of humor," said Ray Ellis. "About five years ago I was in the hospital and he let me watch some surgery. One man needed his lungs tapped and he and Dr. Tigert asked me to hold his arm down. They removed two pieces of rib to insert a drain into his lungs. That evening for dinner we had ribs, and I just couldn't get them down. Doc laughed and looked at me over the top of those glasses. He said it was to get even with me for catching mice on the window sill and putting them in the waste basket where he could see them." He smiled as he thought about the incident. "It will never be known about all the good things that man did for unfortunate people and others, with little or no compensation."

"We owe my husband's life to the doctor," said Erma

Sappington. "He was in a car accident, and thrown out onto the pavement with such force it crushed his skull on the left side and battered his whole head. Dr. Kackley, who was always on the job, rushed him into surgery and opened up his skull. He removed splinters of bone and debris from his brain and cleaned out the wound. When he was finished he gave Dee one-half hour to live, and said if he survived after that, it would be by the grace of God and his will to live. He was unconscious for nearly a month, but he made it. We will always remember and be grateful to Doctor Kackley."

"My husband got hit by a roller skate on his ankle, and the injury turned into osteomyelitis," said Irma Nugent. "It could have caused him to lose his leg, and the doctor had to operate several times, but he kept the infection down, and he kept his leg. Bob often says that to a small boy, Doctor Kackley was a giant heart and soul."

"My late husband helped get the doctor to come here," said Mrs. Eastman, "and it was a wonderful thing for the community."

"He was a great neighbor," said Earl Petereit. "We've lived across the street from him for years, and the girls, Carol and Dorothy loved to go over after supper and listen to Amos and Andy on the radio with him. He loved children."

"He was a wonderful neighbor. We relied on his help so much, even for picking a musical instrument for Pharis," said Otto Petersen. "Evan is quite a doctor, too. This old house has been the home of two great doctors and benefactors to the community."

"I helped Dr. Kackley with confinement cases for several years. When I had my seventh child, I sent for him, not knowing he was in bed with blood-poisoning. He had a bed made for him in a sleigh, and supervised the birth from a stretcher," said Iona Mikesell.

"As far as I'm concerned, Doc. Kackley was a 'real' man," said Johnny Wallace.

"I'm afraid there isn't any left like him," said a little old lady, hobbling past with the use of a cane. "I think we've seen the end of the country doctor, and a shame it is.

Everybody loved Doc Kackley. I don't think he had an enemy in the world."

As the crowd thickened, the dogs, whose sanctuary had been invaded, became more and more restless. All of a sudden a fight broke out between the two massive animals. They clamped their jaws on each others necks, and all efforts to separate them were in vain. People backed away from the area and overflowed onto the lawn and into the other rooms and hall, half filled with the numerous floral offerings carried in by the Mormon ladies of the Relief Society. Others took refuge on the great winding staircase leading to the second floor and its landings. The great staircase went north to south, bent back east to west, and north to south again up the wall. Bill Gagon and Jack Minty grabbed the dogs by the legs and tried to pull them apart, but the dogs would not release their hold on each other.

Lois walked out and got the old fashioned brass teakettle and poured a few drops of heated water on the noses of the animals.

The dogs yelped and released their hold, but in the ensuing scramble, bumped the casket which began to roll on the dolly, then shifted and tilted to one side. As it did, Ellis' glasses slid down his nose, his body shifted slightly making it seem as if his head had turned toward the dogs, and his carefully combed hair stood up in it's usual position.

Ed Whitman, who was protecting the casket throughout the rumpus, caught it just in time to keep Ellis from being dumped out. He looked at his friend's slightly ruffled appearance, and realized he looked much more natural that way than he had before, so he didn't try to rearrange him.

The crowd thinned as the dog fight sent many people home. The dogs were shut into separate rooms, and order was again restored. People continued to pour in from all over the country. An estimated two thousand five hundred people came for his funeral—several times the population of the town—which was held in the high school auditorium. A small percentage of the crowd was actually able to get into the services.

It was about a week later when Evan got word of his father's death. He did not return to Soda Springs until early in the following year, with two weeks leave. A short time after his return, he was reassigned to the historic old venerated Naval hospital in a great ship yard. There he became Chief of Urology. To the Naval hospital came the human casualties and to the yards ships, from the catastrophe of Pearl Harbor, to be repaired and returned, if possible, to duty. It was a place where members of the staff of the hospital and shipyards often had to make grave and final decisions.

When Evan arrived, casualties were coming in from the now sweeping naval attacks on outer fringes of the Philippines and Japan. In another year, the Pacific Fleet would be riding at anchor in Tokyo Bay.

Here with the advent of the great miracle drug, penicillin, the terrible effects of infection could be counteracted and debilitating affects of venereal diseases could be controlled if treated early in the progression of the disease. Whole wards of early gonorrhea patients were cleared out in as little as four days, and early syphilis infections were cured in a week, emptying numerous beds for other afflictions. Great new strides had been made which would again revolutionize the practice of medicine. Doctors could hardly believe what a thousand units of penicillin could do.

After being discharged from the Navy, Evan and Lois went to Montana where Lois had been raised. They eventually settled and retired in Boise, Idaho, spending summers on Williamsburg, where Ellis had met the Cassidy gang so many years before. When Evan heard about the dog fight at his father's viewing, he slapped the thigh of his right leg and said, "And that's the part Dad would have liked best."

Epilogue

A memorial to Ida Kackley, in honor of Lois Kackley was established at Idaho State University as a foundation to study and add to the knowledge of Bear River and its antiquities. It was set up by Dr. Evan Kackley and his sons, Ellis and Alvin.

Dr. Evan Kackley's collection of transurethral prostatic instruments was presented by him, in memory of Ellis Kackley, M.D.,as a permanent display in the Administrative Faculty Room of the Brady Urological Institute of Johns Hopkins Medical School. The faculty room is part of the Hugh Young Memorial Library, itself a part of the Brady Institute.

The collection dates back a century and a half. The work of Dr. Hugh Young, the "Father of Urology" — with his instrument in the first successful rechanneling of the prostate under vision — resulted in completely revolutionizing the treatment of prostatic obstruction during the next 30 years.

The instrument display, in its walnut case, is mounted horizontally on a fine old lecturn in the Memorial Library, where dignified simplicity is permeated with heritage. The oil portraits of Hugh Young and James Brady hang on one wall near the lecturn.

Four instruments designed by Dr. Evan Kackley are in the instrument collection, with the adaptation of one by Dr. John Patton, in miniature size to correct congenital bladder neck obstruction in infants, both male and female.

Scholarships have been established in memory of Dr. Ellis Kackley by some who were helped to get a college education through the generosity and forethought of the country doctor.

The author is willing to speak
or give seminars about the book
or the history of
Southeastern Idaho.

New drug alters eye color

Glaucoma

CONTINUED FROM PAGE 1

such danger and voted 4-2 to approve the drug. "It is very effective" at fighting glaucoma, said Dr. Emily Chew of the National Eye Institute.

The FDA is not bound by advisory-panel decisions but usually follows them.

Glaucoma blinds 80,000 Americans a year and steals some sight from 900,000 others. It is caused when fluid builds up inside the eyeball and causes dangerous pressure. Over time that pressure pushes against the delicate optic nerve until it is damaged and the person begins to lose eyesight.

Standard therapy is a drug called timolol. This eye drop makes the eye produce less fluid, thus keeping the pressure down. But it has numerous side effects, from breathing problems to irregular heartbeat. And people with heart or respiratory problems cannot use it.

Latanoprost is the first of a new class of drugs based on a natural chemical called prostaglandin, which helps the eye drain its fluid.

In a study of 829 patients, those who took latanoprost had a 37-percent greater drop in inner-eye pressure than timolol patients. They also had significantly fewer side effects.

But some had a startling side effect: blue eyes turned brown, as did green, hazel and even yellowish ones. The color change hit 15.5 percent of patients after a year of latanoprost use.

"This is a very strange side effect," acknowledged Dr. Johan Stjernschantz, the company's lead researcher. "There is no other drug or agent that can cause this side effect."

And it is not a reversible change, even when patients stop taking the drug. The question is whether the change is cosmetic or dangerous.

The company theorizes that latanoprost increased the amount of melanin in people's eyes. Melanin is a chemical that gives people skin color, and everybody's eyes have some. But lighter-colored eyes don't produce as much of the pigment, allowing light to better diffuse through the eye and reflect back as, for example, a blue color.

The company gave high levels of latanoprost to monkeys for a year and counted the number of melanin-producing cells, finding no increase. But these cells were producing more of the kind of melanin that causes a dark color than the kind that causes yellower colors.

The company notes that 10 percent of the population experiences an unexplained eye-color change by adulthood anyway.

But critical panelists asked whether the melanin-producing cells would eventually get so full that they burst.

The company noted that if a patient's eye color does not change by 18 months of therapy, it probably will not change.

TALLS CAMERA

"Value & Quality Since 1917"

YASHICA

EXCELLENCE IN OPTICS

Ultra Compact Power Zoom Camera

38-70mm power zoom lens, active infrared auto focus system, 5 mode flash system with red-eye reduction, automatic film load, advance and rewind.

ON SALE

99.99

verdict was read in U.S. District Court but showed no other reaction. His wife, Robin, cried.

Rep. Walter Tucker III

The 38-year-old Democrat was charged with selling his vote on a proposed $250 million waste-to-energy conversion project while mayor of Compton in 1991 and 1992.

He was accused of taking $30,000 from a businessman-turned-informant and demanding $250,000 from an undercover FBI agent posing as the proposed conversion plant's financial backker.

His attorneys maintained that he accepted funds only as a consultant.

Jurors deliberated nine days before finding him guilty on seven

prison ministry – people in there saved."

Tucker, a no minister who is bla the trial that he authorities becaus Christian beliefs.

Defense attorn said he was unsu would seek a nev

Tucker faces u prison when he is 18.

He was electe sent the 37th Distr the working-clas Compton, Watts, C Long Beach.

He said he wou an expulsion heari

Corrections: A headline in some editions yesterday mis ized the Galileo mission to Jupiter. Galileo's probe entered the atmosphere and relayed data during a 75-minute plunge until i destroyed by atmospheric pressure.

Douglas County Superior Court Judge T.W. "Chip" Small v present when a girl witness was interviewed outside of court i rape case against Pastor Robert Roberson and his wife, Conni containing incorrect information about the interview ran in so

Drug backed even though it turns blue eyes brown

TIMES FOCUS HEALTH

BY LAURAN NEERGAARD
Associated Press

SILVER SPRING, Md. – A new type of drug to battle vision-stealing glaucoma works significantly better than standard therapy – but has the startling side effect of turning blue eyes brown.

Despite not understanding the cause or significance of the eye-color change, the Food and Drug Administration should approve latanoprost, a panel of scientific advisers decided yesterday.

But the FDA panel insisted that manufacturer Pharmacia & Upjohn Inc. continue to study the drug's long-term safety and clearly label that it can cause the eye color change so doctors and patients understand the risk.

"This could turn out to be a major public-health hazard for glaucoma patients," said Dr. Alexander Brucker of the University of Pennsylvania, who opposed the drug.

Other panelists countered that there is no proof of

PLEASE SEE ***Glaucoma*** ON A 10

PREVENTION'S
Quick & Healthy
HOLIDAY
FAVORITES
FREE